When Dreams Come True

~

Sort Of

By Earl Snort

Barlow Adams Series Book II

TotalRecall Publications, Inc.
1103 Middlecreek
Friendswood, Texas 77546
281-992-3131 281-482-5390 Fax
www.totalrecallpress.com

Copyright © 2020 by Earl Snort
Cover Design by Bruce Moran

Not a speck of this is true. It's all a figment of my imagination.

ISBN: 978-1-64883-000-6
UPC: 6-43977-40006-2

Printed in the United States of America with simultaneous printings in Australia, Canada, and United Kingdom.

FIRST EDITION
1   2   3   4   5   6   7   8   9   10

To My Wife and in Memory of Mosby the Cat

"Baby, I can't make it without you. And I'm telling you, Honey, you're my reason for laughing, for crying, for living, and for dying . . . ." - (You're My) Soul and Inspiration - The Righteous Brothers - 1966

"Those were the days, my friend. We thought they'd never end. We'd sing and dance forever and a day. We'd live the life we choose. We'd fight and never lose. Those were the days. Oh, yes! Those were the days." - Those Were the Days - Mary Hopkins - 1968

"Lonely days, lonely nights. Where would I be without my woman?" - Lonely Days - The Bee Gees - 1970

"Youth. When I had more energy and stamina than a kitten. When there was a mystery behind every closed door. When Life was full of flavor. When I thought I was bulletproof." - Earl Snort - 2019

"I swear. Every time my pen touches paper, the lies keep stacking up. You can't believe a word I've written." - Earl Snort - 2019

Prologue

The Town of Arlo, in the Texas Panhandle
1958

"Dad, can we get a horse?"

"What do you want with a horse?"

"I'm going to be a cowboy, like Gene Autry. No! Roy Rogers!"

"I never heard of a nine-year-old cowboy. Can't you wait until you finish school?"

"I need to learn how to ride now. Then I'll be good enough when I get older."

"I see. Where would we put a horse? Mom's not going to let it in the house and the garage isn't big enough."

"Come on, Dad. He'll live in the backyard. We have a fence."

"Horses eat a lot of food. Food costs money. A lot of money to feed a horse. They have big appetites. Mom's not going to cook for a horse."

"Come on, Dad. He'll eat the grass. It won't cost a thing. Then you won't have to mow the yard. You'll have more time to hunt and fish and play softball after work. That's another reason we need a horse."

"Who will clean up all the horse poop? Horses poop big piles without a thought as to where it lands. It burns holes in the grass. Flies eat it and then they fly on people and deposit germs on them which makes them sick. I don't want holes in my grass and none of us wants to get sick."

"I'll scoop it all up. Put it in the mulch. It helps to grow flowers. Mom will love that."

"No doubt. Who's going to scoop it up if you're sick?"

"Chloe will. She likes horses. I'll let her ride Buster when I'm not riding him."

"You little liar! I never said I wanted a horse. I just said they're nice when someone else has one. I'm not getting my shoes all messed up trying to clean up horse poop! Yuck! If you get a horse, you'll have to pick up the horse poop all by yourself. I have better things to do."

"Yeah, like making moon eyes whenever you see Dallas McGraw."

"Do not."

"Do too."

"Hey, you two! Knock it off! You're supposed to help each other out. Not stir up trouble. Some kids aren't fortunate enough to have a brother or sister. When things go haywire, that's who you turn to for help. Family. That includes cleaning up horse poop if that's what it takes. Someday you'll understand.

"And another thing. How did you get from asking if we could get a horse to already having it named Buster?"

"That's a good name. Don't you think, Dad?"

"Maybe so, but I haven't heard yet where the money's coming from to buy a horse. Horses cost a lot of money. Who's going to pay for it?"

"How much do they cost, Dad?"

"Well, let me ask you this. How much money do you have?"

"I have $1.61. Plus I have eleven empty soda pop bottles I haven't sold to the market yet. That's another 22 cents. If that's not enough, would you chip in? I'll pay you back."

"Well, let me see. How much money do I have in my wallet? Here's $26. Plus 43 cents from my pocket. Nope, I don't think that'll cover it.

"Besides, I thought you all wanted to go to the movies tonight and see 'Chisum' with John Wayne. That's 35 cents each for Mom and me and 25 cents each for you two. Then there's popcorn and Cokes. That's $1.40. Altogether that's $2.60. Plus, we'll probably need to buy some gas this week and I expect we may need a couple of items at the market.

"I'm pretty sure we don't have enough money to buy a horse.

Besides that, we'd have to get a saddle and blanket and a bridle. I'd say we might have to wait awhile before we can afford a horse."

"Well, how much does all that cost?"

"Oh, maybe $200 for the horse and another $40 or $50 for the tack if we bought it used."

"That much?"

"That much. That's more than my old truck is worth. Besides, where would you ride a horse?"

"I'd ride him to school."

"That's 13 miles. You'd have to get up at 3 in the morning to get there in time. Then you wouldn't get home 'til 6 o'clock. By the time you groomed the horse it would be 7 o'clock and the rest of us would have already eaten supper. Yours would be cold.

"Not only that, you'd have to get a job to pay for the horse. What would you do?"

"Mr. Jeffries has cattle on his ranch. I could get a job working for him as a cowboy."

"You know, that's a great idea. Thing is, he probably wouldn't hire you until you're fifteen or sixteen.

"I tell you what. You start saving your money now and I'll help you buy a horse in a few years. That sound okay to you?"

"It sounds like a long ways off to me, Dad. I ain't forgetting. Someday I'll have a horse and I'll ride it to work. And you know what kind of job it'll be?"

"I couldn't guess."

"I'll be a range rider, like a cowboy with a six-shooter and I'll chase bandits on Buster and if they don't give up, I'll fill 'em full of lead. They won't get away from me 'cause Buster's gonna be too fast. We'll catch 'em all. I'll be like the Lone Ranger but I won't wear a mask."

"You should be just about old enough to take over when the Lone Ranger decides to hang up his spurs. And Son, when that time comes, maybe I'll get a horse and we could ride along together just in case you need some help. Sound like a plan?"

"It's a plan, all right, and I'm holding you to it."

"I wouldn't have it any other way."

CHAPTER 1
Trapped in the Life of an Owlhoot
One Night in the Winter of 1970

Follow the leader. The driver in the second rig was lighting one cigarette after another trying to calm his nerves. He was trailing his older brother along gravel roads close to the Mexican border in the middle of the night with no headlights. El Jefe said no lights until they were back on the main US highway. The driver navigated by the light of a nearly full moon and his brother's brake lights whenever he tapped them. If he botched this up, El Jefe would probably kill him.

After an hour of choking dust and nearly rear-ending the rig his brother was driving, they braked to a halt along a lengthy stretch of empty road. El Jefe and Segundo got out of the new Ford pickup truck and scanned the area for signs of human activity while the driver and his brother waited in their rigs.

Satisfied that they were all alone in the correct location, El Jefe began cutting the farm fence wire. He rolled it back post to post. Then he signaled for the driver and his brother to follow him and Segundo onto the ranch. They putzed along a couple of miles to a canyon with a makeshift wire fence. The driver and his brother opened the back doors to their trailers and put out the ramps. Then the four of them and the sheepdog herded well over a hundred sheep into the trailers.

When they were done, he helped roll up the makeshift fencing and place it in the bed of the pickup. They drove back to the road and waited while El Jefe and Segundo rolled the farm fence back into place and spliced it together. When they were done the fence was good as new.

Each minute they delayed, the driver feared someone would drive past and know what they were up to. He did not want to go to jail, nor did he want to be lynched by an enraged rancher or wrathful lawman for getting caught red-handed rustling. Some of the old timers still subscribed to roadside justice. An eye for an eye. A tooth for a tooth. It sent a chill up his spine.

He had long since realized that El Jefe and Segundo could probably outrun the police and escape in the souped up pickup. However, the driver and his brother would be left 'holding the bag.' They'd never get away driving tractor trailers loaded down with stolen sheep. If he got caught he would be 'swinging in the breeze.' What would his mama or Dolores think if they knew what he was doing? Heaven forbid! He hated his brother for getting them mixed up in this.

Finally, after an eternity which lasted at least fifteen minutes, they slipped away in single file like a jackal leading a pair of bison, still without any lights. Then, after what seemed like his entire lifetime, during which he was too scared to breathe, they came to the intersection of US 90 where they turned their lights back on. When they arrived at US 285, they turned north to Fort Stockton and thence to Pecos and on into New Mexico.

It was daylight when they offloaded the livestock into a holding pen for an Anglo driving a new, white-over-red, GMC Jimmy. The Anglo paid a fistful of dollars to El Jefe. The two of them shook hands. El Jefe returned to his truck. They followed him to Loving, where they stopped at a small diner and ate a ranch hand's breakfast washed down with a carafe of coffee each. The driver was beginning to relax.

When all were sated, El Jefe peeled off twenty $10 bills and gave the driver and his brother ten each. He said for them to drive the rigs back to Pecos and return them to the lot where they had picked them up.

El Jefe pointed his finger at big brother and said to make sure they cleaned out all the sheep dip before locking up or it would be his ass. They would never find his body. The threat was duly noted, as evidenced by expressions of youthful horror. El Jefe said he would get in touch when they had another load. Then he pointed his finger at each of them and said, "And you better be ready, pendejos. Comprenden?"

The look on El Jefe's face chilled the driver all the way down to his stones. He got an involuntary shake and dribbled a small squirt of pee down his leg. El Jefe was surely first cousin to El Diablo himself.

El Jefe paid for everyone's breakfast and walked them into the parking lot back between the rigs. He told Segundo to show them Esperanza.

Segundo pulled out an ornate switchblade with silver and turquoise grips. He flicked open the five-inch blade. It was mesmerizing. Then he grabbed the driver by his hair and jerked his head backwards so forcefully that he lost his balance. Segundo slowly ran the blade across the front of the driver's neck less than an inch from his throat. Then he released the driver with a little shove. He flicked the blade back into the handle and returned it to his hip pocket. He smiled like this was a big joke.

El Jefe spoke softly. "Bad accidents happen to people with big mouths. Real bad things. Sometimes they even happen to their esposa or los niños. Muchachos who can keep a secret earn mucho dinero and live to become grandfathers and great-grandfathers. Comprenden?"

"Sí sí, Jefe."

"Bueno. Make sure you're both available when I need you again. It won't be long."

Chapter 2
Another Day in the Life
Monday, March 9, 1970

It was almost 8 o'clock. Barlow had finished another midnight shift with Archie and was headed to classes at West Texas Junior College (WTJC.)

The semester was half over. So far, so good. He was making all A's and B's. He was content, but at the same time, restless. He concentrated on accentuating the positive. He certainly had a lot to be thankful for. Even so, he was hungry for a little excitement. Bells and whistles were going off in his head. He was fully aware. Be careful what you wish for. You might actually get it to your own dismay!

It had been almost three months since the shootout with the El Diablos Motorcycle Club.

Sarah had said yes and they were engaged to be married next year. Things were going gangbusters between them. She was able to spend more time at his house than before the engagement, which meant more time for dot, dot, dot, which might also mean that her folks knew what their new, number one recreational activity was and had tacitly accepted it so long as they were discreet. Or maybe not. Probably not. He supposed it was better to pretend that he and Sarah had not discovered the wonders of passionate love until they were wed, and maybe not even then to some folks. Small town gossip could be cruel.

Barlow had recently turned 21. He was now the legal owner of the revolver he had carried daily for the past eight months. This seemed like a rather stupid bit of red tape for which to be thankful, but nevertheless, there it was. The last thing he needed after two on-the-job shootouts was problems with the federal government's branch of the IRS known as Alcohol, Tobacco, and Firearms, acronymically known as ATF. Best to stay on Uncle Sam's good side.

Also, he had been surprised and honored that Sheriff Sol had notified the Army about his rescue of Sandra Taft on the next-to-last day before his ETS (expiration term of service) expired, which resulted in him being awarded the Soldier's Medal for valor and the Good Conduct Medal, as an afterthought, he supposed. This was humbling all the way around.

In addition, Sarah would graduate in May. She was trying to find a better paying, full-time job in addition to helping her folks run the sheep ranch.

Sarah had overheard her folks talking. For the past several years the sheep industry had been on a decline that wasn't expected to reverse itself. For centuries the warmest and most durable garments had been made from wool, unless you got yourself a fur coat made from bear skin. At any rate, science (many said progress) had developed new synthetic fibers at least as warm as wool which were a lighter weight, but more importantly, cheaper to manufacture than wool.

Wool mills were closing one by one because the demand for wool garments was diminishing. That meant the price for wool had fallen for the sheep ranchers. At the rate it was going there would be virtually no demand for it after the next ten years.

That left only one thing. Raising sheep for meat. The price per pound for lamb was higher than for mutton. This was the direction sheep ranching was headed. Nevertheless, neither lamb nor mutton were in as high demand as either beef or pork.

The Bakers hadn't decided yet what they planned to do to remain viable. With times getting lean for sheep ranchers whose primary source of income came from wool, it would be in the best interests of the Baker family if Sarah found outside employment. Of course, she would help out as unpaid labor at the ranch whenever she could.

Another concern for the Bakers was that they employed three loyal ranch hands. The last thing they wanted to do was to let them go. They had worked there for so long that they were like family.

Fortunately, Sarah had a line on a potential full-time job at the rodeo grounds. Dennis DeBerry, the director, had run the operation solo for at least thirty years but he was getting up in age. The county supervisors were considering the employment of an event planner to assist him. This would be a seismic shift in thinking for those tightwads. Plus, there was a good chance the assistant could become the director whenever Mr. DeBerry decided to retire. Sarah was a local favorite in the barrel racing circuit and Mr. DeBerry was fond of her. Besides that, she was getting her associate's degree in animal husbandry. That should help. Barlow was keeping his fingers crossed.

But back to being restless. Barlow needed some action. Just about any kind of lawful action. Yes. He was thankful for the opportunity to attend college and he was determined to graduate on time next year. Also, he was riding horses with Sarah once or twice a week and sometimes this could be a little dicey. He wasn't anywhere near being up to rodeo circuit standards but he was working in that direction.

He had no right to be even a little bored, not with everything going so smoothly, but there it was. Besides Sarah, who really got his juices flowing, he needed some adventure or a small brush with danger.

Barlow was becoming something of an adrenaline junky. Not so bad that he wanted to be a bull fighter or jump out of airplanes or engage two or more outlaw bikers in a fight at the same time. He needed just enough excitement to get his heart racing to feel really alive.

Good grief! He had to get himself in check.

He knew this was the wrong thing to wish for, but he just couldn't help himself.

CHAPTER 3
Dipping Into the Same Well Twice
Tuesday, March 10, 1970

It was darker than Hades. No moon and overcast. This was the ninth foray the driver and his brother were involved in. So far, they'd rustled sheep for El Jefe from eight different counties in West Texas. Tonight they were returning to the big ranch in Quayle County because that had been their motherlode, both in terms of numbers and in quality of sheep. This ranch specialized in Rambouillets, which were like the Arabian horses of sheep. Primo.

Crazy! This was just begging for trouble. They never rustled from their home county in Reeves and they always delivered to the same Anglo in New Mexico. This was wise on the part of El Jefe. But tonight? This was a tremendous risk! If this rancher had noticed his count was short from the first expropriation, he'd probably have taken preventative measures such as assigning some of his vaqueros on nighthawk. They could be walking into an ambush. The rancher could shoot them all dead and his neighbors would celebrate. There would be no mercy if they got caught.

He was just a peon. A worm. He had no say. El Jefe would kill him if he chickened out.

Tonight they entered from a different section of fencing. Nevertheless, they picked up well over a hundred sheep from the same canyon as before. It was crazy but everything went off without a hitch and he was another $100 richer.

This time when they made the delivery, he memorized the license plate number from the white man's Jimmy - 864321. He wrote it down and hid it in the cigar box in his sock drawer where he kept his cash, small keepsakes, and important papers. It might come in useful if he ran into some bad luck in the future. Pray to God that never happens.

CHAPTER 4
Thursday, March 12, 1970
The Alert is Sounded

"Quayle County Sheriff's Office. Miss Youngblood speaking."

"Loretta, this is Sheriff Waters from Brewster County. How's it going over there?"

"Just peachy, Sheriff. How's everything your way?"

"Pretty good, but there's something I need to run by you all. Sheriff Sol or Chief Alex in?"

"Chief is. Hold on while I fetch him."

"Thanks."

"Hey, Leland! How's it hanging?"

"Loose as a goose. What about you?"

"Hanging in there like a hair in a biscuit. What can I do you for?"

"Well, you all have any complaints of sheep gone missing your way?"

"You mean like rustling?"

"Yep."

"Well, I haven't heard of any. I take it you have."

"Yeah. One of our big spreads in the southwest corner along the Rio Grande is missing about seventy head. They didn't discover it until roundup a couple of days ago."

"Any leads?"

"Well, it's on the river but there's no indication the fence was cut along there, and there's not nearly enough hoof prints near the water to indicate a herd that big crossed over, so it looks like they were trucked out somewhere on our side."

"Any wheel tracks?"

"They found some but they could be from their own vehicles, plus they're old. They got no idea when the sheep were taken. It could have been a month ago. Even longer."

"Have you spoken to any of the other sheriffs?"

"Six so far and no one else seems to have been hit."

"Which counties?"

"Pecos, Presidio, Jeff Davis, Reeves, Hudspeth, and now you."

"Well, I'll put the word out and nose around. If anything comes up, I'll let you know. I bet some ranches around here will decide to do a headcount just to make sure they haven't been ripped off."

"Good idea. Some of our ranchers are doing the same thing as we speak.

"You know the cattle ranchers association couldn't give a hoot if sheep are rustled. I guess I can understand their point, especially since no one's ever heard of sheep rustling, particularly on a large scale, not to mention that the sheep ranchers aren't paying their overhead; but rustling is rustling the way I see it, no matter if it's horses, cows, sheep, goats, pigs, or unicorns, and the prison sentence is the same. It just doesn't seem like there's enough money in sheep rustling for the risk if they get caught."

"You're probably right about that, but consider this. Cattle are branded; horses are tattooed if they're worth much, plus horsemen recognize horses they know; pigs have notches in their ears, but nobody marks sheep. That means if you can acquire the sheep legally or illegally, no one's the wiser when you take them to market, especially if you go to an auction far enough away from where they were rustled. The risk is in the stealing, not in the selling. That's not true of the other animals."

"You got a point there. Guess I never really thought about sheep rustling before. What you say makes sense. I guess we better start checking stockyards where they auction sheep to find out if any new sellers have suddenly emerged on the market. Have ta be careful how we do that. If the auctioneer is pals with the rustlers, he'd tip them off for sure."

"I 'spect so. Let me know if anything develops or if there's any leads you want us to run out for you all. You know we're always glad to help.

"I can save you a little bit of trouble. We don't have much of an auction for sheep in Quayle County, and if someone new showed up with a trailer full of sheep, we'd know about it right away."

"Thanks. I figured as much. I'll call if we need something. You give my regards to that sweet little wife of yours."

"Thanks. I will. Give Muriel my best."

"I will. Stay in touch."

"We will. Take care."

CHAPTER 5
The Week Ends With a Double Bang
Saturday, March 14, 1970

It was a typical week. Archie and Barlow spent their midnights together protecting Quayle County from bandits and rapists and all types of evil doers by holding down the fort in the jail. They drank coffee, smoked, chewed the fat, cleaned all the weapons, tidied up the office like it was about to undergo an SAMI (Army slang for Saturday Morning Inspection), and generally frittered away their time on duty. They never received even a single call all week.

Barlow not only got caught up on homework assignments, but he was more than a week ahead in all of them. He went to school, paid attention in most classes, and ate lunches with Sarah. She was busy with her part-time job in the afternoons, so they didn't have any time for play before he went to bed. Such is life.

But on Saturday afternoon when her ranch chores were done, she went to see Barlow at 4 o'clock at his house in town. The plan was to eat before going to see the 7 o'clock movie at the Bijou. Tonight it was 'Kelly's Heroes' featuring Clint Eastwood and Donald Sutherland, first among many notables, as the stars.

Sarah let herself in as quietly as freshly falling snow while Barlow was still in Dreamland. She slipped off all her clothes and put on some red high heeled shoes. Then she put on an apron. She began making biscuits. She got them in the oven and set the timer before she heard Barlow start to rouse.

She looked in on him. Now he was stretched out on top of the wadded up sheets in his nudies. It looked like he had a massive missile ready to launch. She smiled and said, "Hey, Deputy, you have time for a little R and R (military acronym for rest and relaxation) before we eat?"

"When have I not had time for you, you naughty girl?"

"Well, all righty, then. You just lie there and have pleasant thoughts while I check on these biscuits. They have another couple of minutes before they're done. I don't want them to burn. As soon as I take them out I'll come back and see if I can relieve any of your obvious tension. Actually, I feel pretty tense myself and I might need you to see what you can do for me." She turned around and wiggled her bare caboose before she went back into the kitchen.

"Oh, my gosh! Hurry up! Pleasant thoughts in and of themselves are not nearly enough to relieve all the tension I feel right now."

When she checked the biscuits, they were perfect. She turned off the oven and placed them in a wicker basket and covered them with a dinner napkin to keep them warm. She returned to the bedroom, slipped out of her heels, and slowly removed the apron. Her nipples were as erect as his nuclear-tipped, M-28 Davy Crockett tactical missile.

She got on the bed and gave him a teaser French kiss to get him focused (as if he weren't already) before she straddled him. She lingered just long enough and shifted her body just so, to position his missile exactly where it needed to be. She rotated her hips to cause her launching pad to self-lubricate an inch at a time until he was all in.

The rhythm of ocean waves took over. She rocked at a pace from a primal source which was punctuated by his involuntary thrusts. It was like he was trying to knock the bottom out of her most secret part.

The symphony got louder. The cymbals were crashing. The floodgates opened and his missile launched them both into oblivion. The inner, erogenous beast was assuaged, at least for the time being. However, it awakened the hunger beast, who was pounding down the door.

After a few languishing minutes, they rolled out of bed, put it back in order, and shared a shower.

She said, "Hurry up. My folks might stop by. They decided to go to the movie, too."

Barlow's face was the picture of horror. "What? How soon?"

"Gotcha!

"Hurry up! I need to fry the ham and cook the veggies. I'm starved. If you hadn't been so randy, we could have eaten by now."

"You imp! I would have tossed my cookies if I had had anything on my stomach, but don't worry. Your turn is coming."

"Big talk, coming from a nudie boy. Hush up and set the table."

They ate and cleaned up. It was 6:15. They had oodles of time to spare before leaving for the movie. They had just put the last dish away when the phone rang.

Barlow said, "Gosh, I wonder who that is. I hope I don't have to go to work."

He answered the phone. It was Clarice. She said, "Barlow, I'm glad I caught you before you all left. Can I speak to Sarah?"

"Sure thing. Let me get her for you. Everything okay?"

"I think so. This won't take but a moment."

He handed the phone to Sarah. "It's your mom." He watched her carefully for signs of concern. She spoke for about five minutes before she rang off.

"What's up? She didn't find your birth control pills, did she?"

"It could be worse than that."

Then she asked, "You all get any alarming phone calls at work yesterday, or did Sheriff Sol leave any messages for you or Archie?"

"Nope. We never got a call all week. So far as I know, Archie never spoke to the sheriff or the chief for that matter."

"Well, as I understand it, there's an alert in Quayle County for all the sheep ranchers. It seems that somebody rustled seventy sheep from a ranch in Brewster County. Nobody knows for sure when it happened. Sheriff Sol recommended that all the sheep ranchers do a head count to see if they have any missing sheep. He also recommended that the ranchers check their fencing for any signs of fresh cuts or splicing they didn't do themselves.

"Dad's pretty upset. He said we're skipping church tomorrow to make sure we haven't been hit. Can you help?"

"Of course I can. I always wanted to do something like this. I just hope you all aren't victims. What time?"

"8 o'clock sharp."

"I'll be there. Do you need to go on home?"

"No. Mom said to enjoy the movie, but not to stay up late. She said tomorrow could be a long day. Guess it's a good thing I already got what I really came for."

"I thought as much. You probably won't respect me in the morning."

"Probably not. You're damaged goods, you know. Even so, I am a little partial when it comes to you. I think I'll keep you in spite of what they all say about you."

"Oh, and what's that?"

"Oh, you know. A few of the girls in my class said something about I shouldn't get too wrapped up with you because guys as good-looking as you invariably have teeny little winkies."

"And what did you say?"

"I might have said anything more than a mouthful goes to waste."

"You did not!"

"You'll never know for sure, will you? Now shuck those drawers, Deputy. You got me all hot and bothered just thinking about it. Show me what you got. I need a little more loving before we go to the show. We still have enough time to put out my fire before the show begins."

"And I have just the fire hose to do it. I bet you never mentioned that did you?"

"Of course not, Silly! You think I want the other girls trying to cut in on my action? Hurry up!"

"Shuck your own drawers, Little Lady, hike up your skirt, and bend over the bed. Doctor Adams is going to fill your prescription."

"That's what I'm talking about. Shush and mount up, Cowboy."

CHAPTER 6
On the Job Training in Sheep Ranching
Sunday, March 15, 1970

Barlow arrived at the Bar B at 7:30. He was rigged out in his gun belt just because, even though he felt certain that the others wouldn't be packing. He might even carry the 30-30, if the Bakers could loan him a rider's rifle scabbard. He was, just for the day, fulfilling a fantasy from his youth to be a cowboy. What did it matter if they were rounding up sheep instead of cows? Same-same, he told himself. Rams can be as ornery and dangerous as bulls!

Sarah was standing next to the barn when he arrived. It would have been an understatement to suggest she was more than glad to see him. She shoved him into the barn when she was sure no one was around. She gave him a hug and a kiss that were pregnant with promise.

Oh Lordy! He had been trying to stay focused on sheep ranching and just about anything else that wasn't erotic, and in just a matter of seconds she had ripped down all his defenses. They heard footsteps and broke off but they couldn't do anything to wipe off the guilty expressions on their faces.

Sarah's brother, Cordell, walked in and, ignoring the obvious, asked Sarah if they had picked out a mount for Barlow.

She responded, "I was thinking about Boyo unless someone else was planning to ride him."

"Nope. That'll be just fine. Make sure you get Barlow a short lariat. You know Barlow, not trying to put a damper on your enthusiasm, but I think a rope will be a little more useful than your sidearm today. The idea is to herd 'em and count 'em, not shoot 'em."

"Cordell, I've been carrying a gun too long now to leave it behind. I still haven't forgotten about the Diablos. I'd feel naked without it."

"Okay. I'm sure Sarah would like that."

That riled up Sarah. She responded, "Cordell, you're just being awful! I have no idea what you're talking about! What if I said that about you? I bet Darla wouldn't appreciate it one bit!"

"Darla always appreciates me when I'm naked, Sarah. Just fetch him the dang lariat, would ya? We're burnin' daylight."

Twenty minutes later, Arthur, Cordell, Sarah, Pedro, the top hand, Angel, his brother, Pancho, Angel's son, and Barlow were mounted and headed to the southwest range. Arthur said they needed to work in concert to get the most accurate count. Sarah was the tally keeper.

Before the December lambing, they had counted 948 ewes and 51 rams. The ewes dropped 1,659 lambs, although some of them didn't make it, including four breeding ewes. They should round up something in the neighborhood of 2,600 sheep, assuming they hadn't been rustled.

Sarah had told Barlow that in another thirty to sixty days, the lambs would be ready for market. Not all of the lambs would be sold. Normally, they would sell a quarter of the older ewes and replace them with lambs. That's because most ewes delivered twins after their first year of breeding. The ones that didn't would be sold. Also, after four or five years, most ewes became less productive. That was another reason.

Furthermore, the rams which didn't sire an abundance of healthy lambs would be replaced with younger rams. As a rule of thumb, the rams usually lasted a lot longer - 8 to 10 years at least.

Eventually, all the sheep would wind up on someone's dinner table. Lambs were most valued for meat by the pound. It was the most tender. Old rams were least valued by the pound, but they weighed a lot more - about 300 pounds, compared with adult ewes at 200, and lambs at 80 to 100. Figure about 15 cents-per-pound for mutton on the hoof, versus 20 cents-per-pound for lamb.

However, before taking the sheep to market, they all had to be shorn. Although the market for wool was declining, there was still money to be made from it. But more importantly, the sheep had to be shorn before the summer heat to keep them from dying of heat exhaustion. This had to be done even if no one was interested in buying the wool.

Today's mission was threefold: to get an accurate head count; to herd the sheep into some pens closer to the sheep barn so that Pedro, Angel, and Pancho could begin shearing on Monday; and, to check all the outer fencing for signs of recent cutting and splicing (by rustlers) as well as for areas which simply needed repair. The priority was in that order.

It turned out to be a great day by everyone's standards. The weather was perfect. No one (Barlow, in particular) got thrown off his mount. The head count was 2,633. The sheep did not protest being herded into the two near fields, especially when they found an abundance of grain. The fencing was intact and in good repair. They were done by 3:30 and ready to unwind.

As soon as they rode into the corral, they spotted an iced tub full of drinks under the copse of shade trees. Once the horses were groomed and fed and the tack was hung up, by ones and twos, each found his way into the shade and began to quench his thirst with frosty bottles of Shiner Bock and Miller High Life. The Royal Crown Colas were left unmolested, just in case a thirsty Girl Scout troop stopped by to sell some cookies.

Later that night, Arthur grilled T-bone steaks. Clarice and Darla baked potatoes and biscuits and an apple pie. They also made a tossed salad.

Barlow was worn out and sated. It absolutely couldn't get any better than this. The problem was, he needed to be at work at 11:45. The party was still in full swing, but he kissed Sarah good night and made his way home. Lights out at 7:30. His body cursed him soundly when he woke up at 11.

CHAPTER 7
More About Slick
Monday, March 16, 1970

When Barlow woke at 11 o'clock, his head was pounding and his tongue was thick. Generally, he felt used and abused all over. Besides being exhausted, he was hung over. Everything he did was in slow mo and far beneath his normal standards. This added frustration to misery.

When he arrived at work, he was surprised to see Deputy Sheriff Clarence "Slick" Oldman instead of Deputy Sheriff Archibald "Archie" Willis. It seems that Archie's daughter and two of his younger grandkids, both of whom were teenagers, were visiting from Oklahoma City so he decided to take a few days off.

Barlow grabbed a cup of joe and willed himself to wake up. If only it were that easy.

Slick could see that Barlow was hurting so he left him alone until he could see some signs of life. Then he reported that both Pecos and Val Verde counties had had several auto thefts recently. Sheriff wanted them to start calling in DMV record checks on vehicles they don't recognize when they are on patrol. He told Barlow to check the BOLO (be on the lookout for) list for stolen vehicles and to make some notes in his diary.

Barlow said, "Sounds like our region is in the middle of a regular crime wave. Do you personally know of any car thieves or stolen car fences living in Quayle County?"

"Well, the only stolen autos I'm aware of in the past year are the ones you were involved with. You know, the one Rupert Doyle stole and the one you and Chunk recovered at Alberto's Rocking A. The only potential car thieves I can think of might be some of Alberto's clan, and that's just a SWAG. You see, the problem around here is, it's fairly simple to hot wire a car but even easier to sell it in Mexico with no questions asked."

"Roger that. Is a SWAG what I think it is?"

"A scientific wild-ass guess."

"Thought so. By the way, I'm sure you noticed that I'm suffering tonight. I spent all day with the Bakers helping them on their roundup. I had a few beers, probably a couple too many when we got done, and didn't hit the rack 'til 7:30. I apologize if I seem discombobulated."

"No problemo. Been there. Done that. Were all their sheep accounted for?"

"They were. Everyone breathed a big sigh of relief. Mucho grande celebration. It was still going strong when I left for home."

"Glad to hear it. They should hang all the rustlers by the neck until dead, just like we used to do back in the day."

They didn't say another word for about an hour while Barlow worked through the jackhammer pounding away in his head.

Finally, he said, "Slick, I remember when we met, you said you were an ex-gyrene (nickname for a Marine). As I recall, you're a veteran of Guadalcanal and Iwo Jima and it just so happens that I'm a military history buff. I don't want to be nosy, but I was wondering if you would be willing to share some of your experiences. Maybe a little something about what it was like growing up around here when you were a kid. If not, maybe we could discuss something exciting, like who's going to win the Polish National Ping Pong Championship Tournament or if they plan to colorize the old 'I Love Lucy' reruns."

"No biggie. I'm like most folks. I always like to talk about myself. Besides, I'm pretty much an open book. Hell, in this town, like it or not, we all are. How old do you think I am?"

"Sounds like a song I heard in a hillbilly joint by a dude named Tom T. Hall when I first came back from Vietnam. Something about 'old dogs and children and watermelon wine.'"

"Ain't nothin' wrong with all that. How old?"

"Hard to say. I'm not the best judge of guessing a person's age. WWII didn't start until December 7th, 1941. I'd guess you were at least 18 when you joined. If you signed up in the beginning, I'd guess you were born in 1924 or a little before. That would put you late 40's or early 50's. I'd guess you're about 48 or 49."

"Not bad. I'm 50. Believe it or not, my pa and Archie grew up together. They both went to Quayle School, graduated too, except in those days it only went up through the eight grades. Then they cowboyed together on the Whitaker spread. It's long gone now. Broken up into smaller ranches after the old man died. Shame, too. Anyway, Archie had a talent with horses and he became a wrangler but my pa was just your basic drover working the cows.

"WWI got important in these parts around 1917, or so I was told. Archie and my pa, his given name was Aloysius but they called him Li'l Al on account of his height impairment you might say, got all in a lather over it and decided to go fight the Krauts. They signed up together in El Paso. They wasn't drafting here yet in Quayle County when they volunteered.

"They was both assigned to the 2nd Division but eventually they got separated. Archie was sent to the 5th Machine Gun Battalion and my pa was assigned to the 23rd Infantry Regiment. Archie had a lucky rabbit's foot in his pocket. In spite of all the action he was in, he suffered nary an injury. Not saying he never got sick or nothing but he come out of the war without so much as a scratch. A lot of guys wasn't so fortunate.

"My pa wasn't so lucky. He got gassed and he suffered with it until he died in 1925. He just never recovered his health. He couldn't hold down a job after he come back. His lungs was too bad. He did what he could but we was barely scraping by.

"Archie went on to become a deputy. Damn fine one, too. He also took after his dad and become somewhat of a horse whisperer but he'd never tell you that. He's always augmented his pissant deputy wages by breaking and training and selling horses but that's another story.

"My ma never remarried after Pa died. He was her one and only love. She mourned for him 'til the day she passed in 1960. Me and my brother was just tykes in 1925. We all moved back in with her pappy and mammy on the homestead we still live on, which is a half-section. You might say 320 acres is small potatoes for this area but it has good water and it's free and clear of any debt. It's always supported the horses and cattle we raise to feed our family.

"Getting back to my story, we was mostly raised by Grandpappy Dalton and Grandmammy Esther. They was MacGregors. That was their clan. Family originally come over from Scotland. They up and moved here from Arkansas about the same time as Ripsnort Sweeney come in from Mississippi, only my folks wasn't rich like him. Howsomever, Grandpappy Dalton and Ripsnort was two birds of a feather. They pretty much wiped out the bandits in this county afore there was any law. Lots of mutual respect betwixt 'em.

"I finished high school in 1938. My brother, Bernard, we call him Bernie, is just a year younger than me. He got his left eye put out when he was twelve. Not sure exactly how he done it. He was fucking around with this rusty piece of barbed wire and cut his left eye on a barb. It got infected. He dern near died with tetanus, and in the process he lost his eye. He missed a lot of school too, so they held him back a grade. He should have graduated in '39, but he didn't until 1940.

"Anyhow, after I graduated I got me a job as a short haul truck driver transporting machinery parts between El Paso and Del Rio. It was hard work. Tires was made from rubber then and they had inner tubes. We had lots of flats and had to change 'em and pump 'em up by hand. Lots of mechanical issues. I'm sure you can appreciate that. These was just dirt and gravel roads in them days. Plus, I was still cowboying on the side at Grandpappy's. Yessiree! We was living pretty high on the hog once I was making regular wages.

"Then Pearl Harbor come along. Sneaky Jap bastards! I signed up for the Marines right after Christmas. After Basic, I was assigned to the 1st Marines. We was deployed to Guadalcanal on the British Solomon Islands.

"We landed on August 7th, in 1942. We fought them bastards almost everyday until sometime in February of '43. Can't remember for sure. Towards the end I got dysentery, then malaria, and finally dengue fever. Got to where my trousers with a 28-inch waist was about three inches too loose. Japs and germs dern near kilt me. They tried like Hell, but never did. When the fever come along, it looked like it was gonna be curtains for Old Slick.

"I went from sick bay to a Navy hospital ship and then back to Pearl Harbor to the Naval Hospital there. Took me a long, long time to recover. They almost give me a medical discharge but I begged 'em not to and I reckon they was shorthanded at the time. Besides, I was only a PFC (private first class) and they didn't hafta pay me much.

"You know what? You get a Purple Heart for getting wounded in combat, but you don't get squat for dern near dying from disease or chemicals in a combat zone in some godforsaken shit hole where you never woulda been if it hadn't been for war in the first place. Don't hardly seem right. Me and my daddy both should have gotten one!

"Sorry. That still sticks in my craw. Can't help it.

"Once I recovered and was fit for duty, I got reassigned to the 3rd Marine Division. Don't ask me why, but guess what. They sent me right back to Guadalcanal where I just come from! The 3rd was supposedly there on R and R and later on to retrain, but fighting malaria and sand fleas was mostly what we done. Give me a break! What kind of rest or relaxation can a young man get on a jungle island without pussy and whiskey? What was we supposed to do, play checkers?

"We stayed there until July of '44, when we up and went to

Guam. We mopped up the Japs and took over the whole dern island. Lots of combat. Give 'em a helluva lickin'. I was there but don't claim no credit. I was still a little puny, so I was temporarily reassigned from infantry to supply. I never really was in no danger.

"From there we went to Iwo Jima. By then I was completely healthy. Went back to the infantry where I belonged. We landed towards the end of February in 1945. It was godawful bloody. Took a month to root out all them Jap bastards and they fought tooth and nail.

"None of 'em surrendered. Not one! Suicide charges. Killed 'em all. Didn't matter. Kept on fighting. We lit 'em on fire with flame throwers. Still didn't matter. Fought like they couldn't wait to die. Seemed like everyone around me got shot. Being a skinny little fucker saved my ass more'n once. Big fellers couldn't squeeze behind an anthill like I could to avoid being shot at by the snipers. We lost a lot of good men.

"In April, they sent us back to Guam. I was beginning to think I was jinxed to go to everyplace twicet. A few months later, Harry Truman dropped the atomic bombs. Bravo for old Harry! Stones as big as cantaloupes! They don't make Presidents like him no more.

"The Nips surrendered in August. The 3rd was sent back home to California. I got a honorable discharge in November. I done three years and ten months. The division was deactivated in December. They give me the Pacific Campaign Ribbon (Asiatic-Pacific Campaign) and the WWII Victory Ribbon. A year or two later, them ribbons was upgraded to medals and they mailed 'em to me. Put 'em in my safe deposit box at the bank just in case of fire. I'd hate to lose 'em. I didn't come by 'em cheap.

"When the war ended, I come home and went back to cowboying on the family spread. I got married in March of '46 to Clementine Gossett, this fixie little thing that I met in San Francisco on my way home from war. She really turned my head.

She begged me to stay there but I wanted to get back to Texas, so I did. I reckon things must've not been going the way she wanted 'em to in California, 'cause she wrote me a letter and asked what I thought about her taking the bus and coming to visit.

"Of course I said yes. By then, both my grandpappy and grandmammy had passed, so I had my own room. Momma wasn't pleased about me sharing a bedroom with a woman I wasn't married to, so I didn't at first, but that didn't really work out. Clemmie was a city gal and didn't cotton to fucking in the barn or anyplace that wasn't a real bed with sheets, so we went down to the courthouse and got hitched by Judge Sweeney's pappy when he was the judge.

"Then we fucked like minks for several months. Clemmie was a moaner and a screamer and we went at it morning and night. Upset Momma. Bern never said a word about it. He was still single at the time. Anyway, Momma and Clemmie despised each another. Momma said we wasn't a lasting combination. Of course Momma was right but I couldn't see it.

"I was out branding cows the day she run off. I never saw it coming but I should've. She hated the heat and the dust and the cow shit and my momma and dern near ever' thing else about Texas. The main thing she loved was fucking and so did I. She caught the Greyhound bus and went back to San Francisco. Before she left, she cleaned out the stash in my sock drawer. Took over $400! That was a bundle in them days.

"Last I heard, she married a taxi driver whose claim to fame was that he was General Bradley's driver during the war. You know, we never divorced so far as I know but it's doubtful anyone in California would ever find out unless she told 'em. I don't 'spect she would ever do that.

"I never remarried. Hell, there's lots of widow women and divorcees and old maids out there what love to fuck. That's really all I care about. My brother's got a sweet little wife named Theresa Mae and they got three kids. We all live in Grandpappy's house so it's not like I don't have family. His kids will pass on the Oldman family name."

"What about your brother? Did he stay home during the war?"

"Glad you asked. It's a funny thing. Early in the war, no one wanted him because of him only having one eye. Then in early '44, the Army got desperate for more men. Did you know the Army had 108 divisions during the war? They only had three active duty divisions when it started.

"Anyway, they started drafting guys for what they called 'limited duty.' The idea was that these would be the rear echelon, ash and trash, chair-bound warriors. Shoe clerks. Readers and writers, not fuckers and fighters. Free up the healthy guys to do the fighting. Well instead, they put Bernie in a field artillery unit. Wasn't that what you was in?"

"Yep."

"Bernie was a gunner on anti-aircraft artillery, AAA, or sometimes called ack ack. He was in France and Germany. He shot down several Kraut fighters who was strafing. Not all at the same time, mind you. Different engagements. They give him the Bronze Star with 'V' device for valor because he shot one down while he was one of their targets! No telling how many GI's he saved. So who's the real hero now?

"The Army gives Good Conduct Medals to soldiers in wartime with spotless records and more than a year in service. In the Marines it takes four years, period. He got one of them too, plus the European Medal (European-African-Middle Eastern Campaign Medal), and the WWII Victory Medal. Of course they was all just ribbons until after the war, except for the Bronze Star."

"Slick, both of you are heroes, but you fought in different parts of the world in different branches of service and in different types of units. You both have a lot to be thankful for and a lot to be proud of.

"Of course, I hafta add that my ex-gyrene buddies never let me forget how tough they all are, and how everyone's a badass in the Marines, and how all us dogfaces in the Army couldn't carry their water. 'Once a Marine, always a Marine.' I'm sure it's true some of the time, but not always. But maybe it is true in the way medals are awarded, and certainly true for the Good Conduct Medal."

"Well, I'm sore about the Purple Heart, nothing else. I know they follow the letter of the law on who gets one and who don't but the regulations should be changed. I think maybe you missed my point regarding Bernie.

"In the beginning of the war, he wasn't good enough to serve, even as a supply clerk. Then when things get dicey, strategically speaking, just like magic, suddenly he's good enough. You don't have to have two good eyes to have the heart of a warrior and perform acts of valor. I'm very proud of him and I'm glad he had the opportunity to prove hisself.

"Now, let's talk about something else. You got to be bored to tears by now.

"You think the Mets will win the World Series again this year? I bet if they was to play it again with the Orioles, the Orioles would win it."

CHAPTER 8
A Special Assignment
Monday, March 16, 1970

Barlow said, "I doubt it, but Slick, before I lose my train of thought, I'd just like to say you have a real fascinating family history. I really appreciate you telling me. One of these days I hope to meet Bernie and his family. All I can say is, your family is a lot more colorful than mine. Compared to you all, we're as dry as Texas dust.

"Example. I grew up in the Texas panhandle in a one-horse town, not quite as off the beaten path as Mosby, but definitely nothing like Dallas or Amarillo. We lived near cattle ranches but I never learned how to ride a horse. That's always something I wanted to do.

"Now, since I met Sarah, that's something I do every chance I get. Someday I hope to be as good of a rider as everyone in her family."

"That's good thinkin'. I've always ridden horses, and mules, too, for that matter, long as I can remember and generally speaking, I'd rather go a-horseback than in a machine. I'm just not much in love with automobiles.

"Heck, the only one I ever bought is a '41 Ford pickup I got from Mickey Delaney in 1948, thankfully after Clemmie took a powder or no doubt, she'd have stolen it, too. I still drive it whenever I need wheels. Other than that, me and my brother have Grandpappy's '23 Model T pickup, which we still use on the ranch.

"From time to time we have problems getting parts for the Model T. Buck Boyd is pretty good finding 'em but when he can't, we jury-rig it with homemade parts. We just don't take it off the ranch . . . ."

The night, which started so painfully for Barlow ended so surprisingly for both of them. Sheriff Sol rolled in at 7 o'clock. This was early for him. He poured himself a cup of coffee and told them to grab a seat in his office.

"Boys, Judge Sweeney's Triple S Ranch has been rustled. Somewhere between 200 and 300 sheep are missing. These are all Rambouillets. They found four different places where the fencing had been recently cut and spliced back together. The splicing was expertly done. They also found tractor trailer tracks and an area on the north side of a canyon that makes a natural holding pen where they believe the rustlers rigged up a temporary corral. Lots of sheep tracks, plus it has running water.

"Judge Sweeney doesn't want anyone to know about this. No one! His hands have been threatened with death by hanging if word gets out. He wants the two of you to set up on the midnight shift to catch the rustlers. He will have his best and most trusted vaquero, Rico Méndez, as a guide to help you all out. You begin tonight."

Slick asked, "Did he specifically ask for us?"

"He did. He knows you're the best damn cowboy in this county and he's keen on Barlow as a result of the Diablos incident."

Barlow asked, "How do you keep something like this a secret in Quayle County?"

"It won't be easy. Of course Chief Alex and Archie will be in on it. Thing is, Judge Sweeney doesn't know how his ranch was singled out. As of now, no one else in Quayle County has complained about missing livestock of any kind. We do know Brewster County has had at least one victim in which the rancher lost over seventy sheep. So for now, we'll keep this amongst ourselves. I'll figure out something to pacify inquiring minds."

Barlow asked, "Does Judge Sweeney have reason to suspect he might be hit again?"

"Nope, but it looks like they've hit him at least twice. He runs over 60,000 head of sheep. Look. He has more than 150 square miles to protect. Also, this canyon is the perfect holding pen. It's a safe bet they'll hit him again, especially if they think he's oblivious to his losses.

"It goes without saying that he and his brother are extremely influential in Texas political circles. Besides that, it's our sworn duty and he's our neighbor as well as our friend. If this doesn't pan out, we'll shift to something else, especially if we get any other reports of rustling."

Slick asked, "So what's the deal for tonight?"

"You two are now working 9 p.m. to 5 a.m., seven days a week until I decide different. You all meet at Judge Sweeney's new barn on the southwest side off CO 8 near Rattlesnake Trail. Slick, you know where that's at. You show Barlow. Rico Méndez will meet you there at the gate at 9. You will hide your trucks in the barn. Slick, you can take your own mount. Barlow, he'll have some mounts for you to choose from or if you want, I'll bring Arthur Baker into this and you can borrow one from him.

"Find the best vantage points to set up without being spotted. Rico will help you all with that. You can probably safely assume that if the rustlers do return, it will be between midnight and 4 o'clock.

"Fellas, twenty years ago we would have shot the rustlers as soon as they started to round up the stock. We can't do that anymore. You have to wait until they move the sheep off the Triple S onto public property before you can confront them. This way there's proof beyond a reasonable doubt they were rustling.

"These owlhoots are likely dangerous. Arm yourselves accordingly. Don't shoot unless you have to, but don't takes any chances.

"I'll find a hidey hole for my car south of the previous probable entry points on Rattlesnake Trail where I can see anyone sneaking in without them detecting me. If they do show up, I'll cut 'em off at the pass as soon as they exit the property with rustled stock. Your job is to back me up. Of course, you all won't have any commo, but I'll have commo with Archie at Base.

"Boys, the Sweeneys could have called in a half-dozen Texas Rangers on this if they wanted. I'm proud Judge Sweeney has faith in us to get the job done. Any questions?"

Barlow asked, "Sheriff, if it's all right with you, I'd prefer to ride one of Arthur's horses named Boyo. Would you ask him?"

"I will. Slick, I'll get Arthur to bring the horse and tack to your place sometime today. Would you mind hauling him along with your mount?"

"I'd be delighted, Sheriff. I been waiting for an opportunity like this for an awful long time."

Barlow responded, "Me, too. Slick, give me the directions and I'll meet you not later than 8:45."

"You got it."

CHAPTER 9
The Stakeout Begins
Monday/Tuesday, March 16/17, 1970

Barlow was so pumped about his pending assignment that he had a hard time concentrating in class. After three hours of book work, it was a relief to report to PE.

The phys ed instructor had a thing for scheduling punishing runs on Mondays because he knew most of the students blew off physical fitness on the weekends, that is, other than twelve-ounce curls with frosty brown bottles. Today, they ran a brisk eight-minute pace in formation for four miles before running the obstacle course for time. No pain. No gain. This was exactly what Barlow needed and he pushed it hard.

After class, he met Sarah in the student union for lunch. It took everything he could muster not to share his secret with her. He knew she'd smell a rat by tomorrow morning but at least for today, he kept his word and she was happy. What's the saying? Ignorance is bliss? He certainly hoped so, at least for today.

That night, Barlow had no trouble getting up three-and-a-half hours early. For supper, he ate fried bologna and mayonnaise sandwiches with applesauce for dessert, washed down with a pint of milk. He made American cheese and lettuce sandwiches for his early morning meal. He filled one canteen with water and his thermos with coffee. He also put a couple of apples in his poke - one him and one for Boyo.

He arrived for the rendezvous at 8:30. Slick and Rico were already there, parked in tandem. Slick was towing a two-horse trailer on the back of his '41 Ford pickup. Even in the dark Barlow could see that the truck looked like new. The trailer, however, was another matter entirely. Barlow fell in line.

They drove single file along a sheep trail to a new barn bigger than Barlow had ever seen in his life. A ranch hand rolled open the door and they drove inside. The ranch hand closed the door, stepping inside. It was darker than Hades when they turned off their headlamps. The ranch hand lit a lantern and turned it up just enough so they could see each other in the shadows.

Rico introduced Slick and Barlow to his oldest son, Pepe. He said they would go on horseback, first to see where the fence had been cut and mended, and then to the canyon where the sheep had been penned up.

Slick brought his horse, Toby, out of the trailer first. Toby was a big bay with three white stockings. Then he brought out Boyo, a smaller, more compact sorrel, with a cream-colored mane and tail. Barlow was pleased Arthur had included saddlebags and a rifle scabbard and even a short lariat with the tack.

Barlow stowed his gear, to include a bandoleer full of rifle cartridges in the saddlebags and slid his Winchester into the scabbard. Then Slick reached into his cab and brought out an old, but well-maintained Remington, double-barrel shotgun with external hammers, referred to as rabbit ears for obvious reasons. The barrels were at least thirty inches long, with significantly bigger bores than a twelve-gauge.

Barlow exclaimed, "Oh my gosh! What is this? Did it come over on the Mayflower? Did it belong to Miles Standish? Did he use it on any of our Penobscot Indian brethren? Oh! Maybe it's Bernie's ack ack gun."

"This, Laddie, is me grandpappy's full-choked 10-gauge. He bought it in San Antonio in 1910. It patterns double-aught buck out to eighty yards. Her name is Colleen. Means girl in Scottish. I got a saddlebag full of shells for her. She can turn a grizzly bear into hamburger in a New York second. I'm thankful it was handed down to me and my brother.

"You see. It's like this. It's dark. We won't really be able to see our sights until we shoot the first round. Then we'll adjust according to what we can see in the muzzle flash. I don't have to be spot on with old Colleen here. All I have to do is point her in the general direction and pull the triggers. However, if they're more'n eighty yards away, it'll be up to you to bag 'em with that tried and true cowboy rifle in your scabbard there, that is, if you can see your sights."

"Yes, but what if you hit two or three bandits when you only meant to shoot one?"

"They're rustlers, ain't they? We used to string 'em up soon as we caught 'em in the old days."

"Yes, but this is Judge Sweeney's land."

"Exactly. Ever heard of his grandpappy, Ripsnort Sweeney? He has a whole graveyard full of rustlers buried somewhere on this property. Ain't that so, Rico?"

"Sí. It is so, Mr. Slick. Come daylight, I will show you both if you like."

"Well, so long as we're on the right side of the law. I feel so much safer now, knowing that you've got us all covered with your heavy artillery. If it does come down to nut cuttin' and you shoot first, it'll be game over and the rest of us can just head on back to the barn."

"Right you are, Laddie. Methinks it's a wonderful thing to witness when the light switch comes on to those less fortunate than ourselves in the thinkin' department."

Once they were mounted, Pepe blew out the lantern and opened the door. Then he mounted. They paused long enough to let their eyes adjust to the darkness of a three-quarters full moon.

They rode single file. Rico led and Pepe pulled drag. Rico pointed out four recent fence cuttings and splicings spaced about a hundred yards apart. The rustlers did an expert job. Hardly noticeable, at least by moonlight. The cuts were all made on the fence paralleling the east side of Rattlesnake Trail, about halfway between the northern and southern termini on this particular section of land. Barlow was having a hard time trying to pick out landmarks, in case he needed to return on his own sometime in the future.

They rode about two miles east of this fence, which brought them to a semi-circular canyon. Actually, it was like a four-fifths circular canyon, with a small stream running through it from an underground source, providing a shallow pool of water. It could easily hold a hundred sheep, probably a lot more. Forty feet of fencing would be sufficient to enclose it.

How on Earth would a stranger find this natural holding pen if no one showed him? Barlow and Slick both said inside job but Rico swore that all the hands were loyal to a fault. He said it had to be someone else. Maybe a neighbor or long lost family member or a former employee.

Rico said he would slowly and painfully slice the cojones off the guilty employee if it turned out that this was an inside job. Then he would feed his cojones to this mean, ornery sow named Naranja while the cabron watched in horror. This is the best way to punish a traitor, no? Do it in front of his wife and his kids. Make him suffer for the rest of his miserable life.

Slick smiled. Barlow was speechless. Rico seemed too peaceable to even think such a thing. They got back down to business.

Rico pointed out two arroyos close enough to the canyon to keep it under surveillance, and deep enough to conceal a mounted rider. You could keep an eye on the opening from either one, but not be able to see what was going on inside.

There was a third arroyo which could conceal a man on foot but not mounted. A place to hide in a pinch, perhaps.

Another option would be for a man to conceal himself atop the canyon where he could look down inside it. That was probably the riskiest option for fear that the rustlers might shine a light along the rim to scan it for unwelcome witnesses, but it would have the best vantage point after dark.

Slick and Rico put their heads together and talked it through.

They decided to place Barlow and Pepe in the easternmost arroyo about halfway between the road and the canyon. They could ride along the arroyo closer to the canyon if the rustlers showed up.

Rico and Slick would take the westernmost arroyo. It was closer to the canyon, had a better view of the opening, and was plenty deep enough to conceal them if they were mounted.

They also agreed that, absent exigent circumstances, everyone would hold tight until Slick moved in, shouted a verbal order, or commenced firing.

Rico pointed out that it was very possible the rustlers would make a dry run on the first night to herd the sheep into the canyon with plans to bring a tractor trailer to rustle the sheep the following night. Slick hadn't considered that.

They decided if that were to happen, they would sit tight and wait for the actual rustling to occur. They needed the sheep to be in the truck and off Triple S property to confirm beyond a reasonable doubt that the bandits were indeed rustling, and not just playing a prank.

Everyone was on board. They took their positions to wait it out. It was 11:15. If the bandits didn't show tonight, they could be set up by 9:30 tomorrow night.

Barlow asked Pepe about snakes. Pepe said to avoid bushes or rocks with crevices. The best thing would be to lie on a bedroll on the slope of the arroyo and to move slowly. He said he brought a spade if he needed to take a shit or kill a snake. It dawned on Barlow he was more likely to get snake-bit than shot. Tomorrow night he would have a snakebite kit, a bedroll, and his own entrenching tool.

At 11 p.m., exact whereabouts unknown to the surveillance team, Sheriff Sol parked near the southern terminus of Rattlesnake Trail, facing north. He used duct tape to secure an old, wool, Navy blanket across the bumper, grill, and hood of his car. He was a half-mile away from the nearest fence-splicing.

He didn't want the headlights from a rustler's truck to light up the chrome on his car. He rolled down all the windows and turned off the ignition. He might not see the rustlers initially but he should be able to hear them.

At 4 o'clock he called it a wash. It had been as peaceful as Christmas Eve. He went home to catch a few winks before heading to the office.

At 5 o'clock, Slick and company shut it down. They agreed same place, same time tonight. Barlow followed Slick home so he could groom and feed Boyo. He even had time to go home and shower and change clothes before school. Sarah would smell a rat for sure.

She did. She pinned his ears back in the parking lot as soon as he drove up.

"What's going on?"

"School, I guess."

"Don't be cute. Why did Dad loan Slick Boyo and all the tack, to include a saddle scabbard. Slick owns as many horses as we do and he surely doesn't need to borrow any tack."

"Did you ask your dad?"

"Yes. He said 'need to know and you don't need to know.' Barlow, I know for a fact that you like Boyo more than anyone else who has ever seen him, let alone ridden him."

"You trust your Dad, don't you?"

"Yes I do, but I smell a rat. What are you up to? Look at you! You're out of uniform and you've had a shower. Your hair is still wet. I know that you and Sheriff Sol and Slick and my dad are all up to something and I want to know what. Barlow, I'm your fiancé and I have a right to know!"

"Sarah, your dad and I have been sworn to secrecy. You can't accidentally let something slip if you don't know what it is. All I can say is, it's important and I will tell you everything just as soon as I can."

"Barlow, I know it's something dangerous. I have a pretty good idea already because you need a reliable horse on the midnight shift. You could be tracking wetbacks across the river. You could also be doing something related to our roundup on Saturday. I wonder what that could be. Want me to continue adding one plus one? Bet I can figure it out by adding one more one."

"Sarah, all I can say is I hope you will stop adding. If word gets out on what's going on, the repercussions could be serious. Suppose you are on the right track. If the rest of Mosby thought what you are thinking, it would cause a major problem for a lot of folks, including me. Trust me. I will tell you when I can, and I promise to make it up to you."

"Barlow, I already figured out what you're doing. I just don't know where but I have pretty good idea. I'm concerned about you."

"I know you are and for that I'm thankful. You know me better than anyone else in the world. You know I love my job and I would never quit. I'm always careful, and related to what I'm doing now, I have first class help. I love you with all my heart but you have to accept that sometimes I will be in harm's way. Please don't fret about it. Just keep me in your prayers, okay?"

Sarah walked up to Barlow even closer and fully embraced him. She kissed him passionately. She broke off and said, "Barlow Adams, I love you so much it hurts. Don't get yourself killed, okay? You want to know why?"

"Because you'll miss me?"

"That's right, but that's not the only thing."

"What else?"

"Well, if you have to know, angels don't engage in sex in heaven. I know how much you love it. I'm just looking out for you. If at all possible, you don't want to arrive there until you are way too old to get it up anymore."

Barlow smiled wide. He squeezed her left buttock. "You know what? Sometimes you really slay me. That's one of the reasons I love you so much. And who said I'll ever not be able to get it up?

"Come on. We'll be late for class."

CHAPTER 10
Sunday/Monday, March 22/23, 1970
The Rustlers Return

They had been on surveillance six nights now with nary a nibble in this fishing hole. The work was exciting, no comparison with pulling the midnight tour in an empty jailhouse, but Barlow had scarcely seen Sarah all week. Therefore, he was grateful for the invitation to stop by the Baker's for dinner before shoving off to meet Slick.

Not a peep was mentioned regarding Slick's and Barlow's assignment, but within this small circle of intimate family, it was obvious this was another one of those secrets everyone knew about, but out of courtesy, never mentioned. Light and stimulating conversation has a tendency to stagnate when everyone is trying real hard not to notice the 800-pound gorilla sitting with them in the room. Looking on the bright side, Barlow was happy that he hadn't encountered any snakes so far!

Way too soon, it was time to go to work. Sarah stepped outside with him as he walked to his truck. She said, "Missed me this week, Deputy?"

He replied, "More than you know. I'm hornier than a triple-peckered billy goat with no relief in sight."

"Is that all you miss?"

"You know better than that, but it would certainly help take the edge off so I could concentrate on other things."

"Like what?"

"Like doing it again and again and again."

"You rat! And here I thought you loved me for my winning personality and sterling character and witty charm and ravishing good looks and for all the domestic things I do to make life more pleasurable for you."

"What you said, plus how you make me feel ten feet tall when I'm with you. That's exactly what I meant to say. Did I not convey those very thoughts?"

"Well, okay then. I know it's getting late and you need to go. If you hadn't been such a chatterbox during supper, I would have brought you out here earlier and refined my expertise in the erotic art of fellatio while you gave me a neck and shoulder massage. But now it's too late. Give me a peck on the cheek so you can go out and slay some dragons. Better not be saving any damsels in distress, Deputy. You're running off and leaving one here who is in dire need of satisfaction in terms of tender, loving care."

"Oh Girly, now this is all I'll be able to think about until we get some alone time. I'm getting a white-out. A screamin' semen headache! I won't be able to see clearly until you give me some relief. You are such a tease!"

"Yes, but I always deliver on satisfaction in a big way, wouldn't you say, Deputy?"

"You do, but until you do deliver, I'll be suffering with each breath I take."

"Well, that's the way I feel when I don't get to see you." She pressed her body next to his and wrapped her arms tightly around his waist. She gave him a long, lingering, French kiss. When she broke off, she reached down and squeezed the throbbing muscle between his thighs.

She said, "Goodnight, Deputy. You better have something equally as nice as this for me after school tomorrow. I just might need your ministrations so badly that I blow off work, no pun intended, and keep you romantically engaged until such time as it's necessary for you to resume fighting crime and corruption to keep America safe for democracy. Do we have a date?"

"We do. Better get back to the house. You've been out here so long they'll probably think you did what you said you didn't have time to do."

"Well, I wish I would have gone ahead and done it, especially if I'm going to be maligned as having done it. Until tomorrow."

"Until tomorrow."

Barlow kicked it in gear and met Slick at 8:55.

"Sorry I'm late."

"No worries, Laddy. I'm hoping you been doing what I'm usually doing when I'm running behind."

"If only I were."

Each rider took up his position. Barlow tried to clear his mind by studying the stars, looking for constellations besides the Big and Little Dippers. Hard to do. It took a truly creative mind to identify Taurus or Orion and the others.

It was 2:35. Sheriff Sol was back at his regular vantage point. He was all ears when he heard the truck approaching. He eased out of his cruiser and crept silently up and then down the slope so he could see.

The truck had stopped on the road. It was still idling, but the headlights were off. He saw the passenger exit the vehicle and stoop down by the fence. He cut it and moved it out of the way so the pickup could enter Triple S land. Once it moved away from him into the pasture, Sheriff Sol returned to his unit and radioed Base.

Archie answered right away. Sheriff Sol ordered, "Wake Chief Alex and get him to set up out of sight on Highway 90 west of 651. He's to be on the lookout for a dark pickup truck with two men. I want to know which direction this truck goes. He can tail it for a short distance to see if he can get a plate number, but tell him it would be better that he doesn't get anything than to get burned. Don't follow it for more than a mile at most. I will radio when the vehicle departs the goldmine. Copy?"

"Copy, Quayle 1. Quayle 2 will contact you when he's on location."

"Quayle 1 out." He stepped out of the car to take a leak. Then he lit a cigarette and waited patiently for human nature to follow its course. He wished he had a way to contact Slick. No matter. Slick knew what to do. If all went well, they'd be rounding up rustlers tomorrow night about now.

It was 2:50. Barlow and Pepe heard a vehicle in the distance long before they saw it. The sound of the engine gradually escalated. Finally they saw it silhouetted in the moonlight. A dark pickup was creeping their way. They lost sight of it when it dipped down on the back side of a low rise. The sound of the engine died down until they could hear it no more. Once again, it was as quiet as a graveyard. The silence was deafening.

Barlow wondered what they were supposed to do next besides not get detected. He deduced that this was a dry run but certainly there must be something they could do. He could tell that Pepe was keying off him. Tick tock. Tick tock. Tick tock. His orders were to sit tight. They sat tight. Geez, this was killing him.

At 3:20, they faintly heard the baa-ing of sheep. Patience. The volume was increasing! The sounds of a moving flock got stronger and stronger. Finally, a medium-sized flock crested the rise. They saw two men with staves on foot with a dog. The dog was doing most of the work. The flock stayed together.

Barlow and Pepe left their mounts tethered where they had been watching. They scrambled along the arroyo to the end closest to the mouth of the canyon, going as far as cover would allow. It wasn't close enough but it would have to do.

They watched while the dog and the men herded the sheep into the canyon. One man and the dog remained at the mouth while the other man walked back over the rise.

A little while later, the truck crested the hill and stopped near the canyon opening. Both men retrieved a roll of fencing and some stakes, and began closing off the opening. As soon as they finished, they returned to the truck and began to make their way back to the road.

For just a few seconds, Barlow could see the men more distinctly when the interior courtesy lights illuminated them. It happened too fast and too far away. All he could make out was that they were of medium height and build and that they both were wearing jean jackets and cowboy hats.

Barlow and Pepe ran back to their mounts. They were about to follow the truck when Slick and Rico rode up. Slick said he and Rico would follow the truck to see if they could make out a license plate. He said Barlow and Pepe could follow behind them at a safe distance. The idea was that no one gets burned.

This killed Barlow's soul but he did what he was told without complaint. He knew this was the right thing to do. If they didn't spook the rustlers, they would arrest them all tomorrow night. Otherwise, this was just an exercise in futility.

It was 4:15. Slick and Rico swung wide to the north so as not to be in direct line of sight from the rear view mirror when they closed the gap. They could hear the truck but not see it.

They saw the taillights in the distance when it stopped at the road. They watched as both rustlers got out and spliced the fence. These guys were good. They were done in ten minutes.

They watched the truck drive north on Rattlesnake Trail. When it was beyond eyesight, they saw Sheriff Sol crawling along behind. Neither vehicle was running with lights.

They rode back to Barlow and Pepe and passed along what they saw. Slick said everyone did a great job and that tomorrow night should be their big payday. They rode back to the barn and loaded the horses. Slick said the drill would be the same tonight unless Sheriff Sol or Chief Alex contacted them and said otherwise. The deputies and vaqueros parted ways, full of anticipation as though this were Christmas Eve.

Slick and Barlow drove straight to the jail. Sheriff Sol, Chief, and Archie were already there sipping coffee.

Chief said the truck drove north on 651. He followed it as far as Washington Avenue. He said it looked like the license plate had been removed. He could tell it was a Ford F-100, either a '68 or '69, and it was either black or navy blue. It was similar to

Delmar Logan's truck but it wasn't Delmar's because his is kind of tore up and this truck looked brand new. He did see that the tailgate had a white oval sticker on the left. It looked like a car dealer's sticker, but he couldn't make it out. It didn't look like any of the stickers from dealerships he was familiar with.

Sheriff Sol thanked everyone for their diligence and hard work. He said he would have help tonight in marked units after the rustlers showed up. The marked units would be pre-positioned to make traffic stops once the rustlers drove away from the ranch. No contact would be initiated until the rustlers were on the highway. Finally, he reminded Slick and Barlow to update their diaries so they could write their statements regarding what they saw and did tonight.

It was 7 o'clock. He told Slick and Barlow to split. Slick tried to get Barlow to go onto school, saying that he would groom Boyo, but Barlow said "Thanks, but nothin' doin'. That's my responsibility."

It was 8:10 when he slipped into class. He met Sarah at noon when they were both done for the morning. They didn't tarry. They booked it back to his house and were both naked as jaybirds by 12:15.

This was no time for slow hands. It was akin to a house on fire. They came together and rode the tidal wave for all it was worth. They locked into the pupils of each other's eyes and saw the reflections of themselves in the throes of ecstasy. They pursued their needs with the ferocity of a tornado, never stopping, violent thrusts, soaked in sweat, out of breath, overwhelming sensations, out of control, finally erupting like a volcano before they both expired as a result of overexertion.

They both lay on their backs, gasping for breath, their senses of touch on overload, sated for a brief while, like halftime in a football game, recharging batteries, wanting more, needing more, nothing else in the whole wide world more important than what they were doing now, unable to keep their hands off one another.

Fifteen minutes. Not a word uttered. Barlow rolled over and mounted her again. He pinned her arms to the mattress. He started slowly but Sarah's urgent thrusts upward moved him from first to second to third gear. They were running up the mountain again. She was urging him to move faster.

"Keep up. Don't stop. Go faster. Push harder. Please don't stop. I love you. Right there. Deeper. Keep going. I can feel it. It's happening. Oh, please don't stop. I'm coming . . . . Oh Lordy, please don't stop. Oh, thank you. Thank you. Thank you. Ohhhh. You can stop now. You can stop. Did you come? Oh, good. Hold me tight. I love you so much."

Silence. Reflection. Thirty minutes passed.

"Barlow."

"Wha?"

"Are you hungry?"

"I think so. Are you?"

"Starved. What have you got to eat?"

"I have some hamburger patties in the fridge. Buns in the bread box. Ice cream. Chocolate chip. Several cans of baked beans and corn and new potatoes and English peas. Limas too, I think. Oreo cookies. Potato chips. Barq's root beer. What do you want?"

"I'll fry some hamburgers. You interested?"

"Yes."

"Okay. I'll fix some lunch. Also, sorry, but I didn't beg off from work. I need to be back by 3."

"It's okay. I'm completely worn out, plus I need some sleep before work tonight. Hope you don't mind."

"Can we do it just one more time? I wasn't through yet."

"Give me a few minutes? I'm running on fumes. My tank is empty. Let's eat first. Need some energy."

"Wouldn't you rather do it first?"

"Oh, Babe . . . ."

"Gotcha! Really had ya going."

"What?"

"Just kidding. I'm a little tender down there right now. I probably will be out of service for three or four days at least."

"Oh, don't say that. I'll be ready for more fun and games tomorrow. Promise."

"Nope. I don't think so. Sorry."

"Oh, Geez."

"Gotcha again!"

"Sarah. Fix food. You keep teasing me and I'll get all horny again and now that I've gotten off twice I should be good for at least another thirty minutes, maybe an hour. Probably two. Then your brand new saddle really will be worn out."

"Big talk from someone who hasn't slept yet but I'm too hungry to see if you're bluffing. I'm headed to the kitchen now. In my nudies, Smartypants. It's so exhilarating to walkabout unencumbered by clothes. I might even step outside and check the mailbox. Hope Mrs. Peabody isn't watching."

She bounced out of bed and made sure she had his undivided attention before she wiggled that perfect, tight, round derrière of hers in his direction before she skipped to the bathroom en route to the kitchen.

Barlow thought once again, "It just doesn't get any better than this. Absolutely no way."

CHAPTER 11
Monday/Tuesday, March 23/24, 1970
Several Unexpected Developments

This night Sheriff Sol and Chief Alex met with Slick, Barlow, Rico, and Pepe at the barn. Deputies Ernie Atwater and Noble "Chunk" Bustamante had already been briefed at the jail earlier in the day.

Sheriff Sol said it was all he could do to persuade Judge Sweeney that he needed to be as far away as possible from tonight's festivities. Not a solitary soul in this group believed that a single rustler would be taken alive if Judge Sweeney were present.

The plan from Day One to present remained the same. Allow the rustlers to load the sheep and drive off of Triple S property before effecting the arrests.

The rustlers would have to go north because they were only a mile-and-a-half from the Mexican border. Furthermore, they could never drive a tractor trailer loaded with livestock through the river without getting it bogged down even though it was shallow here. Therefore, the assignments were the same except for the following addendums.

First, Chief Alex would set up about three miles north of Mosby on Highway 651 behind an abandoned roadhouse. He would radio Base when he saw the rustlers headed south. Afterwards, he would take backroads to Range Road a couple of miles east of Rattlesnake Trail and about four miles south of CO 8. He would vector in to Rattlesnake Trail once the rustlers departed the Triple S.

Second, Chunk would be in a marked unit. He would set up at the old entrance to Casey Salazar's spread on Rattlesnake Trail north of the Triple S, once the rustlers entered Judge Sweeney's ranch. He, too, would vector in for the anticipated traffic stop(s) once the rustlers made their departure.

Third, Ernie would be in a marked unit, set up behind the co-op on Highway 90 about a mile west of 651. He would be there in case the rustlers took a different route to the ranch from their departure route as indicated the night before. He would also close in for the bust, coming from the farthest southern departure point.

Sheriff Sol would be in his usual location. He would give the signal to move in.

The mounted men would be there to observe the rustling and just in case things went amok before the rustlers departed the property, or on the remote chance they tried to double back if things didn't go as planned.

Everyone was ordered to be alert and armed with a long gun. They should not overlook the fact that desperate men have used motor vehicles as weapons to avoid capture in the past. If push came to shove, everyone needed sufficient firepower to shut down a truck.

There were no questions. Barlow noticed that for the first time, Rico and Pepe were armed. Rico had a WWI military surplus M-1903, bolt-action Springfield rifle, in 30-06. Pepe had a WWII military surplus Winchester Model 12, pump shotgun in 12-gauge. Barlow knew it was military surplus because it had a lug nut on the barrel for fastening on a bayonet. As long as there weren't a dozen rustlers or one armed with an M-16, the arresting officers should be all right.

By 9:15 everyone was in his assigned position except for Chunk, who was at the jail pending Sheriff Sol's instructions to man his post.

The sky was clear with a thousand stars and a full moon. Pepe said there were 126 sheep in the canyon. Most of them were lambs. He said figuring low, at an average weight of 80 pounds per sheep and 15 cents per pound on the hoof, the heist was worth at least $1,500.

Barlow was pumped so he ate his sandwiches early. Besides, he figured if he waited too long he'd never have a chance to eat.

At 1:25, Ernie reported that a black Ford pickup with two men, followed by two eighteen-wheelers with stock trailers, just passed his location headed eastbound towards 651. He couldn't see how many people were in the big rigs.

Quayle 1 told Quayle 2 to shift to his back door post. He told Chunk to wait fifteen minutes before leaving for his post.

Slick and his crew were still unaware.

At 1:50, Sheriff Sol watched the trucks stop on the road a quarter-mile farther away from him than the night before. Slick's crew could vaguely hear, but not see the vehicles. The diesels made a lot more racket than last night's pickup truck.

About 2:15, Barlow and Pepe watched all three trucks drive towards the canyon in single file. The pickup swung wide to the right. Two men disembarked. The big rigs maneuvered one at a time until their trailers were close to, and facing away from the canyon.

Once they parked, a driver disembarked from each tractor. They went to their respective trailers and opened the doors. They set up ramps. The other two men from the pickup rolled back a portion of the fencing. The dog and one of the men from the pickup truck entered the canyon and began herding the sheep into the trailer on the right. When it was full the driver pulled out of the way. The men on foot rolled the fencing back some more and began herding the rest of the sheep into the second trailer. It didn't take twenty minutes.

The men rolled up the fencing and placed it in the bed of the pickup. Then two men and the dog got back into the pickup and began leading the big rigs out the way they came in.

All four of Slick's crew mounted in a rank facing west. Adrenaline was coursing through their veins like a raging river.

Holding back while every fiber in their bodies screamed, 'Attack!' took monumental discipline. Now the only thing they could see of the trucks were taillights. Finally, they began following slowly at a safe distance, or so they thought.

Sheriff Sol watched the trucks approach the road. He radioed for all units to begin to move in. Then things began to come unhinged.

"The best laid schemes o' Mice an' Men, Gang aft agley. An' lea'e us nought but grief an' pain, For promis'd joy." Put another way, "Man plans and God laughs."

The two rigs pulled out on the road northbound and stopped. The pickup was parked westbound just outside the fence. The two men from the pickup got out and began splicing the fence. Apparently one of them heard or sensed the horses even though they were still more than two hundred yards away, because they both looked up just as the riders crested the low rise.

Slick was out in front. The others were spread out behind him. Once the riders got within range, the driver pulled out a handgun and began shooting at them. The other bandit ran back to the passenger side of the pickup and returned with a shotgun. The dog jumped out of the pickup and began running toward the riders.

Barlow galloped ahead like this was the Charge of the Light Brigade. When he was within thirty yards, he drew his revolver and traded shots with the driver. This was absolutely unacceptable to Boyo, who reared up and began to buck before turning about face and running lickety-split back to whence he came.

It suddenly dawned on Barlow that he had unwittingly committed a faux pas in common horse courtesy, thus precipitating his very first bucking bronco ride. He couldn't believe he was so dense! No wonder the other riders held their fire!

In fact, the other three, more experienced riders dismounted before engaging. The passenger had already fired two shots at Slick, who reciprocated by unleashing both barrels from his antique smoke cannon. He blew his adversary back six feet into oblivion, showering body parts in every direction.

Father and son also returned fire. Pepe shot at the same bandit as Slick but likely did little, if any damage, due to the extended range for a twenty-inch-barreled, open choke shotgun.

The driver may have been out of ammo or he may have decided that discretion is the better part of valor. Whichever, seeing that his partner was blasted into tiny morsels of buzzard food, he ran back to the pickup and began to go adios amigo. Rico shot at this villain once while he was on foot to no avail, and three more times at the fleeing truck, slaying the back windshield deader than the proverbial doorknob.

During the melee, the two big rig drivers also deduced that it was time to 'cut a chogie.' They had been sitting on 'G' waiting for 'O' in high anxiety and shots fired was like waving the green flag at Daytona or Indy. Big brother led and little brother followed - for a hundred yards. Big brother muttered, "Mieda! Joder!"

They could see red flashing lights coming fast from the south and now, off in the distance, red flashing lights coming from the north. Big brother went way beyond just a little berserk with good reason. He had unhappily experienced run-ins with the law in his brief and wicked past. He opted to bulldoze straight ahead, hoping for a miracle.

Little brother, the virgin, started and then stopped dead in his tracks, passively waiting like a sheep being led to slaughter, either to be shot or hung. At this point what difference would it make? His mama and papa would be so disappointed and ashamed! His life was over either way and he only had himself to blame. Had he not heard over and over and over all his life to stay away from Rudy, who was a bad seed? Why, oh why, didn't he listen?

To the north, Chunk pulled across the roadway to establish a roadblock. He soon realized that the big rig was picking up speed with no intention of stopping. He managed to scoot out of the way by a whisker but this cost him valuable time getting turned around to pursue. The radio traffic was chaotic. Too much was happening all at once.

Chief vectored in from the east and Atwater was flying south as fast as he could from Highway 90.

The rig had just passed Chief at the intersection of CO 8 with Chunk in hot pursuit right on his tail. He fell into line behind Chunk.

Ernie had heard about Chunk's near miss on the radio, so he decided to stop where he was and set up his own roadblock. The difference was, Ernie had the Remington, 30-06 sniper rifle locked and loaded and he was prepared to use it if the rig did not show any indication of stopping. He parked across Rattlesnake Trail and used the hood of his unit as a bench rest.

Within seconds, the rig was in the crosshairs of his scope. It was still picking up speed. Ernie shot the first round in the center of the windshield as a warning. Give the driver pause to reconsider his wicked ways. Jail beats death, or so he reasoned.

The driver never even tapped his brakes. The truck continued to gain momentum and would be on top of him within seconds! Ernie fired the next three rounds rapid fire exactly where he thought the driver would be sitting. The glare of the headlights nearly blinded him so he never actually saw the driver when he fired. He was guessing.

The truck slowed abruptly, as if the driver had eased off the accelerator without touching the brakes. It was too late for Ernie to move his unit but not too late to jump into the ditch beside the road to save himself. Sheriff Sol would not be pleased.

The rig center-punched the cruiser but not too hard. It only pushed the cruiser back about four feet. Ernie pulled his service revolver and leapt onto the passenger side running board. First

Chunk, then Chief, ran up on the driver's side, weapons drawn. Fortunately, Chief had remembered to bring a flashlight.

They yanked both doors open almost simultaneously. The driver was slumped over the steering wheel. Chief lifted his head back by his hair to get a look at his face. The back of his head was missing due to a shot in the center of his forehead. Nevertheless, his features were recognizable.

Chief asked, "Recognize him?"

Ernie said, No."

Chunk said, "I do."

Ernie queried, "Who is he?"

Chief responded, "Rodolfo Gómez. One of Alberto Gómez's boys."

Chunk added, "He's one of the ones we thought stole the car from Pecos last summer."

Chief concluded, "Well, whether he was or he wasn't, we know for sure that he's out of the bandit business now."

Chunk concurred, "You got that right."

CHAPTER 12
Tuesday, March 24, 1970
Sheriff Sol Enters the Fray

Stakeouts are multifaceted. Busted stakeouts even more so. While the north end deputies were engaged with Rodolfo, Sheriff Sol, being the only other lawman in a motor vehicle, was engaged with the pickup driver.

As soon as the sheriff heard shots being exchanged at the ranch he blasted the half-mile north to where the rustlers had cut through the fence.

The big rigs bolted northbound but the pickup turned south and barreled right past him. Sheriff Sol executed a J-turn, commonly referred to as a 'U-be' and the high speed chase was on. He had the faster, more responsive unit, outclassing the pickup by far, assuming the race were consigned to the highway. Sheriff Sol thought he had the pickup boxed in because they were coming perilously close to the river.

The outlaw had other ideas and he knew exactly what he was doing and where he was going. He was counting on this lawman to follow the letter of the law, not to play loose with it like he'd seen cops do in El Paso or Mexico. Otherwise he'd be a shit sandwich. "Bastardos!"

About a quarter-mile from the river he turned west onto one of the Triple S goat paths before circling back towards the river. Sheriff Sol was so close to his bumper, if he had blown the fugitive a kiss, the driver would have felt it on the back of his neck because his back windshield was largely missing due to three, high velocity, 30-06 rounds.

The rustler plowed right through four rusty strands of barbed wire fencing marking the border into the river, where it wasn't more than three inches deep, even if it was nearly a quarter-mile wide.

Sheriff Sol held up at the river bank and dismounted. He fired six rounds from his 30-30 into the truck but to no avail. In less than a minute, the rustler had forded the river and was hightailing it pell-mell southbound through the Mexican desert.

Sheriff Sol watched for a few minutes and then began looking around with his flashlight. He could see where this very convenient, illegal border crossing had been used in the past. He imagined that coyotes not wishing to bring scrutiny to this route would probably splice the fence each time they crossed so it wouldn't attract undue attention. Then he got back into his cruiser and drove back to where the shootout began. The excitement for the night had come to an end but not the way either side had anticipated.

Just as he arrived, Chief radioed that they had one rig on Rattlesnake Trail about a mile south of 90. He said the rustler was DOA but his load of four-legged hostages was fine. Sheriff Sol responded that he would be there as soon as he could and for Chief to commence with his crime scene investigation.

When he had a moment to glance around, he saw the second rig parked a hundred yards up the road. Ninety yards closer, a young rustler was cuffed behind the back, sitting on the ground holding back tears. It looked like a scene from yesteryear with mounted posse looking for a tall tree to exact frontier justice.

He dismounted from his unit and walked over to where the fence had been cut. He lit a cigarette and inhaled a draw. He motioned Slick aside and asked, "Whatcha got, Slick?"

"What we got, Sheriff, is a low-down dirty rustler named Chico Gómez from Pecos. I was fixing to send Rico up to the barn to fetch a rope so we could go ahead and stretch the neck of this SOB. He's sobbing like a little girl who lost her dolly. He tried to make like he didn't habla but once I squeezed his nuts a little bit his English come back to him real good. He was screaming, 'abogado, abogado,' but I told him we ain't got no avocados out here on the range."

"You know he meant 'lawyer.'"

"Sure I do. I speak Mex like a native but Sheriff, we don't need no stinking lawyer out here. What we need is the name of the prick that started this fandango by shooting at us before he took a powder and the name of the polecat they was selling them sheep to."

"I agree but I think we can catch more flies with honey than vinegar. Besides, this is Alberto Gómez's boy and the dead rustler up the road is probably his brother or cousin. Would you rather hang this pissant or the hombres he works for?"

"Actually, I'd like to do all of the above but you're the boss."

"I am. Did you get a name on that pile of guts over there?"

"His DL says he's Juan Rodríguez from Pecos but it looks a little suspicious to me. Being that his pard skedaddled to Old Mexico, I'm thinking he might be a wetback."

Sheriff Sol took a closer look at the corpse. "What did you kill him with? A hand grenade? He's got pieces of his body scattered ten feet in every direction!"

"That would be Colleen, my grandpappy's trusty, double-barrel 10-gauge. Patterns eighteen double-aught buck per barrel, out to eighty yards. Does a magnificent job, don't it?"

"I'd say. How did young Barlow do?"

"He done real good, Sheriff, 'cept for one little miscalculation."

"Oh? What was that?"

"He learnt the hard way that you can't shoot a-horseback unless the horse has been trained for it. Even so, from what I saw he has the makings of a professional rodeo rider."

The sheriff chuckled. "Is he okay?"

"Oh yeah. He never got un-assed, even though he was reining in with only one hand. His six-shooter was in the other'n. He's still a mite pissed that he only got off two shots afore he earned his new nickname, Bronco Barlow."

"What about Rico and Pepe?"

"I'd ride the river with them two anytime. They're all right."

"Glad to hear it. I'll pass that along to Judge Sweeney."

"What do you plan to do about the asshole who hightailed it into Old Mexico?"

"Well, he might think he got away scot-free but he'd be wrong. First thing I'm gonna do is bring young Chico straight to Jesus. I can just about guarantee that right about now he's praying with all his might for salvation. Once he understands that the only possible way he can avoid spending the best thirty years of his life in Huntsville, maybe only get ten or fifteen, is through me, he'll beg me to give him a chance to redeem himself and maybe I will.

"Tell you the truth, I doubt this kid really wanted to take up the Owlhoot Trail but he was too weak to stand up to his dearly departed kinfolk. I'm gonna take him with me when I check on Chief and the others.

"Look, we got a mountain of work to do before we can call it a day. I got a camera and a notebook in the car. How about you get a head start on photographing and diagraming the scene here to save Chief some time?"

"You got it, Sheriff."

"Also, once you tally and photograph the sheep, tell Rico they can return them to the pasture. As soon as Chief's done the same up the road, they can repatriate those sheep as well and commence to mending the fence."

"Gotcha."

"Oh, yeah. If you get all that done before Chief takes over down here, would you ride over to where I chased Pancho Villa and do the crime scene over there? You can assign Barlow to take care of anything you need done."

"You bet."

"One last thing. You and Barlow check in with me at the jail before you go 10-7 (out of service)."

"Roger that. Oh, yeah. Take a look at this. I damn near forgot."

"What is it?"

Slick pulled a bandana out of his jacket pocket. He opened it carefully, revealing a switchblade with an ornate sterling silver and turquoise inlay handle. "We found this on the dead man's body in his right back pocket. I put it in my bandana to preserve any latent prints."

"Will you look at that? I've never seen a knife with such a beautiful turquoise handle. Maybe it will help us ID him. Might even be stolen."

"Maybe so. Heck, it has to be worth at least $100. Maybe more."

"I agree. Chief has some evidence envelopes with him. Don't forget to sign the chain of custody when you turn it over to him."

"You bet. I'm all over it."

"Thanks."

CHAPTER 13
Tuesday, March 24, 1970
Sheriff Sol Touches Base With His Troops

Sheriff Sol patted Slick on the shoulder and looked over at Barlow. He motioned for him to come over as Slick walked away to begin complying with the sheriff's orders.

"I understand they call you Bronco Barlow now. I think it fits. What do you think?"

"Guess I earned it, Sheriff. I embarrassed myself. I never considered that a horse had to be trained before a rider could shoot a gun off of him."

"Now you know. All's well that ends well. You'll probably be in for a little ribbing for awhile."

"Well, I've been called things a whole lot worse. This actually wouldn't be so bad, if I actually had ridden a bucking bronco in a rodeo."

"Barlow, whether you realize it or not, you were in your own private rodeo with about a half-dozen spectators. Unless I heard wrong, you rode that tornado until it stopped of its own accord. The fact that you set out to vanquish bandits who were slinging lead at you without understanding the finer nuances of horse etiquette, from a horse's perspective mind you, probably made this ride more difficult than one at the rodeo grounds. It earned you some respect as well as ribbing for months or even years to come, especially from the horse's owner and also probably from your betrothed."

"Oh, geez. By now I bet Arthur wishes he never loaned me that horse."

"I doubt that. In fact, now that he understands you want to be a mounted shooter, he'll probably help you train that horse for his own self preservation. He does not want his future son-in-law to bite the dust and get all busted up before he ties the knot and sires a half-dozen grandkids. He'd lots rather have Sarah on your ass than on his. Mark my words."

"I hope you're right, Sheriff. Maybe I'll wait to see if one of them brings it up first. I don't want either one of them pissed off at me. By the way, what happened to the first rig? They arrest the driver?"

"Don't say anything around the prisoner. The driver didn't make it. He's probably related to Chico. I'm headed up there now. All the sheep were recovered and none of our guys got hurt."

"That's a sigh of relief. I wondered why none of them came down here to check on us."

"They're dealing with a very similar situation as your own. Chief will be down here as soon as he can. I'm taking Chico with me. You help Slick clean up here. Whatever he needs.

"Yes, Sir."

"Rico might need you to help drive the sheep back to their pasture. You might learn how to splice a fence. Also, I'll have Archie call the school and let them know you're 10-6 (busy) with police business.

"Listen up. We need to tie up all the loose ends at three different crime scenes. We have two bodies that need to go to the morgue, and one prisoner to process and determine what to charge him with. We can't book him in Quayle County because Judge Sweeney's the victim. He can't hear the case. Conflict of interest. It complicates matters.

"I want these crime scenes completely processed and all traces of dead bandits sanitized before the press or gawkers get wind of this. Any questions?"

"No, Sir. I'll get to work. You can count on me."

"I know I can. Good job. Don't forget. I need your signed statement before you clock out. Talk to me before you head home."

Sheriff Sol walked over to Rico and Pepe. They were keeping a very close eye on Chico. It was obvious they knew him and what his fate would be if the deputies weren't here to uphold the law.

Sheriff Sol asked, "Not what we expected, was it fellas?"

"No, Sheriff."

"Rico, Pepe, I want you both to know how much I appreciate everything you all did in helping us catch these rustlers. One of 'em's in the wind and we don't know yet where they planned to sell the sheep or who paid 'em to steal 'em, but we will. The investigation is just beginning but we wouldn't be anywhere near this far along without your help."

"Gracias, Sheriff."

"Look, we need to photograph the sheep on the rigs and as soon as we do, you all can herd them back to where they belong."

"Sí."

"And you all will mend the fence?"

"Sí, sí."

"Good. It's getting late. I need to check on the rig they stopped up the road. I'm sure that by the time you move these sheep back to their pasture, the other sheep will be ready. Will you herd them on horseback?"

"Sí, but first Pepe will go fetch our dogs."

"Okay. When I finish up at the other crime scene, I'll stop by The Big House and speak with Judge Sweeney. I'll make sure he knows just how much we appreciate all you've done this week."

"Gracias, Sheriff."

"By the way, do you recognize Chico or the dead guy?"

Rico responded, "We never saw this cabrón but we know Chico. His older brother, Rudy, used to work here for Judge Sweeney. We fired him because he was lazy and untrustworthy. He lied many times. I told him I would cut off his cojones if he ever set foot on the Triple S again."

"How long ago was that?"

"Oh, maybe a year ago. Perhaps a little longer."

"Do you think he might have fingered this job?"

"What do you mean, 'finger'?"

"You know. Provided the knowledge about the canyon. Set the job up. That kind of thing."

"Sí, sí. That would be just like him. He worked here long enough to know about this canyon. That's the sneaky, backstabbing kind of thing he would do. He is no good, Sheriff."

"That's what I thought. Thanks. And oh, yeah. Chief Alex will need to take sworn statements from you both. Once you take care of the sheep, can you come to the courthouse?"

"We will be there, Sheriff, as soon as we can."

"Thanks, Fellas."

CHAPTER 14
Tuesday, March 24, 1970
Sheriff Sol Checks In With the Rest

Sheriff Sol drove eight miles north. He saw the chief's car behind a marked unit behind the rig. He parked and walked around to the front. He saw the other cruiser sideways in the road with the tractor smashed up against the passenger side. It could have been a whole lot worse. The car could have been totaled and Ernie could have been a bug on the windshield.

He stepped up on the running board and looked in. He recognized Rudy immediately. The shot in the middle of his forehead told him everything he needed to know.

"Ernie."

"Yes, Sir."

"That was some fine shooting at nighttime, especially with the headlights glaring into your eyes."

"Thanks, Sheriff. I gave him a warning shot. You can see it in the middle of the windshield. Then he really goosed it. I didn't have any choice. I thought I was a goner."

"I can see that. You did what you were trained to do. How are you holding up?"

"Okay, I think. I never shot anyone before. It feels different. I didn't hate that guy. He was trying to run me down. I wish it never happened. I'm responsible for the damage to the car, too."

"Don't worry about the car. We'll get her fixed. She'll be as good as new in a week or two. Look, how about I take you back to the jail. I'm headed that way in just a few minutes."

"I don't know. Chief probably needs me here."

"No. He and Chunk can handle this. Get your gear and ride back with me. I'll be leaving in just a couple of minutes."

"Sure thing, Sheriff."

Sheriff Sol walked over to Chief Alex. "Got a minute?"

"I got all the time you need, Sheriff."

"What do you think?"

"I think it was a good shoot. Ernie's pretty torn up over it but he'll be okay. He tossed his supper after he saw the mess a 30-06 can make in a skull. It's a good thing he never knew Rudy."

"I agree. Listen, Rico and Pepe will be here in a little bit to herd the sheep. I got Rudy's brother, Chico, in the backseat of my car. He's white as a ghost but savvy enough to say 'abogado.'"

"We also got a dead bandit who foolishly decided to trade shots with Slick and his double-barrel 10-gauge. There's pieces of him scattered all the way across the border. He's a real mess. I got Slick taking pictures and making a diagram. Barlow's helping. How long do you reckon before you can mosey on down there? I want both bodies gone before the newsies and gawkers show up."

"Probably an hour. I got to get the coroner rolling for Rudy and I need Buck Boyd over here to pick up our unit and both rigs."

"Okay. Once Pete Ricketts picks up Rudy, tell him to come back and pick up the other dead bandit down the road. By then, Rico should have the sheep penned up from the rig down there. Chunk can stay here with this rig, so you can head down there. Also, I need you to take a look-see where I chased Pancho Villa up to the point where he forded the river. My eyesight must be getting bad. I sent six 30-30's in his direction but apparently none of them hit pay dirt because he just kept on trucking."

"Where's Barlow when you need him? Ha!"

"No kidding. Say, I'm headed back to town to drop off Ernie and to lodge Chico in the Crossbar Hotel. Then, as soon as I get done, I'm headed back to the Triple S to talk to Judge Sweeney. I don't want anyone punching out until after we have a chance to debrief."

"I'm on it, Sheriff."

"Alex, no shit. I don't want any newsies taking pictures of dead rustlers."

"No worries, Boss. I think we can be done by dawn."

"Good."

The sheriff walked over to speak to Chunk. "What do you think, Chunk? Everything okay?"

"I think so. Tell you the truth, I never imagined it would come to all this."

"Nope. It turned out a whole lot worse than I thought, too.

"You know that Chico Gómez was one of the rustlers? I've got him cuffed in the backseat of my car waiting to assume his new life as a jailbird. Hard to believe, isn't it?"

"It is."

"Look, I know Rudy tried to run you down and then Ernie to escape. Think about it! You need to wrap your arms around this! He was willing to kill you both, turn you into grease spots on the roadway, whatever it took, just to get away! Thank goodness this didn't go his way. Now he's paid for all his sins, at least on this side of the holy veil. So much for knowing these boys since the day they were born!"

"I know, Sheriff. What is this world coming to? I'm good friends with the family. I feel so . . . sorrowful."

"Thinking back, did you ever get wind of anything that would lead you to believe that either of these two boys would be tangled up with something as serious as this?"

"No. Not really. I always knew Rudy was crooked but Chico seemed to have his head screwed on tight. I did think Rudy, in particular, might have been involved with that stolen DeSoto from Pecos last summer. I never even considered Chico for that. Besides, he's four or five years younger. I know he graduated from high school. I think he's in the National Guard now. Rudy dropped out in the 9th or 10th grade, plus I think he did some time in prison. Not positive about that, though."

"How do you think Alberto will take this?"

"It'll break his heart. Also Rosalita's. Chico was her baby. Is he talking, Sheriff?"

"Not yet.

"There's something else. We got another dead rustler from the pickup truck who's higher up the food chain than Rudy. When he bought the farm, the ringleader chucked it all and vamoosed across the river. I'm pretty sure he never got even so much as a scratch, driving a truck that we riddled like Swiss cheese! He has more lives than a cat! We don't know who either of these two hombres are yet but we will. This is just the beginning for us but it's the beginning of the end for our fugitive.

"I'm pretty sure the sheep were not destined for Mexico because the rigs went north. Plus, that's the way the recon went last night. I believe the bossman went south because it was the only chance he had of escaping. Wouldn't surprise me to learn he's got family or friends over there who are probably lending him aid and assistance as we speak.

"We need to identify both of these rustlers, plus we need to find out where they were selling the sheep. Who owns the rigs? Who's the money man? Hopefully Chico will shed some light on this in return for consideration at sentencing. Otherwise, he could be doing some serious time. Sorry, I'm rambling, thinking out loud."

"De nada. Want me to talk to Chico to see if he'll give it up? I know him pretty well."

"I thought about that, but he's already asking for a lawyer. When he finds out that Rudy's dead, he might lose it. I don't want him blaming you. You're my ace in the hole if Alberto bows up, although I don't think he will.

"This is what I need. Go down and see if you can identify the other dead rustler. Then come back. Chief's headed that way as soon as he wraps up the crime scene here. I need you to stand by here for the coroner and the wrecker. Once this scene is clear, go down there to see if they need any help. Rico and Pepe should be up here soon to herd the sheep back home. Come back to the jail when you're done. Write your statement. We'll have a debriefing before anyone goes home. Savvy?"

"Savvy."

CHAPTER 15
Tuesday March 24, 1970
Sheriff Sol Briefs Judge Sweeney

It was nearly 5 a.m. when Sheriff Sol pulled into the driveway of The Big House, as Judge Sweeney's residence was known locally. It probably wasn't any more than 8,000 square feet indoors, with three floors of living space, not including verandas and screened in porches and patios and perhaps even a cellar. Judge Sweeney was on the front veranda, drinking coffee and smoking an aromatic Churchill while he rocked in his favorite chair.

He was already attired in a beige linen suit reminiscent of Colonel Sanders of Kentucky Fried Chicken fame, except in a size 40, not a 48, to include a black string tie and spit-shined Tony Lama, alligator skin cowboy boots, and a beige 25X Stetson without so much as a smudge on the brim.

The end table to his right was the temporary repository of his nickel-plated, Model 1877, Colt Bird's Head 'Thunderer' revolver, with a three-inch barrel, in .41 Long Colt caliber with genuine ivory grips. The revolver was a classic work of art, crafted in 1908, with factory engraved, ornate scrollwork and a scene depicting a lawman dispatching a bandit in a desert shootout.

The revolver was the second thing Sheriff Sol noticed, having been surprised to see the judge all dressed up for the courtroom or a proper hanging so early in the morning.

"Good morning, Sheriff. Can I offer you some coffee and a cigar?" The judge motioned to an end table on his left side with a humidor and a carafe of coffee.

Before he finished speaking, the judge's head housekeeper

stepped out on the porch and set down a fresh carafe of coffee with clean cups and saucers, while removing the old. She poured both men fresh cups. She smiled pleasantly at the sheriff and disappeared back inside as silently as she had appeared. Nary a word was spoken.

"Good morning, Judge. Don't mind if I do. He selected a Punch Puro with a Maduro wrapper. He clipped the end and lit up. He drew a few puffs and exhaled, ensuring that it was properly lit. Very pleasing. He smiled and nodded at the judge.

Judge Sweeney smiled back. "What do you think of my Bird's Head?"

"From what I can see in this light, it's absolutely beautiful. A museum piece for sure."

Judge Sweeney unloaded and handed it to him. The Bird's Head grip fit perfectly in his hand. It had a nice balance for a revolver with a three-inch barrel. The scrollwork was exquisite. The yellowed ivory grips helped set it off. After a couple minutes of close examination, he returned it. Judge Sweeney reloaded it and placed it back on the table.

"It was my grandpappy's. He bought it in 1908, direct from the factory the year before this model was discontinued. By then he had semi-retired. He carried it concealed, mostly for personal protection. I'm pretty sure he never shot anyone with it.

"He also had a Colt Model 1873 Peacemaker in blue steel with a six-inch barrel. It has hand-carved stag grips. That was the gun he carried most of his life. He dispatched many a villain with that gun. Some of them are buried in our own owlhoot graveyard. My brother, Darnell, took that one so I took this one. Darnell carried his when he was a Texas Ranger. This is the gun I used when those bikers tried to murder Monica and me."

"Well, with its history and classic beauty, it's easy to understand why this is your weapon of choice."

"You're darn tootin'.

"By the way, Rico stopped by about an hour ago and told me

what he knew. He said you were busy supervising two different crime scenes. I knew you'd stop by once you were clear."

"Rico and Pepe are two first-class vaqueros, Judge. It was a pleasure to work with them."

"That's why I assigned them to you. What can you tell me?"

"Well, I'm sure you know already what happened at your ranch, so I'll move on.

"The ringleader got away. He led me on a high speed chase back onto your property on the west side of Rattlesnake Trail down to the river. He must have had this as a backup plan because he busted through the fence and crossed at the shallowest part of the river in this whole area.

"Rico had already ventilated his truck shooting at him and I put six more in it from my Winchester while he was fording. All I can say is, he must have had a four-leaf clover in his pocket to get away, and as far as I can tell, completely unscathed, especially with as much lead as we threw in his direction."

"Well, I'm a little surprised that our young, expert marksman, Deputy Adams, didn't snuff his lights out."

"Oh, maybe Rico forgot to mention it. Barlow was riding hell-for-leather, shooting his revolver over the shoulder of a horse that hadn't been trained for that. The ringleader and Barlow were trading shots, while Slick was fighting his own shotgun duel with the other unknown bandit, now deceased. After Barlow's second shot, the horse transitioned into bucking bronco rodeo mode. Barlow managed to stay seated and get the horse back under control, but that was the end of his gunfight."

"Well, for Heaven's sake! Deputy Adams didn't know you have to train a horse for that? How can that be?"

"No, Judge, he didn't. You might not realize it, but he never rode a horse until he moved down here and started dating Sarah Baker. Apparently nobody ever thought to mention it."

"Well, my goodness! He's much too good a man for us not to rectify that lapse in his education! We know he has heart. That's why I requested him. We need to get this corrected right away or get him another mount! This rustling business isn't over yet! Not by a long shot! See to it, will you?"

"Of course, Judge. He's pretty humiliated. He's already talking about training that horse he borrowed from Arthur."

"Well, if he can't train that horse fast enough, let me know. I have several which are well-trained when it comes to shooting on horseback and I'd be glad to loan him one."

"Will do. Well, to fill you in on the rest of the story, like I said, we have not identified the bandit Slick killed or the one who got away yet but I'm pretty sure we will.

"Alberto Gómez's boy, Chico, surrendered peacefully at your ranch after the shootout. He was unarmed and he was one of two tractor trailer drivers. The other was Rudy Gómez, his big brother, who I understand used to work for you. He attempted to run down Deputy Bustamante and Deputy Atwater in the rig he was driving at two different roadblocks. Deputy Atwater drilled him between the eyes with our sniper rifle."

"I remember Rudy. He was pretty lazy and basically worthless. Rico says he thinks Rudy was the 'inside man.' I'm inclined to agree. No loss regarding his demise. How's Ernie doing? I don't read him as the sort of guy who slays dragons and then goes back to playing checkers."

"Right you are. I think he'll get over it but it will take some time. We'll have to wait and see."

"Well, he's a good man. Been around at least fifteen years as I recall. Tell him I appreciate his service and dedication to duty. If you can think of anything I can do for him, just let me know."

"Thanks, Judge. I will."

"Anything on the tractor trailers yet?"

"No. We're just getting started. We've impounded them. They have no markings on them, nor do they have license plates. We'll have to track them down by VIN's. You can just about count on the owner claiming that they were stolen. No matter.

We'll get down to the bottom of this and I'll let you know."

"Any idea as to who the buyer is?"

"Nothing yet. That's something I wanted to discuss with you. I think we have a good chance of flipping Chico if we cut him some slack. You can't be the judge on this. Do you have a preference on which county I call to handle our venue problem?"

"I do. Call Sheriff Waters in Brewster County. The DA over there, Bradford Delaney, did a good job handling my little dust up with the Diablos. Judge Wilson Roberts is a friend of mine from law school. He'll be receptive if you need a search warrant signed or things like that. I'd call him myself, but it would be considered an ethics violation if I did."

"Understood. Besides, Brewster County already has a rustling case and it's probably related to ours.

"Judge, what about the shootings? Do we present them to the Grand Jury in Brewster County, too?"

"No. I don't have a dog in that fight. You can present the case here, but get it done as soon as possible. Tomorrow if you can. Thursday at the absolute latest. Are Oldman and Atwater the only two deputies involved?"

"Yes."

"Get it done quickly. Otherwise, they have to sit in the penalty box and you have a lot on your plate. You need them back on the job."

"Judge, if it's all the same to you, I'll have Archie present the case tomorrow morning after he gets off his midnight shift."

"Call the clerk and set it up for 8 o'clock then.

"By the way, do you want me to get the Rangers involved?"

"Not just yet. It kind of depends on where our investigation leads us. If we wind up with a half-dozen counties or a terminal market in Mexico, then we'll probably need their help."

"The dead bandit on my property have a name?"

"I believe his license says Juan Rodríguez but Slick thinks it's a forgery. We'll send his prints off and see if we can ID him. Plus, his license shows a Pecos address. We'll touch base with the Reeves County SO (Sheriff's Office) and make a trip up there to check a few things out.

"Also, if Chico doesn't waive his rights, we may have to wait until he gets court-appointed counsel. I'm hoping Sheriff Waters will be kind enough to lodge him for us since the court case will be over there. Can we expect Judge Roberts to set a high bond?"

"You can bank on it unless you need it lowered to put him to work for you. He loathes rustlers as much as I do."

"Well, okay. I guess that's it for now. We have a truckload of work to do before anyone gets to sleep today."

"Thanks, Sol. Tell all your men how much I appreciate the good job they've done."

"I will, and don't forget to give your two vaqueros a pat on the back."

"I won't. I let Rico run a few head of sheep on my ranch. I have a ram he dearly loves. I've loaned it to him several times for sire services. Today I plan to give that ram to him. And as for Pepe, he's a senior this year. He wants to go to WTJC. I'll let him know if he's serious, I'll pick up his tuition and books and make sure he has time off to go to classes."

"That's mighty generous of you, Judge. That's why your employees are so loyal to you."

"Sol, as you well know, loyalty is a two-way street. You're well recognized for that yourself."

"Thanks, Judge. I'll be in touch."

"Adiós."

CHAPTER 16
0-Dark-30, Tuesday, March 24, 1970
A High Price to Stay in Business

Humberto Pavón was not El Jefe right now. Right now he was El Conejo, the rabbit, fleeing from El Lobo, the wolf. Bastardos! They shot his truck to pieces and killed his best friend! He was fortunate the American lawman chasing him respected international boundaries. He knew from personal experience that some in El Paso did not.

His truck was coughing on fumes when he arrived at his cousin's house. It was 3:30. Soon it would be light. He needed to conduct his business quickly and get back across the border before daylight.

He pounded on the door until the front porch light flicked on and the door opened. Hector was standing in the doorway in his underwear holding a machete.

"You trying to wake the dead, Cousin?"

"I need some help. Fast!"

"Keep your voice down. We'll talk outside."

They walked into the backyard and stood next to Hector's antique, worn out, truck. Even the junk man had a newer truck.

"What's up?"

"I had some trouble with the pendejo cops in Texas. They shot up my new truck. They don't know who I am but they know my truck."

"So how's that my problem? Why are you pestering me?"

"I need some wheels. I'll trade you my truck for this piece of shit straight up."

"My piece of shit runs good and it's not shot up and the cops aren't looking for it."

"Come on, Man. You owe me. They shot out the glass and it has some bullet holes in it but it runs just fine. Nothing but body damage. The engine's not even hurt. Even shot up, it's worth at least $1,200. Your truck wouldn't fetch $200. I'll swap you straight up."

"You got the papers?"

"Yeah, in the glove box."

"Lemme see the truck."

They walked to the corner lot where the truck was parked. Hector examined the truck carefully. It looked like Humberto just might be telling the truth. Hell, the chrome mag wheels were worth more than his beater!

"Gimme the keys. I want to hear the engine."

"It's outa gas. I got here on fumes."

"We shall see. I will fetch the gas can for my lawnmower."

Hector poured a half-gallon into the tank. He pumped the accelerator. Vroom! It fired up with the deep, resonating roar of Ford's 390 cubic-inch engine, boosted with a four-barrel carb and dual exhaust. It ran just fine. Plus, it had a four-on-the-floor transmission! Maybe Humberto really was telling the truth!

"Okay. Sign the title over to me. I'll go get the title to mine."

Hector went back inside the house. A few minutes later he returned wearing jeans with the title, registration, and two sets of keys in hand to his faded green, 1948 Chevy. It had over 600,000 miles on it, but it ran good and it didn't burn oil. They each signed and swapped documents and traded keys.

"Muchos gracias, Hector. I owe you."

Hector had a cat-eating-a-canary smile on his face. "No, Cousin. I think we are even. Come see me sometime when you are not running from the law. We'll drink some tequila."

"I'll do that."

Humberto fired up the Chevy and left. It had three-quarters of a tank of gas. He took a different route back through Brewster County. He needed to get back to Pecos as fast as he could.

CHAPTER 17
Post Op Briefing
Tuesday March 24, 1970

It was 8:30. The crime scenes had been photographed and diagramed. The sheep had been returned to their pastures. The fence had been mended. Slick and Barlow had fed and groomed the horses. They returned Boyo to his daddy. Barlow spoke briefly with Arthur, Clarice, and Sarah.

The Sears and Roebuck shotgun belonging to the deceased John Doe #1, also known as Juan Rodríguez, and his turquoise-handled switchblade knife had been inventoried and placed into evidence along with the other items collected by Chief Alex.

The big rigs and Unit 81 were like two mastodons and a sabertooth tiger taking up most of the 'museum' space in the secure lot behind Boyd's Phillips 66. Rudolfo Gómez was on a slab at the mortuary. So was John Doe #1. Chico Gómez was huddled in the corner of the stark jail cell #1, hugging himself and rocking back and forth.

Archie stayed over for the briefing. Dewey Carruthers was there as the day shift deputy. Deputies Kirk Shoemaker and Randall Meacham also showed up after Sheriff Sol decided to make this an all hands on deck meeting. Miss Loretta Youngblood was the only SO staff person not attending. She handled the phones and walk-in traffic.

When District Attorney Able DeWitt arrived, Sheriff Sol got down to business. He brought everyone up-to-date on the origins of the stakeout, as well as what had transpired in the wee hours of the morning. He insisted that the staff know the unvarnished truth about what had occurred because they all knew that the Quayle County grapevine would be full tilt before lunchtime.

Sheriff Sol was a detail-oriented person. He insisted that no stone be left unturned. Everything exposed. No 'fog of war' lapses. Each deputy who had been involved presented his own participation in minute detail.

Ernie was first. He had a difficult time discussing the shooting of Rudy. Before Ernie got too choked up, Sheriff Sol shifted the bright light onto Barlow, who sheepishly segued into his misguided efforts to eliminate the threat of the ringleader while blazing away aback a gunshot-averse mount. That took the pressure off Ernie when the other deputies started to good-naturedly break Barlow's chops. No way around it. Barlow from Arlo would be Bronco Barlow forevermore, unless something even more embarrassing came to light.

Slick's recitation of the demise of John Doe #1, a/k/a Juan Rodríguez, brought the crowd back down to serious business. Sheriff Sol stated that the deaths of the two outlaws were unavoidable and fully justified. DA DeWitt concurred but reminded everyone that these two deaths still had to be ruled a justified homicide by the Grand Jury for it to be so legally.

Sheriff Sol took his own licks when he described the escape of John Doe #2, otherwise known as the ringleader. Archie suggested that the sheriff start checking out one of the Thompson choppers with him whenever he decided to go on a stakeout. Slick concurred. No one else had enough time on the job to feel comfortable about breaking the sheriff's balls so they remained mute.

Chief Alex was next. He reported that neither the tractors nor the trailers had license plates, nor external, commercial markings anywhere. However, according to their VINs, both tractors and trailers were titled and registered to Pluto Incorporated, P.O. Box 1612, Dover, Delaware. Neither rig was listed as stolen in NCIC or DPS, but it wouldn't surprise him to learn that they would be later this morning. Simply put, neither Sheriff Sol nor he thought either of the Gómez boys had the savvy or the balls to steal two eighteen-wheelers. Ergo, they believed this was probably done either for Pluto or with Pluto's guilty knowledge.

Chief said he didn't know anything about Pluto Incorporated, yet. Since the Gómez boys were from Pecos, he had a call into the Reeves County SO requesting information on them, Juan Rodríguez, and Pluto Incorporated. He hoped to learn something later this morning.

He confirmed that neither Gómez brother had a commercial driver's license issued by the State of Texas, further suggesting that Pluto might be a criminal enterprise, assuming the rigs were not truly stolen. Chico had a military driver's license with a Class A endorsement, but it was only valid if he were driving a military vehicle. Chief planned to make an inquiry with the Texas Commercial Carrier Section within DMV later today in an effort to trace the history of both vehicles.

Chief said that John Doe #1 was in possession of a Texas driver's license in the name of Juan Rodríguez, with an address of 1517 Allen Street in Pecos. Unfortunately, a close visual examination of the license confirmed that it was a forgery. Furthermore, a check with DMV confirmed that no such license had ever been issued in that name at that address and that the license number was bogus.

He said later this morning, he would send Rudy's fingerprints to the FBI and DPS. He planned to hold up sending John Doe #1's prints, hoping they could get at least a tentative ID on him first. Whereas they normally get a two or three-week turnaround for confirmation of known prints, they would be lucky to get a six-week turnaround on unknown prints absent exigent circumstances. Therefore, he would make a trip to the Reeves County SO just as soon as possible to see if anyone could ID him from his morgue photograph.

Chief said they had no leads on John Doe #2. He was Hispanic, probably of Mexican descent, somewhere between 5'8" to 6'0" tall, regular build, with no facial hair. They were at

Ground Zero with him. He was driving either a black or navy blue 1968 or 1969 Ford F-100 in excellent condition, other than the shot out back glass and numerous bullet holes in the body. It had a chrome cattle guard on the front and a step bumper on the back. It did not have a license plate on it, front or back. The damn thing was last seen in Mexico, so odds are it probably would not resurface in the U.S. but they put a BOLO on it statewide, anyway.

Unless someone spoke out of school, Chico doesn't know that Rudy's dead although he probably suspects it. He definitely knows that Rudy's rig was recovered, plus Rudy is not in jail with him. Problem is, Chico lawyered up so no efforts have been made to interview him yet.

Continuing, Chief said that after the meeting, Sheriff Sol and Chunk would go to the Rocking A to notify Alberto and Rosalita of Rudy's death and Chico's arrest. Hopefully, Alberto will be cooperative. Chunk knows the family intimately and if all goes well, Alberto will persuade Chico to cooperate.

It's possible he could be too scared. John Doe #2 and John Doe #1 initiated the shootout, in that order. Keep that in mind. Both Rudy and Chico were present, at least initially. They both took off. Then Rudy kept on going and Chico stopped. They both witnessed the beginning of it. They were both parked facing north. It took place behind them but they definitely heard it and probably saw it in their side mirrors. If so, there's a good chance Chico fears the bandits more than he does jail. We will remind him that life in prison sucks big time, and we will clue him in that we have enough influence to get his potential sentence reduced substantially if he cooperates, but in the final analysis, it will be up to him.

Something else. Brewster County reported one incident of sheep rustling before we became aware that Judge Sweeney had been rustled at least once, but more likely twice. We initiated the stakeout due to Judge Sweeney's loss. There is no evidence at this time to suggest these incidents are related. However, we are coordinating with Brewster SO to examine this more closely. We know that Brewster has been calling regional SOs in an effort to determine if other venues have been rustled. So far, Quayle and Brewster are the only two that we are aware of.

Sheriff Sol took over the briefing and said he thought the rustlings were connected. In the days to come, deputies would be tasked to canvass all the stockyards in adjacent counties to find out if any have had suspicious sales or newcomers with thirty or more sheep for sale, particularly Rambouillets, since that's the breed the Triple S raises.

"This is a long shot but maybe we'll get lucky. It is doubtful that our four rustlers would have been dumb enough to try to pass themselves off as having a large enough spread to sell a couple hundred or more sheep. That means they probably sold the sheep to someone who's legit and could sell this big a flock without raising suspicion. We hope Chico will cooperate so we can cut to the chase without doing all this legwork.

"But this is the kicker. Since Judge Sweeney is the victim, he can't try the case. We have to go to another venue. Judge Sweeney recommended Brewster, so we're going to Brewster. Therefore, this afternoon we will transport Chico to Alpine. The good news is, we don't have to babysit him. The bad news is, we will be running back and forth a lot. We're down one marked unit right now and that may have an impact. Everyone needs to be prepared for some long days in the short term. Hopefully, it won't take too long to get Unit 81 rolling again.

"That reminds me. We can present the line-of-duty shootings of both deceased bandits in Mosby since Judge Sweeney has no involvement with that. Archie, I want you to present both cases tomorrow as soon as you go end-of-shift. Grand Jury will be scheduled for 8 o'clock. Able, can you line that up and Archie, make sure you have all the relevant facts."

Able responded, "Will do."

"I'd love to give Slick and Ernie a few days off to take some personal inventory but we really don't have that luxury right now. Ernie, Slick, you boys good with that?"

Ernie never looked up from the floor but he muttered, "Okay."

Slick said, "I made my peace with this as soon as that no-good rodent rustled the stock. I'm glad he pulled that shotgun and gave me the opportunity to send him back to his Maker."

"Arch?"

"Consider the Grand Jury a done deal."

"Good. Anything else? Does anyone have a question?"

Kirk asked, "Are we getting DPS or the Texas Rangers involved?"

Sheriff Sol responded, "Not yet. We may need to, but I'd rather not. I do anticipate that we will coordinate more closely with some other SOs." He paused and looked at each deputy directly in the eyes, one at a time.

"You know, Judge Sweeney asked me this same question before we initiated the stakeout and again this morning. It's no secret that he has the Rangers' backdoor, unpublished, telephone number direct to their top dog memorized. Probably has his home phone number, too. Both times I politely said I'd let him know if we needed help. He told me to press on but to keep it in mind.

"Gee whiz, fellas. Is that what y'all want? Wouldn't you all rather solve Quayle County crimes yourselves and not ask Big Brother for help? Do you all think those guys are better than you because they draw their paychecks from the state?

"Heck, we both wear a silver star! Ours is even sterling! I'm not sure a badge made from a Mexican peso is sterling, but it does have a circle around it. Does that make them better? Do I need to buy you all badges with a circle around it?"

Archie answered. "Sheriff, there ain't a man here who would ask another man to come in and pleasure his wife even if she is fat and ugly and ornery. I think you misunderstood Kirk."

Kirk responded, "Sir, Archie has a colorful way of expressing himself. I was just asking if we were going to get squeezed out. That's all. This is an important case to all of us. I daresay everyone here wants in on the action. We can do this, lock up everyone involved, tie the case up with a ribbon if we are permitted to do so without Big Brother's assistance."

Sheriff Sol asked, "Everyone on board with what Arch and Kirk just said?"

What he heard was a resounding chorus of "Yes, Sir!"

"Good. I thought so. Everyone will be involved. Our department is too small to work this case with just one or two people. That being said, I will be more pro-active on this case than on any others that I can think of since I was elected sheriff. Don't take it personally. If the Rangers are called in, it will be because I failed, not any of you.

"In the meantime, we still have to take care of the normal course of business while this investigation is ongoing. Don't get upset if you aren't tasked right away with an assignment specifically related to this case.

"Also, I want each of you to be aware of the status of this investigation on a daily basis. You could be called to jump in at anytime and you must be current. At the same time, I expect you to keep the nitty gritty details within our tight little circle of need-to-know. Avoid town gossip, and for crying out loud, don't add to it. Solving the case, or maybe even saving somebody's life will depend upon us not telegraphing our every move to someone outside this circle or without the need to know.

"Think about it. Two of Alberto Gómez's boys were involved. Our objective is to wrap up the rest of the gang to include the money man behind it. 'Loose lips sink ships.' I expect we will conduct more stakeouts or send somebody in undercover before we wrap up this case. If someone had mentioned to Alberto, or to one of his friends that we were staking out Judge Sweeney's ranch, we probably wouldn't be here today. Savvy?"

"Yes, Sir."

"Any other questions?"

Randall Meacham asked, "Have you drafted a new work schedule yet?"

"No, but I will before I head north. Nobody leave until you know what your schedule is. Also, everyone who worked last night, I need your statements before you go home. I have to write mine as well. Turn them in to Chief. We have to drop off copies at the Brewster DA's office the same time we deposit Chico in their jail.

"One last thing and then I'll let you get to it. Rustlers are desperate men. This used to be a hanging offense! Two of those pendejos began busting caps just as soon as they spotted our horseback surveillance team. But guess what? Horses can't outrun motor vehicles! They didn't have to shoot to escape!

"Maybe they thought these were just ranch hands. Maybe they thought they were deputies. Who knows? They'd be right on both counts. Simply put, to a rustler 'it's mind over matter. They don't mind and you don't matter.' Plus, Rudy tried to plow over Chunk and Ernie in a 60,000-pound truck. Same thing.

"Dead is dead. Stay vigilant!

"Okay. Let's get to work.

"Give me fifteen minutes and I'll have a do-able work schedule. Consider it chiseled in jello. I'm sure it will be amended more than once."

The meeting broke up. Miss Loretta said, "Barlow, Judge Sweeney's office is on the line for you."

Barlow picked up. "This is Deputy Adams speaking."

"Deputy Adams, this is Judge Sweeney. I was wondering if you would do something for me."

"Yes, Sir. What is it?"

"Well, Rico and Pepe caught the rustler's dog. I expect it belongs to the one who expired. I'd guess it's a two-year-old border collie. We're plum full up on dogs over here. I was wondering if you would consider adopting him. Even if the owner were the rustler who escaped, I doubt he'd come back looking for him. Despicable behavior! What do you say?"

Barlow was caught unawares. It was obvious that the judge was an animal lover. He could have asked anyone, but he didn't. Barlow was honored. "Yes, Sir. I'd love to have him. I don't have a dog. Thank you for thinking of me."

"That's quite all right. This is a well-trained, first-class dog with a great disposition. If we didn't have so many dogs here right now, I'd keep him myself. Same for Rico. Stop by The Big House sometime today. We'll have him up there."

"You bet. Thanks again, Judge."

"That's quite all right. Happy to oblige. Good day."

"Good day."

Wow! He came to Mosby nine months ago with nothing but his clothes and his truck. Now he had a job he loved. He was enrolled full-time in college. He had a nice house to live in, plus a beautiful, loving fiancé, the world's best in-laws-to-be, and now a dog! Life can sure turn on a dime.

Owning a dog. Did this make him a family man now?

CHAPTER 18
Tuesday, March 24, 1970
A Surprise for Sarah

Barlow was running out of steam. His mind was darting all over the place. He wanted in on the action. Being on horseback surveillance with Slick for the past week had 'ruint' him for desk work. He was a little behind in his classes at school and he was way behind on spending quality time with Sarah.

He got busy writing his statement. It didn't take as long as he thought. He realized that in the grand scheme of things, even though he had experienced a tremendous adventure, his participation was minimal, albeit sufficient to corroborate the statements of Slick, Rico, and Pepe.

He left the jail at 10 o'clock. He was scheduled on mids for the rest of the week. He was hoping the schedule held because as of now he would be off on Saturday and Sunday. He knew that was a bone tossed his way from the sheriff. In the fog of fatigue and suffering from an adrenaline dump, he concentrated hard to recall Sarah's schedule. He was pretty sure she was free from 11 until 3. That decided it.

He stopped by the Food Lion to buy both wet and dry dog food. Alpo's canned horse meat looked delightfully yummy. Then he went to Caine's Hardware where he purchased three ceramic dishes, a leash, and a leather collar. His last stop was the college. Since he was cutting class he decided to wait for Sarah in the parking lot.

He saw her come out the front door and bounce down the steps. She spotted him as soon as she entered the parking lot. She made a beeline straight into his arms.

"Missed you at school this morning."

"I know. I got off late. Why don't you put your books in the car? I have an errand to run. We can do that and I'll catch you up. Then maybe we can get something to eat or dot, dot, dot."

"I like the dot, dot, dot part."

He filled her in on the way to Judge Sweeney's house. She was horrified that Rudy Gómez tried to run down Chunk and Ernie. She thought it was rip-roaringly funny that Barlow didn't understand horse etiquette with respect to the use of firearms. She wished she could have seen him in full bronco riding mode.

That gave her two ideas. First, they needed to train Boyo so he would let Barlow shoot while he was riding. Second, maybe Barlow would be interested in training for the bucking bronco event at the Cowboy Days Rodeo.

Barlow quickly endorsed plan one. He was skeptical of plan two but said he would consider it.

She responded, "And before you think I've skipped over the most important part of last night's adventures, I haven't. I thank God that you didn't shoot anyone, but more importantly, that you didn't get shot. By the way, you never said why we are going to Judge Sweeney's ranch."

"Well, I told Rico, one of his top hands, that you said Judge Sweeney had an owlhoot cemetery and I wondered if this were true. Apparently he said something to the judge about it and just before I left the jail, I got a call from the judge's office. When I answered, Judge Sweeney was on the line and he invited me to bring you to his ranch so you could come see 'the rustler cemetery,' as he calls it."

"You didn't!"

"I did."

"Barlow Adams, I am so embarrassed! Turn this truck around! We're going back to your house. How could you?"

"Gotcha!"

"What?"

"Just kidding."

"You rat!" She began shoving him into the driver's door. "Why are we really going?"

"Well, it's like this. The rustlers left a young border collie behind. The judge actually called me at work and said he wanted me to adopt it. He said something about me having all the earmarks of a good dog daddy. He caught me off guard. I didn't know what to say, so I said 'thanks.' Then he said something about this helping to prepare me to be a real daddy. So I said that right now I'm just in it for the sex and he said . . . ."

She started pounding on his chest, hard. "Barlow, I never know when you are telling the truth or joking but I know you didn't say that or you better not have! Tell me the truth, now!"

"Truce! Truce! You're gonna cause me to run off the road.

"You know, Judge Sweeney thinks you're a hot chick. I told him no one can fill out an apron in her nudies like you do. You should feel flattered."

"Stop it, now! Tell me the truth. What did you really say?"

"All I said was I'd love to have the dog."

"That's it?"

"That's it, but . . . ."

"But what?"

"Well, I'm kinda overwhelmed. I haven't had a dog since I was a kid and it was really my uncle's dog. I hope it will like me and not poop on the floor or anything."

"You scaredy cat! You'll be a great dog daddy. We have a couple of sheepdogs. Pedro, too. You get along fine with them."

"I guess so."

"What will you call it?"

"Not sure yet. I guess it depends on its demeanor or characteristics."

They arrived at The Big House. Barlow knocked on the front door. It was answered by an older, gracious Mexican woman who walked them all the way through the house to a large screened-in verandah in the rear. They were greeted warmly by

Mrs. Sweeney, who asked them to please call her Monica.

She said, "Please have a seat and join me for lunch."

What they had was actually a gourmet feast of Mexican cuisine preceded by frozen margaritas. Two large ones each, to be exact. By the time they were done, besides being tipsy, they had consumed enough for two meals. More importantly, the conversation was cordial and stimulating throughout.

Afterwards, Miss Monica had a young house servant bring in the orphan dog who had been bathed, examined, and vaccinated by the local veterinarian (who makes house calls.) The dog was a well-behaved, captivating, brown and white heartthrob. The 'tail wagged the dog.' Both Sarah and Barlow were smitten.

Miss Monica asked, "Have you thought of a name?"

Barlow responded, "I didn't have to. He just pantomimed to all of us what to call him. His name is Happy."

The soirée concluded with Miss Monica wishing them all well and inviting them to stop by anytime.

Barlow dropped Sarah off at the college so she could pick up her car. She followed him back to his house.

He wasted no time. He began peeling off her clothes the minute they were inside. Then she undressed him. Happy was all eyes, ears, and wags.

They attacked and consumed each other like starving Ethiopians at their first luau. By 2:25, both were sated and exhausted. Sarah jumped in the shower, then rushed off to class. Barlow set his alarm and fell deep into blissful slumber. Happy waited patiently at the side of the bed until Barlow was peacefully counting sheep. Then he softly jumped on the bed and snuggled next to Barlow's feet. He, too, was asleep in minutes.

CHAPTER 19
Tuesday, March 24, 1970
Notifying the Parents of a Deceased Bandit

Monday had been an extremely long day and night. Tuesday was already a very long day by noon. Most of the sheriff's office staff were functioning on adrenaline and coffee.

Sheriff Sol and Deputy Bustamante rolled up to the Rocking A Ranch. It was a pretty sad affair consisting of fifty acres of scrub. It was bounded by rusty fencing which enclosed three ramshackle outbuildings and a small wooden house, on which the white paint was faded and windblown to memories of better times. Chickens were pecking in the yard. An aging grey donkey was grazing in the back, warding off the coyotes which otherwise would slaughter the three grizzled cows penned in. A derelict Aermotor windmill overlooked the whole affair in silent testimony.

Rosalita was watering a hardy variety of desert flowers in her garden. They portended hope for better times. Alberto walked out of a three-sided garage, wiping his hands on an oily rag. His dilapidated truck was jacked up in the rear. Tools were scattered everywhere.

It's seldom a good thing when the sheriff and a deputy stop by uninvited and unannounced even if they are friends, unless it's just prior to an election. Out of courtesy, Sheriff Sol and Chunk waited for Alberto and Rosalita to straighten up before walking up to the house. Rosalita's face had panic written all over it.

"Hola, Sheriff. Hola, Chunk." She mimicked a smile. "Would you like to come in?"

"Thanks, Rosalita. We'd appreciate that."

They went inside. The house was cozy and tidy. Inviting aromas emanated from the kitchen. Coffee was on the stove. The men took seats around the kitchen table while Rosalita poured the coffee. Though there was plenty left, she did not take any for herself. She sat down and offered a weak smile.

Alberto asked, "What can we do for you, Sheriff? Is anything wrong?"

Chunk looked down at his hands clasped together on the table. Sheriff Sol paused while he looked both Alberto and Rosalita in their weary eyes. "I'm afraid so. Some men tried to rustle sheep from Judge Sweeney's Triple S Ranch last night. They got into a shootout with me and some of my deputies. One tried to run down two deputies with the rig he was driving which was loaded with stolen sheep. Two of the rustlers were shot and killed. One surrendered without a fight. He's sitting in jail. One escaped across the river into Mexico."

Rosalita was quietly weeping and wringing her hands. Alberto grabbed the sheriff's forearm and squeezed. "Which of my boys did this, Sheriff?"

"I regret to inform you that Rudy is dead. Chico is in jail."

Rosalita collapsed in anguish. Her sobs shook the table and nearly spilled the coffees. Alberto blanched from cinnamon brown to ghostly white. He said, "Ay, Dios Mío! They live in Pecos! What were they doing on Judge Sweeney's property? They have jobs! Rudy works as an attendant at the truck stop. He's got a wife and baby boy! Chico works at the feed store there. He has a girlfriend! Are you sure, Sheriff?"

Chunk said, "It is true. We are both so sorry for your loss. Chico is alive and unharmed. We haven't spoken to him yet. We don't know who the other two men are. We came to bring you both back to town if you want to go. You can speak to Chico. You can view Rudy's body at the mortuary."

Rosalita's sobbing increased. She was barely breathing.

Sheriff Sol said, "Alberto, Chunk and I will wait for you all in the parlor while you gather your thoughts. Take a few minutes and decide if you want to come to town with us."

"Thanks, Sheriff."

Sheriff Sol and Chunk poured the remains from their coffee cups into the sink and rinsed them out. They retreated to the parlor. Sheriff Sol whispered, "Do you know if Alberto has any guns?"

"Not sure, Sheriff, but he's bound to have at least a rifle or shotgun to kill coyotes. I don't think he will be a problem, though."

"Well I wouldn't want him to have a change of heart and shoot us or kill himself. Grief can cause a person to do some crazy things he never imagined he was capable of."

"I don't think there's much chance of that. Is that why you didn't want to wait in the car?"

"Pretty much."

"Tell you what, Sheriff. Let me see if I can spur them on a little bit. I wouldn't be surprised if Rosalita decides to stay at home. We can see if one of her daughters or daughters-in-law can be with her. I'm sure Alberto will want to see Rudy's body and talk with Chico. We'll probably have to carry him back home. His truck is jacked up on blocks. Right now they have no transportation."

"Of course we will bring him home. I'll wait right here while you find out."

Thirty minutes later a daughter-in-law was consoling Rosalita. Alberto gratefully accepted the ride to town.

They stopped by the mortuary first. Alberto stood and wept silently when Mr. Ricketts pulled the sheet down from Rudy's face. The bullet hole in the forehead was unpleasant to behold but not nearly as unpleasant as the back of his head which thankfully, he could not see.

Finally, he asked, "What's next?"

Mr. Ricketts said they were waiting to see if an autopsy would be required. If not, Rudy's body would be released for burial. Otherwise, it might take a few days. He asked if Alberto had a funeral home in mind.

Alberto said, "We want you to handle it. I need to talk to Father Francisco at St. Stephen's about conducting the service."

Mr. Ricketts said he would contact Alberto for further details on the arrangements as soon as the body was released.

Sheriff Sol asked Pete to show Alberto the unknown rustler to see if he could make an identification. Alberto shuddered when he saw the body. He made the sign of the cross. He shook his head no. "Is this the man who got my boys involved in this wretched business?"

Sheriff Sol replied, "We don't know for sure. It could have been the hombre who escaped."

"I hope they both burn in Hell, Sheriff. Rudy was impetuous but he was not evil. I know he did not devise this scheme. He doesn't own a cattle truck. He doesn't even know how to drive a big one like that! Someone paid him to do this. Chico, too!

"Rudy never minded me. That's why he moved so far away. I put my boot up his ass when he did wrong. He talked Chico into this! I know he did!

"Chico is a good boy, Sheriff! He joined the National Guard! They taught him to be a truck driver. He was going to make something of himself. That's probably why Rudy talked him into getting involved. Now it's come down to this!

"Please, Sheriff, you have to catch this bastardo and make him pay! Chico is Rosalita's favorite. Now if he goes to prison, she will mourn herself to death!"

"We will do our best, Alberto.

"Thanks, Pete. You can cover him up now. I'll let you know about autopsies as soon as I get an answer from the Brewster County DA's office. They're handling this case since Judge Sweeney is the victim. It wouldn't surprise me to get orders to transport them both to Alpine."

"Of course, Sheriff.

"Mr. Gómez, please accept our heartfelt condolences. We will take good care of your son. I'll be in touch as soon as we know something."

"Thank you, Señor."

Sheriff Sol and Chunk escorted Alberto into the jail. As soon as Chico saw his father he burst into tears. Sheriff Sol told Alberto they would give them a few minutes alone and to holler when he was ready to go or if Chico wanted to talk. Then he and Chunk went to the jailer's room in back to wait.

It did not take long. Alberto said Chico wanted to talk.

Sheriff Sol said, "Let me call DA DeWitt and Sam Davis, the defense attorney, to come over. Alberto, you and Chico are my friends but this case will not be heard in Quayle County. I'm going to bring the lawyers over in an abundance of caution to make sure everything is handled correctly. There's a lot at stake here."

"It's okay, Sheriff. Chico knows he did wrong and he wants to make amends. He would prefer that you call Father Francisco."

"Tell you what, Alberto. Let me call the lawyers first. Soon as we're done I'll get Father Francisco over here."

Sam Davis was first to arrive. He met with Chico and Alberto for half an hour. Afterwards, he huddled with DA DeWitt and Sheriff Sol. He said Chico had some useful information and he wanted to cooperate. As his temporary counsel, he was wondering what, if any, benefit he would receive for his help.

Able DeWitt said the DA in Alpine, Bradford Delaney, whom they both knew, would be the prosecutor. Able didn't know enough about the case to make any promises, nor was it any longer in his purview; however, he would recommend leniency and suggest that they consider reducing the charges somewhat due to Chico's youth and lack of past criminal behavior, assuming his information proved useful and he were willing to testify against his co-conspirators if it became necessary; further, he stressed that rustling is a serious felony and that Brad Delaney was unlikely to take prison off the table. Chico should understand that he would likely go to prison but not for 20 or 30 years.

Sam said, "Chico and Alberto can live with that. The kid's so ashamed and so is his father, Sheriff, that you might want to consider putting Chico on suicide watch. And he needs to be away from gen pop (general population). This kid wouldn't survive the night if he were put in with the bad boys."

DeWitt said, "Maybe we can help him get out on bond. No promises. Let's see what he has to say first."

CHAPTER 20
Tuesday, March 24, 1970
Chico's Statement

They traipsed out of the jail into Sheriff Sol's office. Once they were all seated, Sheriff Sol advised Chico of the Miranda warning. Both he and Sam signed the waiver.

Chico began, "Rudy and his wife, Maria, and me and my girlfriend, Dolores, went to the Cactus Cantina in Pecos to celebrate New Year's Eve. We were having a great time. Our waitress, this chick named Jasmine, was real busy and having a difficult time keeping up with all her orders. Her boyfriend was this dude named Juan Rodríguez. He was sitting by himself in the corner, all pissed off because Jasmine didn't have time to spend with him.

"Jasmine was afraid she'd get fired, plus she was making a whole lot more money in tips than she would ever make on a regular night. She asked Rudy if it would be all right for Juan to join us since we were laughing and having so much fun. She said he was all mumped up being by himself and that she would make sure we got extra good service.

"Rudy said, 'Yeah, if you can give us all a free round.' She said okay. She brought Juan over and after awhile he loosened up and we thought he was a pretty good guy."

Sheriff Sol asked, "Did you know Juan Rodríguez before then?"

"No. He is in his thirties. I never saw him before but him and Rudy hit it off. I was a little leery of him. He was a muscular guy with some homemade tats, plus he had an edge like he was always looking for a fight.

"Anyway, a little before midnight, this other dude come in

with a Mexican chick who was smokin' hot. She was already drunk. Her dress was practically hanging off of her. It was low cut and she wasn't wearing a bra. It was all any guy could do not to stare. Besides that, her skirt was cut full but it was super short. When she bent over, if you were to her front you could see her boobs. If you were to her back, you could see everything because she wasn't wearing any panties. I'm pretty sure she's a wet. I just knew sooner or later some dude would say something or stare too hard and there'd be blood on the floor."

"What about her date? Was he a wet?"

"Not sure. Maybe. He was dressed up in a fancy black suit with silver buttons and a black cowboy hat with a rattlesnake band. I seen he had a gun tucked into his waist when his coat fell open."

"What kind of gun?"

"I don't know for sure. It was big. It was chrome and had mother of pearl grips."

"Was it a revolver or a semi-automatic pistol?"

"Not a revolver. A pistol. Like a .45 or something."

"What happened next?"

"Well, the guy said something to Juan. I couldn't hear. The music was loud and he was talking low. I saw right away that Juan was very respectful of him. Jasmine brought him and his girl a couple of shooters. He gave her a $10 bill and told her to keep the change. That's more than an $8 tip! Anyway, he and the puta left shortly after that.

"Rudy asked Juan who his friend was, and all he said was the dude likes to be called El Jefe and that it was in everyone's best interest to humor him unless he was looking for trouble."

"What did he look like?"

"You saw him last night. He was driving the black pickup truck."

"Go on."

"Well, Dolores and I left a little after midnight. Rudy and

Maria stayed out with Juan.

"About a week later I went to the truck stop to get a hamburger where Rudy works. He took a break and ate with me. He said Juan and El Jefe were old compadres and that they work for two rich white dudes who are identical twins. Juan works as a ranch hand for one and El Jefe works for the other brother who drills oil wells. Juan asked Rudy if he could drive an 18-wheeler. Rudy lied his ass off and said yeah, a little, but that I was a better driver than him because that's my job driving 18-wheelers for the National Guard as a weekend warrior.

"Juan said they had a little action going on the side and that they needed a couple of big rig operators to help them make some midnight requisitions. He said usually it would only take five or six hours a night but the pay was a flat hundred bucks, whether it took two hours or ten. Rudy said we were both interested."

"What did you say to Rudy?"

"This scared the bejesus out of me! I knew these dudes were some bad hombres. I didn't want anything to do with it."

"Well, why did you?"

"Because Juan said they didn't really want some half-ass like Rudy who didn't know what he was doing driving for them but if he could get me to do it too, they'd take a chance on him. I didn't want any part of this. I knew we'd be hauling some type of stolen shit. I told him I didn't want to go to jail.

"Rudy freaked and said if I backed out, they'd probably kill us because now we knew they were involved in something shady. If we didn't go along, it would indicate we didn't trust them. That would mean they couldn't trust us not to blow them in to the cops. Besides that, Rudy pointed out that neither one of us was making a hundred bucks a week, let alone for just one night's work. We both needed the cash so I said okay.

"It was around the second week in January. It was on a Monday. I remember that because it was the day right after my weekend drill for the National Guard, so it had to be on the 12th.

I was whipped because we worked our asses off that weekend. I was at work. Rudy stopped by at lunchtime and said that Juan called and said we have a job. He said for us to meet them at 10 o'clock at some business called Pluto, like Mickey Mouse's dog, on Carter Street between 5th and 6th. He said for us to pull around in the back if we got there first."

"Whoa, whoa, whoa. You got Juan's phone number?"

"No, but Rudy did."

"Did Rudy keep an address book? Where would he have placed that number?"

"If it wasn't on a scrap of paper in his wallet, he might have written it on this address book his old lady keeps by the phone."

"Where can we find Maria?"

"Normally at home in Pecos. He's lived there for several years on 2nd Street. The number is on his driver's license, except that Maria probably went to Mama's house or her mama's house if she knows Rudy's dead."

"Who's her mama?"

"Frieda Honoré. She lives in Pecos on Pace Street. It's in the book."

"Okay. What kind of business is Pluto?"

"I never heard of it before but it has something to do with servicing oil drilling companies. That's who El Jefe works for."

"That would be one of the rich twin white dudes?"

"I'm pretty sure."

"Go on."

"Rudy picked me up at 9:45. He already knew where the place was. It's a small business with a big lot in the back. When we got there I saw two tractors with stock trailers already attached."

"Did you see any other trailers?"

"Oh yeah. They had several flat beds and a regular 53-footer back there plus some drilling stuff, but they only had two tractors."

"Were Juan and El Jefe there waiting for you all?"

"No. They didn't get there until almost 10:30. I told Rudy that they weren't coming, that this was probably some kind of test and that we should bug out. Maybe they would hire somebody they trusted more than us but Rudy said to hang on, they'd show up, and for me not to get my panties in a wad. He reminded me that this was for a cool hundred bucks each, in cash, and that we'd be done by daylight. I seen this tricked out Ford pickup drive past the shop but it didn't stop. About fifteen minutes later it came back and parked next to Rudy. El Jefe was driving. He and Juan got out and said they were checking us out in case we called the cops."

"Who said?"

"El Jefe. He showed us he had a gun. He said he was always prepared for any situation. Then he asked if we was ready to make a hundred bucks. Rudy said that's why we're here. El Jefe said we were picking up some sheep tonight and dropping them off at another ranch. We would play 'Follow the Leader.' He was the leader. Rudy was 'in the rocking chair' since he wasn't a trained over-the-road driver and I was pulling drag.

"We drove to some ranch in the middle of nowhere in Culberson County. It had a really nice fence. The gate wasn't locked. We went in and drove for several miles and I never saw a house or a building. Finally we come up on this flock of sheep. We all got out. Juan had this sheepdog and he and the dog herded nearly a hundred sheep on the trailers. It only took about thirty minutes and we was ready to go.

"Then we got back on 285 and drove to New Mexico. We only went about fifteen or twenty miles to a county road south of Loving. They call that area Malaga. I don't remember seeing a highway sign. It's easy to miss but the road doesn't cross 285 on the west side. It only goes east. There's an old, broken down windmill just before the road on the east side. That's my landmark. We followed it five or six miles. Then we came to a ranch on the north side. It looked run down but it was right on the Pecos River. I remember that. We unloaded in a corral.

"The first time I never saw the man who lives there. El Jefe went in the house. A little while later he came out and said it was time to vamoose. We drove back to Pecos and parked the rigs where we picked them up. Then El Jefe paid us. He said this was a trial run and that we were on probation. We better forget everywhere we went and what we saw if we knew what was good for us."

"Do you remember the ranch you rustled?"

"Yes. I'm pretty sure I can find it."

"What time did you get there?"

"Maybe 11:30 or midnight. It really wasn't that far from Pecos. Maybe fifty or sixty miles."

"What time did you arrive at the ranch in New Mexico?"

"Maybe 1:30 or 2. There wasn't anybody on the road."

"Can you find it again?"

"Sí, sí."

"What time did you get back to Pecos?"

"4 o'clock."

"And El Jefe personally paid you and Rudy a hundred bucks each?"

"Yes."

"How much did Juan get?"

"I don't know, but I am sure it was more than us. He had the dog plus he herded the sheep. Besides, I think he and El Jefe are partners. Rudy and me, we began calling him El Segundo because he was second in charge."

"How long 'til the next job?"

"A few days. Not even a week. I remember because Dolores' birthday is January 19th. It was on a Monday. I used part of the money to buy a necklace for her. We did it on a Thursday night, but really it was Friday morning."

"That would have been January 15th to the 16th."

"I suppose."

"Where did you go?"

"That trip was a little longer. We went to a ranch in Jeff Davis County outside of Valentine. Same deal as before, except we had to cut the lock on the fence and it took a little longer. We didn't get as many sheep this time. Maybe seventy. It took too long to round them up. Plus it was about a hundred miles to get there. El Jefe was pissed off. He blamed all of us. We didn't get back to Pecos until almost 8 o'clock. I was nearly late for work. Rudy was late. El Jefe said we would start earlier from now on, especially if we had to drive a couple hundred miles to do the job."

"Can you find that ranch?"

"I'm pretty sure. The gate was damaged. It looked like someone had run into it. It was a little hard for Juan to get it open. Same thing for getting it closed."

"What about the third time?"

"That's when Rudy decided to be a big shot."

"How so?"

"Sheriff, could we take a break? I haven't had anything to eat since supper last night."

"Sure thing. Chunk, could you call Betty's and order six Blue Plate Specials? Tell her extra large portions. We'll get the Cokes from the machine here."

"You bet, Sheriff."

CHAPTER 21
Tuesday, March 24, 1970
Chico's Statement (Continued)

"The third time out was when things began to get out of whack."

"How so?"

"Rudy was into this whole bandit thing. He was beginning to see himself as some sort of desperado. He started growing a mustache. He talked about buying a gun. He started wearing this sheath knife everywhere he went. Besides that, he wanted to make more money. He thought he could elevate himself above Juan. He couldn't get it through his thick head that we were expendable - that Juan and El Jefe were compadres from way back.

"The last time out, he saw El Jefe dog out Juan because he was having a hard time rounding up the sheep. He never considered that the sheep were more scattered and that what we really needed was more than one dog. So Rudy has this brainiac idea. He tells El Jefe that he knows of a ranch with a natural holding pen. He said we could round up the sheep one night and make off with them the next. Plus he said this ranch had Rambouillet sheep, which are bigger and have more meat on the hoof."

"You mean Judge Sweeney's Triple S Ranch?"

"Yeah. Rudy used to work there but he got fired and he wanted payback. He blamed the foreman. Said he was a prick."

"Do you mean Enrico Méndez?"

"Yeah, Rico. Rudy hated him. Anyway, at first Rudy convinced El Jefe that the two of them could herd the sheep themselves. All they needed was a roll of fencing and a few stakes to hold it in place. Then El Jefe wanted to know if Rudy had a sheepdog and if he could splice a fence well enough that it wouldn't be noticeable. Of course the answer was no to both questions, so El Jefe said that Rudy would ride with him and Juan to herd the sheep.

"He wanted to know the location of the ranch. Rudy said it was in Quayle County about 120 miles south of Pecos. El Jefe said for him to meet at the regular place at 9 o'clock the next night."

"You mean at Pluto's?"

"Yeah.

"When was this?"

"About a week later."

"Wednesday the 21st? Thursday the 22nd? Friday the 23rd?"

"It would have been Wednesday night. El Jefe said he didn't like pulling jobs on Fridays, Saturdays, or Sundays. Less people moving around on weeknights. His preference was Tuesdays through Thursdays."

"Okay. Let's back up. How did Rudy contact El Jefe to begin with? Did he have a telephone number for him?"

"No. He kept going by Pluto's until he finally caught him there. El Jefe works there all by himself."

"So what happened?"

"Well, the next night when they met, Juan was really pissed off at Rudy. When Juan caught him alone, he told him this better be the mother lode or they might just leave him behind and let him find his own way back. He also said if Rudy ever tried to go behind his back again, he would cut his heart out and feed it to his dog. I'm not sure exactly what all happened except from this point on, Rudy was real scared of El Jefe and Juan. Initially, he was just scared of El Jefe.

"Anyway, everything went as smooth as you please. The next night, Thursday, we all went back and took our biggest haul ever with the fattest lambs. We dropped the sheep off at the same place. This time, El Jefe was in a great mood, so he took us to a cafe in Loving for breakfast.

"After we ate, his mood changed. It was like he got suspicious or something. He told Rudy and me to drop the rigs off at Pluto's but then he followed us out to the parking lot. We were standing between the rigs. It was still dark, about 5 o'clock I think, and he began saying stuff like guys who talk out of school wind up hurt or dead or maybe someone in their family pays the price. Then Juan grabbed me from behind by my hair and yanked my head back. He had this switchblade knife and he ran the blade across my throat about a quarter of an inch away. Then he let me go and put the knife in his pocket and acted like it was just a big joke. It wasn't a joke to me. I thought I was a dead man and I didn't do nothin' wrong!"

"Was this because Rudy tried to cut him out? Were you the family he was referring to?"

"I don't know. I didn't think so at the time. Rudy shit himself. Not kidding. He had to wash himself off with a hose hooked up behind the diner. Anyway, from this point on I knew Rudy and I were in so deep we could never get out. I knew they would kill us if we said we wanted out. Rudy thought so, too. I think that's why he didn't stop tonight. He knew he was a dead man for sure if he surrendered. Me, too. I'm for sure a dead man if El Jefe ever finds me."

"We'll talk about that a little later. Tell me what you all did next."

"I'm positive El Jefe knew how bad he had us scared. He was making a lot of money off of us. We were his cash cows but we were also expendable. If anything went wrong, we would be the ones left behind taking the fall, just like tonight. I don't think he wanted to waste any time. 'Make hay while the sun shines,' so the following Monday night we did a job just inside Pecos County at a ranch near a small town named Coyanosa."

"Monday was the 26th."

"That sounds about right. It didn't take long to get there. We got about eighty Merinos from a ranch. We could see the ranch house from where El Jefe cut the fence. The porch light was on. We were pretty nervous about that one but we got away clean."

"You can find this ranch?"

"Oh, yeah."

"Where did you go next?"

"That was a pretty long haul. We went to Brewster County. We were probably forty miles south of Marathon at a ranch off Highway 385. This one wasn't worth it to El Jefe. We only got sixty sheep . . . ."

"Are you sure? Only sixty? That doesn't sound like much."

"Oh, I'm sure. El Jefe was all pissed off. We worked all night, mostly driving, burning gas, and killing time. Even so, he still paid Rudy and me a hundred bucks each but he wasn't happy about it."

"Can you find the Brewster ranch?"

"Pretty sure."

"When did you hit it?"

"Just a couple of days later on a Thursday."

"That would have been January 29th."

"That's probably right."

"What was next?"

"It was a couple of weeks later. Rudy and I thought maybe after the light haul they didn't think the payoff was worth the risk. We were wrong. We went out again on the Thursday before Valentine's Day."

"That would have been February 12th."

"I guess so."

"Where did you go?"

"It was almost in our own backyard. We went to Winkler County not more'n forty miles from home. That's the one place I'm not sure about. I was sick, throwing up. All I did was follow and try not to barf in the truck."

"Did you?"

"Oh, no! If I had done that, El Jefe would have shot me for

sure."

"Anything you recall about the haul?"

"Only that we filled both trucks. El Jefe and Segundo were happy. But the sheep were small. I remember that."

"Could you find it again?"

"Maybe. I might have to drive around for awhile. I remember we had a hard time finding the ranch road but it was nighttime. It might be easier in the daylight."

"What was next?"

"The next Thursday. We mostly did jobs on Thursday by then. We went to Ward County to a little place called Grandfalls on the reservoir."

"That would have been February 19th."

"Probably so. I remember the sheep were down by the water and it was really muddy. I was afraid we'd get the rigs bogged down and have to leave 'em. We made a mess in that field. A blind man could have followed us halfway to New Mexico. It's a miracle we pulled that one off."

"Can you find the place again?"

"Oh, yeah."

"What was next?"

"We went all the way to Hudspeth County to a ranch near Salt Flats on Highway 180. It was a complete waste of time. We only got thirty head. I drove back empty. El Jefe still paid me. He sent my cut home with Rudy."

"When was that?"

"The next Thursday."

"February 26th."

"I guess so."

"Could you find this place again?"

"Oh sure. This guy had a brand new Aermotor windmill near the highway but his ranch was all run down. In fact, that whole area looked like a ghost town. I couldn't understand why anyone would buy such a nice windmill and put it out there in a shithole."

"Anything after that?"

"We went back to Judge Sweeney's. I thought that was crazy! I was sure he would have put out some nighthawks, especially up near the canyon, but he didn't. I guess they hadn't missed the first batch."

"Did you or Rudy go to scope it out the night before, put up the pen, round up the sheep like last time?"

"No. I think El Jefe and Segundo did all that theirselves. Rudy and I didn't know we were going back there until we met at Pluto's. Heck, I don't know if I would have showed up if I had known we were going back a second time."

"When was that."

"It was on a Tuesday about a couple of weeks after the last one."

"March 10th? That was the second Tuesday after Thursday, February 26th."

"That would be it."

"Okay. What was next?"

"That was it until last night. We thought they quit or something. I was hoping they did. I thought maybe we were free and clear. Sheriff, I swear, I never wanted to do this. You gotta believe me!"

"I do, Chico, and we all appreciate what you've done to make this right. But here's the situation. Your brother and a man whose name you don't even know are dead. Juan Rodríguez is not his real name, so we don't know who to notify.

"To top that off, El Jefe, your boss, got away into Old Mexico and you don't have any idea what his real name is.

"You say you can find the ranch in New Mexico where you dropped off all the sheep but you don't know the names of the twin brothers, one or both of which allegedly paid for the sheep. You only actually witnessed money change hands between one of the twins and El Jefe but you probably can't tell one twin from the other, and I get it. I bet most folks can't. So even with all your cooperation, we still have a lot of loose ends.

"Let's see. It's already 2:30. We've been up more than 24 hours and everyone's dead on his feet. We need to transport you to Brewster County for your initial appearance since we can't try your case here.

"You've admitted rustling sheep in eight counties if I'm not mistaken, and I very well could be. Rustling used to be a hanging offense in Texas, but fortunately for you, that's no longer the case. Even so, a judge could sentence you to twenty or thirty or more years if he took a notion to make an example out of you.

"Not only that, there's a thing called felony murder. What that means is, although you never had a gun and didn't shoot anybody, you could still be charged with murder because two people were killed during the commission of a felony, to wit: rustling sheep, to which you were a principal party. You and El Jefe both could be held legally accountable for the deaths of your brother and Segundo even though that was never your intent or his."

Chico began sobbing quietly.

Sheriff Sol backed off a little. He said, "Chico, you've been very cooperative. I know you personally, and I couldn't make myself throw you to the dogs like some of the rustling victims would probably want me to do. But the bottom line is, if you can't help us make a case that will stick against El Jefe and the twin or twins who were the receivers of stolen property so we can convict and send them all to prison, you're probably going to draw more time than if you did. Savvy? What happens to you is largely dependent upon us convicting them. That's a tall order."

Chico's sobbing became uncontrollable. He choked on his own spit. He gasped for breath. Finally, he spoke softly. "I think I can help you identify El Jefe. He worked for Pluto Inc. If you can get me his picture, I can positively identify him."

More quiet sobbing and shortness of breath. After a long pause, he resumed, "Someone around Loving should be able to identify Juan Rodríguez if Jasmine can't."

Another long pause. Then forcefully, he said, "I remember now! In the cigar box in my sock drawer in the bedroom of my apartment, there's a slip of paper with the license plate number of the twin El Jefe was working for. He drove the same red and white GMC Jimmy several times when we delivered. I'm pretty sure it's brand new. I doubt his brother ever drove it. I'm sure he had his own truck. Does this help?"

"It helps a lot.

"Chunk, get Chico a release to sign so we can search his apartment for that note. We can use his key from his personal property to get in."

"Yes, Sir, Sheriff."

"Chico, we really appreciate you manning up, making amends and so forth. I'm saddened by what happened to Rudy and Juan but they dictated the terms of their own demise. And for the record, El Jefe is real fortunate not to be laid out in the mortuary next to them. Make no mistake. We will put forth all our efforts into making a case on El Jefe and his boss man and putting them in prison for as long as the law allows.

"The thing is this. El Jefe is a smart man. He knows this. It would be in his best interests and those of his boss if you were out of the picture, took the big sleep. You even said so yourself. Savvy?"

"You mean for me to be dead."

"That's exactly what I mean. It would be real hard for us to tie him into this criminal enterprise without your testimony. Probably not impossible, but very difficult. He fully expects you to rat him out. He would rat you out if the shoe were on the other foot. Therefore, he will try to kill you or pay someone else to kill you so you can't testify in a trial against him.

"So to prevent this, I'm going to do two things for you. First, I'm going to ask Brewster County to put you in solitary confinement for your own safety. Second, I'll see what I can do to get your bond as low as possible. However, if you do make bond, you sure as heck can't stay in Pecos. I'm not even sure your daddy's ranch is safe, so if you do make bond we'll have to figure something out. Understand?"

"Yes, Sheriff."

"Okay. Chunk will take you back to your cell until we're ready to transport you to Alpine. I'll be in touch. In the meantime, we'll see if we can get Father Francisco to pay you a visit."

"Thanks, Sheriff."

"Chunk . . . ."

"Yes, Sir."

"Step out of my office for just a minute before you take him back to the cellblock."

When they were both outside and the door was closed, Sheriff Sol said, "When you take Alberto back out to to the Rocking A, I need you to talk to Rudy's wife."

"Maria?"

"Yeah. Chico said her mother's name is Frieda Honoré. Find out where she lives. We may need to get in contact with her later."

"Okay."

"Get Maria to show you her address book. We need Juan Rodríguez' telephone number. He might have listed it under another name, such as the name of the ranch or the name of the twin he worked for. It's bound to have the New Mexico area code, 505. You might have to go all the way back to their home in Pecos to get it.

"We need that telephone number to tie in the money men. In fact, seize the address book as evidence but be as gentle about it as you can. Give her a chance to write down her most important numbers. Tell her you will return the book as soon as we have examined it.

"This is really important. The Gómez family trusts you. Otherwise, I'd send Randy. Can you do that or are you too tired?"

"Sheriff, I'm all over this like white on rice. Consider it done."

"Thanks. I knew you could do it. If Maria's not already your friend, see if you can make her one. It's not her fault that her husband's a knucklehead."

"You got that right. Will do."

CHAPTER 22
Tuesday, March 24, 1970
Time Out

It was 4:30 before Deputies Kirk Shoemaker and Dewey Carruthers departed westbound to Alpine with Chico and a copy of Chief's initial investigative report addressed to Brewster County District Attorney Bradford Delaney. Just before they left, Sheriff Sol called an impromptu meeting with them, Chief Alex, and Deputy Randall Meacham, who was working the 4-12 shift.

He said, "Guys, it's been an extremely long day. Seems like it's been two days since I've slept. Anyway, we have two dead bandits, one in jail, and one last seen hightailing it into Old Mexico. Besides that, we have twin brothers who appear to be the money men calling all the shots, and who will be difficult to convict without a lot more evidence than we have now.

"Chico just spilled his guts and gave us a dozen or so leads we need to run out in order to resolve this case to our satisfaction. We want solid cases on everyone involved in this rustling operation. No sloppy police work. Think about it. This is the biggest ongoing crime spree that I'm aware of in West Texas. This is a very big deal. Don't lose sight of that!

"As much as I'd like to press on right through the next 48 or 72 hours until we have handcuffs on all the perps, I can't think straight and I venture to say neither can Chief Alex. So, unless they all die first and go to straight to Hell or they move permanently to Old Mexico, we will catch these oxygen thieves, if not tomorrow, the day after that, or the day after that. Believe it or not, Time is on our side. This is what we get paid to do and we do our jobs very well.

"Okay, guys. That's all. I'm going home to get some rest.

"Chief, you should go home, too. When I see you next, I'll be chomping at the bit, ready to kick ass and take names. Thanks for all you've done today.

"Adiós."

Chief responded, "Vaya con Dios."

CHAPTER 23
Wednesday, March 25, 1970
Barlow Suffers to Learn Patience

It was midnight on the dot. Technically, Barlow was not late for work. He was precisely on time, except for the mores of his culture which dictated that anything less than fifteen minutes early was late. Archie was pouring a cup of freshly brewed coffee when Barlow sailed through the door. Randy Meacham was already gone, having been relieved at 11:30 by Arch.

Archie looked up and said, "Long time, no see, Stranger. Are you that bronco busting dude I been hearing about?"

"I am one and the same. I thought you would have brung me up better than that knowing that I'm a tenderfoot and never learnt all these cowboy tricks as a tyke."

"Heck. Even if I hadda showed ya, ya wouldn't have paid me no never mind nohow. Did ya miss me?"

"You know I did. Did you miss me?"

"Nah. Not too much except for when it was time to sweep and carry out the trash. That's one thang you learnt well as a tyke."

"Get outta here, you old coot. Tell me where we stand with the investigation."

"Well, draw up a cuppa joe and I'll fill you in."

Barlow complied.

"First off, Chico saw the light and he come running back home to Jesus. Hallelujah!

"He told Sheriff Sol the general locations of all the ranches they rustled, which are in eight different counties, the approximate dates they done it, plus the location of the ranch in Eddy County, New Mexico, where they sold the sheep. He didn't know the real name of the dead varmint but said he was a ranch hand where they delivered the sheep.

"Apparently the ranch is owned by twin white dudes, identities unknown, and this is where it gets real interesting. The rigs Rudy and Chico was driving supposedly belong to a wildcatter/oil rig service company named Pluto Incorporated, located in Pecos, which is where our fugitive works. Chico doesn't know his name, just that he likes to be called El Jefe. His employer is one of the twins so connect the dots. Both twins must be involved with the rustling. If Chico's information is solid, they own the ranch and the company which owns the rigs.

"Lastly, Chico wrote down the license plate number of the vehicle driven by the twin who accepted delivery of the sheep. It's on a scrap of paper he put in his sock drawer and he signed a consent to search so we can go get it. Does that float your boat, or what?"

"That sounds great! What does Sheriff Sol want you and me to do tonight?"

"Well, there ain't much we can do, stuck here. We already run FBI and DPS record checks on Carlos "Chico" Gómez and Rodolfo Gómez. Chico's clean, but it might surprise you to learn that Rudy got popped in Crockett County in '63 for grand larceny when he was eighteen years old. He got a year in prison, served six months, and got released on parole backed up by a three-year suspended sentence. He got off parole in '67."

"Well, I never met him before. Did he ever serve in the armed forces?"

"Oh, Hell no! He quit high school in the ninth grade at age sixteen. He was IV-F. Nobody was desperate enough to enlist him because he was always in trouble. A real shit magnet. He never got charged here locally because what he done was always chickenshit, petty stuff, plus everyone loved his old man. Finally, it got so bad, Alberto had to run him off. I never heard about him getting busted in Crockett. His family kept that real quiet."

"Did you ever think he had it in him to run down Chunk or

Ernie?"

"Nope. I never saw that coming."

"How's Ernie doing?"

"Oh, he's a little shook up but he's coming around. He'll be okay."

"Good. So what's the agenda for tomorrow. I don't want to get benched because of my rodeo trick."

"Oh, you're not benched. It's Catch-22 for you. You work mids but right now the sheriff needs leads run out which can only be done during regular business hours. Besides that, you and Slick already had a week's worth of fun and games. Sheriff needs to spread the wealth around a little bit. Not only that, but from what I recall, you're still a full-time college student."

"You're absolutely right on all counts but that doesn't make riding the plank any easier. Arch, that asshole shot at me and I'd like a second chance at making him an honest man."

"You mean dead."

"Not if he surrenders peacefully."

"Fat chance of that happening!"

"Well, I know what he looks like. I'd recognize that sidewinder anywhere. If he's up in Pecos, I know I can find him."

"Well, Corporal Adams, Dragon Slayer Extraordinaire, did you ever think Sheriff Sol doesn't want you or anyone else to find that shitbird and scoop him up before we got stronger cases on the shot callers? Wouldn't you like to wrap them all up in one big bundle with a bow? Bust and convict ever' last one of 'em? Send 'em all up the river?"

"Oh, yeah! Dern! I got ants in my pants. Sorry. I'm not thinking straight."

"Barlow, you got great instincts and someday you're gonna be Wyatt Earp and Eliot Ness all rolled into one. But right now you're still a rookie who hasn't even got a year on the job yet. You still got a lot of learning ahead of you. Savvy?"

"Savvy."

"As if Sheriff Sol doesn't know it already, but no never mind, I'll let him know you're chomping at the bit to get back in the game. In the meantime, since we ain't got anything else going on right now, why don't you hit the books and make straight A's this semester? Make everyone proud."

"Not much likelihood of that. I confess that I am definitely behind the power curve with my schoolwork. Thanks, Arch. I appreciate all your insight and advice. I been acting kind of like an asshole and I didn't even realize it."

"De nada. Go get caught up. Not kidding. Make as many A's as you can. A lot of eyes are on you, Kid. There's a bunch of ways to be a hero, but dozens more to be a zero. Comprenden?"

"Comprenden."

CHAPTER 24
Wednesday, March 25, 1970
Picking Up the Pieces in the Office

It was almost 9 o'clock when Sheriff Sol and Chief Alex strolled into the jail. Deputy Atwater was buzzing around, far more energetic than usual, one might even say manic, straightening files, pushing in chairs, dusting bookshelves and desktops and doing all kinds of housekeeping which really didn't need to be done and 'whistling while he worked.' Nobody ever did that in the jail before.

Miss Loretta was quietly biding her time, 'maintaining radio silence,' pretending that all this hyperactivity was normal for Ernie. Truth be known, he was driving her to distraction. She was supportive of his situation but didn't know what to say to him since the shooting. She was relieved when the bosses finally showed up.

Sheriff Sol took time to check on Miss Loretta and Ernie, asking after their well-being and that of their families. He listened patiently to what they said and showed a genuine concern for things which were important to them. He never said a word about how he was feeling. With Sheriff Sol, it was all about you.

This was SOP (standard operating procedure) for him. He liked to ease into his workday. Different from Chief Alex, who had uttered the perfunctory 'hello' and was already at his desk on the telephone, Sheriff Sol always took time for the troops no matter what and probably would have, even if they were directly in the path of a cyclone. That was one reason why nearly everyone in Quayle County loved him and why he never had to campaign during election years. In fact, Miss Loretta never understood how he could maintain this level of grace, especially under pressure or difficult circumstances.

Chief Alex hung up the phone. He said, "I just spoke with one Harriett Morgan at the Texas Secretary of State's Office in Austin. She said Texas does not have a record for a corporation named Pluto. However, she said a lot of companies incorporate in Delaware and South Dakota and one or two other states because it's easy and cheap there.

"I told her what we had going on. She said as a favor to me, she would check both states and the others most likely if she didn't have any luck there. She'll call back and let me know if she has any success."

Miss Loretta said, "If she comes up with anything, you better send her some flowers. Just think how long it would take you to check out the other 49 states. Heck, first you'd have to call the long distance operator for telephone numbers. That alone could take days if you had to work your way through all of the states."

Chief responded, "You are so right. It'll be well worth it."

Sheriff Sol piped in. "Loretta, if she calls back while we're gone, take the message and chat her up. Make a friend. Find out if she has a direct line and what her office address is. Then send her a nice planter on the office account. We'll follow up later with a thank you letter."

"That's a great idea, Sheriff. I'll take care of it."

"Good. Listen you all. Chief and I are headed up to Pecos in Reeves County to run out some leads. We may even drive up to Loving in Eddy County, New Mexico, if we have time. We won't have radio coverage for most of the day. I'll touch base by phone first from Pecos either way.

"Ern, you'll be in charge. You got everything under control?"

"Yes, Sir. Any idea when Chico will get arraigned in Brewster County?"

Chief Alex spoke up. "Sometime this morning. We won't need a presence there. Nevertheless, will you check on this sometime later this morning?"

"Will do."

"Good. If the DA's Office calls, tell them we'll stop by tomorrow with the rest of what we have on Chico. Also, find out if they plan to conduct autopsies on either Rudy or Rodríguez. If so, we need to notify Pete Ricketts since he'll probably be tasked with transport."

"Consider it done. I'll give you a heads up via radio if I get an answer before you all leave Quayle County. Ditto for anything else that's urgent."

Sheriff Sol responded, "Please do, but don't put out anything sensitive over the air. Too many folks have police scanners. Just ask us to give you a call. Also, it goes without saying. If you have something that can't wait and we're out of range, leave me a message at the Reeves SO and I'll call once we get there. If all else fails, call Archie. He speaks for us if we aren't here. Savvy?"

"You got it, Sheriff."

"One last thing. We're not ready to release information about the other ranches that have been rustled. Keep that in house. If anyone asks, tell them to call me or Chief Alex. Make sure the other guys get the word, too."

"Yes, Sir."

"See ya tomorrow."

CHAPTER 25
Wednesday, March 25, 1970
Following the Leads in Pecos

They took Chief's Wagoneer just in case they needed to go off road. It took just a little over two hours to arrive.

The first thing they did was to recon Pluto Inc. It was just like Chico described. It appeared to be closed for the day but they didn't knock to find out.

The next stop was Chico's tiny apartment. They let themselves in with his key. Poor kid. It was bare bones. Not even a TV. Nevertheless, it was straight and it was spic and span.

The single bedroom was spartan. It had a neatly made twin bed, chair, and dresser. That was it. On top of the dresser was a gold metal, folding, double picture frame. The photo on the left was Chico's basic training picture dressed in his Class A uniform with the American flag to his left. He stood ramrod straight and looked so proud. The photo on the right was a high school graduation picture of a sweet-looking Mexican girl. This was most likely Dolores. Sheriff Sol made a note to self that they needed to interview her. She might have additional information on the two unknown bandits.

They found the sock drawer right away. It was the one on top. The cigar box contained small keepsakes, including his high school ring, a few wallet-size photos, crucifix, receipts, pen knife, $240 in cash, matchbooks, ballpoint pen and several scraps of paper. Only one was noteworthy. It had the number 864321 written on it. Chief Alex put it in an evidence envelope.

They searched the entire apartment in ten minutes. They left things as they found them. Chico's National Guard uniforms and his TA-50 (field equipment) took up most of his closet space. The uniforms were pressed and hanging in military order. His boots and low quarters were shined.

They locked up and left. Time to make their official presence known to Reeves County Sheriff Wilbert J. "Willie Joe" Whalen and Chief Deputy Winston Ledbetter.

Both were in the office. They greeted Sheriff Sol and Chief Alex warmly and without fanfare, like it was commonplace for a county sheriff and a chief deputy to drive two hours to visit without an appointment. Chief Alex had called the day before requesting information on the two Gómez boys and a John Doe, AKA Juan Rodríguez, but he never said anything about coming for a visit. Since the noon hour was nearly gone and no one had eaten, they quickly agreed to break bread together at El Gato's Genuine Mexican Food Cafe and to catch up there.

The meal was a scrumptious feast of beef burritos and cheese enchiladas with Mexican rice and pinto beans washed down with sweet tea, not cerveza, which each of them would have preferred.

During the meal, Sheriff Sol gave a redacted version of the investigation to his colleagues. He provided a detailed account of the rustling in Quayle County, to include the shootout, and what little he knew of the rustling incident in Brewster County.

What he held back was the extent of Chico's cooperation, particularly as it related to rustling in the other seven counties, nor did he mention the drop site ranch in Eddy County, New Mexico. He needed more time to develop Quayle's case for successful prosecution of all the gang members. He had decided to come clean with any sheriff who had an ongoing investigation of a rustling by this gang, if, and this was a big if, they reported their case to him first. He decided that Sheriff Whalen didn't have a need to know at this time since his county appeared to be unaffected.

At the conclusion of his briefing, Sheriff Sol asked, "Willie Joe, what do you know about this company in Pecos called Pluto Incorporated?"

Chief Ledbetter spoke up. "Interesting that you should ask. Yesterday morning one of our deputies made a run over there. It seems like parties unknown absconded with two tractors and two stock trailers.

"The Pluto employee who filed the report said they disappeared from the back parking lot sometime Monday night. It sounded a little fishy since this is an oil field servicing company. What on God's green Earth do they need with stock trailers? Besides that, the complainant says he resides on the premises but he claims he slept over with a girlfriend over in Barstow in Ward County Monday night."

"Do you know the name of the person who filed the complaint?"

"No. We can go back to the office and look it up. I just can't recall."

Sheriff Whalen added, "Pluto is a funny name for a company, if you ask me. I never really paid much attention to it. The business is usually closed. It's only a one or two-man operation. Mexican, I think. I can't see how they make enough money to stay in business."

Chief Alex asked, "What about a Mexican fellow, about 30 to 35 years of age, about six feet tall, 180 pounds, jailhouse tattoo on his upper left arm of a rattlesnake striking a javelina? He had a fake driver's license identifying himself as Juan Rodríguez of 1517 Allen Street in Pecos."

Chief Ledbetter asked, "Ain't that the guy you mentioned yesterday? If it is, you got a lot more information today. Got a picture?"

Chief Alex responded, "Yeah, he's the same dude but I'll save his photograph until after we eat. He's kind of a mess."

Sheriff Whalen responded, "Doesn't ring a bell to me. How about you, Winston?"

"Nope."

Sheriff Sol said, "Supposedly he has a girlfriend named

Jasmine at the Cactus Cantina."

Chief Ledbetter replied, "Oh, yeah, we definitely know her. Jasmine Estrada. Some call her Jasmine Erotica. She's, shall we say, voluptuous. A real looker. We think she may do a little freelance hooking on the side. I'd be surprised if her employer, Francisco Robles, is pimping her out, but it wouldn't surprise me to learn he's turning a blind eye so long as she satisfies his carnal desires. We can grab her and have her waiting for you in the interview room if you want."

Sheriff Sol replied, "Thanks, but we'd prefer to do it low key, if she's cooperative. I doubt she knows Don Juan is dead yet. At least I hope she doesn't. If we can't get her to talk to us at home, then yeah, we'd really appreciate it if you all did haul her in."

Sheriff Whalen said, "As you wish. We'll point out her house on the way back to the office. She'll probably cooperate unless it would get her arrested or beat up."

Chief Alex responded, "Well, so far as we know, she's not in any jeopardy unless it would have been from her boyfriend who we heard was extremely jealous, but he's dead. Maybe she knows his real name or where he hung his hat."

Winston responded, "Once you see her, you'll know why her boyfriend would be jealous. Besides putting Miss Texas to shame in the good looks department, she just exudes raw sex. She's a young man's wet dream. Heck, she could give the Pope a diamond cutter in a matter of seconds and turn him into a sex fiend in a matter of minutes. She's that seductive."

Sheriff Sol said, "We appreciate the insight. I'm glad she lives in your county and not mine. From the sound of it, she probably has a whole remuda of young studs. We don't need anymore knife fights in Quayle County than we have already."

On the trip back to the courthouse they passed by Jasmine's house. A blue, 1964, Plymouth Valiant, two-door sedan was parked in the driveway. Chief Ledbetter identified that as her car. They saw movement inside through the curtains in the windows so they felt like she was probably at home.

They also went to see Juan Rodríguez's house at 1517 Allen Street, except no such address existed. The last house was at 1515.

At the Reeves County Courthouse, Chief Alex showed a morgue photograph of Juan Rodríguez to Sheriff Whalen and the other five employees who were present. Nobody recognized him. This wasn't surprising, in that he worked in the Loving, New Mexico area, plus the photograph was even worse than the ones taken by the police as mugshots. The buckshot holes in his face didn't help much either.

Chief Alex obtained a copy of the RCSO incident report taken by Deputy Irwin Trevino, regarding the alleged grand theft auto of Pluto's two tractor trailers. The complainant was one Humberto Pavón, age 30, listed as Pluto's operations manager, who cited the business address and telephone number also as his home address and telephone number.

Mrs. Sebastian, the clerk, ran him through the FBI's NCIC, and the Texas DPS and DMV databases. She estimated the month and day of birth as June 1st, and used 1939 as his year of birth (knowing he was thirty years old), hoping to get a hit. Running a record check required the exact month, day, and year to get a match, but on some occasions, if the name was somewhat unique a close miss would work.

No luck from Texas, but she got a hit from the FBI's NCIC. Humberto Pavón had one arrest in 1960, by the Eddy County Sheriff's Office in Carlsbad, New Mexico, for aggravated assault. His date of birth was listed as May 5, 1939. However, the disposition of the arrest was not recorded.

Next, she called the Eddy County SO and spoke to a counterpart in their records section named Phyllis Rafferty. Mrs. Rafferty pulled up their case file on Pavón, which included a fingerprint card, three mugshots, a personal history sheet, crime scene photographs, incident report, rights waiver, evidence sheet, witness statements, investigative report, investigative notes, and criminal complaint, but no indictment or judicial action documents. She noticed that the arresting officer was Deputy Morris Doolittle, who died in an auto accident a month after the arrest. She said that whoever assumed responsibility for the case after Deputy Doolittle's death must have been asleep at the switch, and she apologized for the incomplete file. She said she would call the district court clerk's office to see if she could get a final disposition.

In the interim, with the correct date of birth, Mrs. Sebastian conducted a new records search on Pavón in the Texas DPS and DMV databases. He came back clear on the criminal and wanted record checks. But this time it turned out that he had a valid commercial driver's license (CDL), also known as a Class A license, with no recorded traffic citations. The bad news was that his license also listed Pluto's office address as his home address.

Mrs. Rafferty called back. She reported that Pavón was convicted on the aggravated assault. He was sentenced to ten years of incarceration in the Penitentiary of New Mexico. The conviction date was February 8, 1960, so he probably's been out of prison for a couple of years or more. She said the penitentiary could probably provide more information.

Chief Alex spoke with Mrs. Rafferty. He thanked her for everything. He said Pavón was a suspect in a shooting in his county. He asked if it would be possible for her to send him one of Pavón's photographs, a copy of the incident report and the judgment and commitment order. He said he knew it was a big request, but the problem was that Pavón had taken a powder and they were desperately trying to locate him before he hurt someone else. Mrs. Rafferty understood only too well. She would put all those documents in today's mail at close of business. With any luck, he'd have it by Friday.

While Chief Alex was thus engaged, Sheriff Sol and Sheriff Whalen spoke with Deputy Irwin Trevino. He described Pavón as being about 5'10" tall, 160 pounds, with black hair, black eyes, handsome, no mustache as he recalled, dark-complected, a sharp dresser, and he spoke with a heavy Mexican accent. In fact, it had been easier for Irwin to take the incident report in Spanish.

The guy seemed okay. He said they needed the rigs to haul oil well servicing equipment and until they were recovered or they got some new ones, he was basically out of business. He said he was taking some vacation time, going to Ojinaga, Mexico, until they decided. In fact, he said he might even be fired already and just hasn't been told yet. They might have blamed him for the loss. Besides that, business had been awfully slow for the past couple of months. He didn't think they were breaking even after paying the overhead.

Pavón never said who owned the company. Irwin didn't think to ask. He would recognize Pavón if he saw him again. Irwin didn't think it was all that odd for the dude to be living in the office. Saved himself some money that way so long as his boss didn't mind. Left more money for him to chase beaver.

Irwin didn't notice what type of vehicle Pavón was driving. It sure wasn't no new, souped up, black and chrome F-100. He would have noticed that.

Pavón seemed very sure of himself. Acted like if he got fired it was no big deal. Irwin had never seen him before. Also, he didn't know anything about the company except for what Pavón said.

Irwin did know of a young Mexican gal named Dolores who works at the IGA. It's possible she's Chico's girlfriend. He knows who Chico is but he doesn't really know him. He thinks he might be in the National Guard unit. Oh yeah, Dolores' last name is Dugas.

Sheriff Sol kept his thoughts to himself but knew for a fact he would run off any Quayle County deputy who was such a low wattage lightbulb with no more curiosity than Irwin displayed in taking this alleged theft report of $60,000 worth of motor vehicles. Hell! He didn't even get a DOB or a DL number from Pavón or the name and address or telephone number of the corporate owner! Irwin Trevino was a real slug! Too dull of a knife to be a deputy. Probably a county supervisor's brother-in-law or something.

Before leaving the SO, Sheriff Sol said his office would report the recovery of the stolen rigs via NCIC tomorrow. Both sheriffs promised to stay in touch if there were any further developments.

Before leaving town, they stopped by Jasmine Estrada's small stucco house on 2nd Street. She invited them to come in and sit down. Her home was neat as a pin. Chief Ledbetter was right. Jasmine was definitely a ten out of ten.

She said she was widowed with a seven-year-old son. Yes, she did have a boyfriend named Juan Rodríguez. It's not an exclusive relationship. She last saw him Saturday night. He lives on a ranch near Loving, New Mexico. She seldom sees him except on weekends.

Jasmine finally asked, "What is this all about?"

Sheriff Sol said, "We're trying to locate him regarding a stolen truck we recovered. Do you have an address or a phone number for him?"

"No. He always calls me. Besides, it's long distance to call in New Mexico. Plus he lives on a ranch. Maybe they don't have a phone. Lots of ranches don't. He has a friend in town. Sometimes he stays with him. That dude lives in his business. It's called Pluto, like the dog in Mickey Mouse."

"What's his friend's name?"

"I don't know. Juan always calls him El Jefe. That's really strange, because Juan is a ranch foreman. He makes a lot of money. Why would he call his friend 'The Boss?' That's very odd.

"Look. Juan is very good to me. He gave me this turquoise necklace and we took a long weekend in El Paso once. We stayed in a fancy hotel with a pool and everything but our relationship isn't exclusive. He never gave me no ring or anything but I know he likes me a lot.

"I do date other men when he's not around but we keep it as quiet as we can. I'm afraid Juan might hurt me if he saw me with another man. He's kind of jealous. Maybe he even loves me. Why else would he give me this necklace?

"If you talk to him, please don't let him know I spoke with you. He hates the cops. Besides that, he's never mentioned anything to me about a stolen truck. He always drives a silver Chevy pickup truck. Was his truck stolen? Oh, my gosh!"

"No, not his truck. By the way, why does he hate the cops? Has he been arrested before?"

"I don't know. Maybe once a long time ago. He never said, but El Jefe was on edge one time when we were partying and I overheard him ask Juan if he wanted to go back to the joint. Juan said 'no' and then El Jefe told him to get his shit together. I pretended I didn't hear this. I didn't want to get slapped around by either one of them. That's all I know."

"Thanks for your time, Mrs. Estrada. If we see him, we promise to not let him know that we spoke to you. Have a nice day."

"Thanks, Sheriff. You, too."

They went to the IGA where Dolores Dugas worked as a cashier. She wasn't there. The assistant manager said Dolores needed time off to take care of a sick relative out of town. Basically she'd quit but they'd hire her back if she returned.

It was 5 o'clock. It had been a fruitful but long day and they had a long drive ahead of them. They decided to go on back to Mosby.

Before leaving, Sheriff Sol called Sheriff Whalen to thank him and to fill him in on what they had learned. Then he called the jail and spoke with Deputy Carruthers. Nothing major going on. Chico had been arraigned. His bail was set at $25,000. His family couldn't post that much so Chico's in solitary confinement. The Brewster DA and sheriff were standing by to see them tomorrow.

The ride back gave them time to review the facts and to

discuss their next lines of inquiry. Both Sheriff Sol and Chief Alex believed that Pavón was their unknown shooter. If Slick or Barlow or Rico or Pepe could identify him from the mugshot photograph, that would give them enough probable cause to arrest him. However, it was dark during the shootout, which lasted less than a minute, and the distances were less than optimal. Without a doubt, eyewitness testimony would be called into question.

Even so, they could probably convict but Sheriff Sol preferred more corroborating evidence than just Chico's testimony. Locating the black F-100 would go a long way toward sealing Pavón's fate, but it would not make the case against the money man (or men) behind this. The $64,000 question was how to build a strong enough case to convict them, too.

CHAPTER 26
Thursday, March 26, 1970
Chief Alex Lets His Fingers Do the Walking

It was 8 o'clock. Sheriff Sol was busy filling in Miss Loretta, Archie, who was still there from the midnight shift, Ernie, Archie's replacement, and Kirk Shoemaker, who was assigned to work with the sheriff today. Chief Alex was staying behind to conduct telephone inquiries.

It was a little before 9 by the time Sheriff Sol and Kirk left for Brewster County. By then, Chief had already called Mrs. Rafferty at the Eddy County SO, and asked if she could run a license plate number that he thought was from New Mexico. She was happy to oblige. She checked and reported that license number 864321 was registered to Gemini Enterprises, Incorporated, with an address of Post Office Box 966, Loving, New Mexico, on a 1970 GMC Jimmy, red in color. Chief thanked her and hung up. Hmmm. Just like Chico said.

Next he called Harriett Morgan, who had left a message with Miss Loretta yesterday, that Pluto Incorporated was a Delaware Corporation with a legal address of P.O. Box 7912, Dover, Delaware. The president was listed as one Donald Mallard. The registered agent was April Lundgren, who listed the same post office box as her address, also.

Harriett was happy to hear from him. She said, "Chief Snodgrass, I'm so glad you called. The flowers are beautiful. I put the planter on my desk for all the ladies to see. You didn't have to do that."

"Miss Harriett, it was a small enough gesture to let you know just how much we appreciate your diligence in helping us to identify who we need to contact in order to repatriate two stolen tractor trailers. No telling how long it would have taken me to locate this corporation without your willingness to go the extra mile. Sheriff Pratt is so appreciative that he mailed a letter today to the Secretary of State himself commending you."

"Oh, Chief Alex, I don't know what to say! That's so sweet. You don't know how much I appreciate that. If you ever need anything, you just call. You hear?"

"Well, I do have a question or two, if you don't mind."

"You go right ahead."

"Well, for one thing, what's a registered agent?"

"Chief Alex, there're literally thousands and thousands of corporations. Most of them are small. Just a couple of employees. Folks create corporations as tax shelters sometimes but mostly as a way to protect their assets if they get sued.

"For example, a one-man residential contractor might incorporate himself to protect his personal assets, like his home. He might list his truck as a corporation asset if he got a tax break. Now suppose a purchaser isn't happy with the house he bought from the corporation. The contractor doesn't want to make it right for some reason. The purchaser sues the corporation, which is whom he has the contract with. If the purchaser wins a settlement, the contractor declares his corporation bankrupt. The only assets the purchaser can seize would be whatever are listed as corporate assets, like maybe a truck, or office furniture. Generally, the purchaser doesn't get a dime on a dollar. Then the contractor creates a new corporation and goes back to work just like nothing ever happened."

"That's really rotten. It ought to be a crime."

"Tell me about it. Anyway, the registered agent is responsible for receiving any registered mail sent to the corporation, which they forward to the president. Sometimes they file the annual report for a small fee. Basically, all they do is function as a screener for the corporation. That's about it."

"So in other words, since I don't know anything about Donald

Mallard, who he is, where he lives, even if that's his real name, I have to send a registered letter to April Lundgren in Dover to let her know we recovered their stolen trucks, and she passes the message to Mr. Duck, I mean Mallard, and we wait for him to get back to us."

"You're a quick learner.

"Besides being cheap, lots of folks incorporate in Delaware because their businesses are less than reputable and they want to make it more difficult for the police or skip tracers from their home state to find them.

"Anything else I can do for you today?"

"Yes. One more search if you don't mind. It's really quite a conundrum, I suppose. Maybe it will whet your interest.

"I just learned that another company related to our case is called Gemini Enterprises, Inc., and the company's address is a post office box in Loving, New Mexico, physical location unknown. I have a hunch it is also incorporated in Delaware. Would you be a dear and check for us? It would be a big help."

"Of course I will. That doesn't sound too difficult. I'll call you back as soon as I find something."

"Thank you, Miss Harriett. We really appreciate it. Good day."

Next, he called the U.S. Postal Inspection Service in El Paso. He spoke with Inspector Bud Wagner, asking if he could get subscriber information for Post Office Box 966, in Loving, New Mexico. He told Bud he was working on a shooting related to stock rustling, and he had a lead which indicated the subscriber to that box might have some involvement.

Bud said he could get it but it might take a day or two. He had to call the postal inspectors in Albuquerque, and they, in turn, had to make contact with the postmaster in Loving. He asked if this were a confidential inquiry.

Chief said it was; further, that the last thing he needed was to alert the subscriber that he was a strong person of interest, but more likely a suspect in the shooting and rustling.

Bud replied, "No worries. By chance would there be a mail fraud angle or theft of government mail which would give me jurisdiction to join in on the investigation?"

"Not that I'm aware of at this time; however, if we uncover anything that even smells like a postal violation, I'll give you a call. You know we're a small SO and we can always use the help."

"Good enough. We'll be discreet. Let you know when I get a response."

"Roger that. Appreciate it. Adiós."

Chief called Mrs. Rafferty back. "Mrs. Rafferty, it's Chief Alex again. Sorry to bother you. The mail arrived today but unfortunately the packet on Humberto Pavón didn't. Probably be here tomorrow or Saturday. I was just wondering if any of your deputies who were on the job back in 1960, are around. I was hoping someone could tell me something about the case."

"You might just be in luck. Deputy Clive Knobel is here. He was on the job back then. Let me get him for you."

"Thanks."

Silence for two minutes. "Knobel here. How can I help you?"

"Deputy Knobel, this is Chief Deputy Alex Snodgrass from the Quayle County, Texas SO. The reason I called is this. We had an officer-related shooting in Quayle County Monday night. The suspect escaped after a high speed chase into Old Mexico. Sheriff Pratt and I were running out leads in Pecos yesterday. We believe our suspect is from your bailiwick and we hope you might be able to shed some light on him."

"Sure thing. How can we help?"

"Do you recall an agg assault investigation back in 1960, involving a Mexican named Humberto Pavón?"

"Yeah, I do, but that was a long, long time ago. We sent him up for about ten years as I recall. He was just a hotheaded kid back then. Got a little too big for his britches and paid the price. He's probably gotten a lot worse since those days."

"That's what I heard. Mrs. Rafferty has already been kind enough to put some documents in the mail for us but we don't expect delivery for another day or two. I was just wondering if there was anything that you could tell me about him. We believe he's still hiding out in Mexico but we think he'll come back home, wherever that is, after the heat dies down. We would be very surprised to see him back in our county again."

"Well, that's probably right. He's your basic macho Mexican outlaw, except he's a lot more clever. Not worth the cost of a funeral plot. But just so you know, I haven't seen that cockroach in quite some time. Maybe five or six months. He was driving a new Ford pickup truck, black, I think, more chrome on it than a Mexican saddle has in silver conchos, way more truck than he could afford, so he has to be up to something underhanded. He was headed south almost to the Texas state line when I saw him. I guarantee you he didn't use honest means to earn the dough to pay for that truck."

"The truck matches the description that we have. Do you have a license plate number?"

"Nope. Sorry. Wish I did. It didn't seem important at the time."

"Understood."

"Okay. Getting back to Pavón, I knew his mother. She was an illegal alien, but Humberto was born here. Her name was Lucia Pavón. Not a bad sort. Earned her living by doing laundry for folks. She's dead now.

"They have ten or twenty acres full of half-ass relatives living in Malaga. Most of them are farmhands. They don't cause anyone no trouble. There's a couple of bad eggs, but so far as I know, none of them are chummy with Humberto. He's an arrogant jackass who thinks he's better than the rest of them. Even so, just as you might imagine, none of these hardworking citizens would give him up even if he raped Mother Theresa in the county square in broad daylight. Know what I mean?"

"I know exactly what you mean."

"I know he's got family in Old Mexico but I'd be a liar if I told you who or where. Wouldn't surprise me at all if he's holed up there. Dollars go a lot farther in Mexico."

"Anyone connected with his clan ever mention a little town called Ojinaga, just south of the border at Presidio on US 67?"

"Not as I can recall but I can nose around discreetly if you want. That where you think he is?"

"Could be. That's where he told someone he was going since he was temporarily unemployed but it might be a misdirection."

"I'll check around.

"Anyway, getting back to 1960, Humberto was a good looking dude, thought very highly of himself, dressed like a pimp. He was pretty good with his fists and the ladies. He used to hang out at a hole-in-the-wall cantina. I don't even remember it's real name. We used to call it the Greaser Pit. It's long gone now. One night Humberto showed up there and some stranger was making out with a barmaid that Humberto considered his own private stock. Understand that this was one of those places that, for ten bucks, any girl in the joint would have hauled your ashes on the pool table right in front of the whole crowd if that was your thing.

"Words was exchanged. One thing I thought was cute.

"The stranger knew Humberto's name, and he kept calling him Pavón Cabrón. If you don't know Mex, cabrón means cuckold - a guy whose wife is screwing around on him behind his back. These was fighting words. It's the worst insult you can say in their culture.

"The stranger, being a Mexican in a Mexican bar, pulled a knife, but Humberto, being an Americanized Mexican, pulled out a .45 auto. It was close quarters and some would say the advantage went to the stranger, but Humberto was quicker and he shot the stranger in the head. No doubt he intended it as a kill shot, but Humberto missed the fatal area and shot the asshole in his jaw. The bullet went through both cheeks and took out part of his jawbone and some of his teeth but the lucky turd survived. I don't recall whatever happened to him. Guess he went back to whatever rock he crawled out from under.

"Anyhow, this cantina was a trouble spot every weekend and even some weeknights, so our police response was quick. We caught Humberto in the parking lot. Bad luck for him. Some asshole double-parked behind him so he was stuck unless he wanted to flee on foot.

"Judge give him ten years. Never saw him after that until a few months ago. I passed him on the highway. I already told you about that. This is about all I can recall."

"That's a whole lot more than I expected. We really appreciate everything you all have done for us. If there's anything we can ever do for you, don't hesitate to call."

"You got it. I'll let you know if I turn up anyone from Malaga who has a connection with Ojinaga. Take care."

Next, Chief sent a teletype to NCIC and DPS, reporting the recovery of both big rigs.

Following that, he dictated a letter to April Lundgren, Registered Agent for Pluto Inc., to be sent Registered Mail, informing them of the recovery of the vehicles. The letter stated that the vehicles were stored in an impound lot and that storage fees were accruing. If the company did not respond within thirty days, the SO would initiate forfeiture and sheriff's auction proceedings.

After lunch, he received a callback from Harriett at the Secretary of State's Office. Sure enough, Gemini Enterprises was also a Delaware corporation. The bonus information was that it had the same registered agent and address as Pluto. It listed Hugh Mallard as president and Louis Mallard as vice president.

Harriett said, "There's something fishy going on, Chief."

He replied, "I agree. Now I need to find out all I can about the Mallard family. Thanks a million."

Chief Alex was at a dead end at this point, pending a callback from Inspector Bud Wagner, which wasn't likely to come in today. He was fixing to go to the drugstore for a milkshake and call it a day a couple of hours early. It had been four very long days and he was planning to pay himself back a few of the hundreds of unpaid hours he had put in at the SO. Besides that, Sheriff Sol was unlikely to return until well after close of business.

Then he had an epiphany. He had not sent Juan Rodríguez's prints to the FBI or DPS because without a name, the checks would take weeks and weeks for a response. The hope was they would have a name to send with the prints for confirmation because that would reduce the response time to just two or three weeks. It was a long shot but . . . .

He called the Penitentiary of New Mexico. He spoke with a Lieutenant Emmett Little in Records. He requested information on Humberto Pavón, to include a photograph and a copy of his fingerprints. Once Pavón was confirmed as a former inmate and they agreed to send the documents, he asked for names and addresses for next of kin. All he got was Lucia Pavón and her last known address.

Then he wondered out loud if, per chance, the penitentiary kept records on cellmates. Specifically, he was interested in Pavón's cellmates.

Lieutenant Little said that would take a more exhaustive search from the archives. He said they could probably get it by tomorrow.

Chief explained that Pavón was a suspect in a police shooting and that he had escaped. He also explained that they shot and killed his partner, who was a John Doe. They thought that maybe the decedent could have been a cellmate with Pavón.

This gave Lieutenant Little a lawman woodie. He said they would probably have cellmate info if they had been assigned in the same cell for more than just a couple of days.

Chief provided Juan Rodríguez's physical description, hoping that this might assist in identification.

Little told Chief to call him tomorrow anytime after 9 o'clock.

Chief bugged out a happy man one hour early. He went to the drugstore and drank his milkshake at the counter. He chatted up Evelyn, the soda jerk, who was very sweet but definitely not a jerk. As expected, she had the latest rumors about the identity of the unknown rustlers. Listening counted as informant development. Chief smiled to himself. He had high hopes for tomorrow.

CHAPTER 27
Thursday, March 26, 1970
Sheriff Sol Brings Brewster County SO On Board

Sheriff Sol and Deputy Shoemaker also had a productive day in the field while Chief Alex worked the phones. Like him, they spent most of their time on their asses, but it was mostly in Sheriff Sol's Plymouth Fury and not behind a desk, which was the unabashed preference for them both.

They stopped by the Brewster County SO first and met with Sheriff Leland Waters and Investigator Avery Carmichael. Cutting to the chase once the preliminary greetings were exchanged and coffees were poured, Sheriff Waters asked if Chico and his compadres were the crew who rustled the Ramirez' Twisted Oak Ranch in his county.

Sheriff Sol asked, "Where is it?"

Sheriff Wiley said, "It's down near the Big Bend National Park off US Highway 385."

"Well, they very likely did then. That's one of the things I need to talk to you about."

"We're all ears."

"To back up, you notified Chief Alex about the rustling incident in your county and we passed that along to our ranchers. Judge Sweeney learned he had been rustled at least once but more likely twice. We set up a surveillance on his Triple S Ranch.

"On the sixth night, we watched the two John Does round up about 130 of Judge Sweeney's sheep and pen them up in an almost fully enclosed canyon.

"The following night, the two John Does and the two Gómez brothers came back and herded the sheep onto big rigs driven by the Gómez brothers. We allowed them to drive off the ranch. The two John Does were splicing the fence when they spotted our mounted surveillance team.

"The two John Does decided to shoot it out. One died and one escaped. Chico's brother, Rudy, decided to make a run for it and in so doing, on two different occasions, he attempted to run through a roadblock with the tractor trailer full of sheep. He almost ran over two of my deputies. It was a bad decision and it cost him his life.

"Chico surrendered at the scene, but he lawyered up right away. We lodged him in jail and let him stew. A few hours later, we brought his daddy in to see him.

"We've all known Alberto Gómez and his family since the beginning of Time, or so it seems. He's a good man and despite what Chico's done, he's no gangster. We felt like Alberto would bring Chico around and he did.

"We knew the venue for trying the case would be over here but once Chico broke and was ready to come to Jesus, we decided to milk him for everything he would tell us. In an abundance of caution we got attorney Sam Davis temporarily appointed as his counsel and we brought our DA, Able DeWitt, to sit in with Sam, Alberto, Deputy Bustamante, Chief Alex, and me during the interview.

"Chico confessed that he and Rudy were paid $100 in cash, hand-to-hand, by the escapee, John Doe #2, whom he knows only as El Jefe, each time they rustled a ranch. They rustled eight ranches in eight different counties. Their overwhelming favorite target was Judge Sweeney's Triple S, which they rustled three times.

"The other rustler was decedent John Doe #1, whom Chico knew as Juan Rodríguez, which we know to be an alias. They delivered all the stolen sheep to a ranch in Eddy County, New Mexico, located generally in the vicinity of Loving.

"In terms of hierarchy, we have the owner, possibly owners, of the New Mexico ranch, who purchased and presumably sold all the stolen sheep. Then we have El Jefe, the bandit who escaped, ramrodding the rustling, followed by his partner, Juan Rodríguez, who apparently was a sheep herder by trade, followed by Chico's older brother, Rudy, a convicted felon who brought his little brother into this scheme, and concluded by Chico.

"Chico is an eighteen-year-old virgin in a manner of speaking, too weak to stand up to his brother and especially not the two badass bandits. He surrendered peaceably, copped to everything, and right now is the only one left holding the bag for the whole outfit. We all know he's looking at potential sentences in eight counties which could land him in prison for the rest of his life. He knows he's going to prison but he deserves some leniency. You've seen him. You know he will never survive in the joint.

"I have two goals and a proposal but I need your help to pull them off."

"What is it, Sol? We're not heartless bastards, you know."

"I do know. I hate a rustler about as much as anyone so sometimes I think maybe other folks can't see their way to a little mercy. I apologize.

"My goal is to wrap up all the guilty parties into one neat bundle and to convince the judges to show Chico as much leniency as they're willing to do. Both of these are tall orders but Chief Alex and I hatched a plan that will work if we're discreet and join forces.

"The main sticking point is that we need to stay mum regarding what we know about the ranches in the other counties until we spring the trap. I know this goes against the grain in terms of mutual assistance to fellow officers, but we can share everything and assist in every way possible after we make the bust. Otherwise, we are almost certainly going to lose the money men. Can you live with that?"

"Do you know where these ranches are?"

"Not yet. Chico gave us general locations. That's why I'm just pretty certain the Ramirez ranch is one of them. He didn't know the names of any of them. He only saw them in the dark but he's a smart kid and he thinks he can find each of them except maybe for one. My idea was to check him out of jail and take him to identify as many as he can. It could take two or three days because they're scattered far and wide."

"Have any other sheriffs besides me come forward about having ranches that were rustled?"

"Nope. However, I did speak with Sheriff Whalen in Reeves County about the Triple S and our shootout, plus I mentioned that you all had a rustled ranch but I didn't tie anything together. For one thing, I wasn't sure. I'm still not positive. Sheriff Whalen knows Rudy and Chico, and that John Doe #2 allegedly lives in Pecos but that's all. Since Chico claims they never shit in their own mess kit, I figured that was all Willie Joe needed to know for now."

"You're probably right. So what's your plan? I could see the Rangers swooping in and taking over since it bleeds over into eight counties, New Mexico, and Old Mexico."

"You're absolutely right. Judge Sweeney's mentioned that twice. We both know he has the juice to call in a dozen Rangers if he so chooses. At least for now he's content to let us run with it. Heck, Leland, we can do this and have some fun with it, if you're willing."

"I'm all ears. Heck, Sol, I have to get re-elected, too."

"Leland, you're a shoo-in unless someone has color photos of you romancing a goat. Now, here's a rough outline of my plan.

"Phase I, before Chico changes his mind I want to check him out of jail and have him take me to all the rustled ranches he can remember. He mentioned eight and they're scattered everywhere and like I said, it might take two or three days. At least I have identified the one in my own county. You can send a deputy along to take notes if you want. So far, so good?"

"Absolutely. I'll send Avery. I'm sure we can work that out

with the DA. What next?"

"Phase II, we have the two tractor trailers in our impound lot. They belong to a corporation named Pluto Inc.,with a Delaware address. Pluto has a small office in Pecos. Apparently it's a one-man operation run by a man named Humberto Pavón. We learned that he's a convicted felon from New Mexico. Pavón is the person representing Pluto, who filed a police report in Pecos Tuesday morning alleging that the two rigs were stolen sometime Monday night.

"We've requested a mugshot of him from Eddy County. It's nine years old but I think my guys will recognize him from the shoot out. At least I hope they do. Ditto for Chico.

"Today, I've got Chief Alex sending a registered letter to Pluto's registered agent in Delaware, informing them we recovered their rigs and that they have thirty days to make arrangements to pick them up or we will begin forfeiture proceedings and a sheriff's auction. We're hoping that since Pavón filed the theft report, he will be one of the parties with proof of ownership to claim the rigs. This is where we need to join forces."

"Go on. Nothing too tricky so far."

"Hold on. We have more prep work first.

"I'm jumping to Phase III. I'm 99% sure Judge Sweeney will loan us his airplane that he parks over here at your airport to do a recon of the target ranch in Eddy County. We can do a drive-by once with directions from Chico but I don't want to get burned. From the air we can get a better perspective on how to put it under surveillance and how to plan a raid. We need to do this within the next week."

"Good grief, Sol! Since when did we get deputized to run an operation in New Mexico? That's what the Rangers are for!"

"Hold your horses, Leland. I'm coming to that.

"Once we know the location of the target ranch and get aerial photographs, we examine all possible routes the Pluto employees would use to transport stolen sheep to it. Now back to Phase II.

"Everybody in Mosby knows everything they think there is to know about this case. They don't but I don't want to disabuse them of this notion, especially since this is an ongoing investigation. Therefore, I want to move the tractor trailers from our impound lot to yours. I plan to put an undercover deputy in the lot to do the transaction. It needs to be one of my guys that your citizens don't know, just in case someone from here would walk in to pick up a car or something while the bad guys are doing the transaction. It would be fine if you had a guy inside, out of sight as back-up, but not doing the actual transaction. Are you with me on that?"

"So far."

"Good. Now here comes the delicate part. My guy will check all the paperwork and verify that everything's legit. During the transaction, he will casually mention a local rancher who is looking for someone to take a load of sheep up to Pecos for auction within the next couple of days. Time is of the essence. That sort of thing.

"Phase IV. We need a local rancher not near your victim ranch who'd be willing to loan us some sheep to be rustled. If you don't have anybody, I'm sure Judge Sweeney would loan us some but we still need some place other than Quayle County for them to be rustled from. Otherwise, it smells of a set-up. Capeesh?"

"Go on."

"Phase V. If they take the bait, we need to surveil the trucks and the rustling and follow the sheep all the way to the ranch in New Mexico. That means using personal vehicles and soft clothes and CB radios on a channel nobody uses. Are you up for that?"

"Maybe. Do you all have CBs?"

"What we don't have and need, the sheriff's office will buy. What about you all?"

"Same thing."

"Great! So are you on board?"

"Yes, but what makes you so sure they'd take the bait. Hell, their last fandango was a disaster!"

"Think about it. They haven't made any money lately. Here's a chance to steal a load on the way home. It's perfect. In fact, Pavón might even plan to go back after the fact to pretend he wants to pick up the load that he already stole. So long as he gets away clean, no one could prove a thing!"

"So when's the pay-off for us?"

"Phase VI would be a joint raid with Eddy County to arrest all the crooks and recover the sheep. The best case scenario would be to do it during daylight hours the morning of the delivery.

"We can still charge the rustlers in our respective counties but we won't have to babysit them until we're ready for court. That is, so long as we don't have to kill 'em during the raid. My expectation is that Eddy County would get the money men unless our district attorneys can figure out a way we could do that, too. Also, the other counties could get their licks in at this time if they choose to do so.

"Nothing ever goes exactly as planned, most dramatically demonstrated by the most recent incident at Judge Sweeney's. I'm open to suggestions if you can think of anything else which would rein in the money men."

"What about checking auction lots where the stolen sheep would have been sold? We might get lucky there."

"The main drawback is that a collusive auctioneer might tip off the receivers of stolen property. Also, how do we prove that any of the stolen sheep which were auctioned actually belonged to the victim ranchers? They don't have brands or tattoos. I doubt any of the victims could positively identify their own sheep, which reminds me that we must be able to positively identify any sheep we use as bait."

"Good points. I'm stuck. I think this is a long shot but I'll give it a try. How many men can you dedicate to this?"

"Well, including me, we have a total of ten sworn officers on the Quayle County Sheriff's Office. Obviously somebody has to man the fort, so it would be something less than that, like six or possibly seven. Most likely six. How about you?"

"We have sixteen total but I could probably dedicate up to ten if it didn't take too long."

"The manpower-intensive portion won't begin until the day Pluto has an appointment to pick up the trucks. That day will probably be 48 hours long. I'm guessing we have about a week until then to set things up. If you commit Avery to work with me until then, we will do most of the prep work."

"Consider it a done deal."

"Great. We'll get to work."

CHAPTER 28
Thursday, March 26, 1970
The Brewster Country District Attorney Signs On

Next stop was the Brewster County District Attorney's Office. The DA, Bradford Delaney, was in Judge Roberts' court handling today's criminal docket. ADA Galen Story was holding down the fort.

"What can I do for you, Sheriff? Nothing urgent I hope. We have a full docket today. I have to be back in court myself in just a few minutes."

"We won't keep you. Galen, this is Deputy Kirk Shoemaker."

"I know Kirk. We're old acquaintances. His little brother and I played together on the Brewster County High School baseball team. Kirk was a few years ahead of us. Glad to see you again, Kirk. How's Penny?"

"She's fine. Thanks for asking. How's Bonnie?"

"Doing fine. She's at home almost ready to deliver our first child. I'll tell her you asked."

"Well, my goodness! Congratulations to you both."

"What have you got for us today, Sheriff?"

"Well first, please convey our appreciation to DA Delaney for all your office has done on this case. We dropped by to deliver this file with copies of everything we have to date on Chico Gómez. It's thicker than a New York telephone directory and it's far from finished. This has got each deputy's statement, Judge Sweeney's complaint, statements from his ranch hands, record checks, crime scene photographs, diagrams, and a whole slew of other things which have already slipped my mind.

"We're pursuing a dozen different leads and as we get more information, we'll bring you all more documents."

"Thanks. We've been waiting for this."

"My apologies. We have a small staff and we're going balls to the wall."

"I bet you are."

"I just spoke with Sheriff Waters. We're both on the same sheet of music. Does Chico have court-appointed counsel over here yet?"

"Yes. He's represented by Eric Holland."

"Do you know if Chico's still cooperating?"

"I believe he is. Do you need to speak with him?"

"Well, he gave us general directions to eight different ranches the outfit rustled. Of course, we know where Judge Sweeney's is located. If Chico's willing and his attorney doesn't object, we'd like to check him out of jail and have him take us to the others, to include the one in Brewster County. The eight ranches are in eight different Texas counties, plus the receiving ranch is in New Mexico, so we will probably have to check him out two or three days to locate them all, assuming that he can."

"Have you all identified any victims besides Judge Sweeney and Hector Ramirez from our county?"

"Well, right now we are not even 100% sure that the Ramirez ranch was hit by this crew. That's one of the ranches we want him to show us. But beyond those two ranches, we are ignorant of any other reports of rustling which we find very strange. Some of the other counties were contacted by the sheriff's office here before we arrested Chico but none since and there's a reason for that."

"Why is that?"

"For one thing, we have not yet conclusively identified the unknown dead bandit, or the bandit who escaped, or the receivers of the stolen sheep in New Mexico, or even the true owners of the tractor trailers which were allegedly stolen.

"We do believe we have identified the escaped bandit. We're pretty sure he worked for the corporation which owned the rigs and we have reason to believe the owners of that corporation were the receivers of roughly 700 to 800 stolen sheep.

"We have an undercover operation in mind which we hope will identify all the players and help us to obtain proof 'beyond a reasonable doubt' that they all were complicit in the scheme to steal sheep, which led to the death of two individuals, not to mention the attempted murder of several of my deputies. If we were to notify all the sheriffs of the counties in which we identify victim ranches, you know what would happen."

"You mean a hungry sheriff will jump the gun and we'll lose the money men and maybe the fugitive, leaving Chico holding the bag."

"You got it!"

"I'm with you. Let me call Eric and if he doesn't object, you can get Chico and be on your way."

"Great. Just to make sure we're clear on this, we need to keep all this hush hush. The undercover operation will begin right here in Alpine. The fewer who know about this, the better for all of us."

"Oh, we're eye-to-eye. I'll have to let Eric know, but besides Bradford and me, no one else will be in the loop here."

"Thanks. Much appreciated. I'll fill you all in on details as our plan begins to go into the operational phase."

"Please do."

CHAPTER 29
Thursday, March 26, 1970
Beginning Phase I

At 12:30, after victualing at the McDonald's restaurant in Alpine, Sheriff Sol, Deputy Kirk Shoemaker, Investigator Avery Carmichael, and Chico Gómez piled into Sheriff Sol's Plymouth Fury and headed west on US 90 to Jeff Davis County, looking for the second ranch the outfit rustled on or about January 15 or 16. It was near Valentine. Actually, the ranch was just north of Presidio County.

They had no difficulty in locating it but had to drive four miles past the damaged gate from which the crew had entered to locate the main entrance. It was about 70 miles from Alpine. This was the Double Nickel, owned by T.J. and Cora Moran. Chico said they scored about 70 sheep here. Kirk and Avery were furiously taking copious notes so they could find this place again and to corroborate Chico's statement.

From there, they continued northwest on US 90 and thence north at Van Horn where US 90 merged with TX 54, and then they turned west again onto US 180, a distance of about 115 miles, to Salt Flat in the northeast corner of Hudspeth County.

Chico pointed out an old, abandoned cafe or inn perhaps, at an unmarked gravel road heading north. He directed them right to the Circle E, owners unknown, which certainly did not look like a ranch devoted to raising sheep. This whole Salt Flat area looked run down and deserted.

This was the eighth ranch they rustled, on or about February 26. Chico said they only bagged 30 sheep.

The Circle E homestead looked ramshackle but there were signs of gentrification, like somebody was trying turn it into a hobby ranch. No wonder they didn't make a very big haul. Probably belonged to an overpaid lawyer or doctor in El Paso, which was only about 60 miles farther west, who was looking for a quiet weekend getaway not too far from the Guadalupe Mountains National Park which was just north.

Sheriff Sol wondered how the theft of 30 sheep from the Circle E went unreported. He figured that was probably every single ovine on the ranch. He also wondered who fingered the job. It would have been impossible to steal a flock of sheep from this ranch undetected if the owner were home. He also wondered if the rustlers were acquainted with the victim. He decided that when it came time to notify the sheriff in Hudspeth, he would have to play this a little more carefully than he had previously assumed.

As long as they were in the general area, Sheriff Sol decided to find the first ranch the crew rustled, which was in northeastern Culberson County. They hit it less than a week before the second ranch, which was on January 15/16, putting the first theft sometime between January 8 and 14.

They took US 180 east to TX 54 and turned north to the New Mexico state line, where they turned south and east on CO 652. Then they got to the tricky part.

They were in the middle of nowhere. There weren't any significant landmarks. Chico had driven from the opposite direction in the middle of the night. He was looking for a 'really nice fence and gate.' They drove about 20 miles when Chico saw the gate where they had made their breech that night. They had driven 52 miles from Salt Flat. They continued east for about a mile, where they saw the main entrance, identifying it as the Delaware (from the dry arroyo they drove past) Cactus Ranch, also known as the D Bar C. They would have to identify the owners later, same as for the Circle E.

It was almost 6 o'clock. They had driven approximately 230 miles from Alpine and there was no direct route back. He figured they were 80 miles from Pecos, the nearest place to find a diner, and another 100 miles to Alpine from there, not to mention another 100 or so miles to Mosby.

It was after midnight when Sheriff Sol and Kirk returned to Mosby. They had driven more than 600 miles. They had been in the car so long that they wore calluses on their butts. Besides numb asses, they were both physically and mentally exhausted, too loopy to work calculus problems or to conjugate Spanish verbs in their head. Technically, since it was already Friday, it was also Kirk's day off.

Sol was thankful that he had had the presence of mind to call Chief Alex when they stopped for supper in Pecos, and told him to take Deputy Dewey Caruthers with him today to Alpine to pick up where he and Kirk left off.

They pulled into the courthouse lot. Kirk piled into his POV (privately owned vehicle) and headed straight home without fanfare. He was running on fumes. Sol was in the same boat and he planned to do likewise, but since he was in a county car with a police radio, he heard a call from Barlow requesting back-up that Kirk did not hear.

All thoughts of sleep evaporated. Sol got on the radio and said he was en route. He drove Code 2, oscillating red light but no siren, until he turned onto the street Barlow named at which time he turned off the overhead. No need to alert the bad guys of his presence until he knew what was going on.

CHAPTER 30
Friday, March 27, 1970
No Such Thing as Routine in Police Work

It was after midnight. Barlow had reported for duty at 11:45, anxious for an update on the case from Archie, whom he knew would have the latest poop. They never got around to discussing it.

Archie wasn't feeling very well. He had a 24-hour bug or something. He apologized to Barlow, who begged him to go home, but to no avail. Barlow knew he could handle the office by himself and Archie knew it too, but his sense of obligation overruled his common sense, so he stayed.

The phone rang about 12:15. Normally Archie took all calls but he was in the john calling ralph. Barlow stepped up to the plate as the pinch hitter.

"Sheriff's Office. Deputy Adams speaking. How may I help you?"

"Deputy Adams, this is Mrs. Winona Caldwell. We live at 27 East Washington Avenue. My next-door neighbor died and his funeral was today, um, rather yesterday. He lived alone. His family drove back home to Fort Stockton.

"My husband and I saw some lights on in his house, like flashlights, not lamp lights or overheads. Somebody's in his house. Also, there's a strange car parked down the street. My husband thinks it's a Pontiac. It's too dark to tell what color it is.

"My husband got his gun and he's hiding between our house and Mr. George's keeping an eye out. Come quick! I'm afraid someone might get shot. I'd just die if something happened to Francis."

"Is Francis your husband?"

"Yes! Come quick!"

"What's Francis wearing?"

"He's in his nightshirt and robe. The robe is blue. My husband is 74 years old, and he's feeble, and he's bald. Please don't shoot him by mistake."

"What's your neighbor's name and what's his street number?"

"It's Mr. Theodore George. He's at 29 East Washington. Please hurry! Something bad could happen!"

"We're on our way. Be there in just a couple of minutes. Stay inside."

"Okay. Bye."

Barlow loaded a shotgun and signed out a car. He knocked on the restroom door and said, "Arch, do you know a Francis or Winona Caldwell?"

"Yeah, they live on Washington. He's a retired railroad man. Nice guy."

"Do you know a Theodore George?"

"Yes. Ted died this week. What's going on? Can't this wait until I get done hugging the commode?"

"Well, Mrs. Caldwell just called and said burglars are in Mr. George's house. Mr. Caldwell is out in the yard with his gun. I'm going over there right now before someone gets hurt. I'll give you a call when I know what's what."

"Barlow, I'll be on my way as soon as I can. Be careful. No tellin' what you're walking into."

"Roger that. I'll turn up the volume on the radio before I go so you can hear it from in there. I'll call in as soon as I know something."

The sounds of violent regurgitation sent Barlow scrambling on his way.

When Barlow turned the corner onto Washington Avenue from Texas Street, he turned off his headlights. He slowed down to a crawl and stopped at the curb in front of 26 East Washington.

He turned off the ignition. He left the shotgun in the rack. He figured his flashlight would be handier. Even so, he drew his revolver and held it down by his side. He crossed the street but remained on the sidewalk, hoping Mr. Caldwell would see and come to him.

Sure enough, he did. He scurried over as best he could, being somewhat unstable, suffering from palsy, and wearing open-heeled house slippers. He was carrying an old, well-used, long-barreled, British-made, Webley & Scott, break-down revolver in .455 caliber, probably a trophy from WWII or WWI, or perhaps even before. Barlow knew Webleys went into production in the 1880's before smokeless powder was developed. They used black powder in those days. Barlow prayed the gun and the ammunition weren't that old. He noticed that the gun was cocked.

Mr. Caldwell said, "Deputy, there's at least two burglars in my neighbor's house. I saw them. There could be more. Where's Archie? Do you need some back-up? I haven't seen any action since the Great War, but I'm willing and able. What do you want to do?"

"Have they seen you?"

"I'm not sure but I don't think so. Maybe. They been in there a long time."

"Why do you think they haven't slipped out the back door?"

"Because Ted has two big German shepherds in the back yard. It's fenced in. These dogs never bark but they sure as Hell bite! I been feeding them for him. They know me. Them burglars gotta come out the front unless they shoot them dogs. Otherwise, they'll get all tore up."

"Could you see if these guys have guns?"

"No, but Ted owns three or four pistols and I'm sure that many long guns. He also has ammo galore. If they wasn't armed when they come in, they're well armed now."

"I tell you what. You take up a position in the driveway on

the far side of Ted's car. You can lean over the hood or trunk so you can get a better platform to aim your weapon. Don't shoot unless you have to. Understand? I don't want you to get shot, so take cover. Just like in the war, copy?"

"Oh, I copy, Deputy. I didn't fall off the turnip truck yestiddy. And I got a whole pocket full of ca'tridges just in case this takes all night."

"Well all right then, Mr. Caldwell . . . ."

"Call me Corporal Caldwell. I was a corporal in the Great War."

"Very good, Corporal. Man your position. I'm going to call this in. Then I'll take my position and we can get down to business."

"Yes, Sir."

Barlow walked back to his car. He started it up and drove slowly past 29 East Washington Avenue. The suspicious vehicle was indeed a Pontiac - a 1966 Pontiac Tempest, 2-door sedan. It was either green or blue, tough to tell for sure in the dim streetlight. He wrote down the license plate number - Texas 477549. He drove a few doors farther down, turned around, and parked facing westbound in front of the victim's house. The nearest streetlight was where he turned around, so he was barely silhouetted where he parked. He picked up and keyed the mike to fill in Archie and to see if he could come as back-up.

At that moment, the front door of Ted George's house swung open wide. Two men were sneaking out. They must not have looked to make sure that the coast was clear. The first had an armload of loot. The other had a revolver. Too late, they looked around and spotted the cruiser. Shit! The load-bearer turned and scurried back inside. The pistolero, Mr. Badass himself, snapped off three shots in rapid-fire at the cruiser, shooting out the front passenger door window and putting two holes in the door itself, but none in Barlow, who was showered with little shards of glass but was otherwise unharmed. Then Mr. Badass scrambled back inside and slammed the door. It failed to latch but it did remain pushed to.

Corporal Francis Caldwell didn't hesitate. He returned fire. The first shot was well-aimed, so far as a palsied man can aim steadily, and it occurred immediately after the bandit first shot at Barlow. It definitely got the bandit's attention. He reacted like he didn't expect it.

The second shot took a little longer and didn't arrive until after the bandit was back inside and the door had been slammed shut. Suffice it to say, it was too dark for Barlow to ascertain if either shot had hit their mark. He thought probably not, but nevertheless appreciated that those two shots convinced the shooter to cease fire.

What Sheriff Sol heard besides gunfire was, "Base, this is 7. 10-33 (burglary in progress). Come Code 3 to 29 East Washington. Multiple suspects inside. Shots fired."

Deputy Kirk Shoemaker heard the shots, too. He lived at 26 East Monroe Avenue, one block south of Washington. He was almost home when he heard shots just to his north. He arrived at the scene before Sheriff Sol. He was surprised to see a marked unit with Barlow leaning across the hood, aiming a shotgun towards the house.

Kirk stopped and asked, "What's going on?"

Barlow said, "You might want to move your car out of harm's way. I didn't and this cruiser is all shot up. Don't mind the dude in the bathrobe. He's the next-door neighbor and he's on our side. His name is Corporal Caldwell."

"Roger that. We've met. Who's slingin' lead and what for?"

"The owner of 29 died this week."

"That would be Ted George."

"Yes. There are at least two, maybe more burglars inside. One of them shot at me and Corporal Caldwell over there returned fire."

"Want me to cover the back?"

"Oh, Hell no! According to Corporal Caldwell, the owner has a fenced backyard with two man-eating German shepherds. On second thought, see if you can cover the backyard without going inside the fence or stirring up the dogs. If they figure the front is blocked, they may decide to shoot the dogs and abscond out the back. By the way, we think that car parked on the street down there belongs to the burglars. Also, Sheriff Sol is en route."

"10-4. Gotcha covered. By the way, don't you think my neighbor looks a little too old to be a corporal?"

"Not so much. He's a veteran of the Great War. He deserves the respect he requested. If he had stayed in, he'd probably be at least a staff sergeant or maybe even a major by now. He's got moxie so don't give him a hard time, okay?"

"I'll go park my car and be right back."

Sheriff Sol rounded Texas Street on two wheels and charged in Barlow's direction like a goosed rhinoceros in a three-ring Yugoslavian circus. By now, house lamps and porch lights were flicking on up and down the street like fireflies. In some houses, neighbors were peering out of dark windows unseen and undetected. You could safely bet that a multitude of hands were clutching trusted firearms, prepared to vanquish the threat.

Sol parked in front of 26 just like Barlow did when he first arrived. He walked over and crouched down beside Barlow. "I take it we have some burglars who have already demonstrated they'll use deadly force to get away. Either that, or this is the worst domestic call I've ever heard of in Mosby."

At the same time, Kirk showed up on foot to see how the sheriff wanted to handle the situation. He ducked down beside him.

Barlow responded, "It's a burglary, Sheriff. At least two culprits. One of them took exception to my presence and tried to light me up. I haven't had the opportunity to express my displeasure, yet.

"Kirk said he will take the back door from outside the fence.

Mr. George, the homeowner, recently departed, has a couple of man-eating dogs that patrol the backyard. The dude over there aiming across the trunk of the '50 Ford coupe, is his next door neighbor. He's on our side."

Sheriff Sol asked, "Is that Francis Caldwell?"

"Yes, Sir, only he asked me to call him Corporal Caldwell on account of his service to our country in World War I. He's got a Webley, .455 caliber revolver bigger than Archie's Peacemaker. He popped a couple of caps at the burglar who was shooting at me while I was on the radio with you."

"You know he has palsy, don't you?"

"I do, but you'd never convince the bad guys of that. They took his intentions seriously."

"Oh, for crying out loud! We need for him to go back home before he gets hurt."

"Sheriff, he's a determined, righteous citizen trying to right a wrong. He wants to help. I believe it's better for him to stay where he is so we can keep an eye on him, than to piss him off and send him home where he's likely to figure some other way to fulfill his civic duty, like setting up his .50 caliber Browning machine gun with a tripod on his front porch. He might even break out a flamethrower or Gatling gun. Then he might accidentally snuff out one of us."

Kirk added his two cents' worth. "Sheriff, I think Barlow's right. You know Francis takes good citizenship seriously. He believes this is his civic duty. He might even ask you to deputize him. We ought to leave well enough alone."

"You're both probably right. He's a sweet old man but he's about as helpful as Mr. Magoo. His eyesight is better but his palsy is a whole lot worse. Each time he pulls the trigger, he could be sending a round into any of three or four different zip codes. I hate to think of the collateral damage.

"Barlow, have you announced your police presence and commanded the bandits to surrender peacefully?"

"No, Sir, not because I was trying to circumvent protocol but because they discovered me before I had an opportunity to do so. It seems kind of pointless now. They already demonstrated they're willing to shoot it out."

"Understood, but we hafta do it anyway. Especially you. You already have something of a reputation for shooting first and asking questions later, even if it is undeserved. Before you do, though, I want to hear what you propose to do if they kiss off the order."

"Well, Sheriff, it's a small house, probably not much bigger than mine. They don't have an upstairs or a basement. They do have an attic, but they'd really be trapped if they tried to hide up there, especially since we already know they're present. Of course, we will need to search it anyway once we've cleared the living quarters.

"The way I see it, the dogs and Kirk have the back door covered. I figure once we give them a warning to surrender, if they blow us off, we bust in the front door and take care of business. The longer we pussyfoot around, the more likely this will turn into a goat rope. Newsies show up and maybe a citizen gets hurt and I don't mean Corporal Caldwell. Maybe they start popping caps into the neighbors' houses. By daylight, school kids will be setting up Kool Aid stands and it will look like the Cowboy Days rodeo, except bullets will be flying like a horde of hungry hornets over a honeycomb."

"So, you want to bust down the front door and charge in, pistol blazing like John Wayne or Gary Cooper, taking a gigantic chance of getting blown away yourself? Then, I suppose you expect me to clean up the mess after you're dead and gone. Not only that, you didn't even consider that it is my responsibility to be the first one in the door being the sheriff and all.

"Heck, Barlow, you don't even have a year on the job yet! You got some kind of a death wish? I agree that we need to resolve this soon, like in the next fifteen or twenty minutes, but I am not sold on your tactics."

"Sheriff, consider this. First, I am more nimble than you, probably more nimble than Kirk, in that they are running us like thoroughbreds in training. Maybe Kirk is as nimble as me but there's no way you're gonna cover the back door while we go in the front, as important as that is. You're the high sheriff and I know everybody expects you to go in the front.

"Second, I'm a much smaller target than you.

"Third, I've got the shotgun, although I know you could order me to give it to you or Kirk.

"Fourth, I'm fresh. You all have been up nearly 24 hours. Your reflexes are not as sharp as they otherwise would be.

"Fifth, I am volunteering, plus my plan has you coming in right behind me. Think about it! This really is the best way."

Kirk said, "Or I could trade places with you. I'm the more experienced officer."

"Yes, but this is my squeal and you're already fatigued and I'm not. What do you say, Sheriff?"

"I hate to admit it, Kirk, but he's right. I'll give you five minutes to work your way around so you can cover the back door. On your way over there, tell Mr. Caldwell that we need him to maintain his vantage point no matter what. He needs to stay put. Tell him how important that is to us.

"Barlow, I want you to make sure the shotgun is already chambered with a shell and that the magazine is full to capacity. Then, once Kirk has had a chance to set up, I want you to sneak up as close to the front door as you can without being seen, unless, of course, they rush out, blasting away like Butch Cassidy and the Sundance Kid. Be ready!

"I'll make the announcement from here, just in case they look out from behind the curtains. I want them to think the charge will come from all the way back here behind the cruiser. That should buy you about five seconds in which they will be getting amped up.

"I will give them two minutes to fish or cut bait. That's all! Just two minutes so we can keep the pressure on. If they haven't put down their guns and come out, I will fire off a round into the ground. That's the signal to breach. I'll be running to the front door before you get inside.

"Barlow, be alert. No heroics. Shoot anyone who's pointing a gun at you. I'll be no more than five seconds behind you.

"Kirk, keep your eyes open. If I was one of these assholes, I'da already shot me a couple of dogs and been out the back.

"Everyone savvy? Anything not clear?"

Kirk said, "I got it, Sheriff. I'm on my way."

Barlow replied, "Since the door opens from left to right and the picture window is on the right, I'll be on the left side of the steps crouched down. If someone opens the door with a gun in his hand, I will send him to his Maker. If I make entry, it's same, same. Anyone pointing a gun in my direction is getting a dirt sandwich."

Sheriff Sol said, "Okay, but be careful. Don't forget. I'll be five seconds behind you. And remember, five seconds is an eternity when you're dodging bullets."

CHAPTER 31
Friday, March 27, 1970
Why Cops Make the Big Bucks

Five minutes passed. Kirk and Barlow were in place. Corporal Caldwell was still stretched across the trunk with his cocked, Revolutionary War model, anti-tank weapon. Sheriff Sol had his doubts about leaving him be. He prayed that Francis wouldn't shoot Barlow or him when they breached.

Barlow noticed that the door facing was broken where the burglars had kicked it in. That meant it wasn't latched. This would make his job easier.

"Attention burglars! This is Sheriff Pratt. We've got you surrounded. Lay down your weapons. Come out the front door with your hands in the air and you won't get hurt . . . ."

"Shut the fuck up, Sheriff! Who do you think you're shitting? There's not enough officers in this pissant county to surround an anthill. Why don't you lay your own gun down and drive away and maybe we won't shoot you? We been to prison and we know how this works. We ain't going back."

"Okay. It's your funeral. You have two minutes. Before you die, what do you want engraved on your tombstone?"

"What about, 'Here lies the man who gunned down Sheriff Solomon Pratt in the prime of his life?' I want them to bury me right next to you. We'll be locked together in Eternity."

"Clinton Dumfries, is that you?"

"Maybe. How did you know, Sheriff?"

"I recognized your voice. It's all gravelly. I thought you were still in prison."

"Well I ain't, no thanks to you! I shoulda killed you the last time we crossed paths. Sorry I didn't now. Better late than never."

"Clinton, I knocked you down with my cruiser so I didn't have to shoot you. Instead of being dead, you got two broken legs. Apparently it didn't slow you down too much because here you are. You ought to be grateful. How's your brother, Melton, isn't it? He holed up in there with you, too?"

"Fuck you, Sheriff. You leave Melton out of this. You fucked up his life just like you fucked up mine. He wouldn't hurt a fly."

"So he is in there. Tell him to come on out. I don't want him to get shot by accident."

Barlow could hear some muffled voices from inside. It sounded like an argument but he couldn't make out the words. He decided to breach while Clinton was busy jawboning with Sheriff Sol.

"You got one minute left, Clinton. Lay down your weapons and you and Melton come on out."

"You're pissing me off, Sheriff. You better . . . ."

Barlow bounded up the stoop in two steps and crashed the door. The only illumination within came from a plug-in nightlight. The pistolero was about ten feet inside, looking toward the load-bearer, busy jacking his jaw. He was caught by surprise. He spun around with a revolver in his right hand, seeking a target. Barlow responded by sending a load of double-aught buck into his torso, blowing him backwards into the wall. Lights out for Clinton Dumfries.

The load-bearer scrambled around the corner into the kitchen. Barlow chambered a shell and prepared to shoot again but now his quarry was out of his sight. He paused and crouched down before looking around the corner well below waist-high. He didn't know if this burglar was armed.

Sheriff Sol barged into the living room like an ape in the midst of a swarm of pissed off yellow jackets. He flicked on the switch to the overhead lights. Now everyone could see, for better or for worse.

The load-bearer jerked opened the back door and stepped

outside. Too late. The dogs were waiting. They knocked him backwards and were chewing him up like he was Thanksgiving dinner. Sheriff Sol holstered his weapon and waded in like the dogs were a pair of rag dolls. He snatched them both up at the same time and hurled them about ten feet back into the yard. Barlow dragged the man back into the kitchen. Sheriff Sol slammed the door shut. This one latched, and it was a good thing because the dogs crashed it repeatedly trying to get in.

Fortunately Sheriff Sol only had two bites - one on his left arm and the other on his right hand. Neither was life-threatening, although they were painful. The burglar was a mess but his guts and groin were intact and his face and throat were unharmed. However, he was in shock and losing consciousness.

Kirk rushed in the front door, gun drawn, but winded. The first thing he saw was a crumpled, very dead, Clinton Dumfries up against the wall, oozing blood from nine unnatural, .32 caliber orifices in a six-inch spread over his breastbone. He was sitting in a gallon of his own blood. A Smith & Wesson revolver was lying on the floor next to him.

The next thing he saw was a panic-stricken Melton Dumfries sprawled out on his back on the kitchen linoleum, barely breathing, but with what appeared to be even more holes and tears in his chest and arms than his deceased older brother. He was leaking like a sieve. He had soiled himself and the smell was overwhelming. The odor was strong enough to bring tears to a glass eye.

Sheriff Sol said, "Barlow, you tend to Melton. He should make it. We don't want him dyin' of fright. Then, if the phone works, call Arch and have him get Doc Boykin over here ASAP (as soon as possible). Tell him to get Chief Alex rolling, too. Also Pete Ricketts and his meat wagon. Then I want him to wake up Chunk and tell him day shift is early today and to get his butt over here. Got that?"

"Yes, Sir."

"Good. Kirk, you and I are fixin' to search the rest of the house. You get the honors of climbing up into the attic. There might be more bad guys, so be on your toes."

"Whatever you say, Sheriff."

The house had a living room, dining room, small kitchen, bathroom, laundry room, two small bedrooms and one bigger, master bedroom. It took all of two minutes to confirm that no one else was hiding in the living quarters.

The opening to the attic was in the hallway ceiling. Sheriff Sol pulled the cord to the door. He reached up to the folding stairs and pulled them down. Good thing Kirk only weighed 175. The stairs were too rickety for a 250-pound climber.

Kirk asked, "What would you think about sending the dogs up there?"

"You going to be the dog whisperer and entreat them to go up there without biting us first?"

"I guess not. What's going to happen to the dogs, Sheriff?"

"I don't know. There's some who believe they should be put down for mauling Melton. There's others who believe they should be rewarded for doing what they were trained to do - bite intruders. I'll have to think about it, first.

"Hubba, hubba. There's a light cord up there. Pull it, but look carefully before exposing yourself anymore than you have to. You're too good a man to spring a leak like these two assholes down here."

Kirk did as he was told. The attic was as empty as a beggar man's wallet. Excitement over. Grunt work next. Contemplation later.

Sheriff Sol stepped outside into the cool air and pulled the door shut. He lit up a Lucky Strike and took two, long drags. He exhaled slowly. Francis was still on duty at his post except that his revolver was uncocked, laying inertly on the trunk of Ted's auto as benign as a sleeping puppy dog. Francis was standing with his arms wrapped around his body, warding off the chill in the air.

"Frank, thanks for all your help tonight. You might have saved Deputy Adams' life. We owe you a debt of gratitude. You're the type of citizen every sheriff or county judge wishes would make up the constituency in his venue."

Corporal Caldwell morphed from a feeble old man in his bedclothes to a strack (Army slang for squared away), ramrod straight, World War I doughboy, standing at attention before his commanding officer. "Thank you, Sheriff. That means a lot coming from you. I was just doing my duty as a responsible citizen. It was my honor and privilege. Thank Deputy Adams for giving me an important assignment.

"Sheriff, Winona's been waving at me, trying to get me to come back home but I wasn't budging until I was properly relieved of my duty. You might not know this. It was a long time ago but I was commended in dispatches twice by my commanding officer during the war. That was a big deal in those days. I take my duty seriously."

"Well, you are duly relieved, Corporal. Thanks once again. Dismissed."

"Before I go, Sheriff, I was wondering. Did the man I shot at get killed? What about the other guy I saw?"

"All I can say for now is we have one dead and one wounded. I'm sure you can figure out what happened to whom. Right now we need your discretion. You know how the rumor mill distorts the truth. Will you help us out with this?

"It'll all come out anyway in a few days after our investigation is complete. Your name will be mentioned prominently as a local hero, unless of course, you want us to stay mum in the event that the burglars have family who might be hellbent on revenge."

"I see. Yes. I will keep this to myself except for Winona, of course, until it all comes out in public. And Sheriff, I'm not afraid of publicity. Far be it from me to avoid the press. You know I can take care of myself and mine."

"I do, but if you see anyone suspicious lurking around, give us a call."

"Don't worry. I will."

Nighttime evolved into daylight. Once Chief showed up and was briefed, Sheriff Sol and Kirk went home. The heavy lifting was done. Now the only thing left was documenting the crime scene and the clean-up, punctuated by the mountains of paperwork, their portion of which could wait until after they copped a few hours of shuteye.

Chief and Chunk conducted the crime scene investigation. Easy-peasy except for scrubbing down the wall and floor where Clinton got shot and the floor where the dogs mauled Melton. Normally they wouldn't have done this, except Ted George was dead. He was their neighbor and friend. They had no idea what his daughter, Jolene Tripp, who lived out of town, planned to do with the house but they didn't want to leave this mess for her to contend with, especially if she didn't return right away.

The coroner, Pete Ricketts, picked up Clinton Dumfries' body.

Barlow guarded Melton, who huddled on the floor in a corner of the dining room, eyeing Barlow like he was the mouse and Barlow was the snake.

Doc Boykin made a house call and after checking Melton's vitals, he gave him some antibiotics and a sedative. He cleaned all his wounds and sutured the worst ones. He bandaged all of them. He said to watch Melton closely and if he took a turn for the worse, to give him a call. He said if there were any chance the dogs were rabid, they would have to be put down and have their brains examined for rabies.

Chunk drove Melton to jail. Due to his filth and blood-soaked garments, Melton was sanitized in the shower as soon as they arrived and his clothes were discarded in the dumpster behind the courthouse. He was dressed in horizontally striped black and white prison garb with shower clogs.

Afterwards, he was ensconced in their best suite, otherwise

known as cell #1. It consisted of a stuffy, windowless room and a steel bunk with a plastic-covered, two-inch thick mattress, a flat pillow, and a wool, WWII Army surplus blanket. The commode was in the corner, a wide-rimmed ceramic bowl with no lid, but it flushed well. The ceramic sink was just big enough to hold a quart of water. The walls were the proverbial institutional green. The cell smelled of Lysol. Soon, he was nose-blind to it. He knew the drill.

The best thing one could say about his Spartan accommodations, devoid of all privacy, is that they were clean. Spotlessly clean, and it would be his job to scrub it clean everyday if he expected to eat or shower. This was life with just the basic essentials. No matter. He was quite familiar with this type of living arrangements. Been there. Done that. Besides, he expected to be back in prison soon where life had a few more amenities, such as working on a road gang and punking the sissies.

Chief followed Barlow to Boyd's Phillips 66 service station to drop off the cruiser for repairs. They were now down to one marked unit until the one Rudy Gómez smashed was repaired. Fortunately, it was supposed to be ready tomorrow. Then he drove Barlow to the jail so he could write his statement and finish his shift.

Barlow waited until 7 o'clock to call school to tell them he would be absent due to police business. He was duly excused.

Next, he called Sarah. He said he was involved in a shooting incident. He wondered if she could call in sick and meet him at his house. Before she panicked, he said he was all right. She said she would be there as soon as she could.

At 7:45, Dewey Caruthers showed up to go to Alpine with Chief Alex. Chief was tied up giving last minute directions to Chunk regarding Melton Dumfries' initial appearance, which was scheduled for 10 o'clock. He told Chunk to get Randy Meacham to come in early to lend a hand.

At 8 o'clock, Barlow left for home. He felt guilty leaving while others were working long shifts, but Sheriff Sol wanted him to stay at home at least for the day due to the shooting. It was standard protocol. He couldn't return to work until he was officially cleared, which Sheriff Sol planned to do after he spoke with DA DeWitt later in the day.

CHAPTER 32
Friday, March 27, 1970
Now That It's Over

Barlow got there before Sarah. He let Happy out to do his business in the field on the west side of his yard. Then he fed him a delightful pound of Alpo's canned horse meat with its attendant malodorous gravy. Yum, yum. It disappeared in less than a minute, with the concomitant slurping and wolfing sounds and the smacking of lips. Urgent dog daddy duties concluded, he stripped in his bedroom and dumped everything on the floor. He took a long, steamy shower.

When Sarah arrived, she looked in on him and saw that all his body parts were intact. She knew he hadn't eaten, so she began making grits and frying bacon.

When he got out of the shower, he put on a robe and padded barefoot into the kitchen. He took a seat at the table. Happy followed him from the bathroom and lay down at his feet. At this point, neither Sarah nor Barlow had uttered a word. Neither had Happy. He didn't need to. He wagged his tail and the whole world knew what that meant.

Barlow was physically clean but he felt dirty and all used up. Empty. It had been a helluva week and it wasn't over yet. He had wished for excitement. He got excitement. Geez! Be careful for what you ask for.

Sarah poured him a double shot of Old Fitzgerald from a bottle she liberated from her father's liquor cabinet, which more accurately could be described as a bourbon cabinet. It contained many types of bourbon but nothing else. Who needed anything else? Certainly not her dad.

He sipped it and smiled. Smooth.

She smiled back. Then she returned to the stove and began frying eggs. She put two slices of bread in the toaster and engaged the heat.

He finished the first glass of bourbon as she placed his meal in front of him.

She sat down across from him and watched as he slowly ingested every morsel off his plate. He didn't even leave any egg juice for Happy to lick. That was okay, if not exactly satisfactory to Happy. He had already devoured everything he was due. Still, a little egg juice would have been nice.

She poured him another Fitz. She cleared the table, washed, and put away the dishes while man and his best friend watched. When she was done, she took his hand and led him into the bedroom. She gently shoved him onto the bed. Happy sat at his side on the floor. She poured him a third bourbon and one for herself. She sat in the ladder-back chair across the room and waited.

She had never seen him like this before, so . . . pensive. When he called, she thought he needed sex to unwind. Now she was not so sure. It scared her a little bit. She was doing all she could not to look as frantic as she felt inside. What happened? Was he in trouble? Was he frightened into a state of speechlessness? By now she bet her folks already knew exactly what had transpired, book, chapter, and verse!

The three of them watched one another for as long as it took Barlow to visually soak in Sarah's love and to thank God that he was still among the living, with all his parts still functioning at full capacity.

"I'm so glad to see you. It's like I almost fell off a cliff but didn't. I've been in this place before. It's 'deja vu all over again,' just like Yogi Berra said."

"Are you going to tell me before I die of curiosity?"

"Sorry. I am. It's just that times like these remind me just how tenuous Life is. We go around day by day, doing whatever we do, making plans for the future, getting aggravated over trivial things, not fully appreciating all our blessings, and then poof! You almost get hit by a bus. A rattlesnake strikes at you but misses. You get violently sick but it passes. Someone tries to take your life but he doesn't. In a flash, your life hangs in the balance and it's all up to God. You have no time to pray and ask for more time.

"When it's over, if you survive and take time to reflect, you realize that Life is like being a spider hanging from a single strand of web which is directly over a flame, but not close enough to cause any discomfort. If the thread breaks, the spider falls and gets consumed. But the web hasn't broken before and it's usually not over a flame, so the spider just does his thing and never thinks about how precarious Life really is. That's a good thing, else the spider would worry himself to death and never draw a relaxed breath again. Someday, the thread will break and the spider inherently knows that, but he shoves the thought to the farthest recesses of his mind until he has a day like today."

"I'm so thankful you're alive, Spider Man."

"Me, too. Just not my time, I guess."

"Don't say that. It sounds like you're looking for your time to come."

"No. Not seeking it. Just aware that it can come at any moment. That makes every single day precious. Sometimes I forget. Today was a reminder."

"Are you going to tell me what happened or must I hear it from the grapevine?"

"It was so simple, mundane in a way. I guess that's the part which freaks me out. Not my first rodeo. You know that. It's just that it didn't have to happen, but it did happen, and it went down the only way it could go down, logically.

"The only issue was which of us would wind up in the morgue and which of us would have more time with his woman. It can always go either way. It went my way today. I do not have a lucky charm in my pocket, so therefore, I conclude that God still has work for me to do on this planet. Praise the Lord for that!"

"So tell me! I'm about to come apart at the seams. By now everyone in town knows more than me!"

"Sorry. Archie is sick. He was throwing up. He wouldn't go home. He was in the john. The phone rang. Winona Caldwell from Washington Avenue called. Her neighbor's house was being burglarized. He just died so his house was empty."

"Ted George?"

"Yes. I responded by myself. Francis Caldwell came out to help. He had a gun. I told him to take cover behind Mr. George's car. I repositioned my car in front of his house. I got on the radio to tell Archie to hurry up if he was capable. It turned out he wasn't, but Sheriff Sol heard my call and he came. Also, Kirk lives in the neighborhood and he heard the shots and . . . ."

"What shots?"

"Three shots one of the burglars took at me while I was in the car on the radio. He missed me, but I probably have some glass in my clothes so be careful if you pick them up. Anyway, the burglars went back inside Mr. George's house. He has some badass dogs in his backyard, so they couldn't escape thataway, which meant they had to come out the front.

"It was my plan. Sheriff Sol approved it since there was no better way. Kirk covered the rear in case the bandits shot the dogs and tried to escape out back. I crashed the front door when Sheriff Sol was out by the street parlaying with the burglars. I shot and killed the guy who shot at me earlier. The other guy tried to sneak out the back but the dogs mauled him. Sheriff Sol was right behind me and he picked up the dogs like they were stuffed animals and threw them in the backyard and saved this dude's life. Sheriff got bit up, too. If they ever decide to give out lifesaving medals around here, Sheriff Sol should get one. Melton's in jail. That's it in a nutshell."

"Why did you have to crash the door?"

"Well, for one thing, I volunteered. Besides that, both of them had been working since early in the morning and were headed home when I got the call. Sheriff Sol is a big target and he isn't as nimble as me. Even so, he came in right behind me, otherwise the other guy would have been killed by the dogs. I'da probably shot him too, just to put him out of his misery.

"Also, Kirk volunteered to go in the front, but I'm faster and smaller than him, too. Besides that, I have more experience than he does on things such as this. That's why I said this situation was simple and really just one way to handle it. It was clear as a bell. We all saw it."

She started weeping softly. He tripped over Happy rushing to her and lifting her onto the bed next to him. He stroked her hair. Happy whipped the side of the bed with his windshield wiper tail and licked any bare body part he could find. He barked and tried to weasel his way into their embrace, but Barlow shushed him and told him to lie down on the floor. He whined, but complied.

"Barlow, you're not Superman. You might be Spider Man, but Spider Man isn't bulletproof. Someday . . . ."

"Sarah, listen to me. I don't take crazy chances. I do what I have to do. Nothing more. You should know that by now.

"Besides that, I believe in predestination. It's in the Bible several places. Romans 8, for one. Lots of Methodists don't believe in this but the Presbyterians do. Our chaplain in Vietnam was a Presbyterian. He explained it and I believe it.

"God has predestined all His people. They make their own choices but He knows ahead of time what those choices will be. Some people are predestined for good. Others for evil. Another way some folks look at it is the Book of Life. We're already entered into it. God knows when He plans to call us Home. It's pointless to worry about it. Call it Fate if you want to. Some folks refuse to believe this because they say 'it isn't fair.'"

"Barlow, I don't know what to think, but I do understand this.

A cat has nine lives. If you were a cat, how many lives would you have used up already and you just turned 21? Probably just about all of them.

"Or consider this. Sometimes when you roll the dice, you turn up snake eyes. Or in baseball, three strikes and you're out. Are you listening to what I'm trying to explain to you? It's like you live on the ragged edge and yet you act like you're invincible. Like nothing bad will ever happen to you."

"I'm listening. I know I'm not bulletproof, but neither am I snakebit. Some day Jesus will call me home and that will be it for me here on Earth just like it is for everyone else. I'm neither George Washington nor Adolph Hitler and I don't pretend my story is the same, but I do share some similar experiences with them."

"Such as?"

"George Washington led his troops in battle from the front. Not like the generals of today. He had a boot heel shot off, a saddle horn shot off, and several bullet holes shot in his coat during the Revolutionary War, yet he never once got shot. He wasn't trying to be a hero. He was just doing his job to the best of his ability.

"Adolph Hitler was a messenger, a German Army corporal in WWI. His job was to run through the battlefield with messages to the commanders. Every messenger in his company of messengers was killed but two. One was seriously wounded. Hitler was unscathed. They say that because of this, he thought he was one of God's chosen, immortal in a manner of speaking. Made him a little crazy.

"Washington was a force for good. Hitler was a force for evil. I believe they were both predestined by God. Whatever will be will be.

"My point is this. The odds say that Navy will beat Army in football this year. Why do they still play the game if the odds determine the outcome? Could it be that the oddsmakers are wrong some of the time?"

"Barlow, you're impossible! Just reel it in a notch. Okay? I love you. I don't want to lose you to a force of evil. Understand? By the way, what are the names of the two bad guys?"

"Clinton and Melton Dumfries. I shot Clinton."

"Oh my gosh! No way, Jose!"

"Yes, way."

"Eight or nine years ago they robbed the liquor store here in town. Sheriff Sol was a deputy. It happened early in the afternoon. He just happened to drive up when Clinton was coming out of the store right after he robbed it. His brother, Melton, was the driver.

"Clinton fired at Sol several times and shattered his windshield. Sol never fired back. He just drove straight into Clinton and pinned his legs between his bumper and the barrier in front of the store. He broke both his legs. Melton surrendered without a fight. In fact, I don't think he even had a gun. They both got sent up.

"My, my. I bet Sheriff Sol's glad you killed Clinton. He's a bad one. Also, that's probably why he risked his life to save Melton."

"Well, I dunno. He never said one way or the other. I could tell though, from their parlay that there was history between 'em.

"By the way, now that I've finished woolgathering, I have this sort of ache in my groin area, probably overdid it in all the excitement, or perhaps when I jumped up the steps. Not sure. Could you see maybe if you could make it feel mo' better? I sure would be beholden to ya."

"Mr. Adams! Naughty boy! No wonder! You have an enormous erection! Look how it bobs up and down all on its own accord. Your robe is moving around like it has a kitten underneath it. Let me see if I can do anything to ease your pain. It might take a few minutes. Let me take off my clothes first. It makes it harder . . . ."

"It certainly does. Look at those melons! Show me that

gorgeous fanny! My God, it's all perfect! Oh my gosh! Don't be a tease! Hurry up! Come closer! I need to make sure you're not an apparition or a figment of my imagination."

Once she was naked, she lay across the bed and sure enough, it 'took two hands to handle the Whopper.' She licked all around it like it was an ice cream cone.

"Oh, that feels mighty fine. I might have got snake bit. Think you could maybe suck out all the poison?"

"Oh, I probably could, but I'm too wet and worked up. I need you now. Could it wait?"

"Don't know. About to explode. Wouldn't want to disappoint . . . ."

"Sorry. I can't talk right now. I'm putting a monster willie in my mouth. I'm busy."

Sarah knew his body like it was her very own. She sucked and kneaded and stroked and squeezed his flagpole and both ball bearings with the finesse of a true artisan. She built him up and then lightly let him down until he was crazy with desire.

He was on the verge of rolling her over and ravishing her doggie style, when she quit teasing and took him into her mouth as far as she could go while gently massaging his balls. He convulsed, involuntarily shoving another inch down her throat and then she almost choked. He flooded her with his seed, some of which trickled out of her mouth. When he opened his eyes, she rubbed it over her nipples before licking it off her fingers until every last drop was gone.

He caught his breath and then rolled her onto her back. He spread her legs and licked all around her labia and clit. She started rocking her hips back and forth. It felt exquisite. He took his time, returning the favor. She tasted so good.

She thrust harder and faster and began to moan softly. He continued his ministrations with his tongue, only harder. He inserted a finger in her pink rose and began rubbing her in sync with the rhythm of her hips, while his tongue concentrated on her clit. She squeezed his head with her thighs.

He found her G-spot. She thrust harder. Her lubrication began to gush. Moments later, she climaxed and began to slow down, and then stopped moving altogether. It was over. She collapsed, melting into the bed even though she was already lying down.

He gave her a few moments before gently massaging her breasts. Her nipples were erect. She was coming back to life.

It was just in time. He was harder than an Osage orange billy club, just as thick and nearly as long. Performing cunnilingus on this enchanting and alluring fiancé of his added more lead to his pencil than anything else he had ever done or thought of doing.

He rolled her onto her stomach and pulled her up on her knees. The twin globes of her alabaster bottom were perfection itself. He rubbed the tip of his manhood around her glistening, pink, wet honeypot and gradually inserted it a little at a time. She was already on fire.

He was better able to control himself and so was she. They synced into a mutually satisfying rhythm, each concentrating on the sensations that were pulsating through their bodies. Eventually the train picked up speed and the thrusts went deeper. The passion kept building. Their breathing became jerky. He was holding back as long as he could.

The tingling inside her was becoming intense. He shuddered and hammered home as far as he could go. He emptied his sack. At the same time, she clenched him as tightly as she could. Even as wet as she was, he could not withdraw. She collapsed on her face while he was still inside.

They were both out of air, gasping for breath. Their intimate parts, which moments ago couldn't be rubbed hard enough or fast enough, were suddenly too sensitive to touch.

They cuddled on their sides, face to face, thoroughly sated. Today they had time and could go to sleep without fear of being late or being caught.

He whispered, "I love you."

She whispered back, "I love you more, so you better never ever leave me. I couldn't stand it without you. Promise me."

"I promise, God willing."

"Shush. I don't want to think about predestination while I feel this glow."

She took his hand and placed it between her thighs up close and very personal. "Don't move and go to sleep."

All three of them did. The third party lay at their feet.

CHAPTER 33
Friday, March 27, 1970
Continuing Phase I

It was almost 8:30 by the time Chief Alex and Deputy Dewey Carruthers headed west to meet Investigator Avery Carmichael and to pick up Chico Gómez at the Brewster County Jail. Along the way, Chief mentioned what he knew about last night's shooting incident first, saving updated details about the rustling case for later so it would be fresh in Dewey's mind before they began tracking down victim locations.

Dewey was 40 years old. He was 6'6" tall and weighed about a buck-fifty, maybe a buck-fifty-five after eating Thanksgiving dinner. He had blue eyes and a receding chin. He was bald with closely trimmed brown hair around the sides. You couldn't tell he was bald when he was wearing his Stetson. He had a prominent Adam's apple and long bony fingers and skinny feet which could have doubled for skis. They looked exceptionally long in his pointy-toed, high-heeled Tony Lama cowboy boots. He wore silver-framed glasses with circular lenses for reading and ciphering and Ray Ban aviator glasses with green lenses for the outdoors. Also, he was a lefty.

He carried a blue steel, satin finish, Smith & Wesson, Model 28, Highway Patrolman, .357 Magnum caliber revolver with a 3-1/2" barrel and rosewood target grips, in an Austin holster on an El Paso Saddlery gun belt with twelve cartridge loops filled with brass-cased, copper ball ammo.

The bullets were gleaming, without a speck of tarnish, indicative of an anal-retentive man who regularly polished his ammo with Brasso to keep them shiny just like his military brass. The 3-1/2" length barrel on his sidearm was in juxtaposition to his height. One could only hope that his pecker was longer than his gun barrel.

Dewey was an only child, born and reared in El Paso. His father, Grant, was a foreman at the Tony Lama boot factory and his mother, Holly, was a housewife.

Dewey joined the Army in 1948, after graduating as the salutatorian of his high school class. His GT (general test) scores were high so the Army placed him in the Finance Corps, which is the smallest of all the Army branches, after basic training. He was assigned to a finance corps battalion in Fort Hood, Texas, where he worked in the payroll section.

Although the Korean War was in full swing, he was never deployed. He was honorably discharged with a Good Conduct Medal as a sergeant after three years. He returned home and found work right away as a payroll clerk for the Diamond Cab Co.

The Army Reserve established a finance company at Fort Bliss in El Paso shortly after Dewey was discharged. He jumped at the chance to sign up because he was bored at work. Besides that, they let him keep his stripes. He became a career reservist and by 1970, was a master sergeant with 22 years of total service, in line for first sergeant as soon as Cecil Robles retired.

In 1952, as a lark, he joined the El Paso Sheriff's Office as a reserve deputy. He met his wife, Elsie, responding to a call of a bank robbery where she was employed as a teller. She was all of 5'4" tall and pleasantly plump, so standing side by side, they resembled 'Jack Spratt, who could eat no fat, and his wife who could eat no lean.' He didn't catch the robbers but he did catch a wife who rounded him out (no pun) and made him a very happy man, indeed.

Dewey's father died in 1960. His mother was inconsolable. After a lifetime in El Paso, she sold dern near everything and up and moved to Mosby to help her sister, Hyacinth McLeod, run the Thrifty Scot Second Hand Shop that she and her husband, Angus, owned on Texas Street. Angus was having health issues and on good days was unable to do much more than ring up the cash register. Hyacinth was in dire need of assistance and Holly was in dire need of a new purpose in her life.

Four months later, after many soulful pleas from his mother, Dewey and Elsie, their two kids Dwight and Florence, and their rat terrier, John Wayne, sold out and moved 300 miles away to Mosby, also. It was a long commute to Fort Bliss for his monthly weekend drills and two-week annual training (AT), but Dewey could bunk in cheap at the bachelor NCO quarters. Besides that, he had long been ready to pull the plug at the cab company.

Things worked out for the better. Elsie quickly became employed at the thrift shop, too. Dewey set up an office there doing tax returns and bookkeeping, which turned out to be a far more lucrative part-time job than he had imagined possible. The SO had a vacancy for a paid part-time deputy (no pay as a reserve deputy in El Paso), which dovetailed nicely with everything else Dewey was doing. With the exception of monthly drills and AT for the Army Reserve, his work schedule was flexible.

Also, they found a tidy, compact, four bedroom, one-and-a-half bathroom house, with an unattached, two-car garage on Sul Ross Street for much less than it would have cost in El Paso. Holly moved in with them. The kids were thriving in school. Dwight even made the basketball team as a freshman but he wasn't getting much playing time yet. Maybe next year.

Dewey didn't know it yet, but he was Sheriff Sol's first choice to do the undercover at the impound lot. In civvies, Dewey looked more like Ichabod Crane than a police officer. Also, he was fluent in Spanish and he had a quick mind. He looked like a tall drink of water. Ineffective. Timid. A soup sandwich. He wasn't. He would be the mongoose and the crooks representing Pluto would be the cobras. The crooks were way outclassed.

Just like yesterday, it was closer to 11 o'clock than not by the time Chief and Dewey picked up Avery and Chico. Having been up most of the night, Chief opted for an early lunch before hitting the dusty trail. They stopped at the KFC in Alpine. God bless Colonel Sanders! The grub was tasty and there was plenty of it. Chico ate like a ravenous vulture. So did Chief Alex but he washed his down with black coffee instead of orange soda.

Afterwards, they drove north on US 67 near Stockton, where they picked up TX 1776 to Coyanosa in Pecos County. They found the ranch with ease. It was called Medio Camino, meaning halfway there. It was 91 miles from Alpine, so maybe the name of the ranch was rhetorical. Who knew where all the way there was actually located? Maybe it was halfway between Heaven and Hell.

This was the fourth ranch the crew hit. The house was in plain sight of the gate and the location where Chico said they loaded the sheep. It was a cinch that, had someone been awake at the house, he could have seen or at least heard the trucks and the bleating of the sheep. That meant no one was home or the rancher was a very sound sleeper.

One other possibility was that this was a put-up job. The problem with that theory was, so far as they knew, no one had reported the theft. If it was done collusively for an insurance fraud, surely the rustling would have been reported to the sheriff's office.

From there it was a short jaunt, maybe 30 miles, to the seventh site at Grandfalls in Ward County. This was beautiful country. It was also the place where, due to rain and mud, they nearly bogged down the trucks. You could still see ruts in the pasture. This place was called the Box X. Once again, it seemed impossible that this rustling job could have gone undetected. Chico had no explanation.

They had a hard time finding the sixth theft, which was in Winkler County. In fact, it was only about 40 miles from Grandfalls, if one knew where he was going. They drove 67 miles up and down Highway 115 and three side roads until they spotted it. Chief felt fortunate that they did. This was the gig when Chico was sick, so his memory was hazy.

They located it in the vicinity of a tiny town called Wink. It turned out to be a big operation named the Lazy J in a small county by southwestern Texas standards, not to mention sparsely populated. One could bet his bottom dollar that the owner of the Lazy J would receive a full-court press type of response from the sheriff's office for any complaint whatsoever, no matter how insignificant. One could hardly call the theft of two tractor trailer loads of sheep insignificant. It was possible that the Lazy J, being gargantuan like the Triple S, was just too big to keep track of everything on a daily basis. The other possibilities, without more information, were just too perplexing.

It was 3 o'clock. The final destination was back in Brewster County near the Big Bend National Park. Chief and everyone else working the case believed this would be the Ramirez ranch, known as the Twisted Oak, but until Chico confirmed it that was just an educated guess.

They traveled 192 miles from Wink, mostly on US 385, 43 miles south of Marathon before they arrived. Once they rolled up on it, Chico confirmed that it was indeed the site so they didn't need to spend another minute burning daylight. They made a U-turn and then a beeline back to Alpine.

It was 7:45 when they dropped Avery off at the SO. Chief, Dewey, and Chico dined at the Pizza Hut. They ate like a herd of hungry, hungry hippopotami munching away in a sugar cane field. Chico was returned to his jail cell sated and sleepy. It was after 10 o'clock when Chief Alex and Dewey arrived at the Quayle County Courthouse.

Chief felt like he could sleep for two days without waking. 'No rest for the weary and the wicked don't need none.' Tomorrow was Saturday, but he was way behind the eight-ball on this case and the new one on Melton. He knew tomorrow would be another full day. He decided to wait until morning to check in with the sheriff.

CHAPTER 34
Saturday, March 28, 1970 Catching Up and Plowing Ahead on the Rustling Case

Sheriff Sol rolled into the office about 10:30. He was checking the last couple of days' mail, trying to catch up and to sort through the status of both investigations.

Slick was on duty and, with Melton toasting his plums in cell #1, he was busy running back and forth between the office and the jail. Not the greatest way to conduct business but it was the best they could do for the time being. When Chief Alex walked in about a half-hour later, that freed up Slick to be a full-time jailer, an assignment that nobody relished.

Chief poured a cup of coffee. He brought a file full of papers and his coffee and sat down in front of Sheriff Sol's desk. He filled his lower lip with a dip of Copenhagen. He waited for Sol to light up a Lucky Strike before they got down to business. He asked, "Do you have time to catch up?"

"I do. Let's talk about the rustling case first."

"My thoughts exactly. Sheriff, I think we're finally cooking with kerosene."

"No kidding?"

"No kidding. First, I got the mugshot, investigative reports, indictment, and J and C (judgment and commitment order) on Humberto Pavón from Eddy County. I'm 90% sure he's going to be El Jefe. I'll make a six-pack (photo array with six mugshots of similar looking persons, which includes a photograph of the suspect) and show it to Slick before he punches out. If I have time, I'll stop by the Triple S and show it to Rico and Pepe. I'll need to show it to Barlow, too."

"Very good. I need to stop by the Triple S later on today. After you show it to Slick, give it to me and I'll show it to the other three."

"Thanks. That would be a big help.

"Second, I have a mugshot, rap sheet, and fingerprint card of a turd named Cesar Oso. He was Pavón's cellmate for two-and-a-half years in New Mexico. From what I can see, he looks like Juan Rodríguez, although his face was pretty buggered up from the shotgun blast. I'll compare the prints we have on file to see if I can make a match. Either way, I'll send them to DPS for an expert opinion and if they make a match, I'll send a set of prints to the FBI."

"Let me see the photo."

He handed it to Sol, along with morgue photographs.

"Well, he was a fairly nice-looking guy before he tangled with Slick. I think it's him but I wouldn't bet the family farm. What's his rap sheet say?"

"He's 32 years old. Ranch hand. Otero County busted him on different occasions for armed robbery, burglary, shoplifting, purse snatching, disorderly conduct, and drunk in a public place several times. Two felony convictions. Got ten years. Did five. Out on parole. Not allowed to travel outside of New Mexico."

"Check his prints ASAP and let me know what you think before I go see Judge Sweeney."

"Roger that.

"Third, I think I've identified our financiers."

"Really? That's big news."

"Yep. I had Eddy County run the license plate number we got out of Chico's sock drawer. Remember he said the guy who paid El Jefe drove a red and white Jimmy with that number? Also, that he was supposedly a twin and that one twin owned Pluto and the other twin owned the ranch where they delivered the sheep?"

"Yeah."

"Well, the license plate is registered on a red, 1970, GMC Jimmy, to Gemini Enterprises, Incorporated, address P.O. Box

966, Loving, New Mexico. I had the Secretary of State's office check on the corporation. Turns out it's also registered in Delaware.

"The president is Hugh Mallard and the VP is Louis Mallard. If you recall, Pluto's president is Donald Mallard. Get it? Donald Duck, Huey Duck, and Louie Duck. Dewey Duck is the only one missing. Oh, yeah. The registered agent is the same for both corporations - an April Lundgren. By the way, I sent her the registered letter on Thursday about making arrangements to pick up the trucks."

"So Donald, Huey, and Louie Duck are our financiers? Is Mickey Mouse involved, too?"

"Nope. Not by those names, anyway. I called Inspector Bud Wagner with the Postal Inspection Service in El Paso. I asked if he could run a discreet inquiry on the actual human box holders for Gemini Enterprises in Loving and if he could get us a physical address.

"He did his magic and it turns out there are two key holders to Box 966. One is Gerard Gemini Gough. He runs Gemini Enterprises. The other is Geoffrey Gemini Gough. He runs Pluto. They're twins from Mason City, Iowa. Supposedly Geoffrey is a chemical engineer and Gerard has a degree in agriculture. They both graduated from Iowa State University in Ames. They're wildcatters. They've drilled in Bartlesville, Oklahoma, and in Artesia, New Mexico. Supposedly, they haven't hit any big gushers yet. That could mean they're running out of cash.

"They both live on a small ranch in Malaga, which is just south of Loving. It's on County Highway 132, about six miles east of US 285 on the north side. Supposedly, it's a quarter section. I haven't had time to dig any deeper than that."

"How did Bud get all this information off an application for a post office box?"

"He got it from the postmaster in Loving, who will lose his job for sure and maybe get prosecuted if he spills his guts to anyone. He knows these guys. He says they're both friendly as they can be. And for what it's worth, Bud didn't tell the postmaster why he was inquiring."

"What does Bud drink?"

"Jose Cuervo, as I recall."

"Find out when Dewey's going over there next. I want to send him a bottle of Jose's best. And Chief, great job! Now, how did your little foray with Chico turn out?"

"It went hunky-dory. We located the victim ranches in Pecos, Ward, Winkler, and Brewster Counties. The one in Brewster was the one Sheriff Waters called us about. I can't figure how it is that nobody except the Twisted Oak ranch in Brewster seems to have noticed."

"Ditto. We found the ones in Jeff Davis, Hudspeth, and Culberson Counties. To tell the truth, I'm not sure the one up near Salt Flats isn't really located in Culberson County. With the Triple S that makes eight different locations and, so far as we know, only the Brewster ranch discovered the loss on their own. It just doesn't add up."

"So what do you want to do now?"

"Well, I hate to ask, but I really need for you to spend another very long day with Chico the Amigo. Probably be a 600-mile day. Monday, if possible."

"You want me to take him up to Malaga and identify the destination ranch."

"I do, and this time I'd like you to take Chunk with you to see if he can milk any last little tidbit of information that Chico's holding back or forgot. Besides that, your Wagoneer doesn't resemble a police car. My Fury might as well have 'fuzz' written all over it in flashing neon lights. We only get one shot to scope out this place by ground without the risk of heating it up. Are you good with that?"

"You know I am. Anything else?"

"Not yet. What's your take on Avery Carmichael?"

"Seems like a pretty squared away guy to me. I wish he was working for us instead of Brewster."

"Me, too. I just wanted a second opinion. Make sure he knows everything we've got going on in this case, but not in front of Chico."

"Of course."

"I need Leland Waters to stay on board and if Avery agrees with our plan that will help. Leland says he's committed, that he needs a big play before the next election, but I'm not so sure of that. He's a popular guy. I just don't want him to get cold feet. We need his help.

"In fact, I'm fixing to call him in a few minutes to see if he's considered which rancher over there might lend us his ranch and a flock of sheep for the rustlers. We gotta have the ranch. If we can't get a commitment on the sheep, I'll get them from Judge Sweeney but that means we'd have to transport them over there. Besides that, I already have a couple of big asks for the judge."

"How big?"

"Pretty big. I've never expanded my reach this far on a case before. Never needed to. Even if I had wanted to, I couldn't have because he's the judge on all our cases. A favor from him would be considered a conflict of interest. I would have been way out of line. But this time, since he's the victim and not the adjudicator, I can. Even so, I'm going way out on a limb. If things go sideways you'll be the next sheriff and I'll be trying to get my old job back as a railroad dick."

"Well, we'll just have to make sure they don't. Besides, I'm too young to be sheriff."

"Ha! You were old enough the first time I ran for office."

"Maybe I didn't want it. What are you asking for, anyway?"

"First, and most importantly, I'm going to ask to borrow his airplane. After you've done a drive-by on the ranch, I want to examine the layout by air so we can map out surveillance vantage points. Then, I may ask if we could use it again to follow the rustlers, assuming they take the bait. Plus, now that I think about it, wouldn't it be nice to have an eye in the sky during the raid itself? I think he'd really go for that. He might even want to go on that mission himself, strictly as an observer, of course."

"Good idea. That would probably keep him in our camp and eliminate any second thoughts about calling in the Rangers. In fact, it could give him bragging rights of his own whenever he mentions it to his brother."

"I never thought of that, but it's true. Darnell is always boasting about his days in the Rangers. It might even balance the sibling competition a little bit."

"It should, but then again, ever since Max waxed both those Diablos in a very uneven gunfight, I expect Darnell views him with a lot more reverence.

"What was the other big ask you were going to make?"

"Right. I'm thinking about sending either Barlow or Slick with Rico in one of Judge Sweeney's trucks with a load of sheep to the auction in Loving. I want to see if they can delicately ferret out information about any seller who recently started coming in with large flocks of sheep, particularly someone who brings in a variety of breeds. Not the Spanish Inquisition, mind you, just discreet, off-hand banter from a sheep hand to a worker bee in the auction house. If we don't get anything, we haven't lost anything. Judge Sweeney will get paid for his sheep either way and for all I know, they may even fetch a better price in Loving than in Pecos."

"That's a fabulous idea. My recommendation is Barlow. Slick's a great cowboy but that's why he would not be my choice. He knows too damn much about ranching and a collusive auction house worker might take him for one of the victim ranchers looking for answers. Barlow, on the other hand, is a greenhorn. The best play would be for him to be one of Rico's crew. Nobody would ever suspect a greenhorn. Greenhorns don't know what they don't know. He might get put down if the auction worker thought he was being too nosy but I doubt it would raise any suspicion."

"Alex, you are indeed, a crafty character. You know what? I like the way you think. We'll do it your way, assuming Judge Sweeney is willing to go along with it.

"That brings us up to our sting. Beginning as soon as Monday, but probably more likely not 'til later in the week, we should get a call from April Lundgren or Donald Mallard. It would be too perfect to receive a call from Humberto Pavón even though he is Pluto's general manager, so I won't even imagine that.

"If they're anxious to get their rigs back, they'll ask to pick them up later the same day or the next at the very latest. We gotta be prepared or we'll be scrambling. We need to slow them up just a little bit.

"To do that we'll put them on the defensive by creating a bureaucratic cobweb that we wouldn't normally do. We always ask for proof of ownership and insurance but neither these tractors, nor the trailers have license plates. Of course, they will report them as stolen too, but we'll demand that they provide replacement license plates before they'll be allowed to drive them off the lot. It's not a major obstacle. They can get them right there at DMV in Pecos but it could take half a day. That gives us time to set up our surveillance.

"We'll also demand a letter signed and notarized by Pluto's President, Donald Mallard, indemnifying us and the storage vendor from any damage which may have occurred since they last had possession of the vehicles.

"Finally, we'll demand cash for the wrecker service tows and the storage fees. I know what Boyd charges. Tell him to pad it a little bit because he's going to have to provide two drivers to take the rigs to Alpine. I don't want him gouging, just getting his fair due. I'll send Kirk along to grease things at the storage lot and to give them a ride home. We'll set this up for Tuesday.

"Find out the name of the wrecker lot we'll store them in and what their daily rate is. I want to give Pluto a good idea of their costs. In fact, ask Avery on Monday before you pick up Chico. Check it out. Find out who the point of contact is over there but remember, this is all on the QT. 'Loose lips sink ships.' You know the drill.

"Also, I'm still thinking about Dewey as the u/c. Find out if Avery will be Brewster's. Am I missing anything?"

"What about the commo?"

"Let me work on that. I'll run it by Judge Sweeney and get him to grease the expense with the Board of Supervisors. I'll ask for five CB's. That way, after this is all over we'll have one for each unit. We'll get Boyd to install them. We need to do that ASAP. Once we hear from Pluto and set a date, it's game on. No time to putz around.

"Anything else on this case?"

"Not that I can think of right now."

"Good. Let's move onto last night."

CHAPTER 35
Saturday, March 28, 1970
Update on the Dumfries Case

Sheriff Sol said, "I think we dodged a bullet, no pun intended, regarding the Dumfries case. I spoke with Chunk and Able DeWitt. We both know Clinton and Melton were on parole and this is the rest of the story.

"Melton got out a little over a year ago. He was living with his mother over in Langtry in Val Verde County. Darlene's on Social Security and Melton got a part-time job at the DX service station pumping gas. They had a symbiotic relationship. Melton helped pay the bills and he doesn't drink or whore around and she gave him room and board. They respected each other and it worked out just fine.

"Then Clinton got out a week ago. He went back home, too. You know, a hundred bucks and a bus ticket back home isn't much of a new beginning, especially for a very self-important person like Clinton.

"Darlene and Clinton don't gee-haw. Never did. He's a shiftless bully. She wanted him out but he had nowhere else to go. He threatened to use her as a punching bag if she tried to kick him out, so in a manner of speaking, everything turned to shit in Darlene's little paradise overnight without so much as a warning.

"Now, apparently Darlene was related to Ted George. She went to the funeral. Neither of the boys went but this gave Clinton some big ideas about getting rich quick and skedaddling down to Old Mexico to live it up.

"According to family lore, Ted had an extensive collection of silver dollars and a few gold eagles and double eagles. Clinton, brain surgeon that he isn't, thought the mother lode would still be in the house so Melton, his dimwitted sidekick, was drafted to help steal it. Just like the last time when they both wound up in prison.

"Apparently Clinton never considered that Ted's daughter, Jolene, had already gone through the house and taken home the all the good stuff, like his coins, nice jewelry, bank papers, guns, and that sort of thing. She missed the Colt Cobra that Clinton used to shoot at Barlow. Apparently Ted kept it in a cigar box on an end table in the living room.

"After Darlene went to bed, the boys purloined her Pontiac to make a little midnight requisition over at Ted's. They didn't find squat except for the revolver. Clinton couldn't believe that there wasn't anything of significance worth stealing. No coins. No money. No fancy watches or rings. Just the one gun. He didn't want the television. It was old and only had black and white. So was the high fidelity phonograph. It was older than his mother's. Literally, everything that was left in the house added altogether wouldn't fetch a thousand dollars at a shabby second hand store.

"Melton wasn't so choosy. He planned to take a few hand tools and a Timex watch and some dress clothes that fit him. Also a pair of lizard skin Tony Lamas. That's it. That's why they were in the house for so long. Clinton was in utter disbelief."

"How do you know this?"

"Melton opened up to Chunk. Also, after Randy Meacham showed up, Chunk drove out to Langtry and brought Darlene back here so she could pick up her car. Boyd let her have it for no charge. She was thankful. Also, she despised Clinton. It was all Chunk could do to get her to go in and identify the body. She told Pete Ricketts to bury Clinton in a potter's field."

"Really?"

"Yes indeed. She said he didn't even deserve a marker, but she wanted him to identify the grave with a stick with his name on it so she could piss on it whenever she was over this way. Hell, she wouldn't even stop by the jail and visit Melton!"

"Can't say as I blame her."

"I reckon not. Chunk also handled the initial appearance on Melton. That's when he learned that Judge Sweeney was quite fond of Ted. He held court at 9 o'clock instead of 10 on Thursday so he could go to Ted's funeral. He gave sort of a eulogy of Ted in court on Friday morning. The only defendant was Melton.

"I knew Ted was a Pearl Harbor survivor but did you know he joined the Navy back in 1936, and that he retired with 20 in 1956, as a Boatswain's Mate 1st Class? He served on a cruiser in WWII and on a destroyer during the Korean War. His ship fought in the Battle of the Solomon Islands and in the Battle of Leyte Gulf."

"Well, I knew he was at Pearl Harbor but I didn't know any of the rest. I always thought he worked on heavy equipment as a mechanic or something. I had no idea he was retired Navy."

"Well, Judge Sweeney sure did and he unloaded on Melton in court because he found out Melton was related to Ted. He 'no bonded' him lickety-split. Scheduled grand jury for Monday and said trial would be Friday assuming he was indicted.

"Of course, Sam Davis was court-appointed counsel. He said DA DeWitt agreed to only charge Melton with burglary plus the parole violation. No felony murder. He said Melton wanted to plead guilty and go back to Huntsville, the sooner the better. He said there was no reason to fight it especially since he was caught red-handed and he was still on parole.

"Judge said that was probably the smartest thing Melton ever did, and I quote, 'in his entire useless, miserable, wretched, worthless, bean-eating life.' He said Melton was like 'an abscessed tooth on a carrion-eating coyote at a gut pile next to a chicken slaughterhouse.' He finished up by calling him a 'mistake of Nature.' He told Chunk to have DOC standing by to pick up Melton Friday afternoon right after court and not a minute after."

"Max must have been on a tear!"

"Yeah, he was, so Monday I'll have Atwater handle the grand jury on the indictment and the presentation of Barlow's shooting. Then I can let Barlow go back to work on Tuesday with Archie unless he's taking sheep to Loving with Rico."

"How's Archie doing?"

"He's over whatever he had now."

"That's good. How's Barlow after this latest shooting?"

"Not sure. Okay, I suppose. That's one reason I want to take the six-pack over to him. I need to make sure he's not in a funk.

"I hated letting him go in the door first but that was absolutely our best option. I'm big and slow and not so sure I could have got Clinton before he got me. Kirk's solid as they come but you know he's never drawn blood once, even with a nightstick since he's been on the job here. Maybe in the Air Force but I doubt it. Barlow, on the other hand, has this uncanny ability to size up danger quickly and react lethally without hesitation. It's saved his life before. He really is Wyatt Earp incarnate, or perhaps Marshal Bill Tilghman or a combination of both."

"No kidding. What a standard to try to emulate. Is that everything for now?"

"I think so."

"Okay. I'll pour through some files and find pictures of assholes who resemble Humberto Pavón so we can knock that out today."

"Don't forget the fingerprint comparison. That takes top priority."

"Good deal. Let me see what I can come up with."

CHAPTER 36
Saturday, March 28, 1970
Sheriff Sol Works On His Stratagem

First, Sheriff Sol called Barlow's house. No answer. No wonder. It was noon and Barlow was on ice. It was easy to figure where he would be.

Next, he called the Baker residence. Clarice answered.

"Baker residence."

"Clarice, this is Sol."

"Hello, Stranger! My gosh! How are you? This has been a dreadful week for you. Is everything okay?"

"I'm behind on my sleep but otherwise I'm standing in tall cotton. Thanks for asking. How are you all?"

"Oh, we're same-o same-o. Arthur and Cordell and Sarah are out back with Barlow and Boyo. They're trying to teach Boyo that gunfire in his proximity is nothing he need worry about. Did you call to speak with Arthur?"

"No. How's the training coming? Boyo receptive?"

"Well, Arthur and Cordell and Pedro have been lighting firecrackers around Boyo all week. He finally learned to ignore them. It made the sheep and some of the other horses nervous but that's another story. Today's the first day they've been shooting guns next to him. They haven't come in for a break yet, so I suppose it's going okay."

"Glad to hear it. I know some horses never adapt. I hope Boyo does. I know Barlow dearly loves that horse. Can't say as I blame him. Boyo is a fabulous horse."

"He is. We're planning to give him to Barlow as a wedding present, so it would be nice if Boyo learned to meet his needs as a lawman's mount. Sounds crazy doesn't it? Like it's 1870 instead of 1970."

"It's West Texas, Sweetie. We're just not ready to discard the old ways yet. Just ask Judge Sweeney."

"Right you are. Well, if you didn't call for me, and you don't want to talk to Arthur, I'm guessing you called for Barlow. Want me to go get him?"

"No. I do need to talk with him but now that I know where he is I'll stop by in a little while if that's okay."

"Oh, Sol, you know you're always welcome. If you're here about 6 o'clock we'll be ready to eat a mutton stew that I've been working on all day. Bring Joanna and the kids."

"That sounds scrumptious but I've got too many irons in the fire to socialize today. Thanks so much. Could I have a rain check?"

"Anytime."

"Thanks. Before I ring off, how is Barlow doing? I hated putting him out front on the Dumfries incident. Seems like it's become Barlow's job to dispatch all the bad men who need dispatching in Quayle County."

"I know. He's been through so much. Sarah said he was ruminating yesterday morning after the shooting. Not sad, exactly. Sort of stoic. 'Whatever will be will be.' Fate. Everything's in God's hands. He calls everyone home when it's their time. Nothing to worry about. Press on. That sort of thing.

"He seems dapper today. It's kind of sad. He's so young to have been through so many life-or-death situations. I worry about him. He's so cheerful, caring, and balanced. I don't know how he does it, but I do know he's happy with his life just like it is. You're not planning to let him go, are you? It would crush him."

"Oh, heavens no! He's become like a son to me. I haven't had a chance to talk to him since the shooting and I'm glad to hear your perspective. It's pretty much what I expected. You know, Clarice, you're his mother now whether you realize it or not."

"Oh, Sol, hush up. You'll make me cry. I love him dearly like he is my own son. When will you be stopping by?"

"Not sure, exactly. I hope within the next two hours."

"Great! See you then."

"You bet. Bye."

Next, he called Dewey at the Thrifty Scot Second Hand Shop. He knew Dewey would be there since this wasn't a National Guard weekend. Dewey answered the phone.

"Thrifty Scot Second Hand Shop. How may I help you?"

"Dewey, this is Sheriff Sol. Have you got a minute?"

"Yes, Sir. Do you need me to come in early today?"

"Oh, no. Nothing like that. I was wondering. How would you feel about doing the undercover at the tow lot in Alpine this week?"

"I'd feel great about doing it. I appreciate you considering me. I never did a u/c before."

"Well, I think this one is right up your alley. Dress down and just be yourself. Don't let on that you habla. Investigator Avery Carmichael from the Brewster SO will be your back up but he'll be sub rosa, if you get my drift. Too many folks in Alpine know him so he'll be cooling his heels in a back room. Savvy?"

"I sure do. What day are we doing it?"

"Not sure yet. Probably one or two days after we hear back from Pluto."

"I'll be ready."

"Good. One other thing. I need you to drop off a bottle of Jose Cuervo at the postal inspector's office for Bud Wagner on your next trip to El Paso. Buy a fifth of Jose's best and give Miss Loretta the receipt. She'll reimburse you."

"That'll be in two weeks, Sheriff, unless we're still working on the rustling case."

"Oh, Lordy, Dewey, I certainly hope we'll have this all wrapped up by then."

"Okay, Sheriff. Anything else?"

"Nope. Adiós."

"Adiós."

Next call was to Sheriff Waters' house.

"Hello."

"Leland, this is Sol."

"Sol, do you ever take a day off?"

"Every chance I get except when bandits are preying on my constituency. Look, I won't keep you. I was just wondering if you found a volunteer to let his ranch be rustled?"

"I did. Maurice Favre. Pronounced F-A-R-V-E, but spelled F-A-V-R-E. Don't forget that unless you want a cussin'. He owns the M Slash F just south of Jeff Davis County on TX 118, directly on the way to Pecos. He runs Hampshires. He'll put up 100 if you think it's necessary. All he asks is that he get his sheep back intact and that he be paid fair market value for any that aren't returned."

"That's great, but the M Slash F? Are you serious? That's the real name of his ranch?"

"Sure is. That's a hoot, ain't it? Old Maurice has a real sense of humor, doesn't he? All the licensed vehicles on his ranch are marked MF1, MF2, and so forth. Can you believe it? He calls himself the Big MF. He's big, too. Maybe 300 pounds."

"Well, I'll call him whatever he wants. Please convey our thanks to him when you speak to him next. Tell him 60 should be enough.

"By the way, I'm headed over to the Triple S soon as we hang up. Now all I have to ask for is the loan of Judge Sweeney's airplane and a truckload of sheep we can sell at the auction in Loving."

"That's all? Sure you don't need to borrow a cool million or two just to tide you over?"

"Well, it's not like I want to fly the airplane myself and we will sell his sheep and give him the money. It's all in furtherance of capturing the pendejos who rustled nearly 400 sheep from him. You think that's too much? Heck, Leland, if it were up to him, he'd hang those bastards himself and bury them in his very own owlhoot cemetery that his grandpappy established."

"Just breaking balls, Sol. Ratcheting up the stress. It's not too much. Wish I would've thought of it myself. Do yourself and me a favor. Take tomorrow off. Romance your wife tonight if you're not too old to get it up. Call me on Monday. Capeesh?"

"You know what? Soon as I meet with one of my deputies and Judge Sweeney I'm gonna take your advice. Adiós."

"Adiós."

The last call was to Judge Sweeney's house. He called the judge's private personal line in his office at home. The judge caught the call on the first ring.

"Hello."

"Judge, this is Sheriff Sol. I was wondering if you'd be free to discuss the rustling case this afternoon."

"I am. What time?"

"How's an hour-and-a-half sound?"

"Perfect. See you then." Click.

Sol gathered his papers and stepped out to check with Chief Alex. The six-pack was laying on his desk. "Whaddaya think?"

"Looks great. Did Slick make a positive ID?"

"Sure did."

"Which one is he?"

"It's #3."

"Gosh, that's great. To me #3 and #5 look almost identical."

"I know. Slick surprised me, too. Now we'll see if the rest of 'em can do it."

"What about the fingerprints?"

"There is a God in heaven. Cesar Oso's prints match Juan Rodríguez's. I'm ready to mail Juan's prints off to DPS and the FBI. Now all I need to do is locate a next-of-kin."

"Outstanding! Great work.

"Well, I'm headed to the Bar B to see Barlow. Then I'm going to the Triple S. If everything goes well, I'll talk to you Monday morning before you go to Alpine. Try to finish up as soon as you can today and then why don't you get out of here and spend some time with April? Maybe take her to the movie."

"Sheriff, I'm a gone pecan just as soon as I wrap up the Dumfries case file. As it turns out, April does want to go to the movie. 'Love Story' is playing. Imagine that."

"Yeah, imagine that. If Joanna knows it's playing, I'll probably be sitting in the theatre right behind you. Talk to you Monday."

Sol finally completed his inside chores. Next stop was the Bar B.

CHAPTER 37
Saturday, March 28, 1970
Sheriff Sol Continues To Nail Down His Stratagem

When Sol arrived, the training session was wrapping up. Everyone was wearing smiles so he knew it had been a good day.

Arthur said, "Hey, Sheriff! Coming to put Barlow back to work?"

"Hey, you all. Not today. From the looks of things you already wore him out for today anyway. How'd the training go?"

Barlow replied, "Oh my gosh! I couldn't believe it! All week long, whenever anyone was around Boyo, they lit firecrackers near him to get him used to the noise. They lit some more this morning while I was riding him in the corral and he never missed a step. Then I fired Sarah's .22 over his head and around his neck and that didn't phase him. I just got done shooting four cylinders of .41's over him and he acted like this was all old hat. We'll have a few more sessions, I hope, just for reinforcement and then I believe we'll be ready for another go at it with those rustlers if they take the bait."

Sarah interrupted, "Sheriff, can I get you a glass of tea or lemonade or maybe a beer?"

"No, thanks. I just stopped by for a few minutes to run some things by Barlow. I need to go over to Judge Sweeney's before I can call it a day. Hopefully I'll get home in time to take Joanna to see the movie."

Cordell asked, "What's playing?"

"Love Story."

"Is this the first weekend for it?"

"Yep."

"Maybe Darla and I will go see it next weekend."

Sarah said, "Barlow and I are going tonight."

"We are?"

"You owe me, Mister."

"Heck, I owe everybody! Guess I better pony up and buy everyone's tickets."

Cordell said, "Barlow, if you don't take Sarah tonight, she will make life miserable for everyone except you because you won't be here to suffer her wrath. Dad and I will be the ones she takes it out on. You take her to the movies tonight and you're square with me."

Arthur chimed in, "Ditto for me, too. Tell you what. You settle your business with the sheriff. I'll groom Boyo. Cordell, why don't you go on home and see if Darla wants to go. You have to ask, at least. Otherwise you'll be in the doghouse. Sarah, why don't you go in and get cleaned up?"

Barlow said, "Gee, everybody. Thanks for doing this. Where do you want to talk, Sheriff?"

"How about in those chairs over there under the trees? This won't take long."

Moments later Sheriff Sol and Barlow had the copse of trees all to themselves. They sat and took time for the sheriff to light up and for Barlow to put in a dip.

When both were situated, Sheriff Sol asked, "How are you doing, Barlow?"

"I'm fine."

"Look, I need to say something. I made a serious mistake when I assigned you to guard Melton yesterday before dragging my weary ass back home, especially right after you terminated his brother in front of his very own eyes. I should have stayed around until everything was wrapped up. Not my finest hour. As the sheriff, my most important job is to look after my troops and I didn't do that for you yesterday."

"Not a problem, Sheriff. I didn't mind. He didn't act up. Not once. You must have been bushed. I know I would have been. Really, I hadn't been at work except for a couple of hours by then. Not sure I even finished my full shift. I got off easy. Chief and Chunk did all the heavy lifting. All I did was sit on my can and keep an eye on him. No big deal."

"Oh, you finished your shift all right, and then some. I need to know how you feel about everything that happened Friday morning."

"I'm just fine, Sheriff. You know, I didn't set out to shoot anyone when I went to work Thursday night. It's something which popped up unexpectedly and I just did what I had to do. I'm not proud of it, but I'm also not ashamed of it. Clinton called the play. I guess God decided it was his time to go but not mine. I didn't hate him. Same as with the others. I'm not losing any sleep over it. I'm ready to go back to work."

"What if the very same scenario cropped up next week? Would you be as eager to breach the door?"

"Sheriff, I wasn't eager Friday morning. I just did what I had to do. It's in my job description. I want to be a lawman. I don't want to be a shoe clerk. I know the risks. I do everything I can to minimize them. Sometimes there just aren't any good choices. Surely you understand that."

"Barlow, you're too good a man to die young. You're also too good a man for me to ignore if you're suffering from shell shock. Know what I mean? Get depressed. Turn to the bottle. Hold yourself responsible for things which were not of your making. Start having head problems. Savvy?"

"Believe me, Sheriff. I'm over this. I promise. Sarah would blow me in if I wasn't. You know that. She worries about me way too much as it is. All I do is play the cards that God dealt me and thank Him for all my blessings, like Sarah, this family, my job, you as my boss, coming home safe and sound from Vietnam. All of it. I'm balanced, in harmony with the world. Okay?"

"Okay. I'll take your word for it. Now I'll get down to

business. Take a look at this six-pack and tell me if you can identify the rustler you traded shots with."

"I'm pretty sure it's this one."

"Which one?"

"Definitely #3."

"Are you absolutely sure?"

"Well, #5 could be his brother but I'm positive it's #3."

"Congratulations. You just identified Humberto Pavón."

"Anyone else ID him?"

"Just Slick. Haven't showed the six-pack to Rico or Pepe, yet.

"Next order of business. On Monday, Atwater is going to handle the Grand Jury on Melton. Melton's already stated he would plead out to burglary and parole violation. If he's true to his word, he'll be eastbound back to Huntsville on Friday, courtesy of DOC, and out of our hair for good, I hope.

"Ernie's also going to present the line-of-duty shooting of Clinton on Monday. Once we get a No True Bill you can go back to work.

"What's your situation at school?"

"I'm all caught up, Sheriff. All A's and B's so far. Heck, we're down to seven weeks before the summer break. I can't wait."

"Good. Make sure you keep it that way. So go to school on Monday. Tell them you'll be out Tuesday and possibly Wednesday on official business. Nothing more.

"Be sure to get some rest Monday afternoon. Unless things change, you'll be going to work in the wee hours on Tuesday morning at the Triple S. You and Rico will take a truckload of sheep to the auction in Loving. This is a u/c assignment. You will be Rico's assistant. The auction starts at 10.

"Nose around a little after you pen up the stock. See if you can get one of the auction hands to open up about anyone who has recently had a half dozen or so sales of various breeds of sheep. A seller with a bunch of different breeds would be a little unusual and should set off alarms. Judge Sweeney is one of the few ranches which specializes in Rambouillets. You can use that but be discreet. No worthwhile information at all beats accidentally tipping off the receiver of stolen property. Remember, the seller very likely was Juan Rodríguez as Gough's ranch foreman. They could be regulars and maybe even co-conspirators with the auction yard. Savvy?"

"Savvy."

"Okay. You all will sell the sheep and return home. With luck, you'll be back by 7 or 8 o'clock. Wednesday will probably be a day off for you so you should be able to go to school.

"Before the end of the week, we could be putting the sting into play. I'll have another assignment for you then. That's why I don't want you missing anymore school than necessary. Roger that?"

"Roger that."

"Okay. We're done here. Have some fun tonight. Go to church tomorrow. You have some serious praying to do."

"Thanks, Sheriff, and good night."

"Good night."

CHAPTER 38
Saturday, March 28, 1970
The Big Palaver With Judge Sweeney

Last stop was The Big House. The quiet, efficient, seemingly mind-reading servant named Matilda showed Sol into the judge's study. He was seated at his desk smoking an aromatic, Oscuro-wrapped Churchill with a crystal glass of Kentucky's finest, otherwise known as W.L. Weller, at his elbow, going over some figures in a leather bound ledger.

He motioned Sol to a comfy, leather, wingback chair. Matilda brought a humidor over to Sol as soon as he was seated. He selected a Monte Cristo panetella and lit up while she poured him a tumbler of Weller from an ornate crystal decanter. Then she quietly left the room and closed the door without so much as a word or a sound.

"How is your day, Sol?"

"Fine, Judge. How about yours?"

"I need a diversion from going over these infernal ledgers. I'm going blind double-checking these figures. I do hope you came to give me something more interesting to ponder."

Sheriff Sol quickly brought him up to date on the status of the rustling investigation.

"Sol, this is all falling into place very nicely. I'm pleased to hear it. Do you need any help? Should I contact the Rangers? It sounds like the investigation is headed out-of-state."

"Judge, we could use some help but not from the Rangers."

"Surely you're not considering bringing the FBI into this! This is a local matter that's simply transcended some manmade political boundaries. We can work around that. We would lose control of everything."

"That's my point exactly. The same thing would happen to me and all my deputies if the Rangers came in. We'd be benched. We want to work this case ourselves with a little help, of course, from our friends over in Brewster County.

"I came to ask if you would loan us your airplane to do a flyover of the suspect ranch in Eddy County. I want to see the layout of the land and to identify the best way to launch a raid, if the bad guys take the bait we plan to dangle in front of them. If possible, we might even like to use the plane to track the rustlers hauling a load of stolen sheep to this ranch."

"Of course, you may use the plane. I'll have my pilot, Nicky Nelson, at your disposal. But what exactly are you trying to do?"

"Judge, we're waiting for a call from representatives of Pluto to pick up their trucks. We know the company is dirty but we'll never be able to positively identify any of the stolen sheep which probably have all been auctioned off anyway. We could never prove the owners had any criminal involvement. So, we've worked out a deal with a rancher in Brewster to pen up a flock of sheep set aside for rustling, with the story line that he's waiting for a transport crew to pick them up."

"Who's that?"

"Some fellow named Maurice Favre. He has a funny sense of humor."

"I know him. He's a real character."

"So I'm told. When the Pluto reps pick up the trucks, our undercover will mention that they could get a job hauling Favre's sheep to Pecos if they don't want to deadhead back. If we're lucky, they'll take the bait, rustle this load that night and lead us back to their doorstep. We'll follow and raid the ranch in the morning during daylight hours before they can take them to auction."

"How do you propose to do all that? What's the Eddy County sheriff think of all this."

"He doesn't know anything about this and he won't if the

rustlers don't take the bait. I'll offer him the same thing I did with Leland Waters. He can have all the glory. Eddy County can charge the Gough brothers with receiving stolen property or conspiracy or anything they want. Same with Humberto Pavón. I don't give a hoot. I know damn well my deputies won't be hauling any prisoners back to Quayle County and I'm good with that.

"The very minute I know the rustlers are headed northbound, I'll contact Sheriff Elliott and let him know. We'll already have Slick and Barlow and maybe one other deputy nearby. I'll ask that Sheriff Elliott cross-designate our deputies and Sheriff Waters' deputies as special deputies for Eddy County just to avoid any problems down the road. I can't see him turning me down. We're gonna make him look like Marshal Pat Garrett after he killed Billy the Kid."

"And if he doesn't play ball?"

"Then I'll have to deal with that then."

"Sheriff, I think I can stack the deck in your favor. If you think the rustlers will take the bait, let me know. Darnell will call Colonel Wilson Speir and tell him we need one ranger for liaison with Eddy County, stemming from a rustling incident and shootout which occurred on our ranch. I can absolutely guarantee the Rangers won't take over our case.

"In fact, I will ask for Ranger Sergeant Winfield Taylor III from El Paso. They call him Trey. His pappy is a retired El Paso PD captain in charge of detectives. Trey's a solid lawman and a dear friend. He protected Monica after she got shot. I don't know if you've met him but you'll be glad he's with you. He's an old school ranger. Carries a well-used Peacemaker."

"I've never had the pleasure, Judge, but so long as we control the case I'll be very glad to have him in our camp. In fact, I'd like it if he were one of the fellows we stage nearby the Gemini ranch, so go ahead and make the call."

"Don't worry. You'll like him. He's your age. He's also a Navy vet from the Korean War. He was assigned to a battleship. The USS Wisconsin as I recall. He was a gunner's mate."

"Well, he had more fun than I did. At least his ship bombarded the Reds. Mine stayed underwater except to recharge the diesels at night. Heck, I'm a Korean War vet and I never set foot on Korea, nor did I fire a shot in anger in their direction."

"Maybe not, but your sub patrolled enemy waters and was prepared to sink any Red vessel that dared to enter your area of responsibility. Sol, you know we seldom get to pick our wars or battles. We each do our bit, even if it's nothing more than preparing meals or scrubbing latrines. Not everyone gets to be Audie Murphy.

"Heck, I was a major in World War II, assigned to the Quartermaster Corps in the Army Reserve. I was in the Corps of Cadets at Texas A&M and received a commission in the Reserve before I went to law school. Other than training, I was never on active duty until the war started. By then I was a captain. I always saw myself as a dashing cavalry officer. The Army didn't see it that way. I bet you didn't know that.

"Instead, I was responsible for thirteen acres of warehouses full of war materiel in Baton Rouge. I worked my tail off ensuring that the weapons and munitions were properly loaded on the designated transport vessels to New Orleans. The only time I fired my weapon was at the range. It's not the assignment I would have chosen for myself. I never left the continental United States. That's how I fought my war. Like I said, we all do our bit.

"So, now that we settled the vicissitudes of war, what else?"

"I'd like to send Rico and Barlow to the auction in Loving on Tuesday with a load of your sheep in one of your marked Triple S trucks, just to nose around and see if they can pick up any intel. Of course, you would reap the financial benefits."

"Why on Earth would we haul a load all the way to Loving when Pecos and Alpine and even Del Rio are closer?"

"Well, the Alpine and Del Rio sheep auctions are too small to be worthwhile. Same as Mosby's. What a joke! Besides that, we heard sheep fetch higher prices in Loving and we wanted to check it out for ourselves."

"Good answer. Okay. I'll have Rico set it up. Anything else?"

"One last thing. I brought a photo array which includes a picture of Humberto Pavón. I need to show it to Rico and Pepe and see if they can identify him."

"This is El Jefe, the rustler who rode off across the river?"

"Yes."

"Show it to me."

Sol placed it on the desk. Judge Sweeney examined the photos. Thirty seconds later he pointed to #3 and said, "This is that chili-eating son of a bitch!"

"How do you know that, Judge?"

"Sheriff, I've been studying criminals all my life. I'm seldom ever wrong in my judgment. I can pick out a rustler from an aggregation of miscreants every time. It's him, isn't it, Sheriff?"

"It is. I just hope Rico and Pepe can identify him."

"I'm sure Rico will. I'm not so sure about Pepe. Have you showed this to Slick and Barlow?"

"I have."

"And . . . ."

"They both made positive identifications without hesitation."

"Just as I thought. I'm a good judge of men."

Judge Sweeney picked up the phone and placed a call. "Pablo, would you ask Rico and Pepe to report me at The Big House as soon as they can?"

Twenty minutes passed in cordial conversation while they indulged in another taste of sour mash and more satisfying premium cigar smoking.

Responding to a soft knock on the door revealed both Rico and Pepe with freshly slicked hair and dusted boots standing erect with hats in hand and looks of apprehension on their faces. "You asked for us, Señor Sweeney?"

"Yes, Rico. Thanks for your prompt response. Pepe, would you step outside for a moment and close the door?"

"Si, Señor." He was out like a wisp of smoke.

"Rico, Sheriff Sol brought this folder with photographs of criminals. He wishes to know if you recognize any of these men from the rustling incident. Take as much time as you need."

Rico studied each photograph with care. Finally, he looked up and said, "This is the one who got away." He was pointing at #3.

"Sheriff, would you ask Pepe to come in?"

"Of course."

"Pepe, would you look at these photographs and see if you can identify any of them from the rustling incident?"

Pepe had a sigh-of-relief look on his face. He studied the pictures in earnest. Finally, he said, "I am not sure, Señor. It is either #3 or #5, who was driving the truck that got away. I am sorry. I was concentrating on the man with the shotgun."

"Pepe, you and your father did fine. I appreciate both of your efforts in trying to identify the one who escaped.

"Rico, I want you to select sixty sheep for sale at the auction in Loving, New Mexico on Tuesday. It's a four or five hour drive at a minimum. The auction starts at 10 o'clock. Deputy Barlow Adams will go with you as your assistant. I want you to sell the sheep. Deputy Adams is on an undercover assignment to see if someone from the auction lot will mention anything about a seller of sheep which might have been stolen. All you have to do is your normal job like always whenever you go to an auction. Do you have any questions?"

"No, Señor."

"Okay. What time would you like Deputy Barlow to meet you?"

"3 o'clock at the secondary corral."

"3 o'clock it is. Thank you. Keep this information to yourselves. You all may go now."

"Gracias, Señor."

"Anything else, Sheriff?"

"No, Judge. That covers everything for now. Please let Nicky Nelson know that I'll stop by the hanger in Alpine about 10 o'clock on Tuesday. I'll let Barlow know where to meet Rico at 3 o'clock Tuesday morning."

"Of course. Happy hunting."

"Oh, I almost forgot. The SO needs to purchase five CB radios and have them installed right away. I don't have the money in my budget. Could you call the supervisors and see if they will okay it? Boyd's sells and installs them. We can get it done for about $600. Without them, it will be hard to conduct a moving surveillance with Brewster. In fact, we may have to temporarily install up to three of the CBs in POVs."

"I'll call Dinkins. He's a skinflint but he wants to stay on my good side or I won't back him in the next election. You can go ahead and start the installations on Monday. All expenses will be approved."

"Thanks, Judge."

"De nada. Just make sure you catch these cowardly, thieving, murderous cockroaches."

"Yes, Sir. We will. Good night."

Chapter 39
Monday, March 30, 1970
Deputy Atwater's Fast Forward Day

Deputy Sheriff Ernest Atwater had by and large, recovered from the mental anguish of killing Rodolfo Gómez in the line-of-duty but he wasn't 100% over it yet. Ernie had eagerly sought and embraced the assignment as the SO's designated sniper and it was a tremendous source of pride that he had been selected. This was also the source of his torment.

Truthfully, no one else had really wanted it, and although Randall Meacham was a better marksman, Ernie practiced and persisted until he was nearly as good as Randy. Randy was a part-timer, plus he wasn't all that interested in being a sniper, so Sheriff Sol had given the position to Ernie. It was a no brainer. The department had a competent sniper and both deputies were happy. The honor came with no emolument other than pride and a police expert rifleman's badge, not all that dissimilar from the shooting badges issued by the Army.

For Ernie, being a sniper had simply been a theoretical concept until the night Rudy Gómez tried to run him down with a tractor trailer. Up 'til then, all he ever did was punch holes in paper targets on the range with the rifle and his revolver. No more. No less. Mosby was a sleepy little town with few, if any, genuine bad actors. In sixteen years as a sworn officer of the law, Ern had never fired a shot in anger. He never honestly considered taking a life, even in self defense.

Then Bang! In the spark of a live or die moment, his life changed forever with a pull of the trigger. Now he was a sadder but wiser person. He didn't understand how Slick or Barlow did it without remorse, or so it appeared.

Maybe war inoculated them from the horror. He didn't know for sure. He was a Korean War veteran but not a combat veteran. He had been assigned to the Transportation Corps. He drove a 5,000-pound truck, otherwise known as a deuce-and-a-half. He transported supplies from the wharf to the warehouses or base camps. The only dead bodies he saw were killed long before he was on the scene. He transported some of them too, for the graves registration people. It was ghastly. He used to have nightmares but not for a long time now.

Nobody shot at him so he never shot back. Not once. In fact, in those days he barely qualified with the M-1 carbine that he was assigned as a combat service support troop, otherwise known as a REMF, or rear echelon motherfucker to the bitter frontline troops.

Not all frontline soldiers were bitter. Usually only the ones who were deadbeats or really scared. The real heroes, guys like Archie or Slick or even Barlow treated the ash-and-trash, another derogatory term for a REMF, with respect and appreciation for the supplies they brought or sometimes for the ride back from the front.

That's why he had wanted to be a sniper so dearly - to make up for his lackluster shooting skills in the Army. And that was his internal conflict. If he hadn't been so prideful, he wouldn't have been a sniper. Then he wouldn't have been in the situation whereby he had had to shoot Rudy.

Logically, he knew he might have to shoot someone anytime he suited up for work. He loved his job. Mostly he helped people but that's not why the county paid him. He was paid to shoot people who were trying to hurt folks. Like Rudy tried to do to Chunk and to him. He was working hard to sort this out. The one thing he knew for sure was that he had to cowboy up and put this behind him if he wanted to stay on the job. It was that simple. Thank God, Sheriff Sol had been patient with him.

Now today, Sheriff Sol assigned him to testify before the

Grand Jury, first to present the indictment on Melton Dumfries for burglary and for violating his parole. Afterwards, he would present Chief Snodgrass's investigative report regarding the fatal shooting of Melton's brother, Clinton, in the line-of-duty by Barlow Adams.

It gave him pause to reflect that only five days ago Archie had testified to a similar set of circumstances regarding the line-of-duty homicides of Rudy Gómez and John Doe #1. All three of these shootings were justified. Slick and Barlow and he all likely would have died had things gone the other way. He knew without a doubt that he would have perished, literally smashed like a bug on the windshield of a truck. Still, it made him sad.

Things changed as soon as he walked into the District Attorney's office. Able DeWitt told him there would be no indictment on Melton Dumfries because he signed a Bill of Information in which he acknowledged his guilt in the burglary of Theodore George's house, which resulted in him violating the terms and conditions of his parole. In essence, Melton was ready to move onto the sentencing phase of his criminal case. He wanted to get out of Quayle County's spartan lockup and return to the relative comfort of the Texas State Penitentiary in Huntsville just as soon as he could.

Judge Sweeney was pleased to oblige. He was standing by to convene court on the Melton Dumfries case just as soon as the Grand Jury rendered a decision on the Clinton Dumfries homicide. Thanks to State Senator Darnell Sweeney, DOC was scheduled to arrive at noon to transport Melton back to his happy home.

Ernie's head was spinning. He had never witnessed anything like this. Get arrested for burglary on Friday. Plead guilty on Monday and go directly to prison. Return back to the true Big House in Texas, home of Death Row and the electric chair. This sounded like something out of the Judge Roy Bean era, except Judge Bean was partial to hanging his convicts. Also, he held court in his own saloon. Wham! Bam! Thank you, Ma'am! Justice is served.

Ernie knew this was all legal but didn't know it was actually possible. You know the old saying, 'Don't mess with Texas?' This put an exclamation point on it, except now it said 'Don't mess with Quayle County, Texas!' Even the El Diablos Motorcycle Club finally figured that out, much to their discomfiture. The weirdness was that Melton couldn't wait to get back. Is that sick, or what?

The Grand Jury was seated at 9 o'clock. Ernie testified at 9:15. Essentially, he read Chief's investigative report verbatim. It was detailed and thorough. There were no questions. He was done by 9:30. Barlow was exonerated by 9:35. Heck! His first class at WTJC probably wasn't even over yet! Ernie guessed the World had had enough of Clinton Dumfries and was ready to move onto more pressing matters. Even his own mother had written him off years ago. C'est la vie!

Judge Sweeney convened court at 10 o'clock. The Bill of Information was read into the minutes. Melton acknowledged that the information was correct. He affirmed that he wanted to plead guilty to both counts.

Ernie presented the allocution from Chief's report. Melton affirmed that it was all true. Upon questioning by Judge Sweeney, court-appointed counsel Sam Davis told the court that he had explained the consequences of this course of action to his client and that he had willingly and knowingly decided that this was the route he wished to embark upon.

Judge Sweeney sentenced Melton to ten years for burglary and three years for parole violation, both sentences to run consecutively after Melton had completed his original sentence for accessory to armed robbery for which he still had three more years to serve. At a minimum, under the best of circumstances, Melton was probably facing at least ten years at hard labor before he could get paroled but he would most likely serve the full sixteen-year sentence.

Melton smiled. He didn't care. He was happy to go back to Huntsville. In stir he didn't have to make any decisions except for which sissy to screw in the showers. Some days he screwed two. There were always plenty of sissies to choose from. He had adapted. Life wasn't so bad there.

Ernie took Melton back to his cell and waited for DOC. That went off without a hitch. By 1 o'clock Melton had 'hit the dusty trail like a cow turd.' Ernie completed his shift cleaning the jail and holding down the fort with Miss Loretta. End of shift he went home.

He was over it - almost. Most cops never pull the trigger in the line of duty. If they do, it's usually in a high crime area like Watts in Los Angeles or a barrio in El Paso. Maybe in the coal mine region in Kentucky such as Hazard or Harlan County. Not in sleepy little Mosby. Statistically speaking, he shouldn't ever have to do it again. But what if he did? That's what he had to work out.

CHAPTER 40
Monday, March 30, 1970
Putting the Final Touches on Phase I

Chief Alex had a busy day, also. He learned that the Brewster County SO used Barrymore's Wrecker Service to store towed vehicles. Avery introduced him to the owner, Harley Barrymore, his wife, Ethyl, and his two sons Casper and Derrick, all of whom worked at the lot. They were more than happy to store the Pluto rigs until the rightful owners came to pick them up. Chief made arrangements for Kirk and two of Boyd's employees, Amos Speed and Jonas Rios, to deliver the trucks on Tuesday.

Then he and Avery checked out Chico for the trip to Malaga. They ate lunch at a greasy spoon Mexican diner in Fort Davis where the food was surprisingly tasty.

It was a long ride to Malaga. They found the turn off at the windmill without any problems. They slowed down to 25 miles per hour so they could clock the distance to the gate and to see as much as they could.

The driveway was 5.7 miles east of US 285. The ranch was well situated in good terrain. Lots of grass. The front field must have had forty or fifty sheep grazing. None of them was sure what breed they were but they knew damn well they weren't Rambouillets.

The east side of the ranch was bordered by the Pecos River. It did not appear to be very deep. Also, it was not very wide here. It doubled back to the west just east of the driveway, which went north from the county highway. There were lots of poplar and willow trees on the south and east sides of the ranch.

The house itself, was a medium-size, red brick, one-story

dwelling with a hip roof and grey asphalt shingles. There was a large barn with faded and peeling white paint west of the house. A corral was on the east side of the barn towards the house. Also, there were two other smaller wooden outbuildings behind the house, both with faded white paint, perhaps a garage and a smokehouse or a spring house. They couldn't tell for sure.

The red and white Jimmy was parked by the house. They didn't see any people. The road continued another 1.4 miles and narrowed down to a one-lane track before turning south. They stopped there and turned around. Then they headed back to Alpine, mission accomplished. Now it would be up to the aerial surveillance to figure out the best way to raid the ranch and where they could stage deputies before the raid.

CHAPTER 41
Tuesday, March 31, 1970
Sheriff Sol Completes Phase III

Tuesday was a clear spring day with nary a cloud in the cobalt blue sky. Chief's description of the target ranch was precise and should be easy to locate from the air. Sheriff Sol met Sheriff Waters and the pilot, Nick Nelson, on the tarmac of the airport.

Nick was a small man, maybe 30 years old, 5'7" tall and a buck forty with sandy hair, blue eyes, and a swashbuckler's handlebar mustache. He was dressed in khaki with a lightweight aviators jacket, aviator shades, and a cap with a brown leather bill and a gold military-style hat shield which he wore at a jaunty angle. He looked like a WWII British Spitfire pilot. He wasn't. He was a former US Army aviator, a warrant officer, who had flown the military version of this aircraft to haul high ranking officers over the battlefields in Vietnam, among other garden spots. Sol liked him the minute he laid eyes on him.

Sol didn't know exactly what to expect. He had never flown on a small private aircraft and truthfully, he didn't have much faith in them. He was pleasantly surprised to see that the yellow and white, 1953, Cessna Model 195B, single-engine, propeller-driven airplane with the wing above the fuselage was highly polished, well maintained, and large enough to hold five people including the pilot.

That didn't translate into roomy for a man of Sol's size, but he was able to get situated in the front passenger seat without much difficulty. Leland Waters, being smaller at 5'11" and 170 pounds, had plenty of room in the back seat. Sol noticed right away that having the wings above the fuselage made viewing the ground much easier than it is as a passenger on a commercial airliner.

It took about an hour to fly to Malaga. Nick pointed the aircraft north and vectored in to the intersection of US 285 at TX 652 in the vicinity of Orla and Red Bluff, about fifteen miles south of the invisible New Mexico state line. He dropped down to 5,000 feet. They followed 285, and in a matter of minutes were able to see Malaga and Loving in the distance. He dropped down to 1,500 feet so they could find the windmill at the turn-off. As soon as they spotted it, he began a slow ascent back up to 2,500 feet.

The target ranch was exactly as Chief had described it. The cluster of buildings within the curtilage was the only one like it in the vicinity. The Pecos River was almost a crescent around the ranch, like a backwards C with a short bottom lip. The top lip veered sharply north at what appeared to be the northeast corner of the ranch. There were two, probably donkeys, but perhaps mules or horses, in the back pasture. Another was in the front pasture with a flock of forty or so sheep.

The only entrance was in the front. There were two vehicles parked near the house. One was the white-over-red Jimmy and the other was a silver pickup. The pickup probably belonged to Cesar Oso. There was also a two-horse trailer parked on the east side of the barn.

The ranch was mostly pasture land except near the river, where there were more trees. Just past the tree line on the north side looked like what could be a county park or campground. They could see single-lane dirt roads with four scattered camp trailers and what appeared to be another dozen empty campsites just west of a building, like an office. There was also a smaller building which could have been restrooms or a laundry.

They could see horses grazing near the trailers. They also saw four riders skirting the tree line to the north. This could be the perfect location to stage a raid team, assuming they could do it discreetly and be able to cross the river on horseback. They'd probably have to cut the fence to accomplish that.

Sol took some photographs with a 35-millimeter camera. He didn't know how good they would be. Hopefully they would show the relationship of the buildings to the road and the river and to each other. Leland was busy making a sketch.

They landed back at the airport at 12:55. Leland offered to buy lunch. Nick begged off, citing a previous engagement. Smiles and handshakes all around. Happy campers each. Sol and Leland repaired to the Texas Longhorn Emporium for a medium rare ribeye steak, cold beer, and lots of privacy in a back room.

It had been a long time since Sol had seen Leland so euphoric. Only after the waitress, who was also joint owner of the restaurant with her husband, and a financial supporter of Sheriff Waters, had brought them their first drafts, taken their orders, and sashayed away did they begin to converse in hushed tones.

Leland said, "Sol, this just might work. If your guy can set the hook, I know we can reel them in. We gotta have the Eddy County Sheriff. Do you know him?"

"I do but not well. His name is Dan Elliott. He's honest, hardworking, a straight arrow so far as I can tell. I met him a few years ago at a seminar put on by the Border Patrol in El Paso about how we can help each other combat alien smuggling."

"I remember that. I couldn't make it because my daughter was having our first grandchild. Do you think he will work with us?"

"Oh, I think he probably would even without any arm twisting. Judge Sweeney doesn't want to leave anything to chance so we're getting one Texas Ranger just to grease the skids, not to take over the case. I'm thinking we could put him at the campground along with the rest of our raiding element, assuming it is a public campground."

"What made you change your mind? Do you know who they're sending?"

"Not my call. Judge Sweeney insisted. His brother, the illustrious and sometimes interfering, pain-in-the-ass Texas State

Senator Darnell Sweeney, is requesting a guy named Sergeant Winfield Taylor the Third out of El Paso. Supposed to be a solid guy."

"I know him! He is solid. I'd ride the river with him anytime, anywhere with nothing but a pocketknife. Judge Sweeney's right. We want this particular officer of the law. Old school. He's Captain Frank Hamer only forty years younger. He'd eat Bonnie and Clyde for breakfast and dine on Al Capone and John Dillinger for lunch and supper. Thing is, he's low key. Not a showboat nor a braggart. He'd be great up there with the raid team."

"That's good to know. It's settled then."

"Do you have the CBs yet?"

"Bought them on Monday. Should have them all installed NLT tomorrow. How about you all?"

"Same, except we should be done today."

"Did you tell the Big MF that he needed to mark his sheep so we can identify them without making it obvious to the rustlers?"

"Yep."

"So what did he do?"

"He'd already sheared them for the season but they went back and sheared a small patch about two inches square in the middle of their stomach. He said nobody would notice it unless they turned the sheep upside down."

"Nice. Simple, too."

"Have you heard anything from Pluto?"

"Not yet. Expect a call any day now. I left detailed instructions for Miss Loretta and the duty deputy if Pluto calls and Chief or I aren't there. The letter we sent was signed by Chief Alex, so that's who they will probably ask for. We'll have at least 24 hours to set up once we get the call."

"Did you send anyone to the auction in Loving to sell Judge Sweeney's sheep?"

"I sure did. They should be on their way back home soon. I

told Barlow to call the office and fill us in before they leave town. I'll check in as soon as we finish lunch to see if we got word yet."

"Can you think of anything we haven't covered?"

"Yes. I want my guys to meet your guys so they can lay eyes on each other and see what type of vehicle each will be driving. We need to do that someplace close by here that's relatively private. You and I need to make assignments. I suggest we station units along the route but out of direct line of sight of motorists, so we can leapfrog from a distance if need be.

"Everyone has to have a sting callsign, something like a CB handle, and everyone has to know where everyone else will be when we begin this shindig. Commo will be our biggest problem. Sooner or later, folks are going to be operating incommunicado, at least for awhile, and they need to know where to go or what to do when this happens."

"Let's work this out at my office as soon as we eat."

"That's a big 10-4."

When they arrived at the office, Sol placed a call to his own office. Miss Loretta answered. He got straight to the point, Sheriff Sol style.

"Hey, Loretta, how's everything going?"

"Okay, I guess. Want to talk to Chief?"

"Just okay? Not hunky dory?"

"It would have been if that grouchy old Mr. LaRue Dinkins hadn't showed up first thing this morning raising Cain over the CB radios."

"What did he say?"

"He said we already have police radios and that this would put us over budget. He said you haven't heard the end of this. Then he stomped out of the office."

"I'm so sorry. I'll take care of this tomorrow. If he ever does anything like this again, tell him you are not authorized to speak with him and he will have to talk to me or Chief Alex. If he won't back off, just get up and go to the ladies room. Don't return until you're sure he's gone. Okay?"

"Okay.

"Heard anything from Barlow yet?"

"Not so far."

"Anyone from Pluto call?"

"No, Sir. I know what to say if they do call. Are you coming back to the jail?"

"Not yet. I'll be at Sheriff Waters' office the rest of the afternoon. Call me there if you hear anything. Oh, yeah, call me before you leave for the day. If I'm already on my way back, they'll let you know."

"Will do. Talk to you later."

CHAPTER 42
Tuesday, March 31, 1970
Barlow's First Undercover Assignment

B arlow had no trouble waking up at 2 o'clock for today's assignment. He put on a pair of dirty jeans and a sweat-soiled shirt, his blue jean jacket, and his old, worn out 3X Stetson with all the sweat stains. He wore his Buck knife on his belt.

He made some peanut butter sandwiches for lunch and put them in his Army surplus pack along with some apples, a box of Crackerjacks, his revolver, spare ammo pouch, and his badge which he hid in a pair of rolled up socks. He filled a canteen with water and his thermos with steaming coffee.

He really wanted to take Happy to help herd the sheep but the chance was too great that he might be recognized in Loving, so Happy remained at home, unaware of just how close he came to an exciting day doing what he was trained and loved to do.

Barlow was five minutes early meeting Rico, thus embarrassed that he was really ten minutes late. He had expected to help load the sheep into the trailer but Rico and his dog, Viajero, meaning Traveler, had already accomplished that task. They were sitting in the cab. Rico was patiently puffing away on a self-rolled smoke while Viajero looked out the passenger window, wagging his tail. Barlow brought his gear and jumped in. At 0300 hours they were 10-8 (in service), headed to the big adventure.

It took them five-and-a-half hours to get there. This included a halt in Pecos for refueling and a breakfast burrito at a bustling truck stop. It was a pleasant drive. Once they arrived, an auction lot employee showed Rico which corral to offload the sheep. Afterwards, Rico parked the empty rig and went into the office to make arrangements to auction the flock of sixty Rambouillet lambs which weighed between 90 and 100 pounds each.

It looked to be a busy day. Several other corrals were already occupied with flocks for sale and three more rigs arrived before the auction commenced at 10 o'clock. Prospective buyers browsed the merchandise, taking notes and asking questions. Barlow browsed too, trying to act like he was an old hand but looking more like an 'all growed up' Opie Taylor wandering around the Raleigh Zoo, just like Chief knew he would.

That didn't mean he failed in his mission. Au contraire, he was fabulously successful but not for the reasons he would have imagined. He thought he was a born natural for undercover work. Truth is, he didn't know what he didn't know. He was still a rookie, even if he did possess all the attributes of a good lawman except for one, that being experience.

Barlow had walked around the other corrals and examined all the sheep. There were some nice ones. He did not recognize many of the breeds but it didn't take a braniac to see that the Triple S lambs were bigger and fatter and looked better tended than any of the others. That's because they were.

He returned to the Triple S corral and was hanging over the fence, watching the sheep bleat and mill around as if they were dissatisfied with their current status in life, when an auction worker about his own age ambled over and rested his arms on the top rail next to Barlow. He lit up a smoke and asked, "Are these your sheep?"

"Oh, heck no. These belong to my boss. I'm just a hand."

"You come in with the Mex wearing the faded red vest?"

"Yep. I work on his crew at the Triple S."

"I don't remember seeing you here before."

"This is my first time here. I haven't been doing this for very long. I just got out of the Army."

"Where's the Triple S located at?"

"You ever heard of Quayle County, Texas? We're down on the border."

"Nope. Texas has too dern many counties to keep track of 'em all but I do know where the Mexican border is. How's come y'all drove all this way to auction?"

"Someone told the owner that sheep were fetching a better price here in Loving than they were in Pecos and some of the other places in Texas we go to, so he sent us up here to see if that's true."

"How much y'all been getting on the hoof down there?"

"I'm not sure. Maybe 14 or 15 cents per pound. You'd have to ask my boss to be certain."

"I believe you. You'll definitely do better here. You'll get at least 18 cents per pound, maybe even 20, for these Rambouillets. They're really fine. We don't see Rambouillets that often around here. Last time was maybe a couple weeks ago. Those dudes have Rambouillets but they also raise other breeds, Merinos, Hampshires, Dorpers and probably some I ain't seen."

"No kidding? What ranch is that? I didn't know anyone did that."

"Yeah, it's not done very often, at least around these parts but them dudes ain't from around here. I heard they're from Iowa or Illinois or someplace up north. Maybe they do things different up there."

"What? They moved all the way from Iowa to Loving? What on Earth for?"

"They're in Malaga, not here. I think they wildcat besides ranching. They may show up here today being as they ain't been here in a while. They're a couple o' nice fellas but they have an asshole who ramrods their ranch. Sometimes he comes instead of one of them. Wouldn't mind if I never saw him again. I can't figure why they'd keep an uppity, hotheaded dipshit like him on board. Carries a fancy switchblade he likes to flash around to scare folks. He may know sheep, but he don't know how to treat people."

"Do they have a big spread?"

"Nope. Not that big. A quarter-section I think, maybe a half, but it's got good grass and plenty of water, or so I heard. On the river. They call it the Half-Circle G. Kinda weird. Ever'one else is the circle this or circle that. None of 'em are half-circles. Why would you call yourself a half-circle?"

"That's really odd. Is it a whole family that up and moved here?"

"Nope. Just two brothers. They's twins, but I can tell 'em apart. Get this. One of 'em's a lefty and the other'n is a righty. I bet you never heard of that afore, have ya?"

"Nope. Have you actually seen them together at the same time or do you just know the difference because of which hand they favor?"

"They come together most of the time. The lefty is Jeff and the righty is Jerry. Jerry's just slightly bigger'n his brother. Also, he wears glasses to read. The other'n don't."

"Well I'll be. You really can tell 'em apart."

"Told ya so. Hey, ain't that your boss flagging you over?"

"Yep, I better go. Hey, my name's Barlow. Nice talkin' to ya. Hope we start coming up this way more often. What's your name?"

"They call me Curley on accounta I'm nearly bald and I'm only 23. Don't slow me down none getting poontang. I get my share. Real name's Edgar Evans. I'm Mr. Fix It around here. Anything needs fixin' I'm the one what does it. Nice talkin' to ya. Hope to see ya around, Barlow."

Barlow joined Rico. They watched the auction proceed. It took a few sessions but they finally figured it out. They started with the lowest grade sheep and proceeded to the best. The Triple S was last. They got 22 cents a pound. They had 60 lambs that grossed out at 5,820 pounds. That was over $1,200 minus the auction house expenses. That was at least $200 over what they could have expected in Pecos. Even after the fuel expenses they came way out ahead. Judge Sweeney would be pleased.

He was doubly pleased after he learned the results of Barlow's intelligence gathering mission.

CHAPTER 43
Wednesday, April 1, 1970
April Fool

Ring, ring, ring. Pause. Ring, ring, ring. Pause. Ring, ring, ring.

"Hello."

"May I speak with Mr. Donald Mallard, please?"

"Oh, he's not at home right now. He's out at a drill site. Could I take a message and have him call you back?"

"To whom am I speaking, please?"

"This is his brother."

"Is this Mr. Hugh Mallard?"

"Er . . . yes it is. Who's calling please?"

"This is Mrs. April Lundgren, your registered agent for Pluto and Gemini Enterprises."

"Oh, of course! Long time, no see. How are you doing?"

"Better than your brother, I suspect. Has he misplaced or lost or sold any of his heavy equipment recently?"

"Well, about a week ago someone made off with two of our, er his tractor trailer combinations. We made a report at the Reeves County, Texas Sheriff's Office where they were stolen, but we haven't heard anything yet. We figured they're probably in Mexico where you can buy and sell just about anything without papers. We'll probably never see them again."

"Did your brother file an insurance claim?"

"Not yet. We have a man checking around in the border towns of Mexico. We'd much rather have the trucks back if we can find them, than file a claim and have our insurance rates soar. We figured we'd give it a month and if we can't find them, then we'd file a claim."

"Well, maybe I have some good news then. I received a registered letter from a Texas sheriff's office which says they've recovered your equipment. It's dated March 26th. That was Thursday, I believe. It says you have thirty days from the date of the letter to pick up your trucks or they will be sold at a sheriff's auction. It also said towing and storage fees are accruing. Would you like for me to forward the letter to you at the Pluto office in Pecos?"

"No. The office has been closed since our trucks were stolen. Can you send it to me at the Gemini post office box in Loving?"

"Of course. Should I address it to your brother in care of you?"

"No. He's an authorized recipient there. Which sheriff's office sent the letter? Do you have an address or phone number or better yet, a point-of-contact?"

"Indeed, I do. It says to contact a Chief Deputy Alexander Snodgrass at the Quayle County Sheriff's Office, 1 East America Avenue, Mosby, Texas, telephone number 915-555-7653. The hours are nine to five."

"Thank you, Mrs. Lundgren. I will tell my brother as soon as he returns home today."

"Very well. Good day, Mr. Mallard."

"Good day, and thank you, Mrs. Lundgren."

The telephone receiver never left his hand. Jerry Gough dialed the Quayle County Sheriff's Office, impersonating his brother, Jeff.

"Sheriff's Office, Miss Youngblood speaking. How may I help you?"

"Have I dialed the Quayle County Sheriff's Office?"

"Yes. How may I help you?"

"May I speak with Chief Deputy Alexander Snodgrass, please? I'm calling long distance."

"Just a moment. I'll see if I can find him. Who shall I say is calling?"

"This is Donald Mallard, calling from New Mexico."

"Hold on while I find him."

Loretta pushed the button to hold the call and cradled the receiver. She said, "Chief, it's Donald Duck from New Mexico. He wishes to speak with you. Think he could get us any free passes to Disneyland?"

"Ha! Fat chance, although he definitely likes to play make believe."

He picked up the receiver. "Chief Snodgrass speaking. How may I help you?"

"Chief Snodgrass, this is Don Mallard, President of Pluto Incorporated. My registered agent informed me that you have recovered two of our tractor trailers which we reported stolen in Reeves County on March 24th."

"This is true."

"Thank you very much. When and where can we pick them up and how much do we owe?"

"You surprise me, Mr. Mallard. You never asked where we found them or if we arrested anyone. What do you all do to make a living at Pluto Incorporated, Mr. Mallard?"

"Pardon my manners, Chief. I was just so excited to learn you recovered our trucks. We've been sidelined since the trucks were stolen. Those are the only two tractors that we own. Pluto is an oil field service company, but we do a little wildcatting on the side. Please accept my apology. Where did you find them? Have you made any arrests?"

"Yes, Sir. We made one arrest. It was a Mexican boy who was driving one of the tractor trailers. His brother was driving the other one, but he didn't make it. The truck he was driving has some minor damage. Very minor. The truck is still drivable. Another Mexican, identity unknown, was also killed and a fourth Mexican got away back into Mexico. If you didn't guess by now, we recovered the trucks near the Mexican border. They were both loaded down with stolen sheep. I was wondering, why does an oil field servicing company have stock trailers?"

"Stolen sheep! Oh, my God! I can certainly understand your confusion. Both trucks and trailers, along with a half-dozen other trailers which are set up for oil field operations, all belong to my company. My brother has a small ranch. I bought the trailers at an auction for a song just in case he ever expanded enough to need them. Sorry to say he hasn't reached that point yet. I probably ought to sell them. I could double my money at a minimum."

"Well that explains it then. Do you have any idea how a gang of Mexican rustlers would target your company to steal tractor trailers?"

"The only thing I can think of is that the lot isn't fenced and Pecos has a large Mexican population. We never thought fencing was necessary. Too easy of a target, I suppose. Soon as we get back on our feet we'll have to fence it in. How soon did you say we could pick up the trucks? We need to get back to work."

"Well, that depends on you. Neither of the trucks nor the trailers have license plates. They also don't have any commercial motor vehicle stickers or markings. We'd be happy for you all to pick up your property at your earliest convenience, but before you do we need to see a police report of the theft, proof of ownership, titles as it were, registration certificates, license plates which you will have to install before you can drive off the lot, the charter for Pluto's incorporation since the rigs are owned by a corporation and not an individual, proof of insurance, a notarized letter signed by you as representative of Pluto Incorporated, indemnifying the Quayle County Sheriff's Office and the towing and storage facilities from any damages or loss of use of the equipment since it was stolen, and approximately $400 in cash for towing and storage fees. No checks. One other thing. If you are not personally picking up your property, we will need a notarized letter signed by you that the people who are picking up your equipment are legally authorized to do so. Also make sure whoever plans to drive the trucks has a CDL. Do you need me to repeat all that?"

"My goodness, Chief, the money is no issue, of course, but it could take a week or more to fulfill this list. Apparently the thieves threw away the license plates we had. This is distressing! I'm not sure how long it will take to replace them. Then you want the notarized statements and I don't have the time to drive to Quayle County to pick up the equipment myself. I'll have to hire somebody. Two somebodies. Three, just to transport them to the storage lot. I laid off all my employees when the trucks were stolen. We've been out of business. Is there no way we could minimize this process?"

"I'm afraid not. Those rigs are worth at least $60,000. We don't usually recover stolen property which is that valuable. Isn't your business located in Pecos? That's what NCIC indicated when we made our queries to determine if the vehicles were stolen."

"NCIC?"

"That's the FBI's National Crime Information Center. It's the system law enforcement agencies use to report stolen or recovered property or to request wanted checks on subjects. Things like that."

"Of course."

"Well, things aren't so bad as you might think. DMV has an office in Pecos. I'm sure you know that already. Take your registration certificates for your stolen vehicles and a copy of your police report to them and you will be able to obtain new registrations right there at home. Also, your vehicles are stored in Alpine, not in Quayle County, because we don't have a secure storage lot big enough to accommodate them. That's only a hundred miles from you. Assuming you have a corporate lawyer, you could get your documentation done in a day. If you're really in a hurry, you could make an appointment and pick up your equipment on Friday. The storage lot is closed on weekends. That's the best I can do. The rest is up to you, Mr. Mallard."

"Well, let me see how quickly we can get this all together. My biggest problem is getting my employees rounded up. Do we really have to make an appointment just to pick up our trucks? Don't they have people on the lot? Where are they located, anyway?"

"Yes, you need an appointment. This isn't like picking up a car that was ticketed and towed for illegal parking. The wrecker company has to follow the procedures to the letter of the law on all stolen vehicles. Your rigs are stored at Barrymore's Wrecker and Towing Service at 1115 West Main Street in Alpine. They're open Monday through Friday, 8 to 6, to pick up vehicles. They're open anytime for the police, or anyone really, who needs a vehicle towed. Any other questions?"

"I suppose not. I will call the wrecker service tomorrow if we get our paperwork together. Otherwise, I guess it will have to be sometime next week. Damn!"

"Well good luck, Mr. Mallard. Make sure all your paperwork is in order so you all don't make the trip for nothing. Call me before you go if you want to double check before you send your men all that distance."

"Are you available after hours?"

"Yes, Sir. The sheriff's office is open everyday, 24 hours, except on Sunday. Then we have an answering service. If you need me, call and someone will track me down and I will call you back."

"Well, hopefully it won't be necessary past normal business hours. Thank you."

"You're welcome. Good day."

CHAPTER 44
Wednesday, April 1, 1970
Sol Catches a Break

Sheriff Sol walked in while Chief was still on the phone. He stood in the wings eavesdropping. As soon as Chief hung up, he asked, "What do you think?"

"I think Mr. Donald Mallard is one charming, slick, lying son of a bitch."

"Think he's involved?"

"Oh, heck yeah, along with his brother. He's got himself in a real trick box, too. First, he needs to get two documents notarized while signing a fictitious name. That's two felonies. Second, he needs two CDL operators he can trust. Third, it's clear they're short on money, so he needs to put this together as soon as he can. Maybe that will motivate Humberto Pavón to rustle the M Slash F on their way back home."

"That's assuming Pavón is one of the guys he sends."

"Roger that. We need to keep our fingers crossed. By the way, have you received a call from Ranger Sergeant Taylor yet?"

"Nope. I figured he would call for you. Guess I better track him down then. We have to be ready by Friday. If I can get ahold of him, I'm thinking about asking him to do a discreet check on the Pluto office in Pecos tomorrow just to see if there's any sign of activity there, and then go on up to Malaga and check out that campground. We need to get our guys up there not later than Friday afternoon."

"You and Leland work out the staffing details?"

"We did. I'm leaving Arch back on mids. Ern's got days. Randy's on afternoons. Dewey's doing the u/c at the tow lot. I'm sending Slick and Barlow to the campground with Sergeant

Taylor. I'll be up there with them waiting for a call that they took the bait. That leaves Kirk and Chunk positioned along the route with you to call the shots coming out of Alpine. Also, Dewey can join the surveillance when he's done. Just make sure he's nowhere near the M Slash F.

"Roger that. What about Brewster?"

"Leland's planning to ramrod from the south like you, except he will start at the M Slash F along with Chief Pruitt to eyeball the rustling. However, Pruitt will remain in Alpine to hold down the fort, assuming of course, that they take the bait. Avery will back up Dewey at the tow lot and be his counterpart in the surveillance. Leland's got a deputy named Francisco Rojas, otherwise known as Pancho the Honcho, to be Kirk's counterpart, and one named Cody Carr to be Chunk's counterpart. He's sending Ralphie Camacho and Dirk Melançon up to the campground. He said he could spare a few more deputies if we needed but I said we probably had more than enough."

"Well that sounds like plenty to me. That's eight units for the surveillance. We shouldn't have to leapfrog more than once."

"I would hope not at all. Look, I'll use the campground crew as a stationary surveillance at the turnoff onto Highway 132 and also at the entrance to the ranch. That second team will be on horseback. That way we never lose sight of the sheep door-to-door. Whoever has the eyeball coming up to 132 needs to continue northbound. The team stationed at 132 will remain in place just in case they surprise us and decide to leave early. The rest of us will powwow at the campground for final instructions with Eddy County before the raid at daylight.

"This entire mobile surveillance is on a lonely stretch of road, especially at three or four in the morning. It better not look like the Veterans Day parade or we'll get burned and could be forced to do a vehicle stop. Then we lose the Gough brothers. Also, we've already had one running gunfight with rustlers and besides being lucky that none of our guys got hurt, we were in our own county. It would be a real stretch of credulity to try to purport this as an arrest outside our jurisdiction because we were in hot pursuit."

"Roger that. Brewster only has jurisdiction for the first ten miles or so. Are you sure you don't want to put Sergeant Taylor in the mobile surveillance? At least he has jurisdiction until we cross into New Mexico."

"Good point. Agreed. I'll put him in your group. Guess I better call Sheriff Elliott up in Eddy County and bring him on board. I'll let you know what he says."

"Roger that. Good luck."

Sheriff Sol went back to his office and made the call. Fortunately, the Sheriff of Eddy County was in residence and taking calls.

"Sheriff Elliott speaking."

"Dan, this is Sheriff Sol Pratt from Quayle County, Texas. Remember me from the Border Patrol conference a couple of years back?"

"I sure do, you old hound dog. It's been a long time. How the hell are ya?"

"About the same. Maybe a few pounds heavier with a few more grey hairs now. How about yourself?"

"Just peachy. Hell, at least you still have hair. The more I lose on top of my head, the more I grow on my ass and out of my ears. What can I do for ya?"

"It seems that Brewster County and I have a sheep rustling problem, and . . . ."

"Let me guess. You think the Loving Livestock Auction Yard is receiving and selling stolen livestock."

"What makes you say that?"

"I had another Texas sheriff with those very same suspicions call me right around a month ago. He was probably right, too. A spread in his county got rustled for about 140 Dorper lambs. We don't have many of that breed in this area."

"The Lazy J in Winkler County, right?"

"Right as rain. We checked at the stockyard and initially they claimed they hadn't auctioned any Dorpers in months and months. We threatened to get a search warrant, so they went through the motions of making an exhaustive review of all their records. Finally, they claimed that the clerk who logged in the sale of 131 Dorpers mistakenly listed them as Merinos. That was a crock of shit but we played along. Hell! The receiving clerk is always the owner or his son!

"The purchaser was a slaughter house in Las Cruces. Dead end there. The seller was this startup ranch on Hwy 132. We went out there. The owners had recently relocated here from Iowa. They confirmed the sale. Said they got the sheep from a relative in Iowa who was unhappy with that breed because they don't do well in that climate. They showed us a bill of sale that could have been dummied up but we called the relative and he confirmed it. That still don't prove a thing but we didn't have any proof otherwise, so we closed the investigation.

"The sellers seemed legit. Nice guys. One of 'em has an oil field service company. We checked. They've done some work in Hobbs. They were cooperative but the stockyard was just a little too reluctant to cooperate with law enforcement. I've had my eye on them ever since then. I even got a CI (confidential informant) who spends a substantial amount of time there trying to make a few bucks by making himself useful, but we don't have any proof of chicanery. Nada. So do you or don't you have suspicions about the stockyard?"

"Well, yes and no. We do believe they've sold rustled sheep but can't say with any degree of certainty that the stockyard was collusive. It wouldn't surprise me though, and maybe if what I'm about to ask of you bears fruit, other information that I have may help you to prove your suspicions."

"You have my absolute, undivided attention."

"Sheriff, I'm working a joint investigation with the Brewster County SO regarding ten known sheep rustlings in the Trans-Pecos region in Texas. One of them was the Lazy J in Winkler County that you already know about. Three were in my county and one was in Brewster.

"So far as I know, this group hasn't victimized ranchers in New Mexico. We're pretty sure the gang is headed up by the Gough twins in Malaga. We're setting a trap to catch them but we need your help. If our plan bears fruit, they'll hit a ranch in Brewster County very soon. We plan to tail them back home to the Half-Circle G. We'd like to work this jointly with you but you'd have to cross-designate us as special deputies in Eddy County. Are you good with that?"

"So far. That would mean we'd get the bust. Are you all comfortable with that?"

"We are. We've even discussed it with the DA. Believe me. There will be plenty of satisfaction and bragging rights to go around. Do you know Sheriff Leland Waters from Brewster?"

"No. I haven't had the pleasure."

"He was the first to get a complaint from a victim rancher so far as I know. He notified a half-dozen or so sheriffs from adjacent counties to include me. That's when we discovered that the largest ranch in our county had been hit twice. We set up on it and about a week later the rustlers hit him again. We had hoped to take them alive but we got in a shootout and a couple of running gun battles. We killed two of the rustlers, arrested one, and the other one escaped into Mexico."

"How does that tie in with the Gough brothers?"

"Well, we already knew two of the rustlers. They're brothers. Originally, they hailed from Quayle County but they moved a few years ago to Pecos. We killed one and captured the other. More about them later if you're interested.

"We finally identified the other dead bandit. He was originally from Otero County. A real bad boy. His true name is

Cesar Oso, but he's been working for one of the Gough brothers using the alias name Juan Rodríguez."

"I know that son of a bitch! I didn't know he was dead. Good riddance!"

"Ditto. The Gough brothers know he's dead, I'm sure, but they're not asking any questions. The rustler who got away knows it too because he was there side by side with Oso, exchanging shots with my deputies. It took some digging but we finally identified that scoundrel via photo array identifications by two of my deputies, a ranch hand, and the other surviving bandit.

"This particular rabbit turd hails from Eddy County, originally. Mrs. Phyllis Rafferty and Deputy Cletus Knebel from your shop were both instrumental in helping us to identify him."

"Who is he?"

"His name is Humberto Pavón. Our survivor and an unwitting informant only know him by the monicker, El Jefe."

"I haven't heard Humberto Pavón's name in years! The last I knew he was serving time in the state pen for aggravated assault or attempted murder in some barroom scuffle. Is that piece of shit really back in my county? He's worse than an infestation of cockroaches in a five-star restaurant!"

"I don't think so, but I'm not 100 percent sure. Pavón runs Jeff Gough's oil field service company, Pluto Inc., from an office in Pecos. Right now he's in the wind but I bet old Jeff will reel him in for us."

"Son of a bitch! Just tell me what you want. I'm all in."

"Jeff called my office a little while ago in response to a registered letter we sent informing Pluto that we recovered two of their tractor trailer rigs which were used to rustle sheep. We didn't mention the rustling part in the letter. Long story short, we have the rigs at a lot in Alpine. Jeff is hustling to get new license plates and proof of insurance, etc., so we will release the trucks back to his company.

"When he does, we'll have a u/c casually mention that a

nearby ranch has a truckload of sheep looking for a ride to the auction in Pecos. We have a friendly rancher who set aside sixty sheep which he's marked for identification. If they take the bait, we have a staggered motor surveillance set up to follow them back to the Half-Circle G. We plan to stage some deputies in the campground just north of them and do a coordinated raid from the north and south in the morning during daylight hours."

"Heck, Sol, if this works the way you've planned it, Eddy County gets all the arrests after Quayle and Brewster Counties suffered most of the losses and did 99 percent of the work."

"We're not walking away empty-handed, Dan. You will have the bodies and first dibs on prosecution, but eight Texas counties can file indictments too, and collectively we can pretty well insure that the culprits won't draw a breath of air as free men for years and years to come. In fact in Texas, assuming that all the counties agree, we could probably consolidate our prosecutions into one. Saves everyone money trying the cases, assuming they don't cop pleas anyway to get a sweeter deal."

"How do you maintain jurisdiction in the three or four counties you traverse in Texas before you arrive in New Mexico?"

"We've got a Texas Ranger lined up."

"Who?"

"Sergeant Winfield Taylor the Third."

"You mean Trey."

"Yes. I haven't met him yet but everyone who knows him sings his praises."

"I know him. You will, too."

"That's what they all say."

"Have you been to the Pecos River KOA campground yet?"

"No. I was going to ask Trey to check it out for us."

"Not necessary. I'll take care of it. How many of you will be staying there?"

"Brewster will have two and we'll have two, plus Trey most likely."

"Better bring horses because that's what that campground is all about. Anything else would smell fishy. I'll line it up. Save Trey the trip."

"Thanks."

"Call me as soon as you know something. I'll deputize your guys at the campground."

"Will do."

The next call was to the Texas Rangers office in El Paso. The receptionist stated that Ranger Taylor was headed to the Quayle County Sheriff's Office and that he would be out all day. She offered to take a message. He told her that wouldn't be necessary.

Perfect! Better to meet each other face-to-face anyway.

CHAPTER 45
Wednesday, April 1, 1970
Sergeant Winfield "Trey" Taylor III, Texas Ranger

Trey Taylor strolled into the Quayle County Sheriff's Office at 11:30. Miss Loretta ushered him straight into Sheriff Sol's office. She never uttered a word. She was stunned and blushing like a bride-to-be. She looked like she might catch the vapors.

Trey looked less than 30 years old but had to be at least 35 to have been a Korean War veteran. He stood 6'2" tall and weighed about 185 pounds. He had a narrow waist, small hips, and broad shoulders. His hair was as blond as straw. He had intense blue eyes the color of a cloudless sky on a crisp, autumn day. His teeth were even and pearly white. His skin was taut and weatherburned. In short, he was stunningly handsome like an Aryan god.

He was wearing western cut khaki trousers, a long sleeve, western-style, white dress shirt with mother of pearl snap buttons, highly polished, brown Tony Lama boots, a beige Stetson, and a brown, tooled, El Paso Saddlery gun belt filled with brass .45 Long Colt caliber cartridges. His six-inch barreled Peacemaker was in a right cross-draw holster. He wore a bone handled sheath knife with a seven-inch blade on his right. The small silver star circumscribed by a circle, identifying him as a Texas Ranger, was pinned on the left side of his shirt.

He looked to be every bit of what each Texas lawman wished to be.

He walked up to Sheriff Sol's desk and said, "Sergeant Trey Winfield at your service, Sheriff."

Sol stood up. They gave one another a firm handshake, all the while maintaining steady eye contact, searching for clues regarding the grit in the other man's craw. Satisfied that the other man would stand and fight, they broke off the shake and the stare and grinned at each other like kids who had just robbed the cookie jar and gotten away with it.

Sol said, "Sergeant, please have a seat. I'm pleased to finally make your acquaintance. I've heard nothing but good things about you. Light up if you have a mind." With that, Sol pulled out a pack of Lucky Strikes, shook out a couple of smokes, and offered one to the ranger.

"Please call me Trey, Sheriff. Everyone else does. Thanks. If you don't mind, I've got the makin's and I'll roll my own."

Sol nodded and sat down. He struck a match to light his own smoke. Trey fished the makings out of a shirt pocket, rolled a tight cigarette, and lit up. They puffed for a minute before speaking.

Finally, Trey said, "Sheriff, I remember you from the UTEP (University of Texas at El Paso) football team. You were one helluva center. You really anchored that front line."

"Gosh. That was many eons ago. Did you go to UTEP?"

"I did after I got out of the Navy. I wasn't a ballplayer, though. That was during my rodeo phase. I made the team but wasn't one of the marquee riders. Ate a lot of dust and didn't bring home many belt buckles. I gave it up after I graduated. Joined EPSO. Couldn't go on the PD because my dad was a captain there. Nepotism and all that."

"I understand it all too well. Did anyone fill you in on our little project?"

"Not really. Let's just say that a certain state senator phoned Colonel Speir, who called my captain, and here I am. The word is that you didn't want outside interference but you got it anyway. Makes me wonder, has anyone from the Rangers stepped on your toes?"

"Oh, heck no. The only one I met before today is Ranger McCallister and I barely know him. We don't get many cases worthy of note here in Quayle County, so we haven't had much contact with you all. McCallister left a good impression but this case is very near and dear to me and I don't want to relinquish the reins to the state. No offense. I have nothing but respect for the Rangers."

"None taken. We all know about how your office broke the back of the El Diablos a few months back. Nobody had ever been able to do that. Quayle SO soared to new heights in esteem within the Texas law enforcement community after that dust up. I know for sure that the Rangers were duly impressed."

"Glad to hear it but truth be known, it was all due to one of our rookie deputies who's probably an unknown descendant of Wyatt Earp. They seem to have the same genetic makeup as far as law enforcement goes, anyway. Now I have to worry that someday you all will scoop him up and leave Quayle County the poorer for it. You know what they say. 'One riot. One ranger.' In that scenario, it was one deputy. Five dead outlaw bikers. Same same."

"Oh, you never know. I heard he's pretty interested in one of Quayle County's charming and most beautiful damsels. He might prefer to stay here with family and friends. He could do a whole lot worse. The grass isn't always greener on the other side of the fence."

"This is true. I guess time will tell.

"Trey, getting down to business, we really do need your help and we're very pleased to have you on board. Did you hear about the shootout we had with rustlers down at Judge Sweeney's ranch?"

"Who didn't? When's the last time someone had a shootout on horseback with rustlers? Fifty, sixty years ago? What I haven't heard about is where you've taken this case. I understand that one of the bastards got away."

"One did. We've taken the case to New Mexico."

"You don't say! Which county?"

"Eddy."

"No problemo. Sheriff Elliott is a stand-up guy and he plays well with others."

"That's my impression, too. In fact, I just got off the phone with him."

"Problem solved. What's the op?"

"Twin brothers named Gough in Malaga, originally from Iowa, control the operation from their ranch. They have spotless records and appear to be legitimate businessmen. Apparently they are well received in the community.

"Since January, they've rustled sheep from ranches in eight different counties in the Trans-Pecos region of Texas that we have identified. They hit Judge Sweeney three times. Understand that the brothers didn't go out on any of the jobs, but they did personally auction the sheep at the Loving stockyard.

"The last time they hit Judge Sweeney, we caught the least culpable rustler, killed two, and one got away. It's doubtful we'll ever have proof beyond a reasonable doubt that the sheep the Gough brothers sold were stolen. None of 'em have serial numbers and how would a rancher positively identify his own sheep, which by now have probably already been butchered? That being said, we did work out another way to nail 'em."

"How so?"

"Well, we identified the one in the wind as Humberto Pavón, a bad hombre from Eddy County. Did time in New Mexico for an agg assault which was really an attempted murder. He's also the one who initiated the fireworks at Judge Sweeney's. He's got more lives than a cat. At least a dozen shots were fired at him and he didn't suffer a scratch."

"Dang!"

"We hope he shows up at our little sting.

"One of the ranches rustled was in Brewster County. Quayle's case is being prosecuted there because Judge Sweeney was a victim."

"Makes sense."

"You know Sheriff Leland Waters?"

"Oh hell yeah! A great guy."

"Good. We've been working this case together. The two eighteen-wheelers we seized belong to the twins in Malaga, known as Donald and Huey Mallard as far as their corporations are concerned, but otherwise identified as Jeff and Jerry Gough.

"We're storing their trucks in Alpine instead of Mosby because they got away clean in Brewster. They'll probably feel safer there than here. We have a friendly rancher outside Alpine who agreed to pen up sixty marked sheep for the rustlers to steal."

"Sweet."

"My chief spoke with Jeff Gough today. Alex told him they can pick up their trucks in Alpine, so long as their paperwork is in order and they pay the towing and storage fees. We're making them jump through barrel hoops as far as the paperwork is concerned to give us time to set up a surveillance from Alpine to Malaga. Chief told Jeff he'd have to make an appointment to get their trucks back.

"We've got an undercover posing as the storage lot attendant, who will casually mention that a rancher north of Alpine has a flock of sheep penned up while he's waiting for a carrier to transport them to the auction in Pecos. If they take the bait, we'll follow them home and raid their ranch after they arrive, but during daylight hours. Sheriff Elliott will swear us all in as special deputies. Collectively we will all make the raid.

"Dan gets to keep the prisoners but all the victim counties in Texas will have a chance to pile on, assuming their DA's believe they have irrefutable proof. Right now, I believe that we're the only one who does, at least as far as Humberto Pavón is concerned, because we caught him redhanded and we recovered the sheep. Nevertheless that's a DA decision, not mine.

"We need you in the surveillance in the event they get wise and we have to make an arrest en route to the ranch."

"No wonder you're so protective of this case. I would be, too. I'm honored to be included."

"Good. Did you bring a horse?"

"You mean I get to participate in the raid on horseback?"

"I do."

"Will you be on horseback, too?"

"Trey, I may be a half-blood Apache, but the only horses I care about are the 330 under the hood of my Plymouth Fury. They're a sight less temperamental and they don't shit on my grass."

"Ha! Well, I didn't bring one but I know I can borrow one from Sheriff Elliott, if need be. When do we start?"

"Glad you asked. If you have the time and you're here in a plain brown wrapper, it would help tremendously if you could discreetly check on Jeff Gough's business, Pluto Incorporated, located at 510 Carter Street in Pecos. That's where Humberto Pavón was hanging his hat prior to the shootout. Chief'll show you his mugshot. Jeff claims they closed shop but we'd like to know for sure.

"Then, if Jeff gets his paperwork together tomorrow, he should call to make an appointment to pick up his trucks. We'll set it up for Friday afternoon so they won't have to sit on their thumbs so long waiting for it to get dark.

"If he doesn't call, it will push us back until Monday at the earliest. Either way, I'd like to do a full briefing in Alpine at some remote site Leland has in mind, probably sometime tomorrow afternoon."

"10-4. I'm leaving for Pecos soon as I see the mugshot. My unit is an unmarked, white Ford Bronco. I'll call here tomorrow for further details."

"Got time for lunch first? I'm buying."

"Appreciate it, but I'll pick up something in Pecos. I want to get home tonight and pack some clothes and fetch my own horse. I want a stable shooting platform for the raid."

"Roger that. Thanks, Trey. We look forward to working with you."

"Ditto. Bye."

CHAPTER 46
Wednesday, April 1, 1970
Humberto Returns

Ring, ring, ring.

"Hello."

"It's me, Jefe. Checking in."

"Where are you?"

"Visiting a lady friend."

"Where?"

"Kermit."

"Good. We're going back to work beginning today. Put your dick back in your pants and get to the office now. What are you driving?"

"What else? That piece of shit truck I bought from my cousin. I need some dinero."

"We all need some dinero. You're back on the clock today. We got a lot of stuff to do. Did you scout any ranches during your time off?"

"No. Scouting requires gas. I've been laid off going on two weeks now. Remember?"

"Didn't you have some places you tucked away on hold?"

"One. In Upton County, but I'd need to check it out again to be sure."

"Okay. Look. The cops have our rigs in storage in Alpine. We can pick them up Friday if we get our paperwork together. We gotta get new license plates for both the trucks and the trailers. I can take care of that. Do you know anyone you can trust to take Juan's place? He's gotta have a CDL."

"Why are the trucks in Alpine? That's in Brewster County. They got seized in Mosby. That's in Quayle County."

"Careful, Berto. Did you forget who's the real El Jefe in our little arrangement?"

"No, Señor Jeff, but I wasn't sure you knew what towns were in which counties since you haven't lived here for very long. Besides, these are in Texas."

"Well, I did my homework. They're in Alpine because that dog trot in Mayberry R.F.D. didn't have a storage lot big enough. That saves us a few miles, plus nobody in Alpine should recognize you, should they?"

"No, Jefe, but Señor, I don't trust anyone locally like I did Juan. There are plenty of sheepherders and some have CDL's but they aren't outlaws. They won't stand and fight, plus they'd probably rat me out if I approached them with the same proposition I made with Rudy and Chico.

"Rudy is dead but Chico is in jail and I'm sure he ratted me out. He doesn't know my name but he does know my face. He also knows where I work and it would not be a stretch to think that the cops in Quayle County know my name and are looking for me. That is why I would not wish to be a CDL driver to pick up the trucks."

"Then get me somebody to do it for you, just for this one thing. We're not going out on a job. All we're doing is picking up our trucks. You can be the third driver who isn't driving a rig. You can even drop us off and wait down the street if you're wigged out."

"Señor, Juan had all the contacts with ranch hands. Not me. He was looking for somebody to replace that cabrón Rudy. Rudy had too many big ideas. He was untrustworthy. Chico was perfect because we scared him shitless. Juan mentioned some scaredy-cat who works at the auction who has a CDL. His name is Curley, I think. He thought we might try him out some night. I never been to the auction house. I don't know this dude. He might work out if all you want to do is pick up the trucks."

"I know Curley and you're right. He might work out. Don't

you have a cousin in Malaga who could do this?"

"My cousins in Malaga are all pendejos. I don't trust none of them. I got some cousins in Ojinaga that I do trust but they ain't got no CDL. Some of them would be real good for the nighttime work. They know sheep and everything. They will fight to the death like Juan. I trust them but they cannot do what you need on this trip."

"Very well. I will talk to Curley. Get all the truck papers ready so we can get some new license plates. I will see you there in about two hours."

"Sí, Señor. I will be ready."

CHAPTER 47
Wednesday, April 1, 1970
Curley Checks In

Curley left work on time at 2 o'clock. He drove straight to the Eddy County Courthouse in Carlsbad. He parked two blocks away outside the Green Toad Tavern. He checked again and again for a tail. So far, so good. This was serious. He was on 007 business.

He ran up the steps to the sheriff's office. He asked for Deputy Norman Rubio, one of the detectives, but he was out on an assignment. The receptionist offered to have another detective come out to talk to him, but he had no faith that someone he had never talked to would take him seriously, so he asked to speak with the sheriff. He said it was urgent.

She asked for his name. He said it was confidential. She persisted. So did he. Finally she picked up the receiver and dialed a number. Then she hung up. A minute later Sheriff Elliott walked in. He took one look at Curley and said, "Rita, thanks for taking good care of this gentleman. Could you get us a couple of RC's and bring them to the VIP conference room?"

"Sure thing, Sheriff."

The sheriff ushered him into a small conference room. They sat across from each other and lit up. Rita brought the Royal Crown Colas and left the room.

"This must be awfully important for you to come here."

"It is, Sheriff. Do you know what Deputy Rubio asked me to do?"

"He asked you to keep an eye out at the stockyards for any signs of stolen livestock being sold. He also said this was an important mission and that you should be extremely careful since rustlers tend to be violent men. Is that about it?"

"Yes, Sir. Today something suspicious happened and I might be in trouble."

"For goodness sakes! What happened?"

"Do you know those twin ranchers named Mr. Jerry and Mr. Jeff Gough of the Half-Circle G? They used to have this thug named Juan working for him but I haven't seen him for awhile."

"I do."

"Well a little while ago Mr. Jeff stopped by. The auctions were wrapping up and he didn't bring any sheep. In fact, he drove up in his Jeep."

"What color's his Jeep?"

"It's white. The top is black."

"Okay."

"Well, he didn't have no business with the auction. He was lookin' for me. He said Juan took off a couple of weeks ago and they ain't seen him since. He also said someone stole his big rigs but the cops recovered them and they're down in Texas at Alpine. He said Juan told him that I have a CDL."

"Well, do ya?"

"Yep, but I ain't ever had a real paying job hauling stuff on accounta I'm not real good at it yet. I barely passed the backin' up part of the drivin' test. I've driven some stock trucks on short hauls for a few bucks on the side, but that's it.

"So I told him I did, but I wasn't no expert driver yet. He said that didn't make no never mind 'cause all he needed me to do was to go with him and some other fella to Alpine to pick up his trucks. He said they'd probably drive down Friday and pick 'em up. He said he'd pay me $50 for my time if I could get off from work."

"So what did you say?"

"Well, Sheriff, I don't make $75 a week. I told him I'd do it but then I got to thinkin'. What if he's gonna rope-a-dope me inta some kinda rustling scheme? Mr. Jeff and Mr. Jerry seem like nice guys, but they let Juan work for them and live on their ranch in a room they set up in the barn just for him. I wouldn't put nothin' past that asshole, even murder. What if Juan's actually the other fella but he didn't tell me on accounta Juan saying I wouldn't take the job if I knew he was involved?"

"Well, I think he's telling you true that Juan doesn't work for him anymore. Sounds like he's really in a jam and all he needs is a licensed CDL driver to do this one-time job for which he's willing to pay twice the going rate.

"You ride down with Mr. Jeff and another fella. That's a hundred miles. Maybe two hours. Go to the tow lot. Show them your CDL. Another hour. Drive the truck back to the Half-Circle G. Two more hours. Collect $50. Sounds pretty straightforward to me.

"Did he ask you to bring a gun or be prepared to fight or speed or anything that sounded crooked?"

"No. Not when you put it like that."

"Well, I tell you what. I really appreciate you coming to see me. I'm curious about this. Unless you're just too leery and you've changed your mind, I'd say take the job and earn the money. At the same time, it is possible that this is a crooked operation.

"If you do decide to go, I guarantee you this. If they plan to rustle a ranch, just do what they tell you short of shooting someone. Don't take a gun and don't let them give you a gun. Tell them you're afraid of guns if it comes to that. I couldn't imagine that it would. Then, when you get back, call my office and tell me everything. I'll protect you from prosecution if you get arrested, even in Texas. Understand? If the cops pull you over, do everything they tell you and keep your mouth shut until they give you your phone call. For heaven's sake, do not let the others know you've spoken to me. They might try to take it out on you.

"Can you do that? If you can't, tell me now. It's okay. Nobody would think the less if you. Either way, I appreciate you coming to see me. In fact, here's $10 for gas money."

"Thanks. I can do this, Sheriff. Just do what they say. Keep my mouth shut. Maybe this is just picking up the trucks. Maybe it isn't."

"That's right. One last thing. Would you call me when you find out when they want you to go? By the way, before I forget, did Deputy Rubio give you a code name?"

"I'll call. No. I ain't got no code name."

"Pick one. When you call, give them your code name. Whoever answers will take your message, even a collect phone call if you are in jail in Texas, and I will respond ASAP. You know what that means?"

"Yes, Sir. Cobra. My code name is Cobra. Cobras are deadlier than rattlesnakes. That's me."

"Cobra it is. Be safe. Call me when you know something. Adiós, Cobra."

"Adiós, Sheriff."

CHAPTER 48
Thursday, April 2, 1970
Final Briefing

It was 3 o'clock. Everyone from the Brewster and Quayle County Sheriffs' Offices who were part of the sting plus one Texas Ranger were assembled in the back lot of the Brewster County Rodeo Grounds. Each officer knew what his assignment would be before he arrived, to allow those with assignments on horseback to head north as soon as the briefing was concluded.

This included Ranger Taylor, who convinced Sheriff Sol to leave him on the campground horseback team and to remove him from the highway surveillance team. This did not please Chief Alex but Trey promised to come screaming south if they were compelled to make a traffic stop. In the end, Sheriff Sol and Sheriff Waters decided that they would not make any traffic stop outside of Brewster County. After all, where could the rustlers go? Once they began driving rustled sheep they were screwed wherever they stopped.

Everyone had an instruction sheet with a roster and call signs for the CB radios, which were tuned to Channel 4, with the trucker channel, number 19, to be used if all else failed. Both departments were tuned to Frequency 2, the statewide band, if they were in a departmental unit. This briefing was a fine tuning before they separated and inevitably lost contact with each other. You know, Murphy's Law: 'Anything that can go wrong will go wrong.'

Sheriff Waters introduced Sheriff Pratt. Sol stood in the back of one of the pickup trucks so everyone could see him. With his size that was't much of a problem and neither was hearing him. "Gentlemen, smoke 'em if you've got 'em.

"The kickoff at Barrymore's is scheduled for this time tomorrow. If they take the bait they will have beaucoup time to kill, so if you're in town, lay low. We don't want to get burned before we get started.

"You all know the plan and what your particular assignments are. This get together is so you can lay eyes on one another, put names to faces of those you don't know, and identify the vehicles everyone is driving. It will be difficult to tell in the dark, so take a good look now.

"Stay off the radio unless what you have to report needs to be put out over the air. Think before speaking. Anyone can listen in on a CB and lots of folks have scanners. We don't want our targets, Bugs Bunny, Elmer Fudd, Daffy Duck, or his twin brother, Huey Duck, to get tipped off. Remember, Bugs Bunny is an unwitting informant. If you have contact with him, do not shoot or beat the shit out of him. Elmer Fudd is a known shooter. He shot it out with us the last time we saw him. Put him down fast if he draws a gun. Daffy Duck and Huey Duck are both unknown quantities. Treat them like you would any other criminal suspect.

"For those of you in the surveillance along Highways 118, 17, and 285, park as far off the highway as you can but still see the road with your lights off. That includes interior lights, too. Turn your engines off. Cover up your smokes. Stay awake and keep your ears on. Be invisible.

"We expect to have a motorcade with two rigs and one sedan or pickup. Who knows in which order? As soon as we know what the third unit is, we'll pass it along. At that time of night, it's doubtful you will see anyone else on the highway, at least not traveling together. When you do see it, put it out over the air. Hopefully somebody will be able to hear you. Give it a few minutes for the units who are already following time to pass. Then turn on your lights and fall into succession.

"Remember, we will have an Eddy County SO unit standing

by at Highway 132 and horseback officers watching the front gate of the target location, otherwise known as Hollywood. Just keep going north when you pass 132 and head to the KOA. Eddy County SO will meet us there.

"Gentlemen, nothing ever goes as planned. Nothing! Be flexible. Use your common sense. Remember, we know where they're going.

"Unless someone has questions for me, that's it."

Nobody spoke up. Everybody had his big boy pants on. D minus 23-1/2 hours and counting.

CHAPTER 49
Thursday, April 2, 1970
The Mounted Officers Meet

It was easy for the mounted surveillance team to identify one another. They were the ones towing horse trailers. Barlow and Slick were in Slick's 'new' truck - the pristine, black '41 Studebaker. Ralphie Camacho and Dirk Melançon were in Dirk's pale yellow '67 Dodge 100, and Trey Taylor was in his white '68 Ford Bronco. It didn't take long for them to bond. Since Trey was familiar with the campground, he led the way. Dirk followed Trey and Slick followed Dirk.

It was a pleasant drive. They chowed down and refueled at the truck stop in Pecos. They arrived at the campground just before dusk. Sheriff Elliott and two of his deputies were there with their campsites already set up.

Trey made the introductions to Sheriff Elliott. Sheriff Elliott introduced Sergeant Jaime Cerano and Deputy Cletus Knebel. The deputy's colleagues called him Clitoris, or Clit for short. He was good-natured and didn't seem to mind. He had equally colorful names for them, like Hiney Suprano for the sergeant. It made Bronco Barlow seem tame and Slick even tamer. Barlow decided to stick with Cletus' given name to be on the safe side.

The lawmen had the campground to themselves. The sheriff didn't say, and the Texans didn't ask if this was at Sheriff Elliott's request. Either way, after they set up their tents and stowed their gear, they gathered around the sheriff's campfire and shared a pot of coffee. When it was good and dark they saddled up for a recon of the Half-Circle G, otherwise known as Hollywood.

This was Cletus' neck of the woods so he led the way. Slick was next, followed by Ralphie, Trey, Barlow, and Dirk. Sheriff

Elliott brought up the rear. Jaime already knew the area, so he stayed behind to keep an eye on the camp. He didn't mind. The fire was warm and it needed tending. Besides that, among the eight of them there were two coolers full of beer, five bottles of bourbon, and one bottle of tequila. He brought the tequila, which he sampled just to see if the worm tainted the flavor. Fortunately, it didn't.

The Texans had all seen Sheriff Sol's photographs and Sheriff Leland's drawing. Nevertheless, nothing beats boots on the ground and the recon made a huge difference.

The good news was they only had a quarter moon, so it would be difficult for their quarry to see them. The bad news was they only had a quarter moon, so it was difficult for the Texans to see landmarks since Cletus was cutting his own trail.

The campground was directly north of the ranch with the Pecos River in between. Looking at the ranch from the south, the river circumscribed it from the 11 o'clock position where it turned north, and went clockwise to the 5 o'clock position, where it doubled back to the east. Hence the name, Half-Circle G, with G being the Gough initials.

First, Cletus took them along the northern perimeter of the ranch where they found a good spot to cut the fence. Next, he took them along the northern border to the east, stopping periodically so they could dismount and scan the ranch. The sheriff was the only one who had thought to bring binoculars, but since it was dark, it was difficult to make out the outbuildings. It was easy to see the ranch house because the interior was lit up like Las Vegas. The only exterior light on the entire property was directly over the door of the barn.

They crossed the river at the 5 o'clock position. It wasn't more than eighteen inches deep. By now they were only a hundred yards north of Highway 132. They saw a small flock of sheep grazing in this front pasture.

The driveway came in at the 6 o'clock position. They rode

south of 132 about a hundred yards just east of the driveway where there was an empty, dilapidated outbuilding ready to fall down. The walls were leaning precariously to the west. The roof was already missing in most places. This was the site they selected for the driveway surveillance post. They decided to put two horseback deputies there who would remain until the raid team came barreling past, at which time they would join the festivities. One would be Sergeant Cerano. Ralphie Camacho volunteered to be the other.

From here, they rode west paralleling 132 to US 285. They continued west along a dirt farm road about 300 yards to a cluster of trees, where the Eddy County motorized surveillance team would be posted. They too, would stay in place until the raid team moved in. Sheriff Elliott said he would ride with the horseback team coming from the north.

From there, they continued north back to the campground. After grooming the horses they repaired to the campfire, joining Jaime in a couple of rounds of liquid refreshment and male bonding.

CHAPTER 50
Friday, April 3, 1970
The Dance Commences

It was 2:45 when the rustlers arrived in Jeff Gough's black over white Jeep. Sure enough, Humberto Pavón, AKA Elmer Fudd, was in the group. He was driving. He never exited the vehicle and Dewey pretended not to notice. Ichabod Crane's doppelgänger stayed busy, real busy, wiping clean the lenses of his silver-rimmed, circular reading glasses. Jeff and Curley, AKA Daffy Duck and Bugs Bunny, walked into the office. As soon as Jeff laid eyes on Dewey he thought, "This rube will be a pushover. I let the chief investigator spin me up over nothing."

"Howdy, Gents. You all must be from Pluto Incorporated. We've been expecting you."

"Hello. My name is Geoffrey Gough. I represent Pluto. This is Edgar Evans. He's one of our drivers."

They shook hands all around. "Very pleased to meet you both. Would you all like a Pepsi Cola, 7-Up, or a cup of coffee. I know it's a long ride from Pecos."

"No. Thank you. We're anxious to get back on the road. What would you like to see first?"

"Well, let's start with the incorporation papers."

Jeff pulled a sheaf out of a leather attaché case. It was comprised of six pages which included a seal on the last page. Dewey dragged his heels and read every last word. Ten minutes later he said, "Welp, this is all in order. Do you have the indemnity papers?"

Jeff handed him a notarized two-page document signed by Donald Mallard, attesting to same. Dewey read it and placed it in his folder on the counter. "Do you have a notarized document authorizing the two of you to pick up the trucks?"

Jeff pulled out a notarized one-page document. Dewey read it and placed it in his folder, too. "Well, all that there looks to be in order. Can I see your CDL's, please?"

Daffy Duck and Bugs Bunny retrieved their licenses from their wallets. Dewey examined each carefully and returned them. "Wow! You fellers got your shit together. You're really making my job easy. Lot of folks ain't this organized. Can I see your insurance papers?"

Jeff retrieved them from his case. The All State Insurance papers were valid through August 1st and all the VINs matched with the inventory document Dewey pulled from his folder. "Good deal. Can I see the theft report made by Reeves County?"

Jeff laid it on the counter. It was a copy like the one Chief had brought back from Pecos. "Says here the office manager, a Mr. Pavón, filed this report. He still on the payroll?"

"No indeed! Mr. Mallard fired him for not taking better care of his equipment. Last I heard, he went back to Mexico to visit family."

"Well, I should say so! He weren't no illegal alien was he?"

"Heavens no! I believe he was a local. Now, it is possible that his mama could have been illegal but Mr. Mallard would never hire a wetback! Not in a thousand years!"

"Well, that's good to know. Can I see the titles and registration papers for all four vehicles?"

Jeff placed all eight documents on the counter. The registration documents were dated yesterday. All the VINs matched. "Perfecto! Looks like you all have everything. Did you bring the license plates inside?"

Jeff produced all four. "We did." Once again, everything was in order.

"Welp, that's everything. All you gotta do now is pay the towing and storage fees of $410.59 in cash. No checks."

Jeff extracted his wallet again and placed four $100 bills, a $10 bill, and a $1 bill on the counter. Dewey counted it and placed it in the till. He gave Jeff his change and a receipt. He said, "Thank you very much. It was a pleasure doing business with you.

"Oh, I almost forgot. You also gotta go out with me and inspect the vehicles and sign this here document that we returned them in the same condition as we received them. I hope you remembered to bring a screwdriver and some bolts to fasten the license plates. If not, we've got some around here someplace."

"Thank you, but we brought our own. I can sign that inspection document now if you'd like."

"Well, I'd like, but one of the tractors has a little damage on the front bumper and the windshield has some bullet holes in it. Also, there's some blood on the seat. We did the best we could to clean it out but we couldn't get out the stain. You understand that's not our fault. That's why you gotta inspect it before I release the truck to you."

"Of course. Just show us the way."

Dewey took them to the side lot and watched while Daffy Duck made a half-ass inspection. He scribbled his name on the release while Bugs Bunny began to fasten the license plates on their respective vehicles. Dewey noticed that Elmer Fudd had already driven off the lot and was waiting for them alongside the curb on Mesquite Street.

While they were waiting for Bugs to finish attaching the license plates, Dewey said, "Hey! I don't know if you all are interested. I can see you're in a big hurry, but there's this rancher, Maurice Favre, owns the M Slash F on Highway 118 about four miles north of town. It's on the west side. He's been waiting for his contract carrier to take a load of sheep up to the auction house in Pecos.

"The contractor's wife is in the hospital, so he ain't got around to it yet. If you wanted to pick up a load on your way home instead of deadheading, you might wanna stop by and talk to him. I heard he's already penned up the sheep. He's been waiting for two dang days. I know he feels sorry for Basil and Lisa, that's the contractor and his wife, but he's getting a little impatient. Know what I mean?"

"Thanks for the tip. We're pressed for time but I'll make a call to Mr. Mallard before we leave town. See if it's okay with him. You wouldn't happen to know how many sheep he is sending to market would you?"

"No, but he's got a pretty big spread. I'm sure it's at least 50. Maybe more. Want me to call and find out?"

"No. I appreciate the offer. I don't want to get him excited until I know if Mr. Mallard authorizes it. You understand."

"Yessiree! Bosses is like that. Always gotta kiss their ass. Well, you all take care. Nice meetin' ya."

"You too. Can you recommend a decent place to eat around here for a fellow in a hurry?"

"There's a McDonalds, KFC, Pizza Hut, and a Moby Dicks just to the west on Main Street if you're pressed for time. There's also a great steakhouse and a diner with real good food in town but ya gotta go inside and sit down. McDonalds is probably your best bet if you're really in a hurry. It's just the other side of the Winn Dixie. You could park your rigs there, if you want."

"Thanks. We'll check it out. Take care."

"You bet."

Daffy Duck took the wounded rig, telling Bugs Bunny to drive the other. They squared the block and headed west on Main. Elmer Fudd followed close behind in the Jeep.

Investigator Avery Carmichael put the word out on Frequency 2 and on Channel 4 on the CB. Chief Alex made a telephone call to Sheriff Sol at the campground payphone, passing the word.

Everybody was on hold, sitting tight, except for Ella Mae Jaleski. She was Leland Waters' secret weapon. She was also his sister's 28-year-old daughter from Bakersfield, California, formerly a junior high school girls physical education teacher, recently divorced from a jarhead stationed at 29 Palms, who couldn't keep his zipper closed and took up with a stripper.

Ella Mae was looking for a new start, specifically as a deputy sheriff in Leland's department. Instead, he gave her a job as a property clerk, telling her that he would wait and see how she did on this assignment for at least a year, maybe eighteen months.

Nobody had a female deputy in Texas and he didn't want to be the first one to kick common sense and tradition in the balls. He didn't give a shit how many man-hating, bull-dagger deputies they had in California. Not saying Ella Mae was a lesbian. No indeed. She liked men. She was a nice girl, probably a little of a tomboy, but she was just asking too much. He had a little over a year left to decide what to do. This was her first test.

Ella Mae was a sturdy girl - a female athlete before athleticism was commonplace among girls. They didn't offer organized sports for girls at Bakersfield High School but the YWCA had classes in gymnastics, which she embraced with unbounded enthusiasm all through junior and senior high school. She became stronger and far more limber than the other girls in her class.

Ella Mae stood 5'8" tall, weighed about 140 pounds, was bigger boned than most girls, perhaps more angular, but not fat and certainly not unattractive. She had blue eyes and medium length brown hair normally worn in a ponytail. She had more freckles than she would have liked.

Bottom line, Ella Mae looked like the girl next door except perhaps just a little bit bigger. She also had a personality as big as Texas. Everybody liked her and that was part of Leland's problem. He'd be an asshole to everyone who knew Ella Mae if he didn't make her a deputy. He'd be an asshole to everyone else in West Texas law enforcement if he did. It was the price one paid when one was in charge. Of course, if he did hire her, she'd have to get POST certified. That might just resolve his problem for him.

Ella Mae was parked in her white, 1968, Ford Fairlane, 4-door sedan on Main Street a half block east of Barrymore's. Had anyone bothered to notice, she looked like your everyday housewife. Not a stunner but also not too shabby. Kinda nice. She grew on you the more you looked at her. That was her greatest asset.

She saw the procession of rustlers creep along westbound on Main, pulling into the Winn Dixie parking lot just west of the McDonalds. They parked and went inside the restaurant to eat. She gave them five minutes before she entered.

They were waiting for their orders when she walked in. She wasn't very hungry but she ordered a hamburger and a small coffee with cream and sugar. The rustlers got their meals and sat down. When hers was ready, she found a table nearby.

They were discussing whether to pick up the M Slash F sheep. Daffy Duck and Bugs Bunny were so inclined. Elmer Fudd was not. They needed to get back. The conversation did not sound sinister. Maybe they planned to enter into a contractual obligation rather than steal them. Finally, at Daffy's behest, Elmer Fudd agreed to go check out the ranch. He said he'd be back in a little bit. He bounced out of his seat and hurried out the door.

What now? She was done eating. Her coffee was nearly gone. She walked back to the counter and asked for a refill. Then she asked if they were taking applications for employment. They were, but the manager wasn't in now. She should come back in the morning between 9 and 10. She asked if they had an application she could take with her. They did, and he handed her one along with her refill. She took it back to the table and spent the better part of 45 minutes completing a simple two-page form before Elmer Fudd finally returned.

Elmer said he checked it out. They have one truckload. The rancher isn't there right now. His son said to come back at 6. His dad would probably hire them. The auction lot opens at 6 am. If they got there before then, they'd have to wait. He said one truck was all they needed this time but they would keep him in mind for future loads.

Daffy Duck said that was okay. He told Bugs to go ahead and take the damaged rig back to the ranch and park it behind the barn. He said it had plenty of fuel to get home. He took a $50 bill out of his wallet and paid him in full for his help. Curley thanked Jeff, traded truck keys, and left. Once he was gone, Ella Mae made a leisurely retreat in search of a pay phone.

She called the M Slash F and asked for her uncle. She told him what she learned. Leland said they saw the Jeep parked along the highway scoping out the sheep and the layout. He also said Elmer never spoke to anyone. He said he would pass the information to the rest of the troops. Then he commended her for a job well done and told her to take the rest of the day off.

Daggone it! Things were just getting interesting and she was sidelined. One day . . . .

CHAPTER 51
Tick Tock, Tick Tock
Friday, April 3, 2019

"You didn't really talk to that rancher, did you?"

"No. I just made up a cover story for us in case Curley gets curious. I don't trust him. I think he'd run to la policía if he knew what we were up to. I also don't think we should take this load to Loving. He'll be there, wonder why we didn't drop the load off in Pecos. We'd get busted for sure."

"You could be right. Maybe we sell them in Pecos first thing in the morning instead."

"Señor, that would be even riskier. Everyone knows me there. They know I'm not in the sheep or the sheep transportation business. Besides that, we've always taken the stock out of Texas to make tracking us down more difficult. If we do this job tonight, you will be at risk same as me. You sure you still want to do this?"

"What's the job look like?"

"Piece of cake. The sheep are Merinos. Very common. They're lambs. Maybe eighty-pounds each. Bring in a good price. They're penned in a pasture that runs along 118. The house sets way off to the west, maybe a quarter-mile back. I didn't see any lights. We have a quarter moon tonight.

"We could back in the drive, cut the fence, load the truck, and head for home. Not even splice the fence. The stealing is the easy part. The hard part is not getting caught with the sheep after we steal them.

"They'll know the sheep are missing as soon as they get up in the morning and look out the window. Sheriff will probably check the Pecos stockyard first since it's closest. Once word gets around, that pendejo in the tow lot will remember he told you about this job and he will finger you. You'll get a visit by the sheriff by Monday at the latest. Maybe even on Sunday."

"Damn! Those sheep are worth about a thousand bucks. We're still waiting for K&R to decide if we get the servicing contract for their new site in Hobbs. If we don't get it, we may be out of business for good. Jerry's not making ends meet in the legitimate sheep ranching side of our endeavors. We don't have enough land to raise a flock big enough to be profitable. His last paycheck was same day as yours and I haven't had one in awhile, either.

"We need these sheep to tide us over. I should've sent Jerry down here to pick up these rigs. This is really his side of the house. I just let him use my trucks for a piece of the action."

"Señor, it will be tight, but we might be able to take the sheep and sell them at the stockyard in Roswell. No one would ever check there. Once the sheep are sold, no one could ever prove they were stolen."

"Gee, it's 100 miles from here to Pecos. Another 80 to Loving. Roswell's another 80 or so. That's 260 miles, plus or minus. You have to figure at least five hours to get there. Probably closer to six. We'd have to be on our way by 2 o'clock at the very latest."

"Well, I do not recommend stealing the sheep before 2 o'clock. We want everyone in bed banging his old lady or sawing Z's. We can still make it by 8:30. That's plenty of time. We need to find a place to hide the truck until it's time to go. The longer we hang around here, the more likely things will get fucked up. Didn't you tell that pendejo you were in a hurry?"

"Yeah, let's go. I saw some pay phones at the Winn Dixie. You jump in the truck and wait until I find out what Jerry thinks."

"Okay, but if he isn't home, let's go. I think I saw a place where we could wait without interference."

"Agreed."

They walked over to the parking lot. Elmer Fudd got in the rig and checked the fuel gauge. It was only half full. He said,

"Jefe, we need fuel. Give me some money and I will fill it up while you are on the phone."

Jeff handed him a $50 bill. He said, "I hope that will fill it up. I'm running out of cash. I'll meet you back here when you're done."

"Sí, Señor." A minute later, he was on his way.

Jeff got $5 worth of quarters in the grocery and went back outside to the pay phones. Fortunately, no one else was there to overhear his conversation. He placed his call and waited. Finally, after just enough time to grow a full beard, Jerry picked up.

"Jerry, it's me."

"Did you get the rigs?"

"Yeah, but something came up."

"What?"

"We have an opportunity to execute an unauthorized midnight acquisition of 60 Merinos. Berto already checked it out. We sent Curley back to the ranch in the truck that got shot up because we don't trust him. I already paid him. I told him to park it next to the barn."

"Okay."

"I need for you to come down here to help Berto pick up the load. You'll have to take them to the auction in Roswell. Soon as you meet us, I'll head back home."

"Wait a minute! Why does the load have to go to Roswell? What's wrong with Loving? We have a good situation there."

"Because Curley thinks we got a contract to haul the load to Pecos. If we bring the load to Loving, he'll know we just took 'em. No contract. Capeesh?"

"Okay. That's fine. Why do you need me? You and Berto can handle it."

"Livestock is your deal. All I do is supply the trucks and get a small piece of the action. You're the one that always makes the arrangements with the stockyards. Besides that, Berto's never done that. It was always you and your boy, Juan."

"So now that you're actually getting your hands dirty you're scared and it's all my responsibility? Is that it?"

"Something like that. I wouldn't even have considered this job but it's low-hanging fruit and we need the dough."

"Tell you what. You and Berto do the job and stop by here. I'll take them to Roswell. We give Berto his $200 and we split the rest 50-50."

"Okay, but you gotta sell them in the morning. We can't leave 'em in the pasture overnight or for a day or two like we usually do. This time there's too much risk of getting a visit by the sheriff's office. The rancher will know his sheep were stolen when he wakes up in the morning. The chump at the tow lot is the one who turned us onto this gig, thinking that we're legit. He would probably turn the cops onto us soon as he hears about the job, especially since these trucks were already used in a rustling operation. Now do you understand the urgency?"

"Understood. You said sixty Merinos. Are they lambs or full-grown?"

"Lambs. Berto said they probably average 80 pounds."

"Just as I thought. Berto knows more about sheep than he's letting on. So let's see. Hmmm. They ought to fetch $900, maybe a G.

"How about this? Instead of paying Berto $200, how about we sell him Juan's truck for $1,000? It's a '65, low miles, in good shape. Better than that heap he's driving now."

"The title and registration are in the glovebox and they're in the name Juan Rodríguez. I don't know how he managed that but he did. Anyway, you credit him $200 for tonight's job and $100 each week instead of paying him 'til it's paid off. If he doesn't like the truck, he can sell it in Mexico or anyplace except New Mexico. That way we have more cash ourselves until you get the K&R contract or we do a few more jobs."

"Good idea. I'll see if he bites. Okay, we'll probably get to the ranch about 5:30 or 6. Make sure you're ready to go. It's about 80 miles to Roswell and we gotta get the load sold tomorrow."

"You already said that. I'll be ready. Good luck. See you then."

They hung up. Berto had not returned yet, so Jeff went back inside the Winn Dixie and bought a loaf of bread, small packages of bologna and American cheese, a jar of mustard, a bag of Fritos, some Oreos, a 6-pack of Barq's root beer, a small bag of ice, and a cheap cooler. Berto was waiting when he returned to his Jeep. Jeff filled the cooler and put the victuals on the rear floorboard.

"Need to gas up, Jefe?"

"Yes. I'll stop by the Sinclair over there on our way out of town. I got us some groceries for later on while we're waiting to go back to work.

"This is the deal. You and I will pick up the load and stop by the ranch long enough for Jerry to trade places with me. Then you all go to Roswell and take care of business.

"Jerry also told me to offer you Juan's truck for $1,000. He said all the papers are in the glovebox and they're in Juan's name. I credit you $200 for tonight or any later jobs, and $100 for each week's wages until it's paid off. That sound fair to you?"

"Señor Jeff, Juan's truck is a 6-banger. I always drive a V-8 with more power. Besides, once I transfer the title into my name, I will be the one in possession of stolen property if the authorities figure it out. I will have to sell it in Mexico. Also, I do not think it's worth $1,000. I will take it for $600 in credit plus you give me $100 in cash."

"That means you would buy it for only $500. Tell you what. Jerry won't like it, but you can have it for $700 in credit plus I give you $100 cash. You get it for $600. Jerry will have a shit fit but that's the best I can do."

"Sold." They shook hands.

"Señor. I saw an old gas station about three miles north of the ranch on the west side. I think it was a Sunoco. It still has an awning over the place where the pumps used to be. We could probably stay there until we are ready."

"Sounds good to me. You can head that way. I'll catch up as soon as I top off."

"Okay. One more thing. Juan and I always take a gun with us on a job. You never know if someone will start shooting. You have to protect yourself. I have my .45. Do you have a gun with you?"

"Of course. I have a real sweet Smith & Wesson, Model 19 Combat Magnum in my briefcase. It goes wherever I go. It's loaded with Super Vel, hollow-point, .357 Magnum ammunition. It will open up a hole inside a body at least as big as that .45 of yours. I also have a box with extra cartridges in the glovebox. Tell me. Do you carry extra ammo, Berto, or just the one magazine in the gun?"

"Sí, Señor. I always carry a round in the pipe plus a spare magazine. That's 15 rounds. I am always prepared for anything."

"Good. That should make us both happy. See you up at the old Sunoco."

CHAPTER 52
Friday, April 3, 1970
Cobra Checks In

It was already dark by the time Cobra pulled into the Eddy County Courthouse. The only lights on in the building were in the sheriff's office. It had a skeleton crew. A young deputy asked, "Evening, Sir. How may I help you?"

"I'm Cobra. I just finished a secret mission for the sheriff. I need to talk to him. He's expecting me."

"Oh, yeah, Cobra. I heard about you. Sheriff isn't in right now. Let me get on the radio and see if I can reach him. Wait right here."

"Base to Eddy 1. Base to Eddy 1. Come in please."

"This is Eddy 1."

"Eddy 1, could you call the office at your earliest convenience?"

"10-4."

The deputy told Cobra to have a seat at an empty desk which had a telephone. A few minutes later, he told Cobra to answer line 2.

"Hello?"

"Cobra, this is Sheriff Elliott. What did you find out?"

"Well, Sheriff. Maybe I was wrong. I rode down to Alpine with Mr. Jeff and some Mexican dude called Berto. We got the trucks out of hock. The clerk told Mr. Jeff about a ranch nearby that has some sheep ready for market in Pecos. Berto went and checked it out. Mr. Jeff decided to take the job so they could make some money. He told me to drive the other rig back to the ranch. It had three bullet holes in the windshield and blood on the seat. The other truck was okay. Mr. Jeff and Berto stayed back to pick up the sheep. Maybe my imagination got the best of me. Sorry."

"Cobra. You were right to bring this to my attention. You never know. Bad guys have regular jobs, too, you know. Did he pay you?"

"Oh, Yes, Sir! $50 in cash."

"Good. Look. Before we hang up I'm gonna speak to the deputy and tell him to give you another $10 for your trouble. I still want you to keep your eyes open at the stockyards. Just because nothing happened this time doesn't mean nothing's going on. Understand?"

"Oh, Yes, Sir. Thank you. I'm giving the phone back to the deputy now. Bye."

"Bye, Cobra."

Two minutes later the sheriff hung up. Standing by, Sheriff Sol said, "Any news?"

"Yeah, the CI brought the rig with all the bullet holes back to the ranch. Jeff tricked him into thinking they're going to transport a truckload of sheep to the Pecos stockyards on consignment. Of course, we already knew he brought a rig back. Our guys saw that. Now we know for certain they've taken the bait. The question is, where are they taking the sheep? You know it probably won't be in Loving or Pecos. Also, he'd be a fool to try to stash them on his own ranch."

"You're right. I'd be surprised if they took them to auction in Texas. Too risky. I'll call Leland in a minute and let him know. We may have to reposition a few guys. Where could they take them in New Mexico if not here?"

"Maybe Las Cruces. They'd have to take 90 west to Van Horn and pick up 54 to El Paso. They could auction there but El Paso's still in Texas. Then at El Paso they'd have to switch to 70. I know it's roughly 40 miles from El Paso to Cruces. I don't know how far it is from Alpine to El Paso."

"I'm guessing about 250 miles. That's roughly a 300-mile trip. Maybe 280 at the minimum. Then they'd have to get back home.

How far is it from Las Cruces to Malaga?"

"I'm sure it's more than 200 miles."

"They'll never do that but we can stage a unit on 90 just west of 285 to cover that possibility. Where else could they go?"

"Well, Artesia and Hobbs are oil towns. They don't have a stockyard. They could go to Roswell. It's about 80 miles from Malaga. That would be about 260 miles from Alpine and then only 80 to get back home. That would be the better choice."

"Agreed. I'll call Leland and Chief Alex and see if they can spread the word. We're going to have to play this one by ear. Looks like a lot of planning may have gone up in smoke."

"Well, we don't know for certain yet. No offense, Sol, but this has been one big gamble from the very beginning. Not many sheriffs would go to these lengths to catch a rustler you already own and a couple of snot-nosed college boys from out-of-state. You must really love that judge."

"I do, but that's not the reason. We're doing this because these arrogant bastards think they can jump into our swimming pool and take a big dump. If we don't make them pay the price, every other bad boy in West Texas will think he can get away with it, too."

"Well, no matter how this goes down tonight, we will catch those bastards and put an end to their wicked ways, at least for the next few years."

"Amen to that."

CHAPTER 53
Saturday, April 4, 1970
Stealing Low Hanging Fruit

It was 1:45 a.m. The sky was black with a thousand stars and a waxing moon. Jeff and Berto had been sitting in the dark for so long that their eyes had adjusted and they could almost see like a pair of cats. Jeff was about to break his cherry as a hands-on thief and his bowels were churning like an ice cream maker. It was old hat to Berto and he was all primed to go, just like a hungry wolf waiting for a juicy doe to cross his path. They hadn't seen a single vehicle on the highway for more than an hour. Time to boogie.

Berto told Jeff to drive the Jeep south about a mile past the driveway to the M Slash F to check out the area. He was to turn around and park on the northbound shoulder about a quarter-mile south of the driveway and turn his lights off. His job would be to stall any northbound motorists by feigning engine trouble. If it looked like anyone were nosing around, he was to flash his lights at Berto and then head north. Berto would abort and they would meet back at the Sunoco. It chafed Jeff letting Berto call the shots but he was the expert in this field.

Jeff slid into the driver's seat. He placed his revolver under his jacket on the passenger seat. He pulled out and drove slowly towards the M Slash F and beyond. He didn't even see a slinking coyote along the route.

The sheep were still in the pen. There were no lights on any where near the entrance to the ranch. The rancher and his family must either be away, asleep, or dead. It was so devoid of human activity that a rabbit browsing in a graveyard would have been as riveting as a bevy of belly dancers in a sideshow at the carnival.

Jeff did exactly like he was told before he parked and turned off his lights. It occurred to him that if things went downhill, he could drive away and leave Berto swinging in the breeze to face the music all alone. He embarrassed himself. He wasn't that kind of man, was he?

Before long Berto was in sight. He was running without lights. He slowed down and passed the entrance. He did something Jeff did not expect. He maneuvered the rig so that it was backed up right next to the fence. The front of the trailer extended across the southbound lane and the tractor was turned ninety degrees into the northbound lane facing north, similar to a jackknife. As long as nobody else was on the highway they were in good shape. If anyone blundered along, this could turn western real fast because neither Berto nor Jeff were planning to go peacefully to jail.

Berto jumped out of the truck and began cutting the fence. Then he created an opening just wide enough to open the doors. He set up the ramp and walked to the rear of the flock and began herding them into the trailer. When the last one was in, he replaced the ramp and closed the doors. He walked around to the cab, got in, and drove merrily on his way. Jeff waited about a minute before following. They drove all the way past the Sunoco before turning on their lights. This went off as slick as a weasel going down a rabbit hole.

Woohoo! He wished he had a real beer instead of a root beer to celebrate. He had entered into this with trepidation but now he was euphoric. The thrill of hands-on banditry was better than sex. He felt like a real badass. Ten feet tall. Bulletproof. Damn! This could get addictive.

He was beginning to understand Berto's persona. Berto was so self-assured. He carried himself like a tiger in a world full of llamas. He could devour anyone he wanted anytime he wanted. Of course, Berto had shot somebody before. Nothing scared him. What a way to live!

CHAPTER 54
Saturday, April 4, 1970
The Reason Cops Become Cops

The trap was sprung.

Maurice Favre, known as The Big MF at his own behest, Sheriff Waters, and his chief, Phillip Pruitt, watched the rustling unfold from the comfort of chaise lounge chairs in a barn loft equipped with a stocked refrigerator, table full of food, coffeepot, and a telephone. The loft had a radio and a television set too, but they never turned them on. They stuffed their faces, smoked cigars, solved world problems, and took turns watching the rustling through a huge telescope Maurice purchased just for this event. It was like watching a football game from a Dallas Cowboys skybox except it was dark and only lasted twelve minutes.

For a guy getting rustled, Maurice was ecstatic, having the time of his life. He never thought about how much fun law enforcement could be. He made Leland promise to swear him in as a special deputy. He had the wrong idea, of course, that law enforcement was a continual adrenaline rush but Leland wasn't about to disabuse him of this notion while his sheep were in the hands of the rustlers.

Chief Phil sounded the bugle signaling the beginning of the fox hunt over the air. Leland called Sol at the campground. Not everyone got the word due to the distances involved and the shortcomings of the radios but enough did to be prepared for when the rustlers came their way.

Deputies tried to notify the units north of them via the CBs mostly, like a chain, but the northern units just south of the New Mexico state line never got the word. However, as the procession rambled along at a respectable 50 miles per hour and the distances between moving units and stationary units diminished, contact was accomplished early enough to alert all the stationary units before they arrived except for one.

Disaster was narrowly averted when Elmer Fudd stopped to take a leak on the side of the highway. Daffy Duck pulled over behind him and besides relieving their bladders, they copped a smoke and chatted for a few minutes.

Chief Alex was the first in the parade of unmarked units and POVs driven by deputies who were following the rustlers at what they all assumed was a safe distance. No bunching up, just like a small military unit on patrol in the bush, maintaining separation to avoid everyone getting wiped out in the event of an ambush.

Chief was what he estimated to be at least three-quarters of a mile behind the rustlers. He was running with lights on. The other units behind him were running with lights off except for the caboose, which changed each time they passed a checkpoint.

He crested a low hill and was coming around a curve when he spotted the Jeep parked behind the 18-wheeler. It was too late to stop so he maintained speed and continued on. He saw Daffy Duck and Elmer Fudd taking a smoke break between the units. They both looked up at him so he waved. He had no idea if they could actually see him but it didn't matter.

Chief got on the CB and told the procession to grab a piece of the curb immediately. He explained the situation, telling the next in line, Pancho the Honcho, to wait five minutes before resuming the trip with his lights on. He said he was looking for a side road to resume the surveillance.

Pancho 10-4'ed and when he resumed the trip the rustlers were nowhere in sight. More than one deputy muttered a prayer of thanks for the halt so they could relieve themselves, too.

Chief drove five or six miles before he found a goat track to set up a surveillance post. He had only been there four or five minutes before the rustlers came into view. Apparently all was well. He waited for four units to pass before he turned in behind them, lights off. He was thinking there should be at least one more unit behind him but he didn't know for sure. He could always turn his lights on if someone came up behind him.

In the interim, Sheriff Elliott had sworn in all the Texas lawmen who were at the campground as special Eddy County deputies. Trey and Slick and Barlow had volunteered to mount up and maintain surveillance of the Half-Circle G Ranch in the wood line on the northern perimeter.

They had no commo. They were there strictly as a safety net in the event the rustlers suddenly decided to haul the sheep elsewhere before the northbound units arrived at the campground to get sworn in, and to receive the last minute raid plan briefing. If everything went as planned, Trey and company would be joined by the remaining mounted officers who were standing by at the campground, to include Sheriff Elliott. Sheriff Sol planned to ride his 330 horses right up the driveway to the front door.

It was midnight when Trey, Slick, and Barlow set up. They were surprised to see that the lights were still on in the house. Trey had borrowed Sheriff Elliott's binoculars and they could see one man moving about inside. This had to be the other Gough brother, Jerry, otherwise codenamed Huey Duck, for the sting operation.

Shortly after 3 o'clock, Deputy Cletus Knebel stopped by to let them know that the sheep were in transit and had been for roughly a half-hour. They extrapolated time and distance and guessed at an ETA (estimated time of arrival) of 5:30. It should be getting light by 6. That would probably make kickoff at 7 o'clock.

After Cletus left, Trey suggested that they go ahead and cut the fence while it was still dark to save time for when they commenced the raid. There were no livestock in this pasture so they didn't have to worry that any would escape. If the rustlers put the stolen stock in this pasture, they would detail one of the other deputies to roll up the fence and keep watch there once the raid commenced.

Slick and Barlow both gave a ringing endorsement. As sure as God made little green apples, no one was going to deny this trio from their mounted charge to capture or otherwise dispatch the rustlers. This would be a first time for Trey and probably a last time for them all to ever have this opportunity again. Besides that, Barlow had a score to settle. Pavón would probably be the first to fire a shot. Whether the others would fight was unknown. Barlow just wanted to be close enough to settle the account if Pavón decided to shoot it out.

They cut the fence and rolled it back. They would have to ride through it single file.

Tick tock. Tick tock.

It was 5:37 a.m., and just beginning to get light. Eddy County 38, manned by Deputies Bradley Bergeron and Zach McGillicuddy, hidden behind some trees on a dirt road on the west side of US 285 just south of County Highway 132, where the sign at the intersection was missing but a derelict windmill on the east side of the road marked the spot, first sighted the rustler rig followed by the Jeep when they were still at least a half-mile south of the Highway 132 surveillance post.

Eddy 38 radioed Eddy 1, sounding the alert. All the lawmen within a five-mile radius received the warning and were sitting on pins and needles, except for five. Eddy County Sergeant Jaime Cerano and Brewster County Deputy Ralphie Camacho, hiding in the dilapidated barn 200 yards south of the entrance to the Half-Circle G, otherwise codenamed Hollywood, and Texas Ranger Sergeant Trey Taylor, Quayle County Deputies Slick Oldman, and Barlow Adams were not, since they had no commo. Needless to say, due to the late hour, they were all on high alert.

Sheriff Elliott and Sheriff Sol breathed a sigh of relief when they were notified that the rustlers turned east onto Highway 132. During the next twenty minutes the mobile surveillance units from Texas began arriving at the campground. Order began to fray and the base camp became chaotic due to the excess manpower in an area insufficient to handle them all or to contain the excitement that had been building all night.

Eddy 38 remained on post just in case the rustlers pulled a fast one and tried to leave before the raid team was ready.

Sergeant Cerano and Deputy Camacho watched the tractor trailer full of sheep and the Jeep pull into the driveway. Daffy Duck parked by the back door and ran into the house. Elmer Fudd pulled the rig partially into the back lot and stepped out of the cab. He lit up a smoke but he didn't seem to be in any hurry to let the sheep out of the trailer. The two deputies didn't have a completely unobstructed view but it was still getting light. They decided to go ahead and saddle their mounts to be ready for when the posse did show up.

Trey, Slick, and Barlow were also intently watching. Slick said, "Those pricks are up to something. I think they're here to take a leak and grab a cuppa joe before heading to the auction. If the raid team doesn't get here quick, we're gonna have to scramble before they get that rig turned around."

Barlow asked, "You think the fellas across the road can see what's going on?"

Trey responded, "They can see the Jeep and the ass end of the trailer but I doubt they can see Elmer Fudd. Look, if these owlhoots look like they're bugging out with the sheep, we'll hafta ride like Hell to cut 'em off at the pass. We're basically screwed once that rig gets turned around."

It was getting lighter by the minute. Then a twin wearing light trousers and a white shirt stepped out of the house and yelled something at Elmer Fudd. The northern surveillance team assumed that this must be Huey Duck, because it looked like the other twin was wearing dark trousers and a dark shirt when he got out of the Jeep.

Elmer Fudd yelled something back. Huey Duck responded by

raising his right arm over his head and making a circular motion, just like the wagon master on the TV show Wagon Train when they circled the wagons before camping for the night. Elmer Fudd turned around and began walking back towards the rig.

Trey said, "Come on, boys! Show time! He mounted and began to cross the stream and go through the fence. Slick followed and Barlow was last.

All the men had their long guns in their saddle scabbards, including Slick's 10-gauge double-barrel shotgun named Colleen. This was because they were all mounted on horses that would not shy when the rider shot over his shoulder. It was also because it's easier to shoot a handgun while mounted than it is a long gun.

Trey was riding a black stallion named Grim Reaper, or Grimmy for short. Trey said Grimmy earned his name when he damn near killed him and a couple of wranglers when they were trying to break him. He said Grimmy had more bottom than any other horse he had ever owned.

Slick was riding a different horse today than Toby, the big bay he rode during the previous stakeout. His mount for this assignment was an appaloosa stallion named Fred Hood, Jr. He was sired by Fred Hood, Sr., with a dam named Polly Wag. Fred Hood, Sr. was named after Captain Fred Hood, who was Slick's Marine Corps company commander when they assaulted Iwo Jima. Captain Hood was killed there by a sniper hiding in a cave. Slick identified the cave and a marine with a flamethrower roasted that Jap bastard alive. Slick said Captain Hood was the finest man he ever knew. He also said 'tweren't nobody going to cut the balls off any horse named Fred Hood so long as he was alive,' so he put up with the aggressive nature of a stallion mount to make his point.

Barlow asked one time if it wouldn't be easier just to change the horse's name and cut him for an easier ride, but Slick harrumphed and stomped off.

Barlow was riding Boyo, the same five-year-old gelding who might've been born a bastard because Barlow didn't know the name of his sire or his dam, nor did he know who or when he was emasculated. He only knew that Boyo was a great horse and that he loved him and that now he was trained not to flinch around gunfire.

By the time the three of them breached the gap in the fence, revolvers drawn, riding hell-for-leather towards the rig and the ranch house, they were in a left oblique. Trey was in the lead on the left; Slick was a little behind in the middle; and Barlow was bringing up the rear on the right. They were closing fast.

Both Huey Duck and Elmer Fudd spotted them right away. Huey Duck ran back into the house just as Daffy Duck exited, running straight for the Jeep. Elmer pulled out his nickel-plated, .45 Government Model Colt, and took aim at Trey because he was by far the closest threat. He fired and Trey's hat went flying. Neither Slick nor Barlow knew if that was a near miss or just the wind. Trey returned fire, missing Elmer, but neutralizing the tractor by blowing a gaping hole in the radiator. Game over for the rustlers with just one misplaced shot. Now all they had to do was surrender peacefully and go to jail.

Not! The negotiations and bartering continued via flying lead.

Slick held fire, closing the gap to get a better shot as did Barlow because he was still out of range, too.

At this point, Daffy Duck ran up from the Jeep. He stopped within three feet of Elmer's right side and took aim at Slick with his .357 Magnum revolver. By now, Slick was within his own high probability zone of hitting what he aimed at. Slick picked up on the threat from Daffy and fired a split second before Daffy did. He hit Daffy in the right leg. Daffy missed Slick, but he did hit the ground on his ass, but just for a moment. He scrambled back up and resumed firing at Slick.

Elmer Fudd and Trey traded several more shots but Barlow's attention was diverted to Huey Duck, who emerged from the house with a pump shotgun and thus, Barlow lost track of Elmer Fudd. Barlow was almost close enough to spit on his nemesis, but he changed course to deal with the even bigger threat of the shotgun. Huey Duck chambered a shell and leveled the shotgun at Barlow but before he pulled the trigger, Barlow shot him center mass and he collapsed like a broken gargoyle off the roof of a six-story cathedral without another thought or worry in this world.

The crime scene was in chaos. Bullets were flying like psychotic yellow jackets in every direction. After Huey Duck went down, Barlow turned to his left and saw Elmer Fudd, who was now on his knees bleeding from two bullet holes in his torso, but far from being out of action. Instead, he was in the process of dropping an empty magazine and reloading with a fresh one. Barlow quickly shot him in the side of his head. Elmer never saw it coming. He bit the dirt. Threat eliminated once and for all.

Next, Barlow looked for the third assailant. He saw that Slick had dismounted and was looming over a thrice perforated Daffy Duck, pointing a cocked Peacemaker at his chest, ready to ventilate him again if he so much as twitched, but twitching is something only a live person can do.

Next he looked for Trey.

Trey was still mounted but he was slumped over, nursing a bullet wound in his chest. Barlow and Slick saw him at the same time. They ran over to him and gently eased him off his horse. They half carried and half walked him inside the house and propped him up on the couch. At the same time, Jaime Cerano and Ralphie Camacho galloped up to the scene ready to assist, but the fight was already over, having run its course in less than a minute.

They sized up the situation quickly. Jaime ran into the house and got on the telephone. He called for an ambulance which would be coming from Carlsbad. In the meantime, Slick and Barlow, both of whom had seen many gunshot victims, checked Trey's wound.

The shot went through and through his left chest, but Trey was having trouble breathing. He had blood in his spittle, indicating that his lung had been punctured. Barlow found towels and washcloths in a closet. Ralphie found duct tape in a kitchen cabinet. Slick fashioned two airtight bandages by cutting the duct tape into two six-inch pieces and folding each in half with the sticky sides together. He and Barlow placed the folded tape strips over the entrance and exit wounds. They used towels as compresses which Slick and Ralphie held firmly in place.

All the while, the officers in the campground had reacted to the cacophony of shots as soon as they heard them. They piled into cars in twos, threes, and fours, and drove Code 3 to the ranch. Eddy 38 was closer and arrived first. Barlow met them as soon as they skidded to a halt. He reported that the rustlers were dead, but Trey had been shot and they needed to keep the road and driveway clear for the ambulance which was already en route. The deputies agreed to radio their sheriff and to handle the incoming traffic.

Trey was sinking fast. He was increasingly having more and more difficulty breathing. Slick and Barlow both knew he needed to be aspirated but neither knew how to do it. They were afraid he would suffocate on his own blood before the ambulance arrived.

Tick tock. Tick tock.

CHAPTER 55
Saturday, April 4, 1970
Aftermath

Sheriff Elliott and Sheriff Sol arrived together with Sheriff Waters following. They quickly surveyed the crime scene and looked in on Trey, who was barely holding his own. Sheriff Elliott took charge of the crime scene and began giving deputies specific assignments. Sol pulled Barlow aside for a private tête-à-tête before Sheriff Elliott assigned him a job.

Barlow could see steam rolling out of the ears of both Sheriff Elliott and Sheriff Sol. At least he thought he did. On the other hand, Sheriff Waters casually cruised the crime scene, looking like he was taking a stroll in the park with no worries whatsoever.

Barlow had a brief reprieve when the ambulance arrived sooner than anticipated and not a moment too soon. The medics managed to stabilize Trey before they left for the hospital. Chief Alex and Sergeant Cerano followed in Chief's car to render all assistance as needed.

Sheriff Sol steered Barlow inside the barn and asked, "Are you all right?"

"I am. Slick's fine, too. Trey's the only one in danger. None of the rustlers have a worry in the world."

"Yes, I can see that. I'm glad you and Slick are in one piece and I pray that Trey will be okay.

"Look, Barlow. Sheriff Elliott is livid and I can't say as I blame him. There's three dead outlaws and fifteen deputies here, but not one from his own department was present when the shooting took place. This looks really bad for him. The press is likely to rip him a new asshole. 'Rogue Texas cops massacre New Mexico citizens right under Sheriff Elliott's nose.'

"Understand the optics? It makes him look . . . ineffective at the very least. I need to know exactly what happened to see if I can't help salvage the situation."

"Sheriff, our orders were to conduct surveillance and to wait for the task force to come in from the south before we rode in from the north with more riders, unless the rustlers decided to vamoose with the sheep before the task force arrived.

"When we set up last night, we cut the fence big enough to let us go through one rider at a time while it was still dark, just in case they decided to offload the sheep in this pasture. We didn't want any of the M Slash F sheep to wander off.

"We knew something was amiss as soon as the rig and the Jeep arrived."

"How so?"

"Look, Sheriff. The rig is not even close to the pasture. The Jeep is next to the house. Jeff Gough ran inside the house as soon as he stopped. Probably had to take a leak. Pavón got out of the cab and walked around to the front of it and lit up a smoke.

"About five minutes later, the other brother, Jerry, came out of the house and yelled something to Pavón. We couldn't hear what he said. Pavón said something back, and then Gough raised his hand over his head and began circling it in the air like 'wagon ho!' Pavón threw down his butt and started back to the cab. It was pretty light by now. We knew they were getting ready to bug out, so we did what we were told to do.

"Trey managed to get mounted first and start toward the rig. Pavón spotted him the very second he crossed the river. Slick got through next and I was last.

"Pavón started shooting at Trey right away since he was closest. Jerry stepped out of the house and ran back in. Then Jeff ran out to his Jeep and came back with a pistol and started shooting at Slick.

"Then I saw Jerry come back outside with a pump shotgun. He jacked a round and I lost track of everything else that was happening. I shot Jerry and he went down. Then I saw Pavón on his knees with a couple of bullet holes in his midsection but he still had plenty of fight left in him. He dropped an empty mag and reloaded with a fresh one. I shot him in the head. Then I looked and saw Jeff on the ground, dead as a doornail, with Slick on foot standing over him.

"Then I looked for Trey. His hat was missing and he was still mounted, but he was slumped over about to fall out of the saddle. Slick and I took him inside and about then the guys from across the street galloped up. Jaime got on the phone and called an ambulance and the rest of us began tending to Trey's wound.

"That's it. End of story. What else would you have had us do? In another two minutes they would have been back on the highway. I thought we were trying to avoid that so we wouldn't have another incident like the one we had at Judge Sweeney's. Besides that, even though we are all Texas deputies, Sheriff Elliott did swear us in as Eddy County special deputies. In a sense, we were working for him. He's giving the orders now, so I guess we still are."

"Hmmm. I need to think about this for a minute."

One minute passed and then two. Finally, he said, "Let's go find Sheriff Elliott. We'll see if he wants information directly from the horse's mouth or if he wants my Cliff Notes version."

They began to walk back to the house when they spotted Slick. Sol asked, "What're you doing right now?"

"Looking for splicing tools. Need me for something?"

"Yes. Barlow, wait for me right here."

The sheriff nudged Slick into a corner in the barn and said, "Tell me what happened. This wasn't supposed to go down like this."

"Well, Sheriff, nothing seldom goes as planned. We was never really in control of this situation and you know it. Within five minutes of arrival, them owlhoots was fixing to skedaddle. We all saw it. I know you already bounced Barlow about this and I'll

298 By Earl Snort

bet a dollar to a doughnut hole he told you the same as me. When Trey gets to feeling a little perkier, he'll tell you the same thing, too.

"We was instructed to wait unless they started to leave with a trailer load o' sheep. That's what they was fixin' to do. We mounted and started riding towards the truck and our old pal, John Doe #2, saw us coming and commenced to firing at Trey. It was daylight by then, so it weren't no surprise to any of us.

"It was a little surprising that the two college boys opened up but it wasn't like we was unprepared. Actually, the turd I shot started off shooting at Trey, but I cleaned his gizzard for him. His brother come out with a shotgun, and Sheriff, I'm thankful Barlow was there. He sent him straight to perdition with one shot. That was him ridin' wide open, too. Then he finished off that Mexican desperado.

"I was still tending to the Gough turd and the Mex mighta cleaned my gizzard while I was lookin' the other way. Besides, I thought Trey had done shot him to pieces, but I reckon he was just one of them sons-a-bitches what takes a lot of perforatin' to put 'em down for good.

"I didn't know Trey was hit, but Sheriff, he got way out ahead of us and most of their attention was directed at him. Trey's gotta lot of sand in him and I surely do hope he makes it. He's aces in my book.

"So if you wanna gnaw on my ass, go ahead and do it. Barlow went along with Trey and me. He really didn't have no say in the matter. All I can say is thank God it was him and not some other'n who might not 'ave been as gnarly or proficient with a six-shooter off'n the back of a horse. That's really all I got to say on the matter."

"Slick, this isn't an ass-chewing. I'm proud of what you all accomplished and I'm sorry Trey caught a round. I have the utmost faith in you and Barlow or I wouldn't have assigned you here. Dan is upset, to put it mildly, that if there had to be fireworks his men weren't in on it, and secondly, he doesn't have a swinging dick left standing who can further his investigation of the crooked auction lot. Can you see this from his perspective?"

"I can. He seems like a righteous man and I'd never do anything to cause him no problems. With 20-20 hindsight, maybe he shoulda detailed one of his deputies with me and Barlow. Honestly, I wouldn't have wanted to be out here on this assignment with any other two men than I was, but I certainly wouldn't have objected to a fourth or a fifth or a sixth. I bet he's already thought of this and he's more mad at hisself than he is with us. So what do you want us to do?"

"For now, just mend the fence so they can feed those sheep. I bet Favre will send someone up here to take them to market on Monday. I'll take Barlow with me to settle things with Dan. Also, I'm sending the rest of our guys back home just as soon as Dan doesn't need them anymore. Anyone who wants to stop by the hospital for a moment to see Trey is welcome to do so, but otherwise we need to tend to our own backyard. Savvy?"

"Savvy."

"Good. Oh yeah. Great job. You always do us proud."

With that, Sheriff Sol motioned to Barlow and they went in search of Sheriff Elliott. He was in the house on the phone, so they waited until he hung up. In the meantime, Sheriff Waters walked over, so this was going to be the time to resolve all the issues before heading back to Texas.

"Sorry, Fellas. I was on the phone with our DA. He wants to grand jury this on Monday. Sol, are you okay with that or do you want me to push it back a day or two?"

"No. That would be perfect. I've spoken to Barlow and Slick and I know exactly how this all went down. I brought Barlow over to give you both a full briefing. If you want to get an investigator over here to take notes that would be fine with us."

"No need. I'll present this case myself. If there's any fallout, and I'm not expecting any but I want to be prepared nevertheless,

I don't want anyone to take it out on one of my guys.

"Barlow, you and Slick will still need to make formal statements at the office before you go home, but this will clear things up for me now. I'm ready if you are."

"Yes, Sir." With that, Barlow told Sheriff Dan what he had already told Sheriff Sol. Barlow's recitation was detailed, clear, and complete. The only question Dan had was how long it took for the guys across the road to arrive on the scene.

Dan appeared to be satisfied. He thanked Barlow for his dedication to duty and performance under dire circumstances. He said that Barlow, Slick, and Trey were all a credit to their agencies. Sol and Leland concurred. Then Sol told Barlow to find Slick and see if he needed any help.

Then the three sheriffs put their heads together and had a comprehensive command debriefing. When it was over, Leland and all his men except for Dirk Melançon and Ralphie Camacho went back to Alpine. Dirk and Ralphie stayed behind because they were set up at the campground. They were detailed to watch the M Slash F flock until such time as Maurice Favre sent someone to assume possession.

Sheriff Sol sent all his guys back home except for Slick and Barlow, who needed to make formal statements. They would return on Sunday. Chief Alex and Sheriff Sol went back home after Sol checked in with Trey. He was in pain and woozy from the sedatives, but already well on the road to recovery. His wife and kids and his boss, Ranger Captain Elvis Stillwater, were en route from El Paso to stay with him. He was expected to be released on Tuesday morning, assuming there were no complications.

Eddy County SO took care of everything else.

CHAPTER 56
May, 1970
Life Resumes

The El Paso Bugle and the Carlsbad Clarion and the AP picked up the story. It was carried in all the New Mexico and Texas newspapers and in many other venues. The focus was on Sergeant Trey Taylor because he was the lawman who got shot in the line of duty, and besides that, he was the only Texas Ranger involved. Everyone knows you have to be a hero with a cape and everything just to get selected to be a Texas Ranger. Not only that, he was as photogenic as Tab Hunter, Rock Hudson, and Cary Grant all rolled into one.

The newsies did not fail to mention the deputies who assisted Trey but their roles were not nearly as prominent. The stories did do justice to the investigation and all three sheriffs were given high marks.

Dan was thankful he dodged a bullet. Leland was all smiles because he believed he needed some good press to ensure his re-election. Sol was pleased that the stories were complimentary and relieved that the focus was on someone other than his superstar deputy. It wasn't lost on him that both Slick and Trey might be alive today due to Barlow's quick perception and precision marksmanship. It wasn't lost on Slick or Trey either.

Trey was embarrassed about all the attention and he tried to spread the wealth but the press controlled the narrative because, as Mark Twain is credited with saying, "Never pick a fight with people who buy ink by the barrel and paper by the ton." In essence, they can shout longer and louder than anyone else. Andy Warhol's message that "In the future everybody will be world famous for fifteen minutes," was fairly prophetic in that within a week the story was old news and life returned to normal.

Sheriff Sol contacted each of the sheriffs in the counties that had been rustled by this gang. He stressed that Chico provided the information which allowed the investigators to identify each victim ranch and each person involved in the scheme. All five of the other rustlers were now dead as a result of resisting arrest.

He also stressed Chico's youth and lack of criminal past. He said Chico was pleading guilty to two felonies for theft over $100, otherwise known as grand larceny, for the rustlings in both Brewster and Quayle counties as part of a plea bargain. He said both of those counties had already agreed to leniency. He requested that each sheriff contact his own victim rancher and district attorney to determine if they planned to file charges and, if so, to please consider leniency for Chico.

The news of the Mounted Wild West Gunfight at the Half-Circle G Ranch was the talk of Texas, and all the sheriffs were pleased 'to know the rest of the story' as this would have been reported by Paul Harvey. There were no hard feelings directed at Chico by anyone except for the owner of the Lazy J Ranch in Wink who had reported his loss to Sheriff Elliott and who wanted Chico's scalp on a wall.

As a concession to him, the Winkler County DA added his own charge of grand larceny but agreed to have it incorporated into the Brewster and Quayle charges, stating that he would not oppose leniency if the presiding judge felt so inclined.

The presiding judge, The Honorable Wilson Roberts of Brewster County, was so inclined. Carlos 'Chico' Gómez was given three one-year sentences for grand larceny, all sentences to run concurrently, and then he was released on probation for the length of his sentence provided he kept his nose clean. Judge Roberts even contacted the Commander of the 36th Infantry Division, Texas Army National Guard, the parent organization to the 544th Transportation Company in which Chico served as a tractor trailer driver, requesting that Chico be allowed to remain in the unit.

Major General Phineas K. Campbell, Commander of the 36th, was not so inclined, but he received a surprise visit from a prominent senior Texas state senator from Quayle County, who gently suggested that the major general endorse the judge's request unless he was prepared to retire at his permanent rank of lieutenant colonel. In that the Texas National Guard major general was not 'federally recognized' at his temporary grade of major general and that he only served in that rank at the pleasure of the governor who would not be pleased if he did not concur with the judge's request, it was a no-brainer.

The Ford 'Better Idea' light clicked on in Major General Campbell's lizard brain, and not only did he heartily endorse the judge's request, but in his letter to the judge, he attached a copy of his memorandum to Chico's commanding officer to promote Private Carlos Gómez to private first class immediately.

In addition, at the senator's suggestion, Major General Campbell transferred Chico to Battery A, 491st Field Artillery, Texas National Guard, in Alpine, where they had a vacancy for an assistant driver for one of the self-propelled, 151-millimeter howitzers. The reasoning behind the transfer was that Sheriff Waters and Sheriff Sol were both concerned that Pavón's surviving family or friends might retaliate against Chico.

In addition, Sheriff Waters found a clean, cheap apartment for Chico in Alpine above the TV repair shop. Furthermore, he got Chico a job working for the county works department as a dump truck driver. Then he got Dolores on as a cashier at the Winn Dixie. The rest would be up to Chico.

If, in the long held tradition of the Army that 'no good deed goes unpunished,' is there a corollary that 'no bad deed goes unrewarded?'

April passed and May arrived without notice or fanfare for many. The days passed slowly for Sarah in particular, until Friday, May 22nd, when she walked across the stage at WTJC and received her associate of arts degree along with 122 other new graduates. Her family had a big soirée at the Bar B for all their family and friends. About 100 were in attendance to help celebrate.

That wasn't all. She got the job as the event planner for the county rodeo grounds. It would begin on Monday, June 1st.

Barlow was excited for her. This would put quite a bit more money in her pocket than her part-time job at the college. Plus, they were just a year away now from tying the knot.

Barlow had one year of college behind him. He would graduate next May with an A.A. in law enforcement. Besides that, he would be awarded a Police Officers Standard Training certificate, mandated by Texas state law which articulated that each law enforcement officer hired after December 31, 1967, must be POST certified by January 1, 1972, to remain employed.

Life was sweet for Sarah and Barlow. Neither one of them could think beyond their wedding date next year. They hadn't even discussed potential honeymoon destinations. Doesn't Life stand still once one has reached Nirvana? Who can fault the young for believing that old age begins at 30?

Sarah and Barlow sure did. Life is full of adventures and theirs was no exception.

Tick tock. Tick tock.

The world has no shortage of evildoers. The only remedy for a bad man with a gun is a good man with a gun.

Tick tock. Tick tock.

POSTSCRIPT
Memories of Wednesday,
March 8, 1961 5:15 p.m.

"Barlow, eat up. Chloe's trying to wash the dishes and you have to dry 'em and put 'em up. You know your momma won't walk out this door until every last dish is put away. We're already running late for the tournament."

"Sorry, Dad. Remember what we talked about on my birthday last week?"

"I do. I will buy you a horse very soon. I promise. I've been talking to a man at work with a three-year-old pinto gelding for sale. I've seen his picture. He's a nice-looking quarter horse, about 15-1/2 hands tall, supposedly knows how to cut cattle. We'll see. He said we could stop by Saturday and you could take him out for a short ride."

"Gee, that's swell, Dad! I can't wait!"

"Well, all right, then. Hurry up and help your sister. Your mother and I have gotta go!"

"Dad, will you get a horse and ride with me? I still want to be a lawman, like Marshal Matt Dillon. We can ride together! Catch bad guys. Will ya?"

"All we can afford is one horse right now. I'll get one in a few years when you're old enough to be a deputy. Then maybe we can ride together like Ben Cartwright and Adam or Hoss or Little Joe on Bonanza. You chase the rustlers and after you catch 'em, I'll tie 'em up and we'll take 'em to jail."

"Cool, Dad! I can't wait.

"Mom, Dad's gonna get me a horse!"

"I know. Come here and give me a kiss. We have to go. The bowling tournament starts in less than an hour."

Barlow hugged and kissed his mom. Then he hugged his dad. Then his parents drove off to the Prairie Bowl Lanes in Baileyville for the league championship tournament.

That was the last time he ever saw them. They were killed in a crash that night. He never got a horse. He hadn't thought about this for a long, long time. The aftermath of the raid brought this memory crashing down around him like pounding waves along a rocky beach. He was holding back tears. Thankfully he was alone.

"I did it, Dad, just like I said. I wish you had been there with me. I know you and Mom watched from above. I miss you all. So long for now."

Glossary

10-4 - affirmative

10-7 - out of service

10-8 - in service

10-33 - burglary in progress

AAA - anti-aircraft artillery, also known as - ack ack

ADA - assistant district attorney

Agg - aggravated

ASAP - as soon as possible

AT - annual training, Army National Guard term for two-week summer camp

ATF - Alcohol Tobacco and Firearms, Division of the Internal Revenue Service

BCSO - Brewster County Sheriffs Office

BOLO - be on the lookout for

CB - citizens band (radio)

CDL - commercial driver's license, also known as Class A license

CI - confidential informant, snitch, rat, stoolie

Code 1 - standard call, obey traffic laws

Code 2 - urgent call, emergency lights and siren optional - speed w/caution

Code 3 - extremely urgent, emergency equipment mandatory, speed with caution. (Note - this is normally a life or death situation.)

Commo - communications, normally radio or telephone

DA - district attorney

DL - drivers license

DMV - Department of Motor Vehicles

EPSO - El Paso Sheriffs Office

ETA - estimated time of arrival

ETS - expiration term of service

FNG - fucking new guy

GI - government issue - Army slang for soldier

Gyrene - slang term for US Marines

IRS - Internal Revenue Service

Jarhead - pejorative term for US Marine

KOA - Kampground of America, privately-owned network of campgrounds

NCIC - National Crime Information Center

NLETS - National Law Enforcement Telecommunications System

NLT - not later than

OP - operation

PD - police department

PFC - private first class

POST - police officers standard training

POV - privately owned vehicle

QCSO - Quayle County Sheriffs Office

RCSO - Reeves County Sheriffs Office

REMF - Rear echelon motherfucker

R&R - military term for rest and relaxation

SAMI - Army term for Saturday morning inspection

SO - sheriffs office

SOP - standard operating procedure

Strack - Army term for squared away

Stir - slang for prison

SWAG - scientific wild ass guess

TA-50 - table of authorization - Army abbreviation for field equipment

U/C - undercover

UTEP - University of Texas - El Paso

VIN - vehicle identification number

WWI - World War One

WWII - World War Two

WTJC - West Texas Junior College

Character List

Quayle County, Texas:

Barlow Adams - deputy sheriff, protagonist, Sarah's fiancé

Solomon Pratt - county sheriff, also known as: Sol, Sheriff Sol

Alexander Snodgrass - chief deputy sheriff, also known as: Chief Alex

Chief Ernest Atwater - deputy sheriff, also known as: Ernie, Ern

Noble Bustamante - deputy sheriff, also known as: Chunk

Dewey Carruthers - deputy sheriff

Randall Meacham - deputy sheriff, also known as: Randy

Clarence Oldman - deputy sheriff, also known as: Slick

Kirk Shoemaker - deputy sheriff

Archibald Xavier Willis - deputy sheriff, also known as: Archie, Arch

Loretta Youngblood - secretary to sheriffs department, also known as: Miss Loretta

Sarah Mae Baker - Barlow's fiancé

Arthur Baker - sheep rancher, Sarah's father

Clarice Baker - wife of Arthur, Sarah's mother

Cordell Baker - sheep rancher, Sarah's brother

Darla Baker - wife of Cordell, Sarah's sister-in-law

Pedro - Baker ranch hand

Angel - Baker ranch hand, Pedro's brother

Pancho - Baker ranch hand, Angel's son

Maxwell Sweeney - county Judge, wealthy sheep rancher, also known as: Maximum Max, Max

Monica Sweeney - wife of Maxwell

Darnell Sweeney - Texas state senator, former Texas Ranger, brother of Maxwell

Buck Boyd - owner of Phillips 66 service station

Ian Boykin - physician in Quayle County

Francis Caldwell - husband of Winona, citizen, aid to lawmen

Winona Caldwell - wife of Francis, complainant regarding a
    burglary in progress

Sam Davis - defense counsel

Dennis DeBarry - director of rodeo grounds

Able DeWitt - district attorney

Pete Ricketts - coroner and funeral director

Albert Gómez - small rancher, father of Chico and Rudy

Rosalita Gómez - wife of Albert, mother of Chico and Rudy

Enrico Méndez - Sweeney ranch hand, also known as: Rico

Pepe Méndez - Sweeney ranch hand, son of Enrico

Brewster County, Texas:

Leland Waters - sheriff

Phillip Pruitt - chief deputy

Ralphie Camacho - deputy sheriff

Avery Carmichael - deputy sheriff investigator

Cody Carr - deputy sheriff

Dirk Melançon - deputy sheriff

Ella Mae Jaleski - property clerk in sheriff's office

Francisco Rojas - deputy sheriff, also known as: Pancho the
    Honcho

Bradford Delaney - district attorney

Eric Holland - defense attorney

Wilson Roberts - county judge

Galen Story - assistant district attorney

Maurice Favre - owner of the M/F ranch, also known as: the Big
    MF

Nicky Nelson - small plane aviator employed by the Triple S
    Ranch (Sweeney)

El Paso County, Texas:
Winfield Taylor III - Texas Ranger sergeant, also known as: Trey
Bud Wagner - US Postal Inspection Service inspector

Reeves County, Texas:
Wilbert Whalen - sheriff, also known as: Willie Joe
Irwin Trevino - deputy sheriff
Mrs. Sebastian - clerk at sheriff's office
Winston Ledbetter - chief deputy
Carlos Gómez - rustler, Army National Guard soldier, son of
    Albert Gómez, also known as: Chico
Rodolfo Gómez - rustler, son of Albert Gómez, also known as:
    Rudy
Jasmine Estrada - tavern waitress, also known as: Jasmine
    Erotica
Dolores Dugas - Chico's girlfriend
Humberto Pavón- rustler, also known as: Berto, El Jefe, Elmer
    Fudd, John Doe #2

Travis County, Texas:
Harriett Morgan - Texas Secretary of State clerk

Val Verde County, Texas:
Clinton Dumfries - convicted felon and burglar
Melton Dumfries - convicted felon and burglar
Darlene Dumfries - mother of Clinton and Melton

Eddy County,New Mexico:
Dan Elliott - county sheriff
Bradley Bergeron - deputy sheriff
Jaime Cerano - deputy sheriff sergeant, also known as: Hiney
    Suprano

Cletus Knobel - deputy sheriff, also known as: Clitoris, Clit

Zach McGillicuddy - deputy sheriff

Phyllis Rafferty - secretary to sheriffs department

Edgar Evans - confidential informant, also known as: Curley, Cobra, Bugs Bunny

Geoffrey Gemini Gough - sheep rancher, rustler financier, twin brother of Gerard, also known as: Jeff, Donald Mallard, Daffy Duck

Gerard Gemini Gough - oil wildcatter, rustler financier, twin brother of Geoffrey, also known as: Jerry, Hugh Mallard, Huey Duck

Juan Rodríguez - rustler, also known as: Segundo, Cesar Oso, John Doe #1

Santa Fe County, New Mexico:

Emmett Little - Department of Corrections lieutenant

Pima County, Arizona:

Chloe Adams Kilgore - Barlow's sister

Coahuila, Mexico:

Hector - Humberto Pavón's cousin

Acknowledgements

First, the author wishes to acknowledge his Maker "from whom all blessings flow."

Second, the author wishes to acknowledge his wife and lifelong companion who has always been in the words of the Righteous Brothers, "my soul and my heart's inspiration."

Next, in no hierarchical order, the author wishes to acknowledge DB and LB of Newland, NC, who after the author's wife, were the first to read 'Making Mountains Out of Molehills' and to make suggestions on how to make it better. They also introduced him to the publisher, to whom the author also owes a debt of gratitude.

The author wishes to acknowledge BS of Louisville, KY, for proofing 'When Dreams Come True - Sort Of.'

Furthermore, the author wishes to acknowledge AC of Greencastle, IN, for teaching him the rudiments of sheep ranching, both past and present and BC of Columbia, TN as it relates to training horses for mounted shooting.

Continuing, the author wishes to acknowledge BJO of Louisville, KY; JB, deceased, of Valley Station, KY; JGE, deceased, originally from California, MO; JM, deceased, originally from Hollywood, FL; GG of Grafton, WI, GS, from Cody, WY, JSH of Baton Rouge, LA; and DB of Lafayette, LA, all of whom were law enforcement partners of the highest order.

In addition, the author wishes to acknowledge TW, from Louisville, KY; DT, formerly from Gulfport, MS; JC, once upon a time from Diamondhead, MS; RS, at one time from Miami, FL; SM of Ellicott City, MD; RR of Rehoboth Beach, DE; and DL of Millersville, MD, all law enforcement supervisors who had a major, positive impact upon his professional development as a law enforcement officer.

Furthermore, the author wishes to acknowledge TT of Sulphur Springs, WV; JW of Houston, TX for proofing 'When Dreams Come True - Sort of;' and RW of Urbandale, IA, all of whom are lifelong companions from the author's errant youth in the military.

Last but not least, the author acknowledges many unnamed people who provided him with raw material over the years and whose true life experiences were woven into the fabric of this book and into 'Making Mountains Out of Molehills.' Of course, the accounts were modified to fit the needs of both stories.

The author also wishes to thank those who have taken the time to read his books.

About the Author

Earl Snort is the nom de plume of a retired law enforcement officer with more than forty years experience toting a badge and a gun. Before that he served in the armed forces.

He and his wife have been married nearly fifty years. They reside in the South. They have one son, also a career law enforcement officer, and two grandchildren.

This is the author's second foray into the world of writing fiction. After a lifetime of writing non-fiction to document investigations of true crime, he decided to try his hand in make believe.

He hopes you enjoy the yarn.

April, 2020

Title: *Making Mountains*
Out of Molehills

- Author: Earl Snort
- Publisher: TotalRecall Publications
- Paper Back: ISBN: 9781590954324
- eBook ISBN: 9781590956533
- Pages 320
- Publication Date: 2019

It was 1969. Barlow Adams, age 20, was a recently discharged veteran. He was driving late at night on a lonely stretch of highway in the Trans-Pecos region of Texas. He stopped to render assistance to a motorist with a flat tire. What he stepped into was a vicious attempted rape. He rescued the victim, which catapulted him into an appointment as a deputy sheriff.

Along the way he encounters an enchanting woman who will change his life forever. In addition, he will be confronted by a gang of outlaw bikers who are obsessed with killing him while he is still learning the ropes of becoming a lawman.

This is the story of a young man in the 1960's, an era which has long been forgotten except for those who lived it.

www.ingramcontent.com/pod-product-compliance
Lightning Source LLC
Chambersburg PA
CBHW020330120726
47904CB00002B/360